Bronwyn Parry grew up surrounded by books, with a fascination for places, people and their stories. Bronwyn's first novel, *As Darkness Falls*, won a prestigious Romance Writers of America Golden Heart Award for best romantic suspense manuscript in 2007. Her second and third novels, *Dark Country* and *Dead Heat*, were voted the Favourite Romantic Suspense Novel by the Australian Romance Readers Association (ARRA) in 2010 and 2013, and were both finalists in the Romance Writers of America RITA Awards – the Oscars of romance writing – and the Daphne du Maurier Award for Romantic Suspense. Her fourth and fifth novels, *Darkening Skies* and *Storm Clouds*, were finalists in the ARRA Awards. An occasional academic, Bronwyn's active interest in fiction and its readership is reflected in her PhD research and she is passionate about the richness, diversity and value of popular fiction. She lives in the New England tablelands in New South Wales and loves to travel in Australia's wild places.

www.bronwynparry.com

Also by Bronwyn Parry

As Darkness Falls
Dark Country
Dead Heat
Darkening Skies
Storm Clouds

Sunset Shadows

BRONWYN PARRY

AUSTRALIA

Published in Australia and New Zealand in 2016
by Hachette Australia
(an imprint of Hachette Australia Pty Limited)
Level 17, 207 Kent Street, Sydney NSW 2000
www.hachette.com.au

Copyright © Bronwyn Parry 2016

This book is copyright. Apart from any fair dealing for the purposes of private study, research, criticism or review permitted under the *Copyright Act 1968*, no part may be stored or reproduced by any process without prior written permission. Enquiries should be made to the publisher.

National Library of Australia
Cataloguing-in-Publication data:

Parry, Bronwyn, 1962– author.
Sunset shadows/Bronwyn Parry.

978 0 7336 3331 7 (paperback)

Suspense fiction, Australian.
Romance fiction, Australian.

A823.4

Cover design by Christabella Designs
Cover photographs courtesy of Trevillion and Shutterstock
Text design by Bookhouse, Sydney
Typeset in 12.75/19.75 pt Adobe Garamond Pro by Bookhouse, Sydney

In loving memory of my mother, who accepted people without judgement, seeing that of God in everyone. A truly beautiful soul, who taught me so much about life and love.

CHAPTER 1

Moonlight shone over paddocks glistening with water from the afternoon's storm. Puddles and rivulets ran to gullies, and creeks rushed towards the river.

Detective Sergeant Steve Fraser carefully steered the quad bike through an ankle-deep rivulet and stopped a few metres beyond it while his colleague followed on her quad. He checked the time. Over an hour, it had taken them, to cover fifteen kilometres across paddocks and rough ground in the dark on the quad bikes. Over an hour, when by road it would have taken a few minutes. Except the road was blocked by flooding after the torrential downpour earlier and they'd had to come the long way around, crossing the river at the Derringvale bridge, then along a muddy but passable back road to the grazing property they'd borrowed the quads from. And from there they'd navigated farm tracks, boundary fences, paddocks, stock routes and bush to get this far.

They had to be close. Serenity Hill, the five-thousand-hectare property they were headed for, lay immediately north of the national park, the river marking the border between them. These low ridges – the one ahead, the one they'd passed – were starting to look more like the rougher, hilly country of the national park than the plains they'd been riding over.

Her police search and rescue uniform spattered with mud, Senior Constable Tess Ballard pulled up beside him and reached for the GPS tucked in her equipment vest.

She compared the GPS screen to what she could see of the landscape around them. 'It should be just over that rise,' she said, loud over the noise of the two quads.

Of course she'd know exactly where they were. In the few days he'd known her, she'd proved herself to be thorough and meticulous, with more discipline and dedication to the job than he'd ever had.

She hadn't so much volunteered to come on this lunatic ride as insisted. But now they were going almost blind into the situation, two of them against who knew how many, with no other police back-up, only the support of a couple of National Parks rangers. One of them, Simon Kennedy, had years of experience as a commando so he'd been scouting the place and the people, but Steve had let Erin Taylor go in too, to infiltrate the reclusive group at the farm. With few police resources out here in the bush, he'd had little choice and Erin had proved her practicality and resourcefulness countless times already. But if

Steve had known this morning what he knew now about this community – this *cult* – he'd never have let her do it.

Nothing about this situation conformed to standard operating procedure but there were at least a dozen children in the cult, and all of them at the mercy of a manipulative, lying bastard linked to the deaths of at least two women. A bastard surrounded by followers he'd brainwashed into believing in him.

The whole thing could go pear-shaped in any one of a hundred ways. If he thought for a moment that Tess would listen to him, he'd order her to stay back. But she was a capable and level-headed officer and he had no reason, other than his own fears, to exclude her. And he had way too much else going on in his head to consider why, when he'd only just met her, he had to quiet the he-man protective instincts.

'Looks like there are too many trees on that rise to take the bikes,' Tess said. 'It'll be safer to follow the stock route up to Millers Road. According to Simon's recon, there's a track into the property not far along, straight down to the woolshed.'

The trees along the top of the ridge, silhouetted against the moonlit sky, would make good cover to observe the place, but Tess made a logical point. Responsible. Safety-conscious. Exactly the kind of officer his father thought Steve should have been. If his father knew of tonight's actions – and maybe the Assistant Commissioner did by now – he'd be railing about Steve's recklessness and irresponsibility. But if he knew what – *who* – Steve half-suspected he'd find among the cult members, maybe he'd be stunned into silence for once.

Steve nodded at Tess's suggestion, revved the quad and set off again, continuing along the stock route. There must have been a mob of cattle past recently, for the grass wasn't long and that made riding over it easier. He stopped at the gate onto Millers Road, a dirt back road, holding it open for Tess and taking a minute to flip the chain back over the hook to secure it closed after he'd ridden through. Around a hundred metres down, a rough sign pointed to the Serenity Hill stockyards, and she opened the gate on to a farm track for him.

Good. That put him back in front, where he'd be first to confront any danger. He rode off without waiting for her, the mud-map of the place that Simon had drawn for him clear in his mind. The homestead itself lay around a kilometre east of here, but this track led down to the working end of the property – sheds, farm cottages, shearers' quarters – where the majority of the community lived.

The track crossed a paddock and disappeared into a line of trees. He caught the acrid scent of smoke drifting on the light breeze at the same time he saw light flickering beyond the trees. A fire. *Shit.* As if the situation wasn't complex enough already. At least the ground was drenched and in the cooler night air it shouldn't spread too fast. He hoped.

Accelerating, he sped down the track but slowed again when a dark figure, silhouetted by the fire's increasing light, trudged out of the trees. A tall man, laden with bundles, one on each hip. The guy stepped off the track and halted. As the lights of the quad illuminated him Steve saw that the bundles were kids. Children, wrapped in blankets.

'You're the cops?' the guy asked. Tall, muscular, dressed in black cargo pants and a black t-shirt, his hair buzz-cut. He had to be the mate Simon had mentioned, a former commando, the one helping him to reconnoitre the place and keep an eye on Erin.

'Yes.' Steve swung off the quad. 'You're Kennedy's friend?'

'Yep. Gabe McCallum.' The larger child, a dark-haired kid about five years old, shifted in his arms and whimpered. McCallum adjusted his hold awkwardly.

'Are the kids hurt?' Steve asked.

'Not hurt. Maybe sedated, on drugs of some sort. But they're both breathing fine.'

'Okay. What's happening? Where's the fire?'

Tess pulled up beside him while the guy quickly explained. 'It's the woolshed. They were all there, wild dancing and drumming, but they left before the fire started. I think someone torched it. They've gone to the river. Simon's following them, with Erin and one of the women from the group – Madeleine, they called her. They think something major's about to go down.'

Madeleine.

The world spun around him and Steve closed his eyes to keep his balance while the name pounded in his head.

Madeleine.

It could be her. Not dead. Not drowned off the Kurnell rocks half a lifetime ago. In the hours since he'd discovered the connection between this case and his family, the possibility had taunted him: that she might have been enticed away from her home and her family by a twisted, controlling psychologist who'd spent twenty years playing games with people's minds. And who'd spent the past week murdering women who knew his secrets.

Madeleine knew those secrets. She had to know that Peter Hollywell and Joshua Kristos were one and the same man. *If she was Maddie. If, if, if . . .*

While McCallum still held the children, Tess hurriedly assessed their pulse and responsiveness. Neither showed any signs of injury.

Steve dragged his jumbled thoughts away from the emotional cyclone and squarely into action mode. 'Tess, take the kids and get them somewhere safe. McCallum, show me which way they went.'

Instead of taking the children, Tess stood her ground. 'No, Sarge. We don't want any more civilians around than necessary. McCallum, take my quad and get the kids out of here, up to the road. You could put them in the box at the back, but for heaven's sake drive slowly and don't flip over.'

Dammit, she was right.

The guy started to protest but Steve overrode him curtly. 'Do it,' he ordered, getting on to his quad again, pausing to let Tess slide into place behind him.

'The river's pretty much due south of here,' she said near his ear. 'About four hundred metres at a guess. The waterfall is a little east.'

Tess rested her hands on his hips as he drove and in among all the other racing thoughts, he registered that fact. He skirted the old woolshed, the flames taking hold of the structure and dancing eerily in the night. Nothing at all they could do about that just now, with no equipment or resources. They passed an assortment of cottages and sheds, with no signs of anyone about.

The track ended at a thick belt of trees. Natural bushland with tall eucalypts interspersed with native cypress and smaller bushes, too rough and dense to ride through on the quad. Tess swung off the back the moment he stopped. When he killed the engine, the thunder of the river filled the night air.

Tess took off into the bush and he followed the bobbing beam of her flashlight, heading towards the sound of the waterfall and the glimpses of lights among the trees. The rough ground and the shadowed darkness slowed their progress to a jog but within a couple of hundred metres they heard snatches of voices rising above the rushing of the water, the trees thinned and the light from dozens of flaming torches danced in the night.

He caught up with Tess and they both stopped while they were still in the cover of the forest, edging forward to where they could assess what was going on.

The moonlight shone bright over the flat area at the top of the waterfall. The flooded river – not much more than a creek a day ago, winding in small channels through the rocks – now surged metres deep, a wild torrent throwing mud, branches and debris over the cliff edge of the falls and down into the gorge forty metres below.

On a rock overhanging the falls, Joshua Kristos stood in white flowing robes, with his arms held wide. Around fifty of his followers – men, women, children – danced and chanted on the flat rocks beside the river, their burning torches casting weird, hellish light over faces rapt and ecstatic.

Steve couldn't see Simon, or Erin, or . . . how would he know what Maddie looked like now, anyway? His sister had been just fourteen when she disappeared. When her clothes and a suicide note had been found at the top of the sea cliffs. When that psychopathic psychologist masquerading as a cult leader had somehow stolen her from them . . .

'Water is life! Water is bliss!' Joshua declared to his followers, and the bastard must have hooked up some kind of microphone because his voice rose loud above the waterfall. 'We are made of water, we crave water! Will you embrace the water?'

'Jesus,' Steve muttered, 'they wouldn't, would they?' But a picture of Maddie standing on the sea cliffs with the man she'd hero-worshipped flashed in his mind, and he didn't need imagination to remember the woman's body he'd carried out of that very gorge below the waterfall just days ago. Rage coursed hot through his veins.

'They could,' Tess said beside him. He glanced at her then, saw her face tense, narrowed eyes staring at the man on the rock. 'He's been screwing with their heads for years. He believes he can make them.'

'Will you embrace bliss?' Joshua shouted. 'Who will become water?'

Some of them moved closer to the river, to the metres-deep currents that carried a tree trunk as if it were a matchstick. No one who stepped into that water stood a chance of surviving.

But they were so keyed up, so ecstatic in their devotion, that if he or Tess rushed in and shouted 'Stop!', they ran the risk of making things worse. Instead Steve touched Tess on the shoulder and pointed along the tree line towards the river. 'We'll go round this way. If we have to charge in, that will drive them away from the water, not into it.'

As they moved in the shadows of the trees he saw Erin and another woman coming out of the forest further along, approaching the edge of the group.

The bastard on the rock continued his cajoling. 'Who will become pure? Who will become one with water?'

'I will!' A woman's cry carried over the roar of the water. 'I will!'

Steve swore and ran, dodging tree stumps and jumping over fallen branches, Tess keeping pace with him.

Someone screamed, 'No!'

Through the trees, he caught sight of a young woman in a white dress, arms out wide, whirling on a rock right beside the water.

'I will!' she shouted, and with one more twirl she pivoted off into the raging torrent and was immediately sucked under.

No chance to save her, not a damn thing he could do. She'd have gone over the falls in seconds, down the forty-metre drop to the rocks below.

'Bliss!' Joshua shouted. 'Such bliss! Who will join us in bliss? Beautiful, beautiful bliss! Eternal bliss!'

'Bliss!' the people shouted, dancing forward in ecstatic frenzy. In the crowd, Steve saw Erin struggling to hold back a young woman close to the edge. The woman, shouting out for 'bliss', dragged her forward.

Tess swore aloud. 'They're going to do it. They'll all go in.'

Steve had already drawn his Glock. 'We have to stop him.' No time to cross the distance and confront the man, no way to persuade his brainwashed, possibly drugged believers before the euphoria and the bastard's psychological manipulation sent them all into oblivion. Fifty or more people, some of them just kids . . .

He raised his weapon, aiming at the man on the rock still calling his devotees to their deaths. No choice. No way to save those people but this.

He fired.

•

Joshua shuddered and clutched his chest, slowly falling backwards off the high rock and instantly out of sight.

The blast of Tess's own shot and Fraser's – and maybe another? – still rang in her ears and her hands shook with the power of the kick as she lowered her handgun. She'd shot a man. Shot *at* a man. She had no idea if her bullet had hit her target.

Joshua's followers surged forward towards the water, and Tess sheathed her weapon, ready to run into the crowd, to yell at them that Joshua was a fraud and not worth dying for. But Fraser gripped her arm and held her back as a woman's voice cried out, strong and powerful, 'Stop!'

The woman walked between the people, as commanding as a warrior queen, her long hair fluttering around her in the breeze, her white dress catching the soft glow of the moonlight. At the edge of the river she stood and faced them, lifting her hands.

Next to Tess, Fraser made a small sound, part shock, part pain, and screwed his eyes shut. His sister. It had to be her. The sister he'd only mentioned this afternoon, when they'd uncovered Joshua's real identity. The sister he'd believed dead for close on two decades.

'Joshua has ascended to bliss,' the woman cried, her voice clear over the waterfall's roar. 'But you are not ready. Your work is not done. None of you are ready. None of us are ready. Go. Go home and sleep. Tomorrow we will meet to discuss what is next. Go and sleep now. Go and sleep. Take the children with you and sleep.'

Frustration almost drove Tess to action. Joshua 'ascended to bliss?' Surely she – Madeleine – had to know the truth about him . . . Tess shook her head in disgust at her own almost-stupidity. An angry, armed cop shouting the truth to fifty keyed-up, psyched-up and possibly drugged devotees on the edge of ecstatic suicide could have been a short path to disaster. Madeleine had the right approach. From what they knew about the cult, her white dress signified some kind of authority and for all that she must have her own doubts about Joshua, she used the group's beliefs, repeating her message, speaking gently and giving them a meaning for Joshua's disappearance. With so many poised on the brink of death, the truth had to wait.

'Well done, Maddie,' Fraser murmured. 'They're listening to you.'

No one spoke out against Madeleine, and the intense, ecstatic energy started to dissipate. Even those closest to the water had stepped back a metre or so from it.

'That's definitely her?' Tess asked. 'Your sister?'

He nodded without shifting his gaze from the woman. 'She—' He cleared his throat. 'She looks just like our mother did.'

There was nothing in his face of the devil-may-care, almost-flirtatious man who'd alternately irritated and impressed her for the past seventy-two hours. Just a man who cared, grappling with a revelation that must have struck at his emotions, hard.

Her own emotions weren't totally steady and she couldn't even think of a platitude to offer to fit the circumstance. She took refuge in procedure and action and pulled the satellite phone from its pocket on her equipment vest. 'I'll report the deaths.'

Fraser cast one quick glance at her. 'I ordered you to fire,' he said. 'When the investigators ask, we'll both tell them that I ordered it.'

Lie to the critical incident investigators? She should have been offended that he suggested it. But her temper didn't flare, and she answered, 'You didn't order me. I made my own decision, Sarge. I'll wear the consequences.' She cut off his next argument by asking, 'Did you hear another shot?'

'Yeah.'

Before she had time to worry about another shooter, steady footsteps cracked on the leaves and twigs on the ground and Simon Kennedy stepped out from the trees, stopping a couple of metres away, a backpack over his shoulder.

Fraser gave him a nod. 'Thought it would be you up there.'

Simon's glance went to Fraser's gun, still in his hand, and to hers. 'You both fired?'

'Yes,' Tess said.

'They'll find his body in a day or two,' Fraser said, returning to watching his sister. 'Then we'll know.'

Simon slid his backpack off his shoulder and held it out to Fraser. 'My rifle's in here. You'll have my statement in the morning. If you want to arrest me now, I understand.'

Fraser made no move to take the pack. 'We'll talk tomorrow,' he said.

Maybe she should have taken the bag and the rifle. Maybe she should even have arrested him, cautioned him. He wasn't a police officer and he'd just admitted firing at Joshua. Procedure required it, simple as that.

Tess wished it was as simple as that.

Until the post-mortem and forensic analysis, they wouldn't know which of them had shot Joshua. Fraser, Simon, or her. But she'd fired her weapon, aiming at the man's chest in accordance with police training and procedure, knowing she might kill him.

Madeleine still talked with the group, moving among them, calming and persuading and assuring them. Erin comforted a distressed teenager. Tess recognised the girl from the few images they had. Simon's daughter, the child he'd not known existed until his estranged wife had been murdered a few days ago. Like Fraser, Simon stood silently watching, making no move towards Erin or the girl, as if he, too, recognised that their presence might upset the fragile calm of the cult members.

Tess stepped a few paces away, using the sat phone to report in to the district police inspector. Although she'd been in the region a couple of months and knew Nick Matheson as a fair and considerate officer, she still hesitated when he answered her call. *'I shot and killed a man.'* As soon as she said the words, the reality would hit and the official response would begin. Right at this point, she felt she'd acted professionally and had taken the only course of action in the circumstances, but in two hours, two days, two weeks – after the critical incident team had put her through their investigative wringer – would she still feel the same certainty?

'Ballard?' the inspector's voice sounded in her ear. 'Tess? Are you there?'

'Yes, sir.' She swallowed. Be professional, state the facts. 'I have to report two deaths, sir. A young woman from the group went into the river at the top of the falls. And so did Joshua Kristos. It's a raging flood, sir, and there was no chance for either of them. You'll need to inform the Professional Standards command. I fired at him, as did Fraser.'

'Lives were in danger?'

'Yes, sir. I believed so. He had them worked up, and they were on the edge of the river, ready to die for bliss. For him.' How could she explain that one man could have talked dozens into dying? 'I think he used some kind of hypnosis, of suggestion. They were totally focused on him.'

'I know it can be done, Tess. He's worked on their minds and beliefs for years.' The uncharacteristic hardness in his tone only lasted a moment. 'What's the situation now?'

'I don't think they realise that we're here or that Joshua was shot. One of the women is persuading them to leave the river. We'll need somewhere for them to go, sir. The woolshed at the property is on fire. I presume you'll want Forensics to go over the rest of the place.' She watched Joshua's people starting to drift away from the waterfall, milling in the open area beyond the river's reach. Fifty people, dazed and confused, and probably now homeless. But the flooded roads would be impassable until morning at least.

'RFS and SES trucks are on their way,' Matheson said. 'They should be able to get through along the stock routes, as you did. I've arranged an evacuation centre at the community hall in Derringvale. The trucks will ferry everyone there. Strathnairn Hospital and the rescue helicopter are on standby. Can you and Steve coordinate things there?'

'Yes, sir.'

Neither Fraser nor Simon had moved from the shadows of the trees, both of them observing the women they cared about from a distance. She'd not seen Fraser so still and silent before, no trace of his grin on his face, his usual vibrancy frozen.

'Sir, you need to know – the woman, Madeleine, is the sarge's sister.'

Matheson had never sworn in her hearing. He did now. 'Kristos has a hell of a lot to answer for.'

Persuading a fourteen-year-old girl to fake a suicide and desert her father and brother. Persuading an emotionally vulnerable woman to leave her husband and conceal her pregnancy, as he'd done to Simon Kennedy's wife, Hayley. Perpetuating secrets and lies year after year after year, manipulating the desires and beliefs of his followers. And likely murdering those who no longer served his purpose.

On rare occasions Tess wished she still believed in heaven and hell, because there might be some justice if Joshua – Peter Hollywell – was confronting demons in the afterlife.

Matheson didn't waste time with impossible wishes. 'As soon as I can get relief officers in there, I want you both to come on one of the trucks to Derringvale. I'll meet you there for a debrief before you go off duty.'

'Yes, sir. I understand.' Tess swallowed after she ended the call, staring out into the night. She understood all right. Off duty. Standard procedure for an officer involved in a death. Because of the presence of two armed officers at the scene, both the young woman's death and Joshua's would be regarded as deaths in custody and subjected to detailed investigation. Every aspect of the situation and her responses would be open to question, including her own state of mind.

If they found that her judgement wasn't sound, that she'd acted injudiciously, then it would be the end of her hard-fought-for police career.

She couldn't let them find out about her past. And no way could she ever tell them that at the moment she'd fired her gun, she'd imagined another man as her target, not Joshua.

CHAPTER 2

Steve remained in the dark shadows of the trees and didn't approach his sister. Occupied with the disoriented members of the group, she hadn't seen him, wouldn't know he was here. Confronting her now, with all these people around – not a good idea. Especially when he had no clue whether he'd rage at her for the lies or crumple to his knees and bawl like a baby. And she must hate him, because she'd left and stayed away. If it made him a coward because he wanted to delay seeing that hatred in her eyes, then yes, he was a coward.

One more shortcoming for his father to criticise.

But he had a job to do, and he did take pride in his work, although the Assistant Commissioner might never believe it.

Encouraged by Madeleine and Erin, some of Joshua's followers had started making their way through the trees to the farm buildings, but they appeared dazed, uncertain of their way, and a few drifted in other directions.

Steve spoke in a low tone to Simon. 'Can you and Erin help guide them back? Gather them near the big steel shed? It's far enough away from the fire.'

'Not the machinery shed,' Simon said quickly. 'Your drug squad will want to take a look in there. The rubbish drums out the back have empty containers for drain cleaners, ammonia and paint solvents.'

Shit, one more complication to deal with. 'It's a meth lab? They're making ice in there?'

'It's locked, so I couldn't say for sure.'

Yeah, but a meth lab would make sense of how Joshua had financed the purchase of the property. Steve's thoughts raced. Highly volatile chemicals, a nearby fire, a crime scene to secure, and criminals to identify and apprehend.

Beckoning Tess, he set off at a jog to marshal people to a safe area. He also wanted to check the homestead itself, where Joshua stayed when he visited and where the group of women who ran the place on a daily basis lived. Probably including his sister. When he'd called on official business on Friday night, the only woman he'd seen hadn't let him in the front door and had coolly denied any knowledge of the murdered women. For all their happy, huggy, harmless facade, this mob was neck-deep in lies and deceit.

A meth lab. How much had Maddie been involved in *that*?

As he and Tess came out of the bush, a Rural Fire Service truck drove down the track to the farm buildings, its emergency lights dancing in the night sky with the flickering glow from the woolshed. The crew jumped down from the truck as soon as it stopped and set to work evaluating the fire and planning their strategy.

'Anyone inside?' the captain asked when Steve reached them.

'I don't think so. They were all at the river, I think. It was well alight when we got here.' He nodded across to the other shed. 'Regard that as an explosive risk. Drug chemicals. Maybe.'

The guy swore. 'They're making that shit here? Bastards.'

Bastards indeed. Across the north-west of the state, methamphetamine use had grown from a trickle to a flood these past few months, ravaging towns and communities already struggling with drought and economic hardship. He'd been on his way home from a meeting of regional detectives to discuss the issues when he'd been called in on this case. The criminals who manufactured and distributed the drugs, who callously destroyed lives and communities purely for their own profit, made his blood boil.

That his own sister might be one of them . . . Shit, he needed some answers.

Another truck arrived – an SES one – and after instructing Tess to secure the buildings with their help, he set off at a jog up the track towards the main homestead. Hidden from the view of the outbuildings, as he came over a rise he saw the low silhouette of the single-storey house, with the glow of lights shining from a couple of windows. As he came within a few hundred metres, one of them flicked out.

He sped up, pushing himself hard, his bad leg protesting. The track skirted a large terraced garden and across the moonlit lawn he saw another figure racing, taking the broad stairs up to the back veranda in two athletic leaps. He caught a brief glimpse of the guy, illuminated by a light before he disappeared inside. Young, shoulder-length dark hair in a ponytail, grinning. But Steve was fifty metres behind, and by the time he reached the door an engine was gunning out the front of the house, and the spin of tyres sprayed gravel against windows as a car swung around at speed. Steve bolted through the house to the open front door and caught a momentary glimpse of a woman driving as the car accelerated down the driveway, taillights red in the darkness.

He let out a string of swearwords as he fumbled for his phone, hurriedly snapping two photos of the vehicle before it turned on to the road and disappeared. With luck, they might be able to read the rego plates on the images. More likely, they'd simply show a blur of red against black.

He had no phone reception, and the sat phone was with Tess, but he figured breaking radio silence at this point wouldn't jeopardise anything. Pretty pointless, though, to ask for any vehicles in the area to intercept a white or silver station wagon, probably four-wheel drive – which described almost every family car in rural areas – especially when the chances of a patrol car being out on these roads tonight were next to zero. The Strathnairn station was south of the flooded river; Tenterfield a long way east. And he'd bet whoever was driving that car was heading north, up over the border and in to Queensland. Still, he put in the call, just in case.

He returned to the house, the front door still open. How many rules had he broken tonight? The moment he'd seen Maddie, he should have stepped away from the case. Personal involvement. Lack of objectivity. He knew all the reasons. But still he'd fired at, possibly killed, the man who'd tempted his sister away. Professional Standards would be all over him for that.

Joshua was dead, yet two people – at least two – had been at the main house and made their escape. The young man, and a woman driving the car. Perhaps the woman he'd spoken to Friday night? She'd introduced herself only as Mary, blatantly denied knowledge of the two dead women, and later phoned a complaint of harassment to his superiors. She was in her forties, cool and confident, looking like a model in designer jeans and linen shirt despite the late hour. Not like the two dead women in their home-made white dresses.

Steve kicked off his mud-caked boots, took his torch from his equipment vest and walked back inside the house. He had no search warrant and a procedural misstep could jeopardise a conviction. He'd already left muddy boot-prints through the house, chasing the suspect. He could probably justify that, but an intentional search? Nope. So he didn't plan to touch anything. He just wanted to check there was no one else here. And to see for himself what kind of place Joshua and his companions had set up.

A door to the right off the main hallway stood ajar. A well-appointed office with all the signs of a hasty stripping of evidence.

Teak filing cabinet drawers were open and empty. Power cords lay near empty spaces on the large polished desk, as if a computer and maybe a hard drive had been taken. A wireless modem blinked on a bookshelf above a printer. The rapid on–off–on of the light suggested data was being transmitted somewhere, but he could see no other computers in this room. Simon had mentioned a surveillance system in the cottages down near the woolshed, which could still be transmitting.

A door on the far wall, opposite where he'd entered, opened into a large sitting room. While the office was teak and muted colours, this room was cream leather and vibrant silks, with outsized sofas, low tables and large scatter cushions on the carpeted floor. A huge television screen hung on one wall, with high quality speakers nearby. A bar in one corner was stocked with top-shelf spirits.

Nothing 'simple' about this space.

He went on through other rooms in the north wing of the house: another, smaller, sitting room, a home cinema, a luxury spa room, and three large bedrooms that reminded him of a top-class brothel he'd once raided. But there was no sign of anyone; the place was deserted.

The south wing of the house lacked the deep carpet of the north wing, and as he went from room to room, the stark contrast between the two halves struck him. It was pleasant enough, with cane furniture, polished wood floors and white-painted walls, but much simpler in style. A bathroom. A massage room. Two plain bedrooms with minimal furniture and decoration. Almost monastic. Definitely monastic when he reached a long room partitioned into four small cubicles, each with a single bed covered with a checked blanket, a small table and chair, and a wooden storage chest. There were few signs of personality or belongings. Joshua's books sat on a couple of the tables with notebooks and pencils. But when he reached the last space and flicked the beam of his torch around, the light caught a faded patchwork quilt on the bed. A simple nine-patch quilt, like his mother used to make. And from a corner of the otherwise empty desk, a worn brown teddy bear stared at him with one glass eye.

Steve squeezed his eyes shut. Grown men didn't cry. Hardened detectives didn't weep. Not even a six-year-old boy cried, handing over a much-loved bear to his little sister to keep her company when he went to big school.

He was in control. Tough. Unemotional. Objective.

And lying to himself.

He raised a hand to wave at the bear. 'Good to see you, Pooky.' His voice rasped in the silent house. 'Hope you've been keeping her out of trouble.'

Before he could get any more ridiculous he spun on his heel and strode away. With nothing more to see, he went outside, shut the front door to secure the premises and headed back down the track towards the outbuildings . . . and towards his sister. Although he still had no clue what the hell he would say to her. His only hope, among the rollercoaster of emotions and possibilities, was that a worn bear and a faded patchwork quilt were unlikely to be treasured by a drug-running cult leader.

•

'It's not safe to stay here. We're taking you to Derringvale where you can sleep tonight. You'll all be together. It's okay. It's all going to be okay.' Tess kept up the constant stream of reassurance, keeping her voice steady and low. Whatever was in the drug cocktail Joshua had given them – she suspected GHB – most had come down off their high, becoming lethargic and open to suggestion. She made use of that, encouraging them with hypnotic repetitiveness. Getting them away from here, with minimal anxiety, to where they could be helped, overrode her discomfort in using the persuasive techniques. Support, not manipulation. For their own good. Surely.

Fortunately they were so dazed that no one asked too many questions. Madeleine's explanation that Joshua had 'ascended to bliss' but that they were 'not ready' seemed to make sense in the warped view of the world Joshua had given them. More SES and RFS trucks had arrived, and a four-wheel-drive police vehicle with officers she knew from the Strathnairn station. They'd brought Gabe McCallum and the two kids back with them, and he hung around while one of the SES crew gave the little ones a full first-aid assessment.

Fraser hadn't returned, so Tess briefed the police to secure the machinery shed and other buildings, and told the SES to start organising the transport of Joshua's followers to Derringvale, a few at a time in the trucks.

'I heard what happened,' McCallum said when she'd finished. 'What can I do?'

She eyed him warily. Simon's friend, a fellow commando. Well, an ex-commando, Simon had said. Dark clothes, a two-day growth of beard, and a hard face with shadowed eyes. Strong and powerful and potentially dangerous. But he'd been helping Simon keep an eye on the place, and he'd looked after the two kids.

'Are you armed?' she asked.

He opened out his hands and his gaze didn't waver. 'No. There's a cooking knife in my backpack, which is somewhere up on that hillside. I don't touch other weapons now.'

But he could probably kill someone with whatever came to hand. Nevertheless, like Simon, she trusted him. 'There are still some stragglers. Come and help me round them up.'

She followed the now well-trodden path back to the waterfall, McCallum moving silently behind her. Halfway along they met Erin, her arms around two young women, both of them red-eyed and dazed. They both wore white wrap-dresses like Madeleine, but were much younger than her. Young, innocent and vulnerable.

'I need to get Willow and Rebecca back with the others,' Erin said. 'Madeleine and Tom are checking for any stragglers.'

'Good. Does Madeleine know that Steve is here?' It came out harsher than Tess intended.

'Yes, Simon told her.' As if Erin picked up her mixed feelings and frustration, she added, 'Go easy on her, Tess. She's done her best in difficult circumstances.'

'It's not her I'm angry with,' Tess said. And it wasn't. But she didn't say any more in front of the two young women – barely out of their teens – who'd been among Joshua's acolytes. Their whole world would be torn apart soon enough, and she knew from her own experience how devastating that could be. They would have to come to terms with having been no more than puppets during years of Joshua's deliberate lies and purposeful manipulations. At least Pastor Abraham had believed his doctrine and delusions, but some of those around him had played puppet masters, betraying the trust of their followers as callously as Joshua had betrayed his followers.

In the clearing near the top of the waterfall, the moon reflected off Madeleine's pale dress, making her easy to spot. She was speaking with a man, greying, strongly built, but as Tess and McCallum approached he nodded at Madeleine, then at her, before striding off into the darkness of the bush to the north.

Madeleine was about Tess's own age, early thirties. Although she'd commanded the group a short time ago, now alone, in her simple white dress and with long hair falling unbound, she seemed younger.

Aware of the authority of her uniform, Tess held out her right hand to demonstrate friendliness. 'Hi. I'm Tess Ballard. I understand you're Madeleine Fraser.'

The woman hesitated before she took the offered hand, shaking it briefly. 'Yes.'

'This is Gabe. He's helping us. Erin's explained to you what's happening? That we're taking people to a safe place in the Derringvale community hall for tonight? There'll be help and support there for those who want it.'

'Yes.' Her glance darted to the insignia on Tess's shoulder. 'Thank you, Senior Constable.'

Definitely the AC's daughter, familiar with police ranks. 'The man who just left – is he coming, too?' Tess asked.

'No . . . He . . .' She swallowed. 'That's Tom. There were some people who slipped away into the bush. He's gone to find them if he can. He . . . You can trust him. He helped to stop . . . what almost happened. He will come back.'

Other people had gone off into the bush? Tess suppressed a swearword. Way too much was going on and there were not enough officers or time to deal with it all. 'Okay. McCallum, can you help Tom search for the missing people? I'll get some of the SES crew to come and assist.' McCallum moved off straight away, after Tom. The SES guys wouldn't get here for another ten minutes, assuming she went to fetch them straight away. 'Madeleine, you should come with me now, and we'll get you over to Derringvale with the others.'

'Thank you.' Madeleine didn't move. 'My brother?'

'Detective Sergeant Fraser? He's not far away.'

'Is he . . . He must be furious with me. He probably doesn't want to see me.' She hugged herself, rubbing her hands up and down her bare arms as if the night air chilled her.

Tess sought for words to deal with emotions she didn't want to witness, let alone feel. Not her strength, this touchy-feely side of police work. But keeping Madeleine onside – a key witness to Joshua's crimes – was part of her duty, and that required some sensitivity.

She reached out and touched the woman's shoulder gently. 'Madeleine, I don't know him well, so I can't speak for him.

But I'm sure he understands that Joshua – that Peter Hollywell – manipulated you when you were very young and vulnerable.'

Madeleine began walking, still hugging her arms around herself, her words as jerky as her steps on the uneven ground. 'I believed in him. All these years. I thought he was special. Chosen. I loved him like an angel. But then Hayley found out it was all lies. All of it. And she disappeared and then my son saw him talking to Sybilla – kissing her – before she stepped off the waterfall. Then after what he did tonight – would have done . . .' She stopped in her tracks, and although Tess couldn't see her face in the dim light among the trees, distress racked her voice. 'What kind of evil does that, Constable?' A hard sob broke up her words. 'Everything I thought I knew . . . it's all gone. You must think me such a stupid fool for falling for those lies.'

Disbelief, shame, guilt, anger. So many complex emotional responses when cult victims discovered the truth. Not easy to work through. Tess said gently, 'No, I don't think you're stupid, Madeleine. People like Joshua, their teachings all seem reasonable – often good things we can all believe in. It's how they twist that to serve their own power that's wrong, not necessarily the ideas themselves.'

Madeleine shook her head wordlessly, as if she didn't know what to believe.

That feeling of being on a knife edge – with no longer anything solid behind, and no idea of the future – oh yes, Tess remembered the terror of it, the desolation and uncertainty. Madeleine would have to face all that and more. 'You're strong,' she said, knowing it was lame, not enough. 'You're going to find a way forward, I'm sure of it.'

Madeleine lifted her face, a sliver of moonlight glistening on her tear tracks. 'I have to. I've got two children. I have to make sense of things for them.'

'There'll be help and support. You won't have to do it alone.' Lucky Madeleine. There'd been no one for Tess. No family. Limited support from the authorities. No friends. Alone and ashamed, with little knowledge of the world and only the vague memories of how things had once been – how life *should* be – to guide her. Sixteen years later, and she still felt like a stranger in a foreign land.

The SES had rigged up some lights to illuminate the area around the sheds and cottages. The RFS hosed the still-burning woolshed and police officers from Strathnairn were fastening crime scene tape around the machinery shed. Erin and the two young women had joined a small group of people beside one of the trucks – a couple of guys in the bright orange SES uniform, and three more of Joshua's followers in their simple loose tops and trousers.

'Thank you for your kindness,' Madeleine murmured. 'Excuse me, please, I need to see Erin . . . to make sure my children . . .' Her voice trailed off and she hurried away.

Madeleine might not have seen Fraser and Simon, observing the scene from the shadows of one of the cottages. Or maybe she had, and couldn't yet face her brother. Tess well understood that nervousness. Keyed up and on the edge of exhaustion herself, with old memories stirred by this situation clawing at her composure, she couldn't face Fraser's tensions either.

Tess followed Madeleine, intending to ask the SES captain to help McCallum search the bushland near the falls for any wanderers. Practical, unemotional, *useful* action.

Several of the group with Erin saw Madeleine and watched as she approached. Tess caught the glance of one of the men, and noted the way he stopped and stared. A vague sense of familiarity stirred but he'd changed, grown from youth to man, and she didn't recognise him until she was just a few metres away. Too late to turn back. Too late to ignore him.

'Theresa!' A broad, wide-eyed smile lit his face and in two paces he stood directly in front of her, crowding her.

Shock and fatigue slowed her reactions and she didn't step backwards quickly enough or far enough before he pulled her into a hug, his arms squeezing her tight. Panic flared, almost paralysed her.

'I've found you at last. I've been looking for you.' His breath was hot against her ear. 'Everywhere, I searched for you. All these years. It's so good to see you, Theresa.' He drew back a little to look into her face. 'More beautiful than ever. My beautiful Theresa.'

Not his. Never his. With his hold loosened, she raised her arms to his chest to distance herself from him. 'Isaac.' *Get away from me. Don't touch me.* Her throat tight from suppressing the shout, she forced out a marginally less panicked, 'What are you doing here?'

'I live here now.' The pupils of his eyes were dilated, his grin more wild than natural. Probably still high on some kind of drug. As if her day hadn't been hellish enough already. Oblivious to her body language, he reached out a hand to cup her cheek. 'Joshua's wisdom has taught me about love and bliss.'

Love and bliss? She wanted to laugh or retch or both. She pulled his hand away from her face and stepped back, hands on her hips, professional authority in her solid stance. 'You'll need to go with the others to Derringvale for tonight. It's not safe here at the moment.'

His gaze skimmed over her, as if noticing for the first time her uniform cap, the badges on her sleeve, her equipment vest, her weapon in its holster at her side. 'You're a policewoman? You've joined the *police?*'

'Yes.' She gave him no further explanation. Owed him no explanation. Glancing past him, she called out to one of the SES volunteers. 'Have you got room on that truck for one more?'

'Sure do.' The guy came over and clasped Isaac's shoulder lightly. 'Come on, mate. Let's get you somewhere safe and warm. They've got food and bedding at the hall. You'll be comfy there for the rest of the night.'

Isaac gave her one last puzzled stare but his eyelids blinked, drooped lower, the hyper-energy rapidly fading. Responding to the SES volunteer's continued encouragement he turned away, stumbling slightly so that the guy had to give him a supportive arm across his back, and to help him on to the truck.

Tess scarcely breathed until the truck's headlights flicked on, the engine started and it pulled out and around to head up the track. She remained where she stood, holding her spine rigid because if she didn't her whole body might begin to shake. Control. No one had control over her but herself. Strength, resilience, independence, self-reliance, pride – no one from her past could take those away from her. Not Isaac, not Pastor Abraham, none of them.

•

While Simon briefed him on what he'd learned observing the property for the past twenty-four hours, Steve's gaze mostly stayed on his sister, talking with Erin, and occasionally drifted to Tess.

He'd left the supervision of the police presence to Tess on purpose, his personal involvement distracting and bringing with it the risk of the investigation being seen to be compromised. He trusted her efficiency and professionalism. Not unfeeling, but in control of her own emotions, cool and self-possessed. That composure only slipped for an instant when a guy approached and tried to hug her. The sudden glacial stiffness in Tess's body language put Steve on alert, but she dealt with the guy's unwanted attention adeptly, sending him off to an SES truck. Clearly not a happy reunion. Not as far as Tess was concerned, anyway. Also, none of Steve's business.

He should go and speak with his sister. She was still with Erin, and their conversation must have been involving him because they both glanced his way. Yet he remained where he was beside Simon. A coward. What the hell was he supposed to do? What was he supposed to say to her? *Hi Maddie, long time no see?*

Erin came across, straight to Simon, the two of them holding each other close. Steve turned away. They had a lot to face, with Simon's new-found daughter and the imminent enquiry into Joshua's shooting. They needed space and time together, alone.

But still he didn't walk over to his sister.

Erin lifted her head from Simon's shoulder. 'Go to her, Steve. She thinks you hate her for what she did. For what he made her do.'

A girl of fourteen, grappling with grief and depression and a less than perfect family. Their father had failed her. Steve had failed her. Maddie would have been powerless against the manipulations of the psychologist she should have been able to trust. Yet she'd shown tonight, with everything falling apart around her, that she had courage and integrity.

He didn't hate her. The huge stone in his chest wasn't hate for her. For himself, maybe. For Joshua and what he'd done. For all the grief and loss the man had put them through.

Across the distance between them, he met her hesitant gaze. Maddie. Scared of him. From all the tumbling emotions he drew out some courage and walked towards her. He didn't have words. Eyes blurring, throat clogged, he just put his arms around her. Maddie's tears soaked into his shoulder and they clung to each other, brother and sister together, as they hadn't done since the first harrowing days after their mother had died.

Familiar, yet disconcertingly unfamiliar. The old protective instincts for his little sister surged but he'd been out of his depth then and even more so now. Nineteen years. More than half their lives. Not a young teenager anymore, but a woman in her thirties, a stranger he didn't know.

He hugged her for their childhood, for the bond that had been between them, for the loneliness and grief and guilt of the long, dark years after she'd gone.

'I'm sorry,' his sister said eventually. 'I'm so, so sorry, Steve.'

'Sshh. You're safe. That's what matters.' The answers to the hundred questions he wanted to ask her mattered, too, but not as much. They could wait.

But Maddie had her own questions. She drew back to search his face. 'Dad . . . is he still . . . ?'

She didn't finish, and although she probably meant 'alive', Steve could have filled that gap with any number of words. Severe. Demanding. Judgemental. Uncompromising. Single-minded. Career-driven.

Yeah, definitely still alive. But the fact that she'd asked meant she must have had little to do with the outside world. A simple web search would have produced a zillion hits. Or just a read of a newspaper now and then would guarantee a quote from him more often than not.

'He's an Assistant Commissioner these days,' Steve explained. 'He moved to an apartment closer to the office a few years ago. Last time I spoke with him –' the stilted, obligatory, mercifully short Christmas phone call – 'he was fine.'

'I was so much trouble for him. And for you. He was always angry with you because of me. I thought it would be better if . . . if I wasn't there. I was so miserable. I had everything planned to end it all. But Peter – Joshua – said there was another way.'

Steve still had his arms around her, and he pulled her tighter so that she wouldn't be frightened by the rage in his face. Not at her. At Peter Hollywell. Joshua. The man who was supposed to be counselling her had helped her fake a suicide. Had showed up at the memorial service all compassion and sympathy, when all the while he'd spirited away a troubled teenage girl and broken her family.

'Bastard,' he muttered through gritted teeth. The memories still gave him nightmares. The hellish torment of the long week of searching for her, the extended cold silences between him and his father, the devastation at the discovery of her storm-soaked schoolbag and her suicide note on top of the sea cliffs.

His only regret about shooting the man tonight was that it had been a quick, clean death, with no opportunity to hold him to account for what he'd done.

'I still don't understand.' Maddie shook her head against his shoulder. 'I don't understand what was lies and what was real. I thought I knew him, thought he was special, but I was wrong, wasn't I? Did he murder them? Hayley and Sybilla?'

He had to respond carefully, police officer, not brother. 'We're still investigating their deaths. I don't have answers yet.' Suspicions, yes. But answers and evidence, no.

'He would have let all of us die tonight. He wanted that. He led them all to that. And Callie . . .' Her voice cracked. 'She wasn't even twenty and she's dead.' He tightened his arms around her, wordless. She gulped back sobs and lifted her head. 'Was it you who shot him? Who stopped him?'

A police shooting would be public knowledge by morning. The police would make a statement, the media would pick it up. 'Three of us fired, Maddie,' he acknowledged. 'We all thought it was the only way to save everyone.'

'I'm glad you did. I was terrified that I couldn't stop him. That they'd push me in and I wouldn't be able to save Tristan, either.'

'Tristan?'

Her face flushed, and she dropped her gaze. 'He's my son.'

'Tall lad? Late teens with dark wavy hair?' He'd seen the boy at the waterfall, hovering near her at one point.

She nodded. 'He's seventeen.'

Seventeen. The arithmetic only took Steve a nano-second. Nineteen years since Maddie had disappeared, aged just fourteen. He barely bit back the anger and the questions. Reassure Maddie, not interrogate her. 'He went on a truck just before you got back here. He was with a girl, a bit younger, and a child.'

'Good. That will be Lily, my little girl, and Hayley's daughter – Simon's daughter – Jasmine. Tris promised he'd find them and take them to safety. He always takes care of them.'

Two kids. She had two children. He couldn't get his head around it. But although he still saw his kid sister in her face, she'd left her own childhood far behind. He just had to deal with the here and now. 'You'll see them all in Derringvale as soon as we get you there.' He paused, recalling the image of Tristan carrying the sleepy child and supporting the drowsy teenage girl. 'Maddie – the girls – were they given something? Some kind of drug?'

'Joshua put something in the drinking water. I don't know what. He did it another time, to loosen people up, he said. To enhance their bliss. I told Tris not to drink it but I couldn't warn Jasmine. The little ones – they had their own drinks. Apple juice.' She bit her lip, eyes clouded. 'Once I wouldn't have believed he could ever hurt children. But I was so wrong about him . . . They will be okay, won't they?'

'There'll be paramedics at the hall to check them over.' Paramedics and child protection officers and police. 'Maddie, the police will be there, too,' he warned her. 'I'm sure they'll want to talk with you.' Especially since most of the others weren't in any fit state to be interviewed. 'I'll be off the case now, of course.'

'I understand. I'll cooperate fully. I owe it to my community to answer whatever questions the police have.' She touched a hand lightly to his shoulder. 'Steve, if I'm arrested, or if anything happens to me, could you . . . would you promise to look after Tristan and Lily? You're their uncle. They don't have anyone else.'

Look after two kids? He'd have laughed if the concern in her eyes hadn't been so real. 'Why do you think you might be arrested?'

'I was one of the sisters. We supported Joshua and provided leadership to the others. I believed in him, Steve. I didn't knowingly do anything illegal but maybe . . . maybe things got so twisted that I did. I helped persuade people to join our communities. If that was wrong, then I need to accept responsibility for what I've done. For helping to spread Joshua's lies.'

Steve doubted anyone would charge her, if that was all she'd been involved in. It would take days, weeks, perhaps even longer, for the police to unravel the cult's operations and determine what crimes, if any, had been committed, and by whom.

'I was one of the sisters.' That caught his attention. This morning Simon had reported observing six women in white conducting some kind of ritual outside the main house. Madeleine's simple, sleeveless white dress was similar to the ones the two murdered women had worn; similar also to the dress worn by the young woman who'd thrown herself into the deadly river, and to a couple of other young women he'd seen in the group.

Maddie shivered, the thin dress no protection for the midnight autumn chill. Or from the after-effects of adrenaline, trauma and shock.

'You're cold.' He didn't have a jacket he could give her. He tucked an arm around her shoulder and steered her towards the four-wheel-drive police vehicle. 'Hop in the back seat out of the breeze. I'll see if I can find a first-aid blanket or something.'

He'd been half aware of Tess, on the periphery of his vision. She and two of the Strathnairn officers who'd come in the four-wheel drive stood with the RFS captain, over towards the woolshed. They all watched a couple of firefighters dousing a particular corner of the smouldering structure. Sombre faces, tenseness in the way they stood, only the occasional exchange of conversation.

He'd go and find out what was worrying them, soon enough. First he needed to ask Maddie some more questions, before others started grilling her. He'd be placed on leave immediately, out of the investigation and the information loops, but in order to help her he needed to understand as much as possible.

In the back of the vehicle with the first-aid and rescue equipment he found a space blanket and he took it to Maddie, helping to wrap it around her shoulders. She let her head drop back against the seat rest, fatigue drawing her features tight. Not only fatigue. The interior light shining from above threw stark shadows on her face, highlighting her thinness, the papery frailty of her skin. The outlines of bones and veins showed in the hand clutching the blanket.

She was chronically undernourished. He'd seen the bodies of the two murdered women, and neither of them had carried an ounce of fat either. Standing in the open door, Steve gripped the doorframe, swearing silently. The sooner he could take her right away from all this, the better.

'You mentioned you're one of the "sisters". Were Hayley and Sybilla "sisters" as well?'

She huddled into the seat and turned to face him. 'Yes. He called us his sisters in bliss. But there are others, and now we have six in each community. Tonight's celebration was supposed to be for Rebecca and Callie becoming sisters. Because Hayley and Sybilla were . . . gone. But Callie . . . she's the one who . . . who died tonight.'

She stopped, swallowed, and closed her eyes while she battled emotion. A tear trailed down her cheek and she scrubbed it away with the heel of her hand.

He gave her a moment to compose herself while he reined in his own anger. Six sisters in each community. He hadn't yet tracked down how many communities there were. Even if there were only a couple of others, that meant almost twenty women who were dedicated to Joshua. The three girls he'd seen in white tonight were young and pretty, scarcely out of their teens, if that. He'd lay a bet that some of their names would be found on missing persons lists.

'I was here on Friday night,' he told Maddie. 'Up at the homestead. I spoke with a woman called Mary. Is she one of the sisters, too?'

She drew in a sharp breath. 'That was you? Mary had only just got home. She said it was a cop harassing her about a broken taillight.'

'I asked her about Hayley and Sybilla. She denied knowing either of them.'

Maddie stared at him. 'She lied.' It was as much exclamation as statement. Another betrayal of trust.

'How well do you know Mary?'

'She joined our group a few years ago. She's older than the rest of us, more worldly, and she took over looking after the group's money. We used to be just a few small, informal communities, but our life became more structured, with more rules, and we began encouraging people to join us in earnest.'

This fitted with his impression of Mary: a self-assured woman who expected to get what she wanted. A woman who lied smoothly without any hesitation. 'Where is she now?'

She frowned, concentrating. 'I don't know. She wasn't at the waterfall. Neither was Tamara, come to think of it. She's one of the sisters, too. Her son, David – he was there but he left afterwards. So did a couple of others. The policewoman said she'd send people to search for them, but they know their way around this area. They might not want to be found.'

And at least two people had driven off from the main homestead. Steve would have put his money on the driver being Mary. A woman who 'looked after' the money would likely be only too happy to disappear with the records and evidence. Joshua had been preparing some new strategy, on the brink of some major change. Two of the women who knew his true identity had been murdered in the past week. Joshua presumably hadn't been planning on dying himself, but given his track record in faking death, that whole scene at the waterfall had Steve's suspicions on high alert.

'Tell me more about Mary.'

'I tried to live in harmony with her. But it was hard sometimes. She wasn't like Hayley and Sybilla. She's very . . . determined. She wants everything to be her way. Tamara can be like that, too, but she's not as clever as Mary. They're competitive, the two of them. Tamara didn't like the amount of time Joshua spent with Mary.'

'So Mary is close to Joshua?' he asked. He didn't ask, '*Would she know what he was planning?*'

Maddie nodded. 'Very close. She often travels with him. And David. He's about three years older than Tris. Joshua always said he loved his children equally, but he was . . . teaching David things, more than Tristan. David is more like him than Tristan is.'

Tristan. His *nephew*. Who didn't take much after his sperm donor. Good. He might actually be able to warm to the kid. Maybe. If he could ever get his head around being an uncle.

The lights of an SES truck shone on the track, presumably one of the first ones to have gone to Derringvale returning for a second trip.

'There's a truck coming back now. You'll be able to go to Derringvale.'

She gripped his hand. 'You're coming too, aren't you?'

'I've got to tie up a few things here and then I'll come over.'

'I wish you could come with me. I'd feel safer with you.'

'Erin and Simon will go with you. I won't be far behind. But nothing's going to happen to you, Maddie. Joshua is dead. He can't threaten you or anyone else.' He smiled what he hoped was a reassuring smile. 'Stay here out of the wind for now. It won't be long before they're ready to go.'

Although she nodded, she bit her lip as if holding back a comment, and her eyes were wide, uneasy. She'd never entirely believed his assurances that there weren't monsters under her bed, either. But she'd clutched Pooky and bravely tried to face the darkness.

On his way to join Tess and the others he passed Erin and Simon, sitting on an old log seat outside the shearers' quarters. Erin's dress was as unsuitable for the cool night as Maddie's, and Simon had his arm around her shoulder.

'Go and wait in the car with Maddie, guys,' Steve said. 'You'll be warmer, and I know she'd appreciate the company.'

Simon stood immediately, holding out a hand to Erin as she rose.

'How's she doing?' Erin asked.

'Okay. A little apprehensive, though.'

'Not surprising. Her whole world has turned upside down. It's going to take her a while to adjust, Steve,' she said gently.

He understood that. It was going to take him a while to adjust, too, and he only had his sister's resurrection to deal with. When his superiors suspended him or sent him on leave, he'd have time to think about it.

In the semi-darkness, McCallum and an SES guy came down the track from the scrub, with supportive hands under the elbow of an older man between them, steadying his occasional stumbles.

McCallum left the SES man to take their charge the last short distance to a truck and crossed over to Steve and Simon.

'Is that guy okay?' Steve asked.

'Found him wandering. Pretty upset. Drugs might have messed with him.'

Not a conversationalist, this McCallum. 'Are there any others still out there?'

'Couple of guys at least. But I doubt they're drugged, they actively avoided us. I can go back, if you want.'

Send an ex-commando civilian back into the wilderness at night after men who didn't want to be found? 'No. You've been a great help. Thanks. Where's your gear? Do you need a lift somewhere?'

'No. Camp's not far. I'll head off in the morning.' With a brief nod to Simon and Erin he strolled away, east into the darkness beyond the machinery shed.

The breeze mercifully blew the smoke from the fire away across the paddocks. The firefighters still concentrated their efforts on the corner of the building, the whole shed now smouldering ruins. With a queasy turn in his gut, Steve recognised the strategy. Preserving evidence as best they could. A tough job for any firefighters, let alone volunteers.

Tess introduced him to the two constables from the Strathnairn station. He'd not met them in the few days since he'd been called in to the district, and they regarded him – the detective sergeant from another region – with wary curiosity. He didn't have time or energy for anything but the basic courtesies, and it didn't matter since his involvement in the investigation would be over within hours.

'What's the story?' he asked Tess, indicating the woolshed.

'The crew saw what might have been a body in the sheep pens underneath the shed.' A report, concise and to the point. 'It was too dangerous to go in, and half of the floor collapsed moments later.'

'They're not sure?'

'Not certain, no. Their view was blocked by smoke and by the poles under the floor. But whatever it is, it has something white around it. If we're lucky, it will just be some plastic or an old feedbag.' A slight flicker in the steady grey-eyed gaze betrayed her unease. She didn't expect they'd be lucky. Neither did he.

If they'd stopped at the woolshed when they'd arrived . . . If, if, if. A tiny word that could screw up even the sanest police officer's head.

'We made the right decision in the circumstances, Tess. We reached the waterfall in time to save lives.'

Tess gave a bare nod, her mouth tight. He didn't entirely believe it, either.

As well as the 'ifs' and doubts about his decision, the fact that the object the firefighters had seen was white gnawed at him. Neither Tamara nor Mary had been at the waterfall, both of them 'sisters' who wore white. Maddie had said there was tension between the two women. Tamara had been with Joshua longer than Maddie, longer than Hayley and Sybilla, and must have surely known his true identity. That seemed the most likely motive for the murders. So had Tamara been at risk, also? Or was she involved in whatever Joshua was planning?

More questions he didn't have answers for. It might be a day or two before Forensics could access the body, if it was a body. It would be longer before an ID could be made.

If Joshua had acted alone, then Maddie should be safe now. But if he hadn't, then his sister might still be at risk.

CHAPTER 3

Neither Tess nor Fraser spoke on the drive to Derringvale, other than the occasional brief exchange with the constable who drove them. In the back seat, Tess closed her eyes to discourage conversation. Not that Fraser tried to make any. He sat in front, mostly staring out the window into the darkness, occupied with his own thoughts.

Her body ached from exhaustion. It had been about eighty hours since she'd been first officer on the scene when Simon Kennedy had returned from weeks away to find his estranged wife's body in his house. Three full-on days and nights, with sleep snatched for a few hours here and there, restless and haunted.

She fought against drowsiness, not daring to allow herself to slide into sleep. Home and her bed were a long way off yet. She needed to stay alert for the debrief with her superiors at

Derringvale. She needed to be alert in case she encountered Isaac again.

The jolting drive over rough paddocks gave way to farm track, then gravel road, then the relative smoothness of the main road before the lights of Derringvale appeared. Not many of them at this hour in the small community. Smaller even than Goodabri, with only a hundred or so inhabitants, and most of them, sensibly, sleeping.

But at the end of the scattering of houses, lights blazed at the community hall, and vehicles were parked along the street in front and the paddock behind. Tess unclipped her seatbelt and opened the door as the car stopped.

Only a moment behind her, Fraser matched her pace towards the hall. 'Nick will be waiting for us. I can get someone to take you home if you'd rather not do the debriefing interview now, Tess.'

If she wimped out now they'd think her fragile and have the psychs on to her first thing tomorrow to assess her mental state. And that would be worse than facing the inspector and getting her report over and done with now.

'I'm fine, Sarge. Perfectly capable of telling him what I did and why.' That she'd shot to kill a man. It didn't matter whether her bullet or Fraser's or Simon's had hit him; she'd fired at him with that intent. And she didn't plan on brooding on that until she made it to the peace and privacy of her cottage.

Fraser gave her a sharp, sideways look, but they were almost at the steps to the hall and Nick Matheson, the inspector, was coming down them.

'Come round the back,' Matheson said. 'It's too crowded in the main hall.'

Like hundreds of old halls in country towns, the front doors opened into the large main space, with a kitchen to one side and toilets to the other. Beyond the open door, she could see people sitting and lying on camp beds and mats while paramedics and community workers moved among them. Definitely too crowded for her liking. Especially since Isaac was in there, somewhere.

Rather than walking through the hall, Matheson led them around the outside of the building to the rear, where a smaller door led to a backstage area. Someone had pulled out an old sofa covered in a tartan blanket – maybe a leftover prop from a theatre production – and the inspector invited them to sit.

Fraser settled comfortably at one end, but Tess perched on the edge, rather than being swallowed up by the too-soft cushions.

While Matheson pulled up a couple of rickety folding chairs, footsteps sounded across the stage and within a moment Leah Haddad joined them. A detective senior sergeant from Homicide in Sydney, sent to head the investigation into the murders, Tess had come to respect her in the past three days despite, or perhaps because of, her tough manner and approach.

'This isn't a formal interview,' Matheson said. 'We just need a brief report on what happened out there, and to find out what support you need.'

Fraser spoke up immediately. 'I gave the order to shoot Joshua Kristos. I considered multiple lives to be imminently at risk and there was no other way to stop him. Constable Ballard acted on my order.'

Damn. Now she had to contradict him in front of the inspector and the senior sergeant.

'With all due respect, sir,' she said to Matheson, 'the sarge didn't order me. I acted on my own initiative.'

Fraser turned to her, and despite the professionally serious demeanour, a light that might have been self-satisfaction or triumph flared briefly in his eyes. 'I'm the senior officer, I had my weapon drawn and I said to you, "We have to stop him." I think Nick and Leah would agree that, in the circumstances, those words constituted an order.'

He'd won. Although she hadn't considered his words a direct order then – and he probably hadn't either – the official record would undoubtedly regard it as so. He'd intimated in the immediate moments after the shooting that he intended to protect her and to bear chief responsibility, and now, using his rank and the truth, he'd positioned himself to do so.

Too tired, she didn't argue. He'd told the truth. Later she might be able to make the Professional Standards investigators understand that she, a female senior constable, would have certainly refused an order from a male detective sergeant if she doubted its wisdom or ethics. That she would likely have fired at Joshua even if Fraser had not had his gun ready. That she trusted her own judgement more than others', irrespective of rank. Although this was not an argument she should make now when she could hardly keep a thought straight.

'Thanks, both of you, for your professionalism and honesty,' Matheson said, as if they hadn't just demonstrated some disagreement. 'If you're up to it, I'd appreciate it if you could walk us briefly through what happened. If you can't yet, that's okay. If you'd prefer to speak to a counsellor, either of you, you have that right, with no reflection on your capability. There'll be a police counsellor arriving with the critical incident team in the morning. In the meantime, I've already called in a psychologist from Strathnairn and you can talk with her, entirely confidentially, if you wish.'

Fraser gave Tess a small nod, letting her answer first.

Let down her guard to a psychologist about shooting a psychologist? 'Thank you, sir,' she said with a fair degree of politeness, 'but it's not necessary.'

'I'm not inclined towards trusting psychologists just at the moment,' Fraser said more honestly, with a flicker of black humour. 'So I'll pass for now, too.'

Matheson accepted their decisions and didn't press further. Tess let Fraser take the lead in outlining the events, although she stepped in and explained about the group members who'd gone off into the bush, and the firefighters' suspicions about the possible body in the woolshed. Haddad asked questions and Matheson clarified some points, but all up it was only twenty minutes or so before they'd covered the necessary detail.

Matheson rose to his feet and thanked both of them. 'I'll find someone to drive you home to Goodabri shortly, Tess. Call me tomorrow –' he glanced at his watch – 'this afternoon, after you've had some rest. Professional Standards will want to speak with you, but your health and welfare come first. Don't hesitate to ask for whatever you need.'

Tess let herself out the back door of the hall, into the quiet and dark of the night. A small group of SES volunteers occupied a picnic table in the small park next to the hall, waiting in case of further need. Most of the crews in the wider district must have been called out tonight.

Perhaps she could ask one of them to give her a ride home. But approaching a bored, idle SES crew who'd be full of curiosity and questions? No. They'd likely be more than happy to help, but avoiding people – her colleagues, community services, Joshua's people, *Isaac* – was her preference. She lingered in the shadows of a large gum tree, grateful for some moments alone.

The old hall had installed indoor plumbing some decades ago, but the original outdoor toilets still stood behind it, the small building freshly painted, the paved path to it well maintained. The door on the gents' side opened with a loud, unoiled creak.

Tess stepped further back into the shadows, up against a fence, but the path he walked unsteadily along passed close to her. Isaac. She held herself motionless but he saw her and stopped abruptly, that grin slowly spreading over his face.

'Tess. You came to find me. I knew you would. We're meant to be, you and I, aren't we?'

'No. No, we're not.' She went to walk past him but he lunged and his arms clamped around her from behind. She bent her head away from the sour smell of old sweat and readied herself to break his hold.

His breath hot on her neck, he said, 'You're so beautiful, Tess. More than you were. I've waited all this time for you. You're mine now.'

'No. I'm not yours, Isaac. I never was.' She pushed down the rising panic and put all her authority into her voice. 'Let me go. Now.'

He laughed. 'Still contrary, aren't you? Never mind. I know how to deal with that.' His arms tightened around her painfully.

She raised her foot, kicked back hard into his shins, and as surprise loosened his hold, she rammed her elbows back into his torso. He folded over, winded, and she wrenched out of his grasp, retreating metres away.

'Don't ever touch me again, Isaac. Don't come near me, or I'll have you arrested. I don't ever want to see you again.'

'You won't arrest me,' he insisted. 'You can't. You can't arrest your husband.'

Cold flooded through her veins. 'You're not my husband. You never were. And I will arrest you if you come near me again.'

He was straightening up, regaining his breath. 'You were promised to me. Before God.'

'I made no promises and God had nothing to do with that hell. Goodbye, Isaac.' She strode off down the path, her breathing rough and hard, trying not to run. She refused to give him that much power over her. She hoped no one had witnessed that scene. No witnesses, no explanations necessary.

'Tess! Stop!'

She didn't stop. Running footsteps pounded behind her, and she spun around just as he leapt. But he caught her off balance, and she fell, hard onto the ground, Isaac on top of her.

•

'Are you covering for her, Steve?'

Leah Haddad asked the question, blunt as ever. Technically his superior, they'd worked well together on a couple of investigations, but with all the weight of HQ behind her she could make life hell for him if she thought he'd stuffed up her case.

'No,' he said, with a reasonable degree of truth. 'My actions and words were a clear indication to her and she followed suit. It was my judgement call, and I made it.' And if anyone's career was about to be buried in shit, it better be his, not hers.

'Are you protecting Simon Kennedy?' she persisted. 'You didn't happen to mention him.'

True, he hadn't mentioned him, but that hadn't been intentional. 'You asked for the brief summary, not a second-by-second account.'

'He asked to see me as soon as he arrived here.' She threw up her hands in frustration. 'This whole thing is a bloody mess. Not just two police officers, but an army reserve commando shooting an unarmed civilian. And we won't frigging know until we find the body which one of you succeeded.'

'Police divers will be here in a few hours,' Nick said. 'If the river levels have dropped enough, the SES will start searching after sunrise.'

'Have you got any feeling about whose bullet the pathologist will dig out of him?' Leah asked.

'Off the record?'

Nick nodded. 'This is all off the record. No formal caution, no record.'

'I'm a fairly good shot,' Steve admitted. 'Got a medal or two from the Police Games. But if you want to be honest, then over a distance of more than fifty metres, at night, you'd probably have to put your money on the highly trained and experienced commando with the rifle and the scope, rather than a mildly skilled cop with a Glock.'

'Shit,' said Leah.

'Yeah,' Steve agreed. 'But if it comes down to that, then it will stand in his favour that three of us took the same decision. One young woman was already dead. Kristos – Hollywell – didn't have a gun or a knife but he'd spent years building psychological weapons in their heads. Plus they showed strong signs of intoxication with drugs – euphoria, suggestibility. I'm guessing GHB or ice or similar. I stand by my judgement, and I'll stand by Simon's and Tess's.'

Nick steepled his fingers, a sign Steve recognised. He waited for the long moment before the man spoke. 'Professional Standards,' Nick said carefully, 'will want to know at what point you knew your sister was alive.'

Yes, they would. 'I didn't know, then. I knew in the afternoon that Kristos was Hollywell, her psychologist. All I had at that point was pure speculation – "what ifs?" – and a gap of nineteen years. I didn't know until maybe five minutes before I fired that there was a Madeleine with the group. It's a common enough name. I didn't see her, I didn't know for sure it was her, until after I'd fired at him.'

Neither Nick nor Leah said anything immediately so he added, 'I understand I'll be suspended or placed on leave or whatever. I guess I need to take some leave, anyway, sort out what Maddie wants to do from here.'

'You're due a few days off duty so take those for now. Then see what Professional Standards and your own inspector have to say.' Nick paused, then asked, 'Would you like me to notify your father? About your sister? Or I could arrange for him to be notified in person.'

Steve almost grasped the chance to avoid that particular conversation. But he didn't. 'Thanks, but I'll phone him in a couple of hours after I've spoken with Maddie again. No sense waking him up in the middle of the night when there are only two flights a day to Strathnairn.'

No sense facing his father's cold anger – and he'd be angry, for sure, about Steve's mess with Professional Standards – before he had to. No sense making Maddie face the old man until she'd had some rest. Whether she'd be ready even then was up to her to decide.

He pushed his aching body up from the sagging cushions of the sofa, and unbuckled his holster, passing his service weapon to Nick. 'Thanks for your support, Leah, Nick. You know I'll assist the investigation any way I can. But for now, I'd better go and see my sister.'

As he walked out the door, it occurred to him it might be the end of his last day of active service as a police officer. Fifteen years, too many cases, too many deaths.

But he didn't know if he could imagine himself as anything else.

And he didn't know, if there was still a threat to Maddie, how he could keep her and her children safe when he'd be excluded from the investigation and without access to the resources he'd always relied on.

He heard the shout as he rounded the corner of the hall – Tess's name, followed by a muffled cry. Figures struggled on the ground in the shadows of the hall and he raced forward. Tess – it had to be Tess in that dark uniform – beneath a guy in lighter clothes. Just before he reached them the man jerked and gave a harsh yell, curling on the ground, clutching his balls. Steve grabbed hold of his shirt and dragged him a metre away, but the guy was oblivious.

For a second, Tess lay on her back on the ground, breathing heavily, and Steve dropped to his knees beside her, scanning for injury. 'Jesus, Tess, are you hurt?'

'No.' Abruptly she rolled over to her side, without much obvious pain. 'Just keep that frigging bastard away from me.'

The bastard still lay on the ground. Steve watched him, ready to cuff him. Ready to punch him into last week if he moved so much as an inch back towards Tess.

She pushed herself up to her knees. He offered a hand to help her up but she scrambled to her feet unaided. A woman who valued her personal space, even before this incident. She rubbed at her shoulder, but her face read anger rather than pain as she kept a wary eye on her attacker.

Steve positioned himself between them, his boot conveniently close to the guy's gut. 'This is the guy you were talking to at Serenity Hill, isn't he? You know him?'

She gave a bare nod. 'I did. A long time ago.' She offered no other explanation.

'So, you want to tell me what happened here?'

'No.' Her eyes as grey as cold metal, she looked him in the face and lied. 'Nothing happened here, Sarge.'

It hurt, that lie. As if she didn't trust him after three intense days and nights working together. But she held his gaze, knowing he knew she lied, and that had to be an indication of trusting him. Trusting him to understand. Maybe his brain was too foggy or maybe he was just a dumb jerk but he didn't understand. 'You're protecting him?'

'No.'

The guy started to rise unsteadily, and Steve leaned down, gripped his forearm and hauled him to his feet, keeping a tight hold on him. 'I should be arresting him, Tess.'

'No.'

'You can't arrest me,' the man said. 'She can't arrest me.'

Steve raised an eyebrow at Tess, uncertain how she wanted this handled.

She stepped forward, feet slightly apart, a strong stance facing the man. 'Shut up, Zac. You're bloody lucky I haven't.'

Zac pulled his arm from Steve's loosened grasp but made no move towards her. 'I was giving you a hug. But it's okay, Tess. I forgive you. It's okay between us.'

What kind of loony was this guy, not to recognise those signals? Steve closed his hand around the baton on his hip, his preferred weapon in close quarters. Just in case.

Tess didn't reach for a weapon but the contempt in her glare blazed a warning. 'That wasn't a hug and there is nothing between us. If you come anywhere near me again, be certain I will arrest you. Now get inside. Keep away from me. And when it's daylight go somewhere far away from here and stay there.'

Zac just smiled. 'You can't tell me what to do, Tess. But you're upset. You've been corrupted by the world and you need some time to understand your sins and find the bliss of God again. I'll pray for you.'

With that he walked away, murmuring softly under his breath, his steps not entirely straight as he headed to the front of the hall. Steve clenched and unclenched his fists, itching to go after him, but he had to respect Tess's wishes, even if he didn't understand them.

She let out a long, slow breath.

'You sure you're okay?' Steve asked.

'I'm fine.'

There was a not-entire-truth again. Steve didn't push it. Much. 'Is there a reason you care to share about why we didn't arrest him for assault?'

'There's a reason.' She rubbed her shoulder again. 'Sorry, I'd rather not explain. And please – please don't tell the others about this. I don't want a fuss.'

'Dammit, Tess, he doesn't seem worth protecting.'

'I'm not protecting him, Sarge,' she said. She dropped her gaze, biting her lip, and for the first time in his experience she spoke in a small voice. 'I'm protecting me.'

The shock of her words hit him almost physically. Whatever had happened in the past, she'd been hurt, badly. Seeing self-possessed, assertive Tess admitting that vulnerability rattled him more than he understood.

I'll protect you, he wanted to say. But how could he? He couldn't protect her against a legal system that dragged female assault victims into court to confront their attackers, and then dragged their reputations through the muck. And he couldn't protect her from Zac, other than here and now. She lived and worked in Goodabri. Steve lived and worked in Birraga, two hours away. He couldn't do anything more for her than he'd do for any other officer. Refer her to relevant support. Make arrangements for her safety and well-being. Find out what he could about Zac, assess the threat.

'Come on inside,' he said. 'The paramedics can take a look at your shoulder. And then I'll find someone to drive you home.'

And then he might not see her again. She'd be on leave, he'd probably be heading back to Birraga in a day or so, and there'd be no reason for their paths to cross again until the coronial inquest, if then.

He'd miss her. That he thought of her at all in that way took him by surprise. But he had a ton on his plate now with Maddie and her family and the inquiry into Joshua's death, and he had a lousy track record with women, anyway. A woman like Tess deserved a hell of a lot better than him.

•

Tess tried not to resent the necessity of having someone drive her home to the police cottage at Goodabri. Driving eighty kilometres herself with a bruised shoulder and a high level of exhaustion was not anywhere near sensible. At least Fraser had asked Dee Edwards. In Tess's two months in the district, based out at the tiny one-officer station in Goodabri, Dee had come out from the main station at Strathnairn to be her back-up on a couple of domestic violence visits, and they worked comfortably together.

'Steve said one of the guys in there had been bothering you,' Dee said as she pulled out on to the road. 'Tall, lanky guy in brown? Isaac, I think his name was.'

Bothering her. Fraser had honoured her request not to mention the attack, but he'd mentioned a 'minor incident' when he'd insisted the paramedics look at her shoulder, and she'd seen him having a quiet word with Dee.

'Yes. That's him. He's someone I knew a long time ago.'

'Ah. He was asking about you earlier. Before you came back from Serenity Hill.' She let the words hang in the air, as if they might not be important.

Tess closed her fingers around the seatbelt crossing her suddenly tight chest. 'What did you tell him?'

'Don't worry. Not much. I just said you were a damn good police officer and a friend, and then I made up a reason to walk away.'

A friend. Dee, describing her as a friend. Tess had no clue how to respond.

Socially reserved, unfamiliar with so much of the popular culture others took for granted, Tess still found friendship difficult to navigate. Especially with someone like Dee; cheerful, confident, bubbling with fun and humour and liked by all her colleagues. She probably called everyone a friend.

'Thanks,' Tess said at last, because she owed Dee an explanation of sorts. 'If you come across him again, please don't tell him anything more about me.'

Dee cast a curious glance her way but simply said, 'No worries.'

The silence stretched while they crossed the bridge over the river, the white swirl of rushing water shining in the moonlight, the same torrent that held the bodies of Joshua and the young woman. Had they been carried past this point already? Or were they snagged somewhere further upstream, caught up in trees or rocks? Tess stared at the road ahead, but the images stayed in her mind.

They turned off the main road to Strathnairn and on to the shortcut, the back route that led east to Goodabri. Very little traffic used this road. Only the locals and visitors to the national park that stretched along this side of the river most of the way between Derringvale and Goodabri.

The light from the moon shone through the trees lining the road, flickering across the black ribbon of bitumen in a ghostly dance, much like the memories constantly flitting around in her mind, haunting her. They should have stayed locked away, buried in her past, but Isaac's attack had proven the weakness of the lock, and the memories flooded over her, eroding her hard-fought-for sense of self-worth and confidence.

Memories . . . fear . . . panic . . .

No.

No, she wasn't back there, back then. She pressed her fist against her racing heartbeat, willing it to slow. Breathe deeply in, breathe slowly out. And again.

She might have made some sound because Dee asked, 'Everything okay?'

'Yes. I'm okay. Thanks.'

'It must have been pretty intense out there tonight. Having an unwelcome blast from the past on top of it all wins the jackpot of crap.'

'Definitely not fun,' Tess agreed.

'If you happen to want to talk about anything, I have a sympathetic ear and nothing to do for the next seventy kilometres.'

No way Tess could discuss anything sensitive with a colleague, however friendly and supportive. Not that she thought Dee would betray a confidence or gossip, but she didn't share her private life with anyone.

'I appreciate the offer, Dee, but I really am okay. Isaac turning up was a shit of a surprise –' now *there* was an understatement – 'but I probably won't ever see him again and that suits me fine. As for the other, three of us made the same decision at the same time, and it's not one I'm regretting in hindsight.'

'Good. We're all behind you, you know. You and Simon and Steve. All of you are sane and experienced and the fact you all made the same judgement call says a hell of a lot about the situation.'

She spoke so familiarly of Fraser that Tess asked, 'Did you know him before this? Steve Fraser?'

'I've been down to Birraga district a couple of times when they've needed extras. Birraga is like Strath – a station that covers a large area, with a few smaller communities. I helped search for a kiddie missing from Dungirri a year or so ago. Was back there a couple of months ago when they had some more trouble. Steve used to be a bit of an arsehole apparently but most of the crew down there think he's come up okay. Got a rep as a bit of a flirt, but nothing obnoxious.'

A reputation as a flirt. Not surprising, although Tess couldn't think of any time when his words or his manner had been inappropriate. Not to her, anyway. Maybe he wasn't interested in flirting with her. But the quick flash of a teasing grin she'd seen a few times in the first day or so – yes, she could see how that could border on flirtatious.

Steve Fraser wasn't on her radar. She doubted she was on his. Most guys thought she was frigid or lesbian because she tended to give off 'not interested' signals, whether she intended to or not.

Unfortunately those signals didn't work on Isaac. Perhaps once the effects of the drugs and Joshua's influence wore off he'd forget her again. He'd pray for her, he'd said. That she'd understand her sins and find God again.

Maybe his views of God had been mellowed by Joshua's less theist teachings. She hoped so. Because when she'd known him, Isaac's God – Pastor Abraham's God – had believed in obedience, discipline, punishment and the subjugation of women to the authority and will of men.

Did Isaac seriously consider the unlawful sham of a wedding ceremony a binding one? If he took it into his head that she needed punishment for her sins then he might consider he, as her 'husband', had a duty to exact punishment and ensure her conformity.

He'd been unstable as a teenager. Joshua's drugs aside, he didn't seem much more stable now.

She didn't pray. If God ignored a terrified, broken, repentant seventeen-year-old, he sure as hell wouldn't pay attention to a trained, experienced, thirty-three-year-old police officer.

If she needed to deal with Isaac, she'd have to do it alone.

•

'They want to take Lily to hospital. Jasmine, too. For observation, they said. Will it be okay? Should I let her go?'

Steve steered his sister to a wooden bench under a tree outside the hall. It was more peaceful here, in the still air of the small hours of the morning. More private, without his understandably curious colleagues nearby. The lights from the hall spilled this far, but across the road the paddocks stretched into the darkness and beyond, to the farmland and dry bushland of the western plains.

A world away from the Sydney suburbs they'd grown up in, but here he was, an older brother again, with Maddie to support and reassure. 'Yes, Lily should be checked over in hospital. I'm sure she'll be fine, but it's best to have them keeping an eye on her.'

Someone had given her a warmer blanket and she huddled into it as she sat on the bench. 'But she'll be so scared when she wakes up. She doesn't even know what a hospital is.'

A kid of five or six who didn't know what a hospital was? Steve had no idea if that was normal or not. He'd certainly known, by that age. Hushed visits to their mother, her face as pale as the white sheets. Trying to keep Maddie entertained while solemn doctors talked behind closed curtains with their parents. Extended holidays at their aunt's home near the ocean in Kurnell when Mum had to go back to hospital again and again and again.

Frightening places, hospitals.

'They'll let you stay with her, Maddie. And she probably won't be in there for long. Maybe just a few hours.'

'Oh.' She gave a shaky laugh that bordered on crying. 'Just a few hours? I don't know where to go after that. I guess I can't go back. I don't want to go back. Not now that I know Joshua lied about everything. But I've got no money. Nothing.' Her face fell. 'Nothing and two kids to look after.'

The enormity of the challenges ahead started to sink in. Despite her dignity and perceptiveness in her role as one of the sisters, when it came to life outside the community, her naivety and inexperience would make things tough and leave her open for exploitation. 'We'll sort something out,' reassured Steve. 'I'll book a motel in Strathnairn for us for a couple of nights.'

'I thought maybe we could stay with you,' Maddie said uncertainly. 'But I don't even know if you've got a wife, or a family of your own.'

Just a fraction of what she didn't know about him. 'I don't have a wife, or girlfriend, or kids.' One more failure, as far as his father was concerned. Their father had been married with two kids by the same age. 'I don't live in this area, Maddie. I'm based in Birraga now.' And he had his own accommodation problems at the moment, after the place he'd rented had sold. He'd been living in the pub for a few weeks, pending confirmation of his permanent transfer to Birraga. And now it was through, but he'd not had time to house-hunt. 'Birraga's a couple of hours south-ish from here. I just got called in to help on this case. I don't have to rush back, though, so you can think about where you want to go after this. I guess you're on the supporting parent's benefit or whatever social services call it these days?'

She looked at him, surprised. 'No. No, we support ourselves. I've never claimed benefits. But everything we earned was communal.'

So she truly did have nothing. Just as well he had a decent-paying job and no time to spend what he earned. 'Don't worry. I can help out for now. It'll be okay. Dad will be able to help, too.'

She fidgeted with the edge of the blanket. 'You're going to tell him? About me?'

'Yes, Maddie. It's not something I can keep from him.'

'But he'll be furious with me. Disgusted.'

Steve slung an arm around her shoulder as though they were kids again, and she rested her head against him, trusting. Trusting him to solve her problems. Like he'd ever been any good at that, although he'd always tried. 'Dad always loved you, Maddie. Damned lousy at expressing it, but he grieved hard after you . . . after you left. He won't know how to say it, but he'll be overjoyed to see you.' He'd better be, otherwise Steve would tell him exactly what he thought. 'Besides, you've made him a grandfather. He'll be so excited he might even crack a smile.'

She made a sound that might have been a tiny chuckle. Or a sob. The old joke between them had too much truth to have ever been particularly funny. No wonder she'd preferred Joshua's affection and love – or what passed for it – to the emotional wilderness their home had become after their mother's death. Emotions weren't orderly, and their father needed order more than he needed to express things he didn't understand.

'The important thing is, Maddie, were you happy? Did Joshua's way of life treat you well?'

'Yes, I was happy. I lived simply but I wanted it that way. I had purpose, meaning and love all around me. I might have been a fool, believing him, but I did love him. And whatever else Joshua has done, he gave me two beautiful children. I can't regret them.'

'He was very clever, Maddie. There's nothing wrong with wanting to live a simple, peaceful life. He fooled a lot of people for a long time.' Perhaps the guy had even fooled himself. History was littered with people who had developed god complexes. But the murdered women, and Joshua standing at the waterfall tonight urging his people to their deaths smacked more of homicidal megalomaniac than delusional prophet.

A couple of paramedics had come out from the hall and were retrieving a gurney from the back of their ambulance. Soon they'd start transporting the kids to the hospital, twenty kilometres away. Maddie would be needed with them. That gave him only a short time to ask questions he wanted answers to.

'One of the guys in your group – his name's Zac – what can you tell me about him? Tall, skinny guy, in his thirties.'

'That's Isaac Matthias. He's been with us a few years. Isaac is . . .' Her frowning pause set alarm bells clanging.

'Is what, Maddie?'

'He works hard. He's always helped others.'

Steve waited for the 'but'.

'He's no trouble except . . . Except he didn't always understand Joshua's teachings.' She gave a bitter laugh. 'Maybe he is smarter than I thought. I don't know much about his background, but he was very religious, and sometimes tried to teach the others about God and sin and other things we don't believe in in the same way. We believe that the higher powers are so far beyond us that they are unknown and unknowable.'

'You need some time to understand your sins . . . I'll pray for you.' Steve wasn't concerned so much about the praying as he was about Isaac lecturing Tess on her supposed sins. The alarm bells clanged louder.

'How was he with women?' he asked.

'Women? As far as I know, he didn't get involved with anyone. He said he was married, that she'd lost the path, but that he'd stay true to her.'

Married? Was he *married* to Tess? Steve's gut twisted at the thought. It couldn't be true. He didn't want it to be true.

'The thing about Isaac—' Maddie hesitated. 'Look, he's okay. As I said, no trouble. But he's – well, quite socially awkward. And he can be a bit obsessive about some things.'

He'd certainly missed clear signals. Or chosen to ignore them. If he became obsessive about Tess . . . Steve pulled that thought up short. Not his business. As an experienced senior constable,

Tess had the skills, knowledge and resources at hand to assess the situation and handle it appropriately.

The very last thing either of them needed was for him to become obsessive about her safety . . .

Four hours later, sitting in a hospital room with his laptop, he'd checked every database he had access to and searched website after website but had no more information about Isaac Matthias. The man didn't exist online.

The text on the screen blurred again and Steve yawned and rubbed his gritty eyes. Maddie slept on a hospital bed with a protective arm around Lily. Jasmine, the thirteen-year-old daughter Simon had never met, slept in the next bed. A nurse came in every now and then to check Lily's and Jasmine's blood pressure, heart rate and breathing, but they'd both roused a few times and the medical staff were confident they'd sleep off the effects of the drugs before long.

Tristan sat on the floor, his back against a wall, arms on his knees. Every now and then he dozed off, but he'd wake again after a short while. He and Steve had only exchanged a few words. The lad clearly erred on the side of distrusting this strange uncle rather than trusting him, despite Madeleine's assurances.

Steve wasn't sure what to do with an almost-grown nephew, either, other than murmuring a comment now and then when he looked up and saw the lad watching him.

Steve checked the time on his computer. Six-thirty in the morning. He couldn't put it off any longer. His father would be awake, getting ready for work. He closed his laptop, left it on his chair.

'Just going to make a phone call,' he whispered to Tristan. 'Won't be long.'

The early morning air was cool and fresh after the air conditioning inside, the sun low in a clear blue sky. Outside the hospital's main entrance a couple of wooden benches occupied a small patch of grass in the sunlight. Despite his exhaustion, Steve didn't sit. Phone in hand, he flicked through his contacts list, thumb poised on his father's number.

'Just effing do it,' he muttered to himself.

The phone rang twice before his father answered brusquely.

'Dad, it's Steve.'

'What's wrong?'

'Nothing. Nothing's wrong.' Hell. 'Dad, do you remember the psychologist that Maddie saw? He's turned up in the case I'm working on, calling himself Joshua and leading a group that I guess you'd call a cult.'

'So?' Short, sharp, impatient.

'Ah, there's no easy way to say this.' He sucked in a deep breath, counted to three. *Just say it.* 'We never found Maddie's body because there wasn't one to find. She's not dead. She's been with this group the whole time.'

Steve's pulse pounded in his ears through the ensuing silence. Maybe he should have arranged someone to call at his dad's place. But then his father would have assumed straight away that something had happened to Steve. He wouldn't wish that on anyone.

'Is this some kind of sick joke?' his father growled at last.

'No, Dad. Maddie's alive and well.' And the mother of two. But he'd leave that shock for a little longer.

'It can't be her. Someone's assumed her identity, trying to get to us.'

He heard the incomprehension in his father's voice, the hardly daring to believe. For once, he couldn't blame him for doubting.

'It is definitely her, Dad.' Her and Pooky. 'I've been talking with her for the last few hours. She's the image of Mum. Even has some of her mannerisms.'

'But . . . why? How . . . ?'

He could imagine his father's bewilderment. There were no procedures to deal with this. No precedent. No precedent for Steve to explain in brief words that might answer his father's unspoken questions. 'Dad, she was depressed and grieving and none of us were happy. He manipulated her fears. He's an expert at it. Persuaded her that we'd be better off without her. She was an unhappy, troubled kid and she believed him.'

Again a long silence, but he could hear his father's breathing, small gasps, uneven, battling emotions. Anger won, and his usually rigid, controlled father burst out, 'I want to kill him.'

Birds twittered in the garden nearby, splashing in a bubbling fountain.

Steve gripped his phone tightly. 'No need to, Dad. I already did.'

CHAPTER 4

Six hours in bed in which she managed some sleep, and a mug of strong coffee recharged Tess enough to face the remainder of the day.

Sitting at the kitchen table with the warm mug clasped in her hands, she considered her options. The next few days until she could return to work stretched empty before her. The interview with Professional Standards might take up a chunk of the afternoon, but after that? After that she needed to have projects to do, things to work on, activities to keep her occupied.

The downside of living in the police residence was the limitations on what she could do to the place. Especially since this posting might only be short term. There was no point doing anything other than maintenance, and as the residence had been renovated recently, there hadn't been much of that. She'd already weeded and tidied the neglected garden beds and planted a few hardy herbs. If she was still here in spring she'd plant a few more.

If she was still here. The fact that she'd shot a man could mean the end of her career, especially if the inquiry found that her judgement had been impaired by her past. The past she hadn't mentioned when she'd joined the police force. And now that Isaac had reappeared, the chances of that all coming to light had just skyrocketed.

If Steve Fraser reported what he'd witnessed, there'd be questions. And while he – with his cavalier attitude towards rules – had refrained from asking them, others with a stronger devotion to proper procedure would be ready to grill her.

Steve had lied, or as good as, about ordering her to shoot Joshua. She definitely had mixed feelings about that, but it demonstrated his readiness to do what he could to protect her. Surely he wouldn't discuss her encounter with Isaac with the investigators? Not without speaking to her about it first?

She'd have to see him. Explain . . . something. Enough so that he wouldn't be concerned about her emotional stability.

She tipped the cooling dregs of coffee into the sink, rinsing the mug and leaving it in the drainer ready for her next dose of caffeine. After her shower. When she'd arrived home in the small hours of this morning, she'd stripped off her uniform and taken a long hot shower, washing away the feel of Isaac's hands on her, but she needed another one now. Partly for routine, starting the day clean, even at this late hour. Partly to wake her up further, sharpen her mind. And partly because her skin still remembered the pressure of Isaac's hands and body and she needed that memory erased for good.

With yesterday's thunderstorm easing the town's water supply issues, she didn't hurry under the shower. For the second time in seven hours she scrubbed every inch of her body even while she knew it was unnecessary, pointless, a symbolic gesture to pacify her emotions rather than a physical cleansing. But at least she felt more energised when she turned off the water and slid back the shower screen . . .

Until she saw Isaac, standing in the bathroom doorway.

'Hello, Tess. You're still very beautiful.'

His gaze, wandering over her, alight with lust, made her want to vomit. But no use letting fear and revulsion take over. She reached for the towel on the rack, drew it around her body, holding his gaze defiantly but frantically thinking of what she could use as a weapon. Some spray perfume in the cabinet beside the sink? A full bottle of conditioner on the floor of the shower? A plastic razor in the soap dish on the wall of the shower?

He stepped into the bathroom, between her and the cabinet, still blocking her path to the door. 'I'm glad you've been washing away your sins, because it's time to consummate our marriage.'

•

In the small room at the Goodabri pub that he'd left his gear in on Thursday and hardly returned to since, Steve showered, shaved and dressed in clean jeans and t-shirt before he packed up his light bag.

He had no time to linger, or to sleep. In an hour he needed to be back in Strathnairn, to support Maddie in a meeting with the community services officers. They were going to have a heap of questions about a child raised off the grid. No birth registration, no Medicare card, no vaccinations or health record at all, and taken to hospital because of the effects of some drug. If they became critical rather than helpful, Maddie would need someone to argue her case. He'd don his knight's cloak, unsheathe his wooden sword, and mount his trusty tricycle to ride to save her from the dragons again.

He smiled at the memory as he went down the stairs to check out of the pub. At three years old, she'd loved the pretty princess dress their mum had made her, but she'd been scared of the dragons he told her about. She'd always needed someone to save her.

His smile faded. Joshua must have seemed like a saviour to her. When everything seemed dark and sad, and Steve and their father hadn't been enough, she'd handed Joshua her trust. And, later, her body.

Two kids. He still couldn't get his head around it. At least the community services officers wouldn't be heavily on her case about Tristan. At seventeen he was almost out of their range of concern. But Lily was only just six. Six and small and vulnerable.

He tossed his bag in the back of his car and pulled out of the parking area. The back road to Strathnairn led past the Goodabri police station. He had a good ten minutes to spare. In the midst of the activity at Derringvale there'd been no quiet time to talk with Tess properly and check she was okay behind the brave face. And no time to say goodbye. Nick would follow up with her, keep an eye on her reaction to the shooting, but after the intensity of their work together over the past few days Steve owed her a proper acknowledgement of her contribution and his appreciation of her teamwork. And as senior officer, he should check on her well-being after the shooting.

The small police station stood at the end of the main town block, between the old Mechanics' Institute building and a park that had probably once been the police paddock. The station and attached residence dated from the 1930s, the red brick making it look more substantial than many of the old timber stations Steve had seen in small towns. He'd been in this station – a couple of cramped rooms, inadequate for any serious police work. The residence looked like it had a couple of bedrooms. The cops and their wives of decades ago who'd raised families in these places had his respect. But not his envy.

Tess's car was parked in the driveway, another car – a beat-up old Ford Falcon – out on the street. But the door of the police station was shut, the closed sign on it directing people to the phone link through to Strathnairn.

Steve parked in the street and walked up the driveway, uncertain, now he was here, if this was a good idea after all. Tess might be asleep. He couldn't see the driver of the Falcon in the park, and the Mechanic's Institute was boarded up, undergoing major repairs.

Maybe the Falcon belonged to a friend of Tess's or a boyfriend or . . . he stopped on the first of the steps up to the house, ready to turn around. He could give her a call later in the day.

A sharp cry and a thud came from the house. He took the rest of the stairs in two strides, and pounded on the door. 'Tess! It's Steve. Are you okay?'

Another thud, another indistinct cry. Definitely a woman's voice.

The front door didn't budge, the lock solid. Glass shattered inside. Steve sprinted around to the rear of the house. The back door stood open, leading into a screened-in veranda.

His eyes took a few moments to adjust to the contrast between the bright sunlight outside and the dull light indoors. Two doors and a window led into the house from the veranda room, one of them ajar.

'Where are you, Tess?' he called, reaching for a Glock on his hip that wasn't there. Damn. And there was nothing here to serve as a weapon, only a table, an old sofa and a basket of clean laundry.

Something solid thumped hard against a door or a wall and someone grunted.

'In here!' Tess yelled.

Steve burst through the semi-open door into a kitchen. In the passageway beyond, Tess – *shit*, naked Tess – struggled with a man who dragged her backwards towards the living room at the front of the house. Isaac Matthias. The bastard had one hand fisted in Tess's hair, the other around her waist, jerking her further backwards as she struggled to maintain her footing. He still wore the loose clothes of the cult with no weapon obvious, but with that grip he could certainly hurt Tess. She already had a red mark on her face and blood dripping from a gash on her arm. With her uninjured arm, she clawed at the hand in her hair.

'Let her go!' Steve ordered, rapidly weighing up strategies to get to him. He couldn't just tear Tess out of his grip, not without hurting her, and he couldn't get to her captor easily with her in the way.

'She's *my* wife,' Matthias shouted at him. 'She'll learn to obey *me*.' Despite his skinny build, he had the strength to slam her into the wall, and she cried out as she hit it with her elbow first, then her head.

With Isaac's side exposed, Steve charged in to tackle him, throwing him down to the floor, twisting in an attempt to cushion Tess as she fell with them both. She moved to roll away but Matthias didn't loosen his grip on her hair until Steve punched him under the jaw, hard. The desire to punch him again, to pummel his face into oblivion, almost overrode his good sense, but he stopped with his arm pulled back, ready to strike. The guy was already unconscious. The fly of his trousers gaped open, his cock half out. Fury blazed red across Steve's vision.

With small gasps of pain, Tess struggled to her knees, clasping her arm.

'You're safe.' Steve's voice came out hard from his tight throat. He concentrated on softening it. 'He's out cold. Are you badly hurt?' He didn't want to crowd in and touch her.

'No.' She glanced back at Matthias, but didn't look Steve in the eye.

'Are your cuffs handy?' Steve asked. 'Mine are in the car.'

'In the bedroom.' She nodded towards an open door. 'I need to . . .' She staggered to her feet and, using the wall for support, stumbled to the bathroom. She slammed the door shut, the lock clicking into place.

Matthias lay motionless, eyes closed, his body limp. Steve rose to his feet and pulled his phone from his pocket, thumbing through his contacts for Nick's number while he strode into Tess's bedroom. Neat, sparsely furnished, the only colour an intricate patchwork quilt on the bed.

He looked around for her uniform and equipment vest while he spoke to Nick. 'I need back-up and an ambulance at Tess's place in Goodabri. I'm arresting Isaac Matthias for assault.' He could hear Tess throwing up in the bathroom. Sexual assault? Rape? He couldn't be sure without asking her. 'She's hurt but conscious. And I need a female officer here, stat, Nick.' Where the heck would Tess keep her equipment vest? He checked behind the door while he answered Nick's questions. A white towelling robe, but no vest. 'Yes, she knows him. He's one of Joshua's crowd. They had a run-in at Derringvale.' *She's my wife.* He'd let Tess explain that one. Although the very thought of Matthias touching her . . . Equipment vest. Find it. Where would a neat-freak like Tess put it? He yanked open the wardrobe door, found it hanging with clean uniform shirts, and took the handcuffs from their pouch while he finished the call to Nick.

With the cuffs in hand, he reached for the robe on the back of the door, intending to leave it for Tess outside the bathroom door. But he heard footsteps – Matthias up and moving rapidly.

The guy was already out the front door, bolting down the path to the Ford Falcon. Steve went after him, yelling at him to stop, yanking on the passenger's door as Matthias revved the engine and accelerated.

The force of the car's movement threw Steve to the ground, the tyres spraying gravel around him, stinging his face. He just had time to push himself up on one elbow to look for the car's rego number before it screeched around the corner and raced down Goodabri's quiet main street. By the time he was on his feet again, a more distant squeal of tyres sounded as Matthias turned on to the main road to the east.

With no police radio handy, he called Nick again and asked him to put out an alert for Matthias. He wouldn't normally call an inspector but he didn't have time to find another number, and Nick would get things moving. 'Dark green Falcon station wagon,' he told him. 'Late eighties or thereabouts. Rego ends in four-seven-three. Heading east out of Goodabri.' East could take him to a couple of highways – the main east–west route, or the north–south New England Highway. Or he could turn off, take rural roads, end up just about anywhere. Strathnairn, Derringvale, or even back at Serenity Hill, now the river level had dropped and the roads were open again.

'That's the Falcon stolen from Derringvale a few hours ago. I've got two cars on their way to you. I'll divert one to search for Matthias.' Quick, decisive Nick. All under control in seconds. He made an even more impressive inspector than detective, and he'd been a damned impressive detective. 'I'll alert the teams at Serenity Hill and the search teams at the river.'

The search teams were still at the river? Not good news. 'They've not found the bodies yet?'

'Not yet. Some of the gorge is still inaccessible. How's Tess?'

'I'm just going to check on her again now.' He was back inside the house, could hear water running in the bathroom.

'Good. Dee should be there within fifteen minutes. Ambulance will be a little longer. Keep me informed.'

Steve returned Tess's handcuffs to their place and took the towelling robe to the door of the bathroom. 'He's gone, Tess. I'm sorry I couldn't stop him. Are you okay in there?'

There was a sniff, and the sound of a sink emptying, before she said, 'I'm okay.' The hitch in her voice belied the words.

'Dee's on her way. I'll leave your dressing gown just here on the door handle. I'll go wait in the kitchen. Let me know if you need anything. Or if you want me to call somebody.'

'No. Thanks.'

He closed the kitchen door enough to block his view into the passage and give her privacy to exit the bathroom. Not enough to shut out her voice if she called out to him.

Everything was in its place in her kitchen. Even the fridge magnets were lined up in two straight rows. He found coffee grounds and a plunger easily enough and filled the kettle to boil water. He added more grounds to the plunger than he normally would. In the past few days working with her he'd learned that Tess drank her coffee nuclear strength, black and unsweetened. Sweetened tea was supposed to be better for shocks, but he doubted she'd go for that.

The bathroom door opened. A few moments later, he heard the soft thunk of the bedroom door closing.

He didn't make the coffee just yet. She might need more time. She might want to hide in her bedroom and not face him. Understandable. But Dee would be here soon. A woman – a practical, empathetic woman like Dee – would be more comfortable company for Tess right now than him.

He didn't dare think about Matthias touching her, assaulting her. He hated the thought of proud, independent Tess made so vulnerable, her slight body naked and unprotected, still fighting and struggling against the bastard who'd attacked and hurt her.

If he hadn't arrived . . . Jesus, he needed to keep all this rage and fury at bay somehow. Tess needed him calm, not all worked up and edgy with anger and ready to rip apart Matthias or anyone who hurt her.

He took out the card the social worker at the hospital had given him and made a quick phone call, asking her to tell Maddie he'd be later than expected. And he added a note to the list he was making: to get a mobile phone for Maddie. Just one of many things she was going to need in her return to the world. Accommodation, clothes, household goods . . . He'd be haemorrhaging money to get her and the kids settled. But of course it would be worth it, to give them the opportunity for a decent life.

The bedroom door opened and Tess came through, pausing in the kitchen doorway. She'd dressed in jeans and a loose t-shirt, the cotton robe unbelted over the top as though she were cold, or wanting its comfort.

Her dark hair, damp around her face, framed her grey eyes, reddened but dry, bravely meeting his gaze. 'I'm a stupid idiot and you've got every right to tell me so.'

He stayed where he was, leaning against the kitchen bench. 'No, I don't have any right to say that. You're no idiot, Tess, and you can't blame yourself. You know as well as I do that no one ever asks to be assaulted.'

'But if I'd arrested him at Derringvale—'

'We had no way of knowing he'd steal a car and find out where you were. None of us can anticipate all the "ifs", Tess. They were his decisions, his actions, his crimes. Not yours.'

'I guess so.' She pressed her hand against her upper arm, where Steve'd seen the cut. 'But I am an idiot for leaving the back door unlocked. I mustn't have locked it yesterday morning when I brought the washing in.'

'Before you went in to work at sparrow's fart after only a few hours' sleep? You had other things on your mind. Matthias had no right to open the door and walk in uninvited.' He reached over to the kettle to re-boil the water. 'Do you want some of the nuclear fission you call coffee? Or I could make sweet tea with lots of milk, if you prefer.'

'Coffee. Please. And thank you for being there at the right moment. I don't think I could have—' her control wavered and she bit her lip, averting her face. Her hand went to her arm again. It had to be hurting her. But Dee and the ambulance were probably still only halfway from Strathnairn.

Steve pulled out a chair at the table. 'Sit down, Tess. Have a howl if you need to. Turn the air blue with swearing if you want to. But will you tell me how badly he hurt you, and let me look at your arm?'

'I'm okay,' she said, but she lowered herself into the chair with a small wince. 'Mostly just some bruises. I cut my arm when the shower screen broke. But I've put a dressing on it.' She looked across at him, candid and professional despite the slight flush on her cheeks. 'He didn't succeed in raping me.' Her mouth curved just a fraction. 'So you don't have to tiptoe around me quite so carefully, Sarge.'

He hid his relief by pouring the coffee. And the tiny sliver of hurt. *Sarge*. Not *Steve*. Colleague, not friend. As senior officer, he'd better damn well remember that. The minute Dee arrived, it would be his cue to leave. He didn't make coffee for himself, but took her mug of coffee to the table. Just a police sergeant supporting an injured colleague, nothing more. 'You do want him charged this time, don't you?'

'Yes.'

'You can also apply for a Domestic Violence Order. To keep him away from you while the case is heard.'

'A DVO isn't relevant. He's not my husband, ex or otherwise. I knew him when we were young. Teenagers. That's all.'

'He seems to think differently.'

'Yes.'

Just that one word at first. Acknowledgement, not explanation. He waited without comment, to give her space to explain if she chose to.

She blew softly on her coffee, her breath ruffling its surface, before she took a cautious sip. Her throat moved as she swallowed that sip, and then she swallowed again before she spoke. 'I grew up in religious sects. First the Exclusive Brethren. Then, when my parents disagreed with the increasing emphasis in the Brethren on business and earning money, we joined others in a breakaway group that was even stricter. The True Brethren of the Covenant. We were a small, closed community of about fifteen families in rural Victoria. Abraham Matthias became our leader, our pastor. Isaac is his son. He's a couple of years older than me.'

She paused, her thumbs stroking the smooth sides of the coffee mug she clasped, her eyes staring at some point on the table in front of her. Steve remained silent, but his thoughts raced. Religious sects. A small group even stricter than Brethren? He'd met some Exclusive Brethren in the course of an investigation once. Pleasant people, worked hard, but very devout and insular. They limited their contact with others, did not eat or socialise with those not in their fellowship, and married within their own communities. And they held some beliefs about the role of women – wives and mothers, subject to men – that he couldn't agree with.

Tess glanced up at him before she continued. 'When I was seventeen, it was decided that marriage and motherhood and the discipline of a husband would cure my sinfulness. So I was restrained and taken to a sham of a ceremony officiated by Pastor Abraham in which my father gave me to Isaac. No consent, no licence, nothing of that sort. I escaped and ran away straight afterwards. That's how "married" we are, Sarge. Not at all.'

'Did he—' Damn, he had to clear his throat. 'Did he assault you then?'

'No. I ran straight after the ceremony. Isaac never touched me.' She seemed about to say something else, but stopped.

Steve had the distinct impression he'd only been told part of the story. But Dee knocked and called out at the front door and Tess rose to go and invite her in. Conversation over. Almost.

'Tess,' he said, and she turned in the passageway to face him. 'Tess, you have my mobile number. If you ever need anything, need my help, you only have to ask. You know that, don't you?'

For a moment she said nothing. Then she gave a polite, unemotional nod. 'Sure, Sarge. Thanks.'

She wouldn't contact him. She was grateful for his help, had given him sufficient information to explain what he'd witnessed, but that was that. He'd be gone from the district in a day or two and he'd only see her again on official business. Her personal life – her personal business – was none of his. He pulled out his car keys, greeted Dee, and said a quick goodbye to both of them.

On the eighty kilometre drive back to Strathnairn his thoughts gnawed around what he'd learned. There had to be a whole lot more to Tess's story. A whole lot more history, a whole lot more pain. She'd said she escaped the sect at seventeen. Had she had family to go to? People to help her? It was going to be hard enough for Maddie to adapt to life outside Joshua's group, he had no illusions about that. But from the little he knew of Brethren, they were even more secluded than Joshua's cult. For a girl of seventeen to find herself in a world she had no experience or knowledge of had to have been incredibly difficult. It must have taken courage, endurance and emotional strength – qualities Tess had in abundance.

But no wonder shadows haunted her eyes and she rarely laughed.

He wished he could make sure that Isaac Matthias never hurt her again. But an obsessive guy who'd held on to his belief in their marriage for fifteen or more years? He'd be unlikely to give up his pursuit of her. Ever.

CHAPTER 5

'What do you mean "she's gone"?' Steve tried to keep his voice down, aware of the open door to the room with Lily only metres away.

Alison, the community services case worker, signalled him into a small office and closed the door. 'There's some concern about a missing woman. We've got two children from the group here but there's no sign of their mother. Your colleagues asked Madeleine to go with them back to the property to help with their enquiries. Tristan has gone with her.'

'Which woman is missing?' He asked the question although he suspected he knew the answer already.

'Her name is Tamara. I'm not sure of her surname.'

Tamara. Who'd been with Joshua for longer than Maddie had. Who knew his true identity. The rival of Mary. The mother of David, who had left the homestead with someone in a car after the events at the waterfall.

If there was a body under the woolshed, it might be Tamara. Or perhaps Mary. But if Tamara had left with her son, why had she not taken her two younger children?

'I should go out there. Maddie should have someone with her.' Someone to ensure that no police officers tried to implicate her in anything. She was too innocent of the law, too innocent of her rights.

'Madeleine specifically asked me to ask you to stay with Lily. She wrote a note for you.' Alison handed it over, a folded page with a ragged edge where it had been ripped from someone's notebook.

Maddie's flowing handwriting, little changed from when she was a teenager, filled half the page. *Steve, I have to go and help. Most of the people won't talk to the police. They might talk to me. I've made so many mistakes and done wrong things and I need to do everything I can to help. Please look after Lily and stay with her. She knows nothing of the world and she needs you. I will come back as soon as I can, I promise. Love, Maddie.*

His pulse pounded in his head as he read the words, his fingers gripping the paper tightly. *I will come back as soon as I can* . . . Leah shouldn't have asked her to go out there again. Maddie was overwhelmed already, with an uncertain future, Lily in hospital, and community services to face. And although Joshua was dead, Steve couldn't shake off the sense that Maddie might be at risk.

Shit, he was overtired and hadn't eaten for he didn't know how long and was worrying way too much. Of course she'd be back soon. When he'd had something to eat, he'd phone Leah Haddad and make sure somebody gave Maddie a ride back. Or he'd go and get her himself. Except he hadn't slept and knew he was too fatigued now to drive very far. And their father was arriving on the afternoon plane.

'Perhaps you could take Lily to the hospital kiosk for a milkshake or a sandwich?' Alison said. 'We're a little concerned that she hasn't eaten anything yet. Madeleine left just before lunch arrived and Lily wouldn't eat it. The doctor won't be around for another hour or two yet but if she's eating he may be happy enough to discharge her.'

'You're going to let me take a little girl to the kiosk? She doesn't know me. She was hardly awake this morning when I left. And I know nothing about kids.'

Alison huffed as if he was a delinquent kid. 'Detective, Madeleine has insisted that you are listed as joint next-of-kin for Lily. You're a police officer so you're approved to work with children. And quite frankly we're short-staffed and I have a number of other children from this group to deal with. My colleague is breaking the news to Jasmine that her mother is dead. I must see to Tamara's children. Unfortunately, neither I nor the hospital staff have time to give Lily the attention and reassurance she needs right now.'

Of course they didn't. None of them did. Alison herself had been called in to Derringvale in the small hours of the morning, and working since then. It was time to step up and be an uncle to a barely six-year-old girl. He'd just have to work out how.

Lily sat on the hospital bed, small in an overlarge bright hospital gown, pillows propped behind her. She had a colouring book on her lap, and a pack of pencils unopened. Someone – maybe the case worker, maybe one of the staff or a volunteer – must have given them to her.

Steve stopped at the end of the bed. Start with the basics, right? 'Hello again, Lily. How are you doing?'

She stared up at him, frowning, the mop of dark curls framing her face. She took a moment before she indicated the packet of pencils. 'I don't know what to do.'

That makes two of us, kid.

'I'll open them for you.'

She handed over the small cardboard box. 'But I don't know what the work is. What service do I do with them?'

Service? Work? But the child was serious, biting her lip, looking to him for answers. His clumsy fingers inadvertently tore the box a little as he prised it open. When he passed it back to her, she held on to it but didn't take any pencils out.

'It's just colouring in pictures, honey. It's just for fun.'

Her frown became deeper. A six-year-old kid who didn't understand what colouring-in was? Even if she didn't enjoy it, surely she'd seen other kids doing it?

Then again, maybe not. Maddie had mentioned that Joshua's Simple Bliss philosophy apparently didn't encourage toys and play. Or formal schooling. The cynic in Steve figured it made his communities cheaper to run.

'You can make all sorts of pretty pictures with these pencils.' *Service. Work.* If she'd been taught that only work was valuable, then he had to make this meaningful for her. Somehow. 'Pretty pictures make people happy. That's good service, isn't it?'

'They make bliss?'

Bliss. That bastard Joshua had so screwed with this little child's head.

'Yes, honey. Happy things help make bliss. Hey, how about we go and get some food? I'm really hungry. I bet you might be, too.'

'Madeleine said I have to obey you.'

'I'm your uncle, Lily. I'm not going to ask you to do anything bad.' But as he said the words he wondered how many uncles around the world had said words like that to innocent kids and then gone and done the opposite.

He helped her jump down from the bed, and reached for her sandals, neatly placed just under the bed. He'd paid them no attention earlier. Now he noticed they were made from old tyres. Soles cut from the rubber tread, a lining of felt, and woven cotton straps crisscrossing the foot to tie at the ankle.

He wasn't sure whether to be impressed by the ingenuity or concerned about the extreme approach to recycling. Either way, he'd have to get Lily some new shoes for winter sometime soon. And clothes. Until Madeleine could provide for them, he'd have to.

She managed to tie the sandals on by herself. When she scrambled to her feet, he held out his hand to her, and she took it, her fingers small and cool in his clasp. She hesitated at the door of the room.

'What's up, Lily?'

'Is it safe? Outside?' She said 'outside' as though it was an alien planet. Joshua had clearly followed a key rule of cults: convince people that anything outside the cult is evil and dangerous.

Steve knelt down to be at eye level with her. 'It's safe, Lily. I wouldn't take you out there if it wasn't. I promise that whenever I'm with you, I'll look after you. I won't let anything bad happen to you, okay?'

She nodded slowly, and he led her out of the hospital room, out into the world for which she had no preparation. Everything would be new and strange to her; everything would have to be learned.

Maddie would be back soon. He only had to get the child some food, entice her to eat it, and keep her company until then.

One step at a time. That's all they had to take.

•

Tess had let the paramedics and Dee persuade her to go to the hospital for a check-up, but the wait for a CT scan of her head gave her too much time with nothing to do but think. She leaned her aching head back against the wall in the radiology waiting room.

She'd definitely used up a year's supply of stupid today. Letting Isaac go at Derringvale was only the first mistake. Not securing the residence before she went to bed her second. Freezing out the sarge when he'd saved her from Isaac's attack and only been kind and sensitive afterwards? Yep, that probably counted as stupid, too.

She wished she could blame the blow to the head when Isaac had thrown her against the wall. Or just the shock of his attack. But no, her cool response to Steve Fraser's concern and expression of support came straight from her own inadequacies and her inability to read social cues properly. That, and her embarrassment. He'd seen her naked. Naked and scared witless.

It shouldn't be a big deal. He'd probably seen heaps of women without clothes. But hardly anyone had seen *her* naked. Heck, hardly anyone had seen her *knees*. She'd worn demure, full-skirted, neck-high dresses for the first half of her life. She'd pretty much lived in trousers since then. On the few occasions she'd shared accommodation with other young women, she'd never been quite relaxed enough to wander around the house half-dressed like they did.

She no longer believed most of what she'd been brought up to believe in. She'd certainly rejected the notion that the female body was inherently sinful and bare skin a wicked temptation to carnal evils. But that intellectual knowledge only went so far. Being sequestered from the world with no books, television, or contact beyond her small community for her entire childhood and youth gave her no grounding in all the subtleties and complexities of 'normal', and she was still trying to work them out, sixteen years later.

She hoped she'd given a good enough impression of being matter-of-fact and professional about it. He'd certainly been professional. As if it didn't matter at all. Maybe it didn't. But he'd brought her a robe, and stayed out of sight. Considerate gestures.

The door of the radiology rooms opened and the radiographer called her in. The scan took only five minutes, and the radiographer didn't appear to be concerned when she helped Tess off the bed afterwards, although she stressed it would be a little while before the doctor reviewed the images and issued an official report.

Tess swung her small backpack onto her shoulder and returned to the emergency department, but the intern who'd initially seen her and ordered the CT scans was occupied with an elderly patient. One of the nurses, a kindly older woman, came across to her and ushered her into a cubicle.

'The doctor will be back to talk with you in a little while when we have the results from your scans. In the meantime, why don't you lie down and have a nap?'

Tess smiled wryly. 'I wouldn't be able to sleep. I haven't eaten anything for about twenty-four hours and I'm hungry.' That and the fact that she had far too much on her mind to drift off.

'Oh, you shouldn't eat at the moment. Just in case, you know.'

In case she had a head injury and needed to have surgery. 'It will be at least an hour before the radiologist sees the scans. And honestly, the chance of me fainting from lack of sustenance is far greater than the chance of bleeding in my brain. So, I'll go and get something from the kiosk.' Appreciative of the nurse's genuine concern, she added, 'I promise I'll stay in the hospital grounds and I'll come back in a little while to get the all-clear.'

Maybe she should have stayed and done the cautious thing but there was nothing in her headache that varied from her standard tension headache whenever she'd worked long hours and skipped too many meals.

The small kiosk off the main entrance foyer of the hospital opened on to a garden, with tables and chairs outside. Good. She could have a few minutes of peace and quiet, alone. Her steps faltered when she pushed open the kiosk door and saw Steve Fraser and his little niece, but he glanced in her direction and she couldn't retreat.

As he juggled two milkshake containers and two sandwich packets, he gave her a smile that was half-desperate. 'Lily is about to taste her first ever chocolate milkshake. We're going to sit outside, if you'd like to join us.'

Lily stared at her with unabashed curiosity. Tess remembered doing the same, as a child, on the rare occasions she'd encountered 'others' from outside her community. In her case, she'd half-expected to see devil horns or some other obvious signs of evil.

Everything must be strange for Lily just now. Probably the more friendly faces she saw, the easier it might be to adjust. 'Thanks,' she said. 'I'll be out in a minute.'

She selected yoghurt, fruit juice and a pre-packaged salad sandwich from the kiosk's limited offerings. Reasonably healthy, and enough to go on with for now. She'd get a vegetable-laden meal somewhere later, when she'd decided where to stay for the night. She'd packed some clothes and bedding and her laptop before leaving Goodabri. Surely by tomorrow they'd have Isaac in custody and she might feel safe at home again.

Outside in the sunlight Fraser sat beside his niece at the table, keeping up a mostly one-sided conversation as he opened her sandwich packet for her. He'd never mentioned a wife or kids and she'd assumed him to be single, but despite some awkwardness he seemed to be doing okay with Lily.

'Lily, this is my friend, Tess. Madeleine's gone back to help at the property, Tess, so Lily and I are getting to know each other.'

Tess said hello, but the girl's attention was all on the cheese sandwich in its opened triangular plastic container on the table in front of her. She didn't touch it. Instead she looked up at her uncle and, pointing to the plastic, asked, 'What's that?'

'It keeps the bread fresh by keeping the air out,' Fraser explained.

'Is it cataminated?' she asked.

Fraser frowned, uncertain what she meant, but Tess had read some of Joshua's teachings online. He'd stressed the evil and dangers of the world outside the community, including the contamination of food with numerous chemical additives, and the overuse of non-organic packaging. She didn't disagree with the cult leader on either of those points, but nor was she extreme about it.

Fraser still looked confused so she assured the child, 'No, it's not contaminated.' Not very, anyway. Tess wasn't about to read the ingredients labels too closely just now. 'The plastic protects the bread from germs. It's safe to eat it, Lily.'

While Tess opened her yoghurt – more plastic packaging to clog up the planet – Lily watched Steve take his own sandwich out of its packet and start eating. She cautiously took a bite of her own, and screwed up her face as she chewed. But she took another bite, so it couldn't have been too odd for her.

Fraser let the child eat without fussing over her. Probably wise. Maybe he did have kids, or experience with them. Her only experience had been with her younger siblings, but their family life had been very strict, full of rules and expectations they'd dared not disobey.

'I'm glad you came in for a check-up,' Fraser said. 'You're okay?'

'Yes. Just waiting for precautionary scan results, but I'm fine.' And any minute now the sugars and protein from the yoghurt would hit her system and start their work and she might even begin to feel human again. 'I didn't say thank you properly back at my place. I am grateful for your help, Sarge.' She felt the warmth on her face but kept her head up, anyway.

He waved away her thanks. 'You had things pretty much under control. I'm mad with myself that I didn't keep hold of him. I want to see him arrested and charged rather than on the loose. Have you heard anything since? Have they found him yet?'

'Not yet. I'm going to stay in Strathnairn tonight.'

'Good.' He flicked some crumbs off the table, and took a breath before he said, 'I've just booked a couple of rooms at the motel down the road for the Fraser clan for tonight. They still have vacancies so if you want to book a room there, you know you'll have a couple more cops nearby.'

'A couple of cops? Your father's coming? He's the Assistant Commissioner, isn't he?'

'Yeah, due to arrive in an hour or so. He's flying up now. I haven't seen him for a while. But of course he's not coming to see me.'

'I've met him,' she admitted. 'I worked with him for a few weeks a year or two back.'

'You did?'

'I'd broken my arm and was on restricted duties. Your father was heading up a review of occupational health and safety training at the academy and I was assigned to assist him for a month.'

'My commiserations. I'm sure the broken arm was less painful than working with my father.'

His flippant tone and quick grin didn't quite hide the hurt. Pain, not anger. In her own experience of dysfunctional family relationships the pain mostly outweighed the anger. But whatever the cause of the Fraser family's problems – and maybe it was tied up with Madeleine's disappearance and with the entirely different temperaments between father and son – she'd respected the Assistant Commissioner.

'We got along fine,' Tess said. 'He's a stickler for process and procedure but that made things easier, really.' It wasn't her place to interfere in his relationship with his father but she hated seeing pain, particularly when she respected both men. 'Did you know he has a photo of you on his desk?'

Fraser's eyebrows lifted high. 'He does?' Then he gave a rough laugh. 'He probably throws darts at it.'

The first half of her sandwich finished, Lily touched her uncle's arm. 'Excuse me, can I have a drink, please?'

'Sure, honey. Here's your milkshake.' Fraser passed her the cardboard container but she held it uncertainly in both hands, eyeing the straw poking out from the cap as though she'd never seen one before. She probably hadn't. More plastic for a child unused to it. Straws hadn't been part of Tess's upbringing, either. Food had always been served on plates; drinks in glasses or cups.

Fraser picked up his own milkshake. 'Just suck through the straw, Lily. Like this.' He demonstrated, grinning around the straw when the milk hit his mouth.

The child copied him, her eyes wide. Wider still when she tasted the drink. Her smile after her second taste radiated wonder and pure delight.

'Now I've done it,' Fraser said. 'Started her on a lifelong chocolate addiction.'

'There are worse addictions,' Tess said. Police saw plenty of them – alcohol, heroin, ice. Chocolate and caffeine didn't rate as problematic compared to the addictions that destroyed relationships, families and lives.

'Yep. And Maddie should be back soon so she can deal with the sugar rush. That's probably enough milkshake for now, Lily. How about you eat the rest of your sandwich?'

He'd do okay as an uncle. Beneath his irreverence and his dark humour lay good sense and a gentleness and a concern for others. Lily would probably come to adore her uncle. Lucky girl, to have a family to care for her. Lucky Maddie, to have a brother, and a father who was travelling at short notice to welcome her back.

The last letter Tess had sent her family had been returned, unopened. Just like all the others. She had ceased to exist for them the moment she'd left the community, and they would never forgive her.

So what? She didn't need them. They'd not been there for her in her darkest times and she'd done okay without them ever since. Everything she'd achieved, she'd achieved herself. And she was proud of that.

Yet Lily reminded her of her youngest sister, around the same age the last time she'd seen her. Tess squashed the memory with a dose of reality. Verity would be married by now, with a young family, and most likely as rigid in her beliefs and as unforgiving as their parents.

•

The warmth of the sunshine, the food, and Lily's bright-eyed discovery of new things eased Steve's exhaustion and improved his mood. So did Tess's quiet company, and the absence of fear in her eyes.

It was interesting that she'd worked with his father. Not surprising that they'd got along. Discipline, order and procedure mattered to both of them. In all honesty, it mattered to him, too. Maybe not in his personal life – what there was of it – but certainly in his work. Yet out here in western New South Wales with significant distances to cover, perpetually stretched resources and limited back-up, sometimes the rules simply couldn't be applied. He'd learned to be flexible.

He checked the time. After four o'clock already. Less than two hours before his father arrived. He needed to contact Leah Haddad, make sure Maddie was on her way back soon. Since he couldn't leave Lily until his sister returned, he also needed to arrange for someone to collect his father from Strathnairn's tiny airport.

He could take Lily back to her room, show her how to use the colouring book, and then make his phone calls, but that meant leaving Tess. Besides, Lily still had some of her lunch to finish. So did he. Better to stay out here in the fresh air for a little while longer yet. At least as long as Tess stayed.

He admired Tess's courage. Not only her courage in defending herself against Isaac Matthias, but afterwards. Facing Steve despite the discomfort of their mutual embarrassment. Acknowledging the consequences of her decision not to arrest Matthias earlier. Even joining him and Lily at the table when she probably didn't feel like company, let alone his company, or that of an unknown child.

Fortunately Lily had good manners and, although curious and wary, didn't need constant attention. Whatever their faults, the Simple Bliss crowd apparently didn't spoil their kids. Perhaps the opposite, but other than being a little underweight, none of the kids showed signs of neglect or abuse. Unlike Tess, however, who'd been restrained and taken to a marriage ceremony against her will at seventeen.

As if she knew his thoughts had turned to her, she drew in a breath and switched the conversation back to him. 'When will you return to Birraga?' she asked.

He didn't mind answering. The more she knew about him, perhaps the more she'd feel comfortable with him. 'Maybe tomorrow, maybe the next day. Community services and child protection people have to be happy about Lily and Tristan. Maddie said this morning that she'd like to live near me, at least for a while, so I'm waiting to hear back from a real estate agent about rentals in the district.' About a place for him, too, since he needed to move out of the hotel.

'How long have you worked there? In Birraga?'

'I was working mostly out of Moree, but I had a couple of cases in the Birraga district over the past few years. I came back to fill a two-month vacancy nine months ago and it's only just been made an official transfer. So that's where I'll be for the foreseeable future.'

'Do you like it there?'

Did he like it? His reasons for accepting the position involved bad memories, mistakes and yep, a certain degree of self-punishment. Atonement might take a century or two. Somehow he no longer felt or noticed censure from anyone but himself, but he knew he couldn't articulate the how or why of that, so he fell back on light banter. 'Well, no one's threatened to run me out of town lately.' Not for a couple of years, anyway. 'And we did clean up a particularly nasty bunch of crims last year. So the place is growing on me.' And he had friends. Mostly in Dungirri, sixty kilometres from Birraga, but genuine friends, who'd seen him at his worst and not written him off entirely. Sunday lunches at the pub in Dungirri had become the highlight of his week.

Lily found the bottom of her milkshake with a loud, bubbly slurp that clearly startled her. Her glance up at Steve held an edge of worry, as if she thought he might be angry. Poor kid, navigating so many new and unfamiliar things. Once – in his young and stupid days – he might have played the fool and made an even louder noise with his own. But that wouldn't exactly be responsible or helpful to the kid, would it?

'It's okay, honey,' he said. 'It's always tricky when you get to the bottom. Hold it at an angle, like this, and you can get the last bits.'

His phone beeped with a message. With a murmur of apology to Tess, he checked it. The real estate agent. No suitable houses available in Birraga, but a three-bedroom plus sleep-out with a large yard in Dungirri. The attached photo showed a neat house in good condition, one Steve recognised. Across the road from the police station, just a block from Dungirri's only shop, and a short walk to the school. Decision made. He messaged back that he'd take it and asked for the paperwork. With luck, Maddie and the kids might be able to move in straight away. One problem most likely solved. And if need be, he could stay in the sleep-out until he found something in Birraga. Two problems solved.

Tess finished her juice and began to collect together all their discarded wrappings. She'd go soon. He'd have to take Lily back to the ward soon. He didn't know how to prolong the time with Tess without coming across badly. Some time in the past few days he'd fallen for her, hard. The realisation stunned him, but it made sense of the upside-down state of his emotions around her.

His phone beeped again with an incoming call. Leah Haddad. 'Sorry, Tess, I have to take this. Could you stay—' He indicated Lily, and Tess nodded.

He strolled out into the garden while he answered the call, staying within eyesight but not earshot of Lily. 'What's happening?' he asked Leah.

'No sign of the bodies in the river yet. Forensics still can't get under the woolshed to check that probable body. They're bringing in a dog, should be here in an hour or so. The workshop in the machinery shed was cleared out on Saturday, apparently. Your visit on Friday night must have spooked them. There's not much left that we can pin a drug manufacturing conviction on. According to the little we've been able to find out from this mob, only a few people were ever allowed in the workshop, and none of them are here. Apparently Joshua spun some tale about experimenting with making environmentally sound fertilisers for their crops.'

That coincided with what Maddie had told him when he'd broached the subject during the night. 'Have you found anything that will give reason to search the other communities?'

'No. I've so far got nothing on anybody, other than one of the men, Tom, who confessed to adding an unidentified substance to the water last night, on Joshua's orders. I got his statement but let him go. He might be useful. In the circumstances, I have to let the people here return, at least until we unravel who's behind the holding companies that legally own the place and what money has been flowing where.'

'That could take weeks or frigging months.' Although Joshua would never answer for his crimes, there had to have been others involved. The chances of a conviction became slimmer, the longer it took.

A family of small birds fluttered in and out of a nearby birdbath, playing in the water, oblivious to his frustration. He envied their simple life. His had suddenly developed far too many complexities. 'Have you finished with Maddie and Tristan? Can someone bring them back to the hospital soon?'

'Maddie's helped all she can for now. I'll bring them. She's just getting some of their belongings. We'll be there in around an hour.'

Good. His father wouldn't have to wait long to see his daughter. He finished the call and went back across to the kiosk, where Tess and Lily had gathered the rubbish from their meal and taken it to the recycling bins.

'The pictures tell you which bin to put things in, Lily,' Tess explained. 'See? Plastic and glass bottles go in this bin. And cardboard and paper in this one. They'll be made into new things for other people to use.'

Lily frowned thoughtfully. 'But why don't we just wash them?'

The question stumped Steve for a moment. When had the metal milkshake containers of his youth disappeared? And freshly made sandwiches served on plates?

'People value convenience,' Tess said, and he liked the way she didn't talk down to Lily. 'Using disposable things means that they're always very clean, without germs. But most people, when they're at home, use proper plates and cups.'

He nodded his thanks to Tess for knowing what to say. Maybe she'd thought about it more than him. She probably ate better than he did. He could cook, but rarely did. Never had the time, with the long hours he worked. Birraga had several pubs, a pizza and hamburger take-away, and the ubiquitous Chinese restaurant. He didn't starve. He even ate vegetables regularly. He imagined making some joke about that to Tess but she was checking her watch, and he'd already taken up her time when she should be getting the all-clear from the doctor.

He held out a hand to Lily. 'Time for us to go back and play with those coloured pencils. Mummy –' he corrected himself, because she didn't use the term – 'Madeleine will be back soon. How about we make her a pretty picture?'

Lily nodded and pointed at Tess. 'Can we make her one, too?'

'Of course we can make one for Tess.' He hoped their combined colouring skills wouldn't be too laughable. He gave Tess a brief apologetic smile but then moved to more serious matters to update her in words Lily wouldn't pay attention to. 'Not much news from Leah. Little or no progress on any fronts. Nothing and no one found.'

She understood, her nod solemn. 'Okay. Dee's coming back in a while to see what the doctor says. Hopefully she'll have some news.'

Like Isaac being arrested already. Steve wanted to hear *that* news.

Back in the hospital room, he found that Jasmine was still with the case worker, so he and Lily had the room to themselves. Nothing in his police training had included how to entertain six-year-olds. Especially one with so little experience of the things most kids were familiar with.

He propped Lily up on the bed with pillows and pulled the meal tray across to work on. She hadn't used a pencil before.

He had to show her how to hold one, and how to use it. Which meant he had to dredge up memories from thirty-something years ago. 'Okay, hold it straight up if you want to draw something. See, like this? But for colouring, hold it a bit on the side. Like this. See how you can shade things?'

The colouring book featured Disney princesses. Why couldn't they have given her a colouring book with animals? Something nice and easy. A is for anteater, Z is for zebra. He had no knowledge at all about Disney princesses. Fortunately, neither did she, so he didn't have to dodge questions about their names. Ladies in dresses, that's how she saw it.

'It's a very long dress,' she said, studying the first image. 'Why is it so long?'

The gap between the outside world and her world loomed large. She'd had no TV, no books, no school. No princesses, no fashion. The community made their own clothes. She'd probably never seen a formal dress. Maybe she'd escaped all that pressure on little girls to dress up, to be valued for their pretty clothes. Perhaps the Simple Bliss folk had got something right.

'It's a special dress. For celebrations. What colour do you want to make it?'

She knew her colours, and chose orange, setting to work with determination and focus. Despite her inexperience, she did well. Eye–hand coordination. Was that what they called it? He'd ask someone. Tomorrow he'd get her books with animals. And trucks. And alphabets and numbers. And stories. Picture books and stories to help her learn about the world.

He settled into the hospital armchair beside the bed and added books to the list on his phone for tomorrow's shopping expedition. He had a few lists. Issues to discuss with Maddie, things to buy for the family, tasks he had to do, questions he had to ask counsellors, doctors and community services.

At least Lily was young enough that she wouldn't have fallen too far behind her peers, and her natural curiosity would help her. The cult's practice of everyone being responsible for children meant she hadn't been constantly asking after Madeleine, and had accepted him and even Tess very quickly.

But Tristan . . . Steve had more concerns about him. The lad could read, had read hospital posters, medical charts, and the newspaper in the waiting room. And Steve suspected there was a sharp, questioning brain behind the constant observation and carefully closed expression. But he'd not been to school, nor had access to education and books. As to the emotional and psychological impacts of the past few days' events, Steve couldn't tell what he thought. Tristan had witnessed Joshua – his father – apparently persuading Sybilla to walk off the waterfall several days ago. And he'd not been drugged last night, so had witnessed those moments when everyone else might have done the same thing. While the others possibly hadn't yet realised that Joshua had been shot rather than 'ascended to bliss', Tristan knew the truth.

The only thing Steve had learned for sure about the lad was that he was protective of his mother, his sister, and Jasmine. That had to be a good sign.

Lily's sugar rush couldn't have been too bad because she'd put down her pencil and curled up in the bed, already napping. Good timing. His father's plane would have landed at the airport outside town, and he'd be here in fifteen minutes.

Steve pushed himself out of the armchair and stretched his back and neck. Sometime soon he'd need to sleep. When Maddie arrived back and the father–daughter reunion had been achieved, and Lily most likely discharged from hospital, they could all go to the motel – the Fraser family – together.

With a word to the nurse, he left Lily sleeping and walked along the corridors to the hospital foyer and outside, away from the soporific air conditioning. Fresh air and the last rays of autumn sunlight might give him enough of a boost to get through the next few hours. He sat on a bench, not far from the entrance where he could watch for his father. Aaron Georgiou, the detective constable from Strathnairn, had offered to collect him from the airport so Steve kept an eye out for the detective's car.

Bright lights flickered to life in the playing fields across the road from the hospital as several footy teams began to gather for training. Informal, relaxed friends greeting each other as they left parked cars and walked across to their various teams. Like most country towns, sport brought people together, contributed to building a sense of community. Like Birraga. Even like Dungirri, small as it was, coming together to field its own team in the regional rugby competition this season, for the first time in decades.

The murder, lies and betrayals of Joshua and his cult didn't touch this honest, everyday life, these strong ties of friendship and community. Although some of these players might also be in the SES, or the RFS, or other emergency services that helped the police whenever needed, the fact that footy training went on reminded Steve that there was a balance, good to counteract the evil, and plenty of 'normal' despite the spikes of abnormal now and then.

He spotted Erin and Simon walking along the path towards the hospital, clasped hands a sure sign that they'd resolved the issues that had been holding them apart. After the intensity of working together over the past few demanding days, Steve had grown to like both of them. Despite the shock, Simon hadn't hesitated for a moment in stepping up to accept the changes to his life to care for his new-found teenage daughter, and with a generosity of spirit that Steve respected the man had said no word against his estranged wife, who'd left him years before and concealed their daughter's birth. He would make a good father, and with Erin beside him with her good sense and warmth, Jasmine would be well supported in adapting to her new life.

When they stopped to greet him, they talked for a few minutes and he shared with them the little news he'd received from phone calls and text messages from Leah and Nick during the day. 'The critical incident team arrived earlier – they'll conduct an investigation into the two deaths at the falls,' he told them. 'Nick will be in touch because they've asked to interview both of you. But that won't be before tomorrow. They haven't found the bodies yet and I don't know what they'll decide about Joshua's death, but I'm not stressing about it at this point. I know that if the circumstances were repeated, I'd do exactly the same again.'

'So would I,' said Simon. 'If I'd known you were there, I mightn't have. But I didn't know, and people were about to die. I'd make that same decision again.'

The man sure as hell didn't deserve a murder charge, and Steve vowed to himself to make damned sure that the investigators and the coroner understood exactly how it had been in those few minutes when Joshua had been in control of his people and willing their deaths.

'I'm off the case now. Personal connection and all that. I'll stick around town for a few days though until we sort some things out and Maddie works out what she wants to do. She's helping the police.' He silently debated how much to tell them. Not everything. They had other things on their minds. But they'd been there, might be able to shed light on some things. 'There's no sign of Mary, or of Tamara. Mary at least knew Joshua's plans and she and Tamara had a long-running dislike of each other.'

'I didn't see either of them at the falls,' Erin said. 'The last time I saw Mary was at the woolshed.'

Simon nodded. 'Mary's the leader of the women? I saw her leaving the woolshed. But then I followed Erin and Madeleine. I'm fairly sure Mary torched the woolshed.'

Steve'd pass that information on to Leah. She could get more detail from Simon later. 'Forensics are still waiting for the ruins to be declared safe, but the bad news is they think there's a body. I haven't told Maddie yet.'

'You think it's Tamara?' Erin asked. 'She knew Joshua was Hollywell. If he was silencing those who knew . . .'

'We'll find out, eventually,' Steve said, but his brain raced through the possibilities. Simon had seen Mary heading towards the house when the others were already on their way to the waterfall. Tamara hadn't been at the waterfall. He needed to find out – *Leah* needed to find out – when Tamara had last been seen. Because if Tamara was the possible body under the woolshed, then either she had to have been there before Joshua led his people to the river, or Joshua hadn't killed her. And if Joshua didn't kill her, then they'd be looking for another murderer. And if there was another killer, then as one of the early members of the group – one of the few remaining people who had known Joshua's identity – Maddie might not be safe.

If, if, if. Nothing solid, only conjecture and guesswork. He'd learned the hard way that instinct couldn't be trusted, but uneasiness still rippled up and down his spine. It had to be fatigue. Lack of sleep made monsters out of molehills. And he was too tired to even get his metaphors right.

Erin and Simon continued on inside to see Jasmine as Aaron's car pulled in to drop off his passenger. Steve drew in a deep, slow breath to force some oxygen into his brain and blew it out very gradually, before he walked towards the car to greet his father.

The changes struck Steve as Bruce Fraser got out of the car. Past sixty now, his father still held his back as straight and stiff as if he were on the parade ground although he wore a suit rather than his Assistant Commissioner's uniform. But his once-dark hair had become grey, and his face had become thinner and more lined. His eyes . . . his eyes looked beyond Steve, searching for Maddie around the hospital entrance while he shook his son's hand.

'Where is she?'

'She'll be here in a few minutes. She's been out helping the investigation. Leah Haddad is driving her back now.' Steve indicated the grassed area nearby where he'd been sitting, away from the staff and visitors coming and going through the main doors. 'Why don't we wait over here, Dad? It's more private.'

His father followed him but wouldn't sit, pacing instead. 'The children, are they—' He searched for a word and didn't find one. 'What are they like?'

Had his father been imagining dirty, drug-addicted ferals? Possibly. There hadn't been much time, in their rushed second phone call this morning, for Steve to say much other than tell him he had grandchildren.

'They're good kids. Unsettled just at the moment, especially Tristan. But they're both bright, and curious. Lily's asking questions about everything, and listening to the answers. Tristan – he's going to need some patience, Dad. The man he believed in, his father, betrayed him and now he's not sure what to believe and who to trust. It might take him a while to work that out.'

'Hollywell –' Bruce cleared his throat, as if he needed to clear the taste of the name from it – 'was his father?'

'Yes. Lily's, too.' Hard words to tell him, but at least it saved Maddie having to face her father to deliver that news. 'He seems to have treated her well, Dad.' Lies, manipulation and polyamory aside, but Bruce didn't need reminders of that just now. 'The things he taught weren't wild, and she said she was happy. It's only been this past week or so that she had reason to suspect his motives.'

'He murdered those two other women? The ones you're investigating?'

'Was investigating, Dad. I'm off the case now. I believe he murdered them, yes, but there's no definitive evidence yet.' There might never be proof. Unless they found fingerprints on the knife that had murdered Simon's wife, Hayley, or something else to place Joshua at the scene, there was little other evidence. And only one witness – Tristan – who had seen Joshua speak with Sybilla before she'd walked off the waterfall. From a distance. At night.

'You said you shot him. That others did, too. Have they found his body yet?'

'No. Not yet. The critical incident team have arrived, Dad. They'll decide what action to take.'

Rather than quizzing him further as Steve had expected, Bruce simply nodded, accepting. 'I've taken leave for now. But the Commissioner expects to be kept informed.'

Assistant Commissioner's son shoots sister's lover. Steve could imagine the headlines if things got out of hand. Of course the Commissioner expected to be kept informed. Probably the Police Minister, too. If the media turned it into a circus his father's job might be at risk as well as his own. But if they were lucky, there'd be some political or sporting scandal that would keep the Fraser family off the front pages.

Leah's dark blue sedan pulled in to park across the road, and Steve pointed it out to his father. First Leah got out, phone in hand, then Tristan and Maddie stepped out on the passenger side, both holding cloth bags of belongings. She'd changed out of her white dress into blue trousers and a top, and plaited her hair into one long braid.

Steve drew a deep breath. Maybe a minute, maybe less, until this reunion of father and daughter. A daughter who resembled her mother closely. His own emotions tumbled chaotically. Theirs had to be far more intense.

Bruce made a strangled sound, stepped forward, stopped, his gaze on Maddie, fifty metres away. She couldn't have heard, but she saw them, saw their father, and stood still for a long moment before Leah directed them the short distance to the pedestrian crossing. A safety island between the two lanes made crossing the reasonably busy road safer. Leah remained near the car, deep in her phone conversation, while Maddie checked for traffic before stepping out on to the crossing, with Tristan a pace or two behind.

Maddie directed a hesitant smile at their father and Steve grinned and nodded his encouragement as he walked beside Bruce to meet them.

The roar of an engine accelerating rapidly impinged his awareness as a dark utility sped towards the crossing.

Maddie shouted as she saw it, spinning around to push Tristan back out of its path. But even as Steve ran, the car hit Maddie full-on and hard so that she flew onto the bonnet of the vehicle, hit the windscreen as the vehicle swerved, and he heard his own voice shouting *'No!'* as she was thrown off at speed across the small refuge island and into the path of an oncoming car.

CHAPTER 6

Steve fell on his knees beside Maddie, chaos erupting around him but all he could see was the small patch of road and Maddie lying crooked, broken, bleeding in front of him. He cried and he didn't care, didn't dare to touch her other than her hand, gently, because of the blood and the lacerations.

He straightened her top over the gritty marks on her abdomen and he murmured to her even though her eyes were closed, 'Maddie, it's okay, there's help coming. Just stay still, Maddie, I'm with you.' A hand, not his, touched her face, brushed a strand of hair away from a cut near her temple. 'Dad's here, Maddie, we're with you. We're both here.'

His heart leapt as her lips moved and she whispered faintly, 'Daddy?'

'I'm here, sweet girl. I'm here.'

'Daddy . . . so . . . sorry . . . forgive me . . .'

'Sshh. It's all forgiven. I love you, sweetheart. Always.' His father's voice broke on an anguished sob.

People spoke and shouted and moved around them but Steve ignored them, seeing only Maddie's pale face until a pair of leather-sandalled feet edged into his vision. Tristan. Steve reached up to grasp his forearm, tugged him gently down to kneel by his mother in his place.

Her eyes flickered open and her lips formed a smile as she focused for a moment on her son's face. 'Tris . . . love . . .' Her eyes drifted closed again.

Steve watched her mouth, willing her to breathe in, breathe out.

'Daddy . . .' Just that one, so-softly whispered word.

'Sir, I'm a doctor. Please let me . . .' The woman in a white coat moved Steve aside, and knelt on the bitumen, feeling Maddie's neck for a pulse, running her gaze over her still body, lying so awkwardly. She pushed up Maddie's top a little way, pressed her hand lightly over her abdomen.

'Don't hurt her,' his father said.

Steve put an arm around Tristan's shoulders, then drew him a short distance away while the doctor and a nurse tried to save her and his father begged once more for them not to cause her pain.

But Steve knew she felt no pain, would never feel pain again, would never breathe or smile or hug her children again, and the dagger in his heart stabbed and twisted, tearing it apart.

Time seemed to stretch but eventually the doctor sat back on her heels and reached a hand across Maddie to their father's arm. 'I'm sorry, sir. There's nothing more we can do.'

'No!' his father cried out. He leaned over Maddie, his tears falling on her face. 'No, not my girl. No. No.'

Tristan looked to Steve, face ashen, eyes full of fear and one burning question. Steve could scarcely breathe, let alone lie about heaven or bliss or soften it in any way. 'She's gone, Tris. She was too badly injured.'

'Dead?'

'Yes.' He smothered the howl rising from his chest, stood tall so he wouldn't fall to the ground to keen his grief. He had to hold himself together and be strong. He had to be strong for his father, for Tristan, for Lily. If he fell apart now, he'd fail them. He dragged the heel of his hand across his face to wipe away his tears. 'Do you want to—' Damn, he had to concentrate to get the words out through his swollen throat without cracking up. 'Do you want to say goodbye to her?'

Tris nodded, and Steve gave him a little push, and her father and her son sat on either side of Maddie, wordless.

People milled around and from somewhere nearby he heard Leah swear. He had to move, soon, and until other officers arrived he had to be a police officer and deal with the injured, secure the crime scene, locate witnesses.

But darkness was falling and Maddie lay silent and still and he could not leave her yet. The question she'd asked only last night echoed in his mind as clearly as if she'd just spoken the words: '. . . *if anything happens to me, could you . . . would you promise to look after Tristan and Lily?*'

He hadn't promised her then but he did now. 'Yes, Maddie,'

he whispered. 'I'll look after them. I'll look after them always and protect them with my life.'

•

Police in small communities got to know emergency departments and their staff quickly. Assault cases, accident victims, drunks and drug addicts – even based in tiny Goodabri, Tess'd had to bring a few people in to the Strathnairn hospital. So she'd been invited to wait for the doctor in the staff break room, and help herself to coffee.

Burying her unwelcome thoughts in an ebook on her phone, she didn't properly register the rush of hushed activity in the room beyond the door for several minutes, until Marco, one of the nurses, poked his head around the door.

'Tess – your scans are clear, but things are going to be a mess here and the doc won't be free to tell you that for hours. I know you're not on duty, but there's a major accident right outside. You might be needed.'

Tess stuffed her phone into her pocket, ready to go. 'Car accident?' she asked, following Marco back to the main room where he rapidly stacked gloves and other equipment onto one of the blood pressure monitor trolleys.

'Car ran down pedestrians at high speed. At least three. It's bad. They're triaging out there and the rescue helicopter is on standby.'

High speed car and pedestrians? Always bad. And a small hospital with limited staff and few doctors could only stabilise critical injuries and send them on to larger centres. 'What can I take out?'

'This.' He pushed the trolley towards her. 'The doc's already out there with the rest of the team. They'll need supplies.'

Tess joined the stream of available staff heading out through the foyer to the street. Twilight was deepening into night but the bright lights from the sports fields spread far enough. The locations of the injured were marked by the people around them. One group at the pedestrian crossing. Two more twenty metres down the road. At each end of the street, guys in sports gear blocked the traffic and directed it away from the scene. Small clusters of spectators kept a respectful distance from the activity around the injured.

In the closest group, Steve Fraser stood motionless. She saw the body at his feet, the figures beside it, the medical staff moving away, and dread chilled her.

Someone took the trolley from her and rushed it to one of the other groups.

Steve turned as she approached, his face haggard, drained of light and energy, and it was Madeleine there on the road, and the Assistant Commissioner, holding her hand and weeping silently, and her son kneeling, shoulders shaking as he touched her lifeless face.

Tess swallowed back her own dismay, fought to maintain emotional control in the face of their shock and grief. Dee would probably hug Steve but she couldn't do that, not naturally, and all she had were the standard, useless expressions. 'I'm sorry, Sarge. So sorry. You're not hurt? Or the others?'

He seemed to take a moment to process the question before he shook his head. 'We saw it happen. He drove straight at them. At Maddie and Tristan. He sped up on purpose to hit them.' He dragged a hand through his hair and looked down the road. 'He hit other people, too. I should go and help Leah.'

'You stay here. I'll go.' She could do nothing more for Madeleine. Her priorities right now had to be checking on the other injured, and on assisting Leah to manage the scene.

Whoever had driven the car had hit at least two others without stopping. Tess reached the first, a young woman in sports gear lying on her back, her legs twisted, her face white with pain, a bicycle with a bent wheel on the road nearby. The doctor from the emergency department finished giving the woman an injection and assured her it would take effect soon. With instructions to the nurse with her to monitor the cyclist closely, the doctor hurried on to the next cluster of people on the road.

Tess followed, with a sharp word to a bystander taking photos to put away their phone. Bits and pieces of overheard conversation informed her as she hurried. *'He didn't stop.' 'The bastard swerved on purpose to get her.' 'Is he dead? He must have flown out of that chair.'*

A middle-aged woman sat on the road, leaning against a parked car, distressed but conscious and not, at least at first glance, badly hurt. Another woman knelt beside her, attempting to calm her. *'I tried to pull him back. I wasn't quick enough. It's my fault.' 'No, it's not your fault.'*

Not far beyond the two women, Leah Haddad crouched next to an elderly man sprawled on the ground, metres from an upended wheelchair. She stood aside to make room for the doctor. After a brief handover, the detective senior sergeant saw

Tess hesitating and strode across. 'I'm glad you're here, Ballard. How's Madeleine?'

Tess shook her head wordlessly and Leah swore. 'The boy? I headed straight over here. He wasn't hurt, was he?'

'He's not injured.' Not physically, anyway. But he'd seen two parents die in two days, both violently. How could a teenager get over that? Let alone everything else he'd lost.

The flashing lights of a police car and an ambulance edged around the makeshift roadblocks. With the doctor, the nursing staff and the paramedics, there would be enough skilled people to help the injured.

Leah looked across to where the Fraser men huddled around Maddie's body. 'Jesus, they must be shattered. How bloody cruel for her father. To find she's alive, and then . . . They were just there, on the other side of the road. It happened right in front of them.'

Tess averted her gaze as Leah dashed away a tear. Just a few days since the detective had arrived from headquarters in Sydney to take charge of the murder investigation, and she'd proved to be tough, thorough and often blisteringly honest. Not one to display emotion, but that didn't mean she didn't feel them.

Tess controlled her own with difficulty. She needed to be busy, not standing around, useless. 'Did you see the driver?' she asked Leah.

'I was on the phone and I turned my back. I didn't see it happen. Didn't see the driver. But I'm going to nail that frigging bastard.' She paused, huffing out a breath. The harshness in her voice faded when she added, 'I'd better go talk to Steve. Can you see if you can find any witnesses?'

Tess scanned the surroundings while Leah walked across to the Frasers. Nick Matheson had joined them, clasping Steve's shoulder in masculine compassion.

Dee, still in uniform, spoke sympathetically with a distraught man near a car stopped in the middle of the road. The SES were blocking off the street at both ends. Spectators – maybe witnesses – stood in small groups nearby. She could certainly approach them, ask what they'd seen, except she wasn't in uniform and didn't have her ID with her.

She met up with Dee, who left the driver sitting on the street kerb.

'This is a nightmare,' Dee said. 'You're okay? You weren't involved?'

'No, I was inside. But it seems like a vehicle travelling east deliberately ran down Madeleine on that side of the crossing. After hitting her –' she used her hands to indicate the direction – 'he collected the cyclist over there. Then the old gent on the wheelchair. Looks like he was thrown out of it. The woman pushing it was luckier.' A relative term. The emotional scars would run deep.

'Will he make it?'

'He doesn't look good. Might have a better idea after he's stabilised and inside. The cyclist is conscious, but I'm guessing she has multiple fractures.'

'This poor bloke,' Dee nodded towards the man she'd just been talking to, 'was coming west this way when the sarge's sister was thrown right in front of him. A couple of witnesses have confirmed it. He couldn't have done a damn thing about it.'

A single moment, and it would haunt the driver forever. A few seconds earlier, a few seconds later – so many, many accidents Tess attended resulted from the unfortunate combination of place and time with a moment's distraction, or another driver's negligence, or an unforeseeable occurrence. But this carnage was a criminal act, a wanton act of violence that made her seethe. So much hurt, so much suffering and sorrow because one person made a conscious decision to use a vehicle as a weapon.

On the kerb, the driver of the second vehicle rocked backwards and forwards where he sat.

'He needs to go in to the ED,' Tess said, but when Dee began walking with her she waved her back. 'I'll take him. You're in uniform. Go find witnesses.'

Her arm around his shoulders, she cajoled and half-supported the distressed middle-aged man into the emergency room and handed him into Marco's care with a brief summary. With the nurse's permission, she took a sheet and a couple of blankets from the linen trolley before she returned outside.

Most of the spectators had left, or courteously remained at a distance, but a few gawked at Madeleine and the men around her. She moved them on briskly, requesting their respect.

Aaron, the detective constable from Strathnairn, must have arrived while she was inside. He stood talking with Steve, Leah and Matheson, a metre or so from where Assistant Commissioner Fraser and Madeleine's son still sat by her body.

Tess approached the Assistant Commissioner, laid a gentle hand on his arm. 'Sir, I've brought a sheet. Is it okay if I cover her?'

He faced her slowly, his usually sharp gaze taking a moment to focus and recognise her. 'It's Ballard, isn't it?' His voice scraped, hoarse and uneven.

'Yes, sir. Tess Ballard.'

He nodded absently. 'Yes, cover her,' he said. 'But not her face. Not yet.'

She wanted to weep for him, for the strong man devastated by the cruellest of circumstances. Her vision blurring, she unfolded the sheet. Steve came to take one side, and they draped it softly over Maddie, Tristan helping to bring it up to her chin. AC Fraser didn't move, except to draw his daughter's hand from under the sheet to hold it.

With a worried glance at his father, Steve took Tess slightly aside. 'Tess, could you go and sit with Lily for a while? I need to get Dad and Tris inside, maybe into the hospital chapel for a bit. But I can't tell Lily just yet. Not until I can hold it together.' He gave a tiny, self-deprecating smile that cut straight into Tess's heart with its raw honesty.

'Of course I will.'

'Aaron was just taking a report ten minutes ago of a stolen car that might be the one. There's an alert out for the car already. Maybe we can catch the bastard, and find out if this is connected, or if it was just random.'

Tristan rose to his feet. 'I saw the driver,' he said. 'I know who it was.'

Steve gestured to the other detectives to join them. 'Who, Tris? Who was the driver?'

'A man from our community. His name is Zac.'

'Isaac Matthias?' Tess almost didn't recognise her own voice.

Tristan shrugged. 'I think so. I've heard him called Isaac. But we mostly called him Zac.'

Steve frowned. 'But it wasn't the same car. It wasn't the green Falcon he was driving earlier today.'

'He stole one, he could have stolen another,' Matheson said. 'Aaron, we'll need a search of the area where the second car was stolen. The first might have been abandoned nearby.'

'But why would he go after Madeleine?' Aaron asked.

Leah stood with her fists thrust into her pockets, tense and angry. 'Because the crowd out at Serenity Hill – the mood was getting heated. They know police shot Joshua and now they don't trust us. They were turning against Madeleine, too. It was a risk taking her back out there. It would be wise, Nick, if Steve and Tess left the district for a little while. Somewhere safer.'

'Are you sure it was Isaac, Tris?' Steve asked, but he kept his voice calm. 'Did you see him clearly?'

'Yes. I was just there, just behind her. I saw him. I saw him laugh as he hit her. Laughing as if –' he glanced between them all, searching for understanding, 'as if it was bliss.'

Tess closed her eyes but it couldn't shut out the mental images. Isaac laughing as he murdered Madeleine. Isaac grinning as he'd tried to rape her. Isaac smiling ecstatically as a very young man, preaching fervently of the pure joy in doing the Lord's work.

Isaac considered himself her husband. If he found out she'd shot Joshua, or if he ever found out the role she'd played in his own father's death, he would punish her and murder her with as much joy – or bliss – as he'd murdered Madeleine.

CHAPTER 7

Steve must have slept eventually, because he woke to the sound of a car engine starting outside a nearby motel room, and a low shaft of sunlight beaming through the gap in the curtains into his gritty eyes.

Despite the car noise, his father's rasping breathing didn't change, and Tristan didn't move in the bunk above Steve.

Steve slid carefully out of bed and pulled on his jeans and t-shirt. Tristan slept soundly in the top bunk, wrapped in the patchwork quilt Maddie had brought from Serenity Hill, packed in the cloth bags that had almost been forgotten in the aftermath of yesterday's accident. The quilt, the teddy bear, a few simple, hand-stitched clothes for each of them, and that was it – all Maddie's possessions. All the childrens' possessions.

He took his phone and a bottle of water and opened the door as quietly as he could, slipping out into the morning light.

Tess sat at the small table outside the next motel room, a tin open in front of her, sewing a small piece of fabric. She gave him a wan smile and gestured for him to take the other chair. 'Did you get some sleep?' she asked, placing the fabric into the tin and closing it up, pushing it off to one side.

'Yeah. You?' He didn't have enough neurons firing to comment on her sewing, and it didn't matter.

'Some. Lily's still sleeping.'

The child didn't really understand what had happened – the only upside to the cult's practices of community child-rearing, and their emphasis on a blissful afterlife. She wasn't accustomed to always having Maddie nearby and she didn't, yet, comprehend the finality of death. She'd mostly been upset last night because they'd all been barely coping.

'Thank you for looking after her, Tess.'

She dismissed his thanks with a shake of her head. 'I'm glad I could help. But I kept thinking,' she added, with a hitch in her voice, 'that it should have been Maddie there with her.'

It took him a moment, and effort, to reply without his voice cracking. 'Yes. It should have been.'

A police car turned in to the motel driveway, pulling up beside the one already there. The day shift taking over from the night shift. Nick had insisted on placing a guard overnight. Steve had slept a little better knowing they were there, and that Tess was safe in the room next door.

The car door opened and Dee got out and strolled down to greet them. 'Good morning,' she said. 'Everything quiet overnight here, I gather?'

'Yes.' Steve frowned, trying to think. She'd been at Derringvale two nights ago, and at Tess's yesterday, at the hospital last night. 'How come you're here? Seems like you've been on duty for days.'

'Off and on. The boss sent me off home reasonably early last night, so I've had a good break. We're still short-staffed, though.'

Steve rose and brought a chair from the table outside his room. 'What news?'

Dee accepted the seat with a grateful smile. 'Thanks. Detective Haddad has been on the go all night. She doesn't stop, that woman. She's not letting many others stop, either.'

Yeah, that was Leah. Steve sent out a silent hope that she'd make a quick arrest. He hated being useless, sidelined from the investigation. It was all he knew how to do, police work, and he craved the familiar activity and the frenetic pace, instead of struggling to keep his head above water to deal with the unfamiliar responsibilities of here and now.

But now even the familiar procedures of investigation involved emotions he barely knew how to contain. 'Who's going to Maddie's post-mortem?' he asked through a thick throat. One of the detectives on the case had to be there. Which meant Leah or Aaron. A tough task, but necessary.

'Haddad. She's going down to Sydney this morning.'

'How are the other casualties? The elderly man?' Tess asked.

'They're doing okay. They were both taken to Tamworth but that's mostly precautionary, I think.'

Good news, but Steve focused on his most immediate concern. 'Isaac Matthias?'

'Haven't found him yet, Sarge. The first car he stole was dumped near where he took the second one, which was at a service station. A guy left his keys in his car while he went to pay for fuel, and it was gone when he came out. Security footage showed Isaac just walking up to the car and driving off in it, cool as a cucumber.'

Steve doused the string of swearwords on his tongue with a swig from his water bottle, frustration, tiredness and guilt stealing a more coherent response. If he'd arrested Matthias at Tess's place, Maddie would still be alive. He'd gone over and over that scene in his mind half the night, thought of a dozen things he could have done differently, should have done differently. His fault, his responsibility, that Matthias had got away.

Tess asked into the silence, 'Any news on the possible body in the woolshed?'

'Yes. Confirmed last night. A woman. Post-mortem will have to determine identity and the cause of death. But,' Dee grimaced, 'I did hear there were suspected stab wounds.'

Not an accident, her being under the woolshed. Another murder. But when, and by whom? Joshua? Or someone else? Steve ran through possibilities by habit. But he was no longer an investigator. He didn't have to do this. He just wanted answers.

'There was another development overnight, though,' Dee added. 'Two actually, although they might be related.'

Steve hoped for a breakthrough, but Dee didn't look all that excited. 'Tell us.'

'The two other kids at the hospital – the ones whose mother is missing – they've gone. Things were fairly frantic there with getting the casualties stable and then flown out and when someone checked on the kids around midnight, they'd gone. Security footage from the corridor shows a person in a hoodie leading them out. Could be male or female. But that's all we have so far.'

Damn. Whatever it meant, it wasn't good. 'And the other development?'

'Haddad and the night shift went out to Serenity Hill looking for the kids, and the whole mob have gone. Not a soul there now. The cottages and the machinery shed are cleared out. The truck and the couple of cars that were there before are gone.'

'They've run. Any idea where?'

'Not yet. Haddad's got Aaron working on it. I'm sure Nick will keep you up to date.' She pushed back her chair. 'Now, I'll leave you to your morning. My partner,' she jerked a thumb towards the car, 'is jonesing for some caffeine. The motel restaurant is serving breakfast, so I'd better go and let him get some. Just hoy if you need us.'

Steve ached for caffeine, too, and he'd bet Tess needed a mega-dose, but he had no intention of disturbing the sleepers in the motel room by boiling a kettle and possibly clattering cups. He could hold on a bit longer. Probably.

After Dee left, Tess said, 'None of that was good news.'

She seemed subdued, lacking her usual concentrated energy.

'Nope, it wasn't.' He leaned his elbows on the table, rubbing his neck, taut muscles protesting. 'We still don't know if Tamara is alive or not. Perhaps it was her who took the children.'

'I doubt it.' She blew out a slow breath. 'I think she's dead.'

'Because?' he probed, wanting to know her reasoning.

'She's one of the handful of women who were with Joshua very early on. Three of them are now dead – Hayley, Sybilla and Madeleine. Possibly more, if that murder at the coast last week is connected. If they were killed because they had knowledge that could derail Joshua's plans, then Tamara probably knew it too.'

'But if Tamara is the dead woman, then who took her children away?'

Tess had her hands clasped on the table and focused on them, steepling her fingers as she said slowly, 'There are a few possibilities. If the community raises the children, they're as much the community's as they are hers. If they feel a responsibility for them, or if there's a particular group member who was close to them, they will have taken them when they left. Or —' She stopped abruptly.

'Or?'

'Or someone has a purpose for them.'

'For a thirteen-year-old girl and a two-year-old boy.' It wasn't a question.

She nodded wordlessly. Two kids without a mother, and likely without a father. Vulnerable, innocent and at risk of exploitation. He'd seen the results of that too many times, and the thought sickened him. And Maddie's children, especially Lily, would have been left just as vulnerable if not for the quirk of circumstance that had assigned him to the investigation.

No way would he leave them unprotected. And no way did he want to see Tess unprotected, with Matthias still on the loose and cult members with a grudge who knew where. 'Have you got friends or family to stay with for a few days?' he asked. 'Until Matthias is arrested and things settle down?'

'No. Not really. But I'll sort something out.'

Not his business, and she was a more than sensible adult capable of arranging things for herself, but it worried him that she didn't have anyone to go to.

His father emerged from the motel room, blinking once as he stepped into the sunlight. He wore his suit trousers and a clean shirt, with crisp, straight fold lines from being neatly packed. He came to stand by them, stiff and formal.

'Good morning.' He cleared his throat. 'I must apologise. To you both. For my breakdown last night.'

A 'breakdown'? Sitting for twenty minutes with his daughter in the most tragic of circumstances? For a man accustomed to emotional control, maybe, but Steve didn't consider it as any kind of a failure. The opposite, in fact.

'Dad, sit down. We were all cut up, with good reason. You don't need to apologise to anybody for anything.'

'There is nothing to apologise for, sir,' Tess said in her quiet, sincere way.

His father sat in the offered chair somewhat awkwardly, as if he wasn't sure he wanted to. Steve had never thought of his father as being shy before but perhaps he was, out of the comfort zone of his official role. Come to think of it, he couldn't recall seeing him relaxed since . . . ever. Not even on the few family holidays they'd taken when his mother was well enough.

Tess had left the door of her room open and Lily appeared in the doorway, her hair a wild halo of dark curls around her face and Pooky under her arm. Her too-big t-shirt reached to her knees. One of Tess's, Steve presumed. She hesitated, her thumb creeping towards her mouth as she saw all three adults.

'Good morning, sleepyhead.' Steve gave her the most reassuring grin he could muster and was rewarded with a tentative smile.

Tess stood, and held out her hand to the girl. 'Hello, Lily. How about we go and wash your face and get you dressed?'

Steve added another mental note to his growing list: *Ask Tess what clothes to buy for Lily.* She might have a better idea of the things a little girl needed than he did. He'd got as far as jeans and t-shirts on his Lily list, copied from his Tristan list. He had a feeling it was going to get a whole lot longer.

'Excuse me for a few minutes,' Tess said to his father, but added with a swift glance at Steve, 'I'll make some coffee.'

'Don't worry about coffee yet. We can have breakfast in the motel restaurant. The coffee is probably better than the instant packs in the rooms.'

She nodded and closed the door as she went inside with Lily, giving them all a degree of privacy.

His father cleared his throat again. 'We'll need to decide what to do. About the children. Maybe your aunt—'

Steve headed off that idea, fast. 'No, Dad. Liz has only just retired. She's been planning for years to spend her retirement travelling. I'll look after Lily and Tristan. They'll live with me.'

'You can't raise them. The boy, maybe, he's old enough, but not a little girl. You're on your own. You have a demanding career.'

As always, his father's pointed lack of belief in him landed with a spear of anger and hurt. He'd long ago learned not to snap back, to pretend he was uncaring. To bury his hurt so his father couldn't see it and triumph.

But this morning, for the first time, the hurt didn't last long. He remembered the broken man last night, his grief tearing away his self-control. And when he looked closely at his father in front of him, he saw past the stiff authority and recognised it, finally, for the protective armour it was.

Understanding unfolded and the old hurts began to dissipate. His father didn't so much doubt him as he doubted himself. How many times had those words run through Bruce's mind, after his wife died and left him with two children? *You can't raise them . . . not a little girl. You're on your own. You have a demanding career.*

Whether anyone had told his father that, or whether it had been his own self-talk, without his wife's support and encouragement the negativity and doubt must have eaten away at his confidence, year after year. Throw in two teenagers to raise, both with their own issues . . . No wonder Bruce had escaped into his work. Being a senior police officer might have been easier than being a parent.

Somehow he had to explain to his father what he wasn't even sure he could explain to himself: a gut-deep certainty that it was the right thing to do.

'Maddie asked me to take care of them if anything happened to her, and I promised I would, Dad. I know it's going to be a huge challenge, a huge change for me. But it's important to me. I'm their uncle. It's my responsibility.'

'But Lily is so young. You can't work long, unpredictable hours with a young child. If you were married, it might be different. But you're not.'

'I know, Dad. My career isn't as important to me as this is. I've been a police officer for fifteen years. Maybe it's time I had a career change, did something different. I'll take leave for the next few months. We'll get settled and get to know each other. Then we can weigh up options.'

Steve expected more arguments, but they didn't come. Only a question, 'Where will you go? Back to Moree?'

'No. My place there is rented out on a long lease. I started arranging yesterday to rent a house for Maddie and the kids in Dungirri. I'll go forward with that.'

'Dungirri? Isn't that where—'

'Yes, Dad.' Where he'd failed. Where a little girl had died because the police – because *he* – had focused on the wrong man. Where he'd almost lost a colleague, a valued friend, because of his own anger and arrogance. But also where he'd been part of a team that had cleaned up a criminal mob that had intimidated the town for decades.

'I've got good friends there now,' he explained. 'And it's a community that has every reason to take very close care of its children. Plus it's a small school, only two blocks from the house. I think Lily will feel more comfortable there.'

'Will I have to go to school?'

He hadn't heard Tristan open the door, didn't know how long he'd been listening.

'If you want to, yes. The high school is in Birraga but there's a school bus from Dungirri. We can talk in the next few days about what you'd like to do. There's no hurry to decide.'

Maybe school, if he wasn't so far behind he'd be ostracised. They probably had programs for kids who weren't ready yet for higher school certificate studies. Or he could do general education subjects through online learning. There would be plenty of possibilities. He'd build on Tristan's existing skills and interests, and not push him too hard into anything. It was going to be enough challenge for the lad to find his feet in his new world.

'I can work. I'm not a free-loader. I know farming. Crops and cattle and sheep. And I can build things. Furniture and sheds.'

Either Maddie's influence or the groups' culture had given him a good work ethic, apparently. Or they'd exploited the unpaid labour force.

'Those are useful skills to have, Tris. You're probably handier than me. If you want some paid work, there may be some people in Dungirri who could use your experience.'

His father's chair scraped on the ground as he stood up. 'You've got everything in hand here. I'm not needed so I'll . . .' he paused, swallowed, and then powered on, 'I'll book on this morning's flight to Sydney. I want to be nearby for –' another slight pause, and a quick glance at Tristan, 'for the examination.'

The examination. Maddie's post-mortem examination at the morgue in Glebe, where the pathologist would document her injuries so that there would be no doubt in court that Matthias had killed her.

Steve rose and clasped his father's shoulder. 'Dad, you know you won't be able to attend it, and you wouldn't want to. Leah Haddad will be the observing officer, and she'll keep us informed. I understand if you really need to be in Sydney but to be honest –' he drew in a breath to say words he'd never said to his father, 'I could do with your help and company here.'

Unfamiliar ground, this new relationship with his father. No longer constantly butting heads and seeing the worst in each other. Maybe it wouldn't last, but for now, with his father blindsided by grief and out of his depth, Steve had to take charge and be the stalwart one.

He half expected his father to disagree, if only out of habit. But Bruce only responded with a gruffly honest, 'I don't see how I can be useful.'

'After we go in and give our statements, I'll be caught up with the critical incident investigation. That will likely take hours. Lily and Iris need clothes and other things. If you could keep them company and take them shopping until I'm free, that would be a huge help.'

An expression of horror crossed Bruce's face. 'I know nothing about children's clothes, Steven.'

No, he didn't, because Steve's mother or his Aunt Liz had managed the child-caring tasks until he and Maddie were old enough to shop for themselves.

'Never too late to learn, Dad. I'll give you a list. It'll just be basics for a couple of days. The sales staff will be able to help.'

When Tess brought Lily out, the girl wore one of the two simple shift dresses that Maddie had brought from Serenity

Hill, with her recycled-tyre sandals. Just as well the sun shone and the autumn weather was mild. He mentally added jacket, sweatshirt, shoes and socks to the list. They only needed enough to wear for the next couple of days. Once they went to Dungirri, he had friends with children who could advise him on what they'd need, longer term.

They all walked up to the motel restaurant together. Although the kids were accustomed to communal meals, the motel restaurant, the other guests and the array of dishes engaged their curiosity. Lily's questions about all the different foods on the buffet kept Steve occupied, explaining things to her and steering her towards the healthy choices. Tristan remained quiet, watching and learning, eating toast and drinking juice and declining other food.

Somewhere along the line Tris had learned that watchfulness. According to Maddie the other night, Joshua had favoured David over Tristan. Perhaps the kid's caution went further back than this week's events. Or perhaps he'd somehow inherited his grandfather's temperament.

They ate quickly, with limited conversation at the table. The children displayed good table manners. Although Lily asked a few more questions of Steve, she seemed uncertain of her new grandfather – a somewhat mutual feeling, Steve suspected, from the few stilted comments his father made to them. Bruce treated Tess with old-fashioned courtesy, his default mode for dealing with women outside a work context. Other than polite responses, Tess hardly said a word, toying with her fruit and yoghurt before she ate it.

'Everything okay?' Steve asked her as they left the restaurant.

'Yes. Not looking forward to this morning. You'll be right with Lily now, won't you? After we're finished with the critical incident team, I'll head home to pack some more things. I might have to be away for longer than I thought.'

'Have you decided where to go?'

'Not yet.'

Reluctant to simply say farewell and let her get on with her life, he made do with an earnest, 'You'll keep in touch, won't you? Let me know where you are, how you are?'

She agreed, with a politeness that guaranteed nothing.

Her non-committal distance bruised emotions already battered by Maddie's death. He and Tess ... yeah, definitely a no-go, despite the storm of challenges they'd faced together these past few days. Senior officers behaving ethically didn't make approaches to women officers, especially when he'd witnessed her at her most vulnerable. Maybe later, sometime down the track when this case was over ... No, he wouldn't hold out much hope. She had her own life to lead, and he no longer had the choices he used to have. His father, Tristan and Lily waited for him, and everything had changed. Two children totally dependent on him. For years ahead. He'd be pushing fifty by the time Lily finished school.

So be it. Suck it up and make the best of it. It wasn't as though he'd had any other plans.

He walked back into the motel room to move on with the first day of the rest of his life.

Arriving at the police station with the Frasers, Tess found herself ushered into Nick Matheson's office along with them. The involvement of an Assistant Commissioner's son in a critical incident inquiry and the murder of his daughter apparently merited the allocation of the police force's best detectives. Nick introduced them to Chief Inspector Heather Arundel, sent from the Professional Standards unit in Sydney to head up the inquiry. In her fifties, brusque and business-like, she offered her condolences on Maddie's death with sincerity, but excused herself after the introductions.

Steve and his father needed no introduction to Detective Chief Inspector Alec Goddard, called across from the north coast command to take responsibility for the murder investigations. Tess knew him by reputation – a highly regarded DCI at State Crime Command before he'd transferred to the north. Haddad wouldn't like having someone brought in over the top of her, but Tess doubted she'd be surprised. With the involvement of the AC's family, the investigation had to be, and be seen to be, at the highest level of priority and integrity.

Steve greeted Goddard with some warmth, although neither of them were effusive. 'How's Bella? Keeping well?' Steve asked him.

A woman. A woman who connected them somehow. Goddard's partner, Tess guessed, by the way his solemn face softened with a smile. 'She's very well. At a conference in Melbourne at the moment and trying to get another paper finished before July.'

Steve grinned but Tess thought there might be a touch of wistfulness in it. 'Give her my best wishes.'

None of her business if Steve had a fondness for the senior detective's partner. Especially since Goddard didn't appear perturbed. But whatever their connection, it likely explained why Goddard was on the homicide investigation and not the critical incident inquiry.

With all the on-duty officers busy, Tess kept Lily company while Steve, AC Fraser and Tristan went with Goddard to give their formal witness statements about Maddie's murder.

In the police station break room, Tess found some biscuits and poured a glass of water for Lily. They sat at one of the tables, but neither she nor Steve had thought to bring books or something to entertain the child, so Tess pulled out her tin of patchwork pieces from her backpack. Plain and patterned fabric stitched around cardboard templates made dozens of small elongated hexagons in a variety of colours and designs. She would eventually sew them together to make complex tessellated blocks, but for now the piles of pieces offered endless possibilities.

'Do you think you can make patterns with these?' she asked Lily, spreading out the honeycomb pieces and showing her how to place their edges together in various shapes.

Lily's face lit up and she reached for the pieces, her fingers gently sorting colours and trying out combinations.

Tess sat back and watched, sipping her own water. Lily quickly became absorbed, her brow furrowing as she contemplated options and switched the coloured and patterned pieces back and forth to see what she liked best. Tess's fingers itched to take out her needle and thread and stitch some more pieces because she knew no better way to take her mind off worries, but any of the station officers could come in at any moment, and she kept her patchwork to herself.

Too many people had outdated or misogynistic ideas about the skill and value of women's crafts and she had enough challenges just now without that kind of negative judgement. The rhythms and distractions of paper piecing had helped her through dark times without alcohol or drugs and she had a quilt and a half as an extra bonus. Nothing weak about that.

By the time AC Fraser came to collect her, Lily had grouped three lots of blocks into patterns that pleased her. Tess stood as he entered the room, but Lily straightened a piece before she looked up hesitantly at her grandfather, both proud of her efforts and uncertain of his response.

'Very good,' he said gruffly, almost as uncertain as the child. 'They're called tessellations. They're important principles in mathematics and geometry.'

That made at least four words there that would have gone over Lily's head. He might as well have been speaking a different language.

'Tesslations?' Lily glanced between the two of them as she repeated the only word that sounded familiar. 'Tess?'

'A tessellation is a type of pattern,' she explained, and then stopped short because she couldn't think how else to explain polygonal shapes and flat planes in terms appropriate for a six-year-old. Plus she hated the thought of getting it wrong in front of one of the state's most senior police officers.

Yet he only picked up one of the unused pieces, flipped it over and touched a light finger to the stitches holding the fabric around the paper. 'My wife did some paper piecing. Before she became too ill.' He placed it down, looked around the room, anywhere but at her. 'She taught mathematics and science at high school. Until the cancer . . . She fought it for more than ten years.'

How much he had lost, wife and daughter. No wonder he rarely smiled and even more rarely showed any sense of humour. He'd had little to laugh or even smile about.

There weren't any effective words in any dictionary for his sorrow. Her throat tight, she fell back yet again on the useless, 'I'm so sorry, sir.' In the weeks she'd worked with him, he'd made no mention of his wife, or his daughter. Or his son. Only that one photo of Steve on his desk. Perhaps if their shared grief over Maddie's murder bridged the distance between them, that would be one small good out of too much sorrow.

He gave the briefest nod in acknowledgement of her poorly expressed sympathy and then touched an awkward hand to his granddaughter's curls. 'Lily, put those shapes away now and say thank you to Tess. It's time for us to go.'

With one quick glance at Tess for verification, Lily obeyed without argument. Maddie and her community hadn't raised spoilt princesses.

AC Fraser shifted on his feet. 'Can you recommend where in town I can find children's clothes?'

'There's a Salvation Army shop a block or so down on the left,' she told him.

He stiffened, eyebrows rising. 'I can afford new clothes for my grandchildren.'

'Of course, sir. There's a Target Country nearby. But I was thinking that new clothes need washing before wear and the Salvos will have some clean things she can wear straight away.'

'Ah. Good thinking. I don't suppose you can spare an hour to come with me?'

'Sorry, sir. The inquiry.'

In normal circumstances he wouldn't have forgotten. Nothing about the past twenty-four hours approached 'normal'. 'Yes. Of course. Just speak calmly and tell the truth, Ballard.'

Despite his solemn nature, there was a kindness to him and she had no qualms about leaving Lily in his care. They would get used to each other, those two. Already Lily raised a hand, expecting him to take it. And he did.

Tess saw them out of the station, pointed out the direction of several stores, and then returned inside to wait on the uncomfortable vinyl chair outside the interview room. With nothing to distract her, she breathed slowly and deeply in an attempt to keep rising anxiety in check. This investigation could ruin her career. Her life revolved around her career. She was Senior Constable Tess Ballard and proud of her achievements, but almost all her achievements related to her job or her study – which related to her policing. A Bachelor of Social Sciences with Honours. A Masters degree in Criminology. But what would that matter if the inquiry found she'd acted wrongly in firing at Joshua? She could be disciplined, dismissed, charged with murder. Probably not the last, but if everything went haywire, if the inquiry didn't comprehend how it had been and the police force or politicians or the public needed a scapegoat, then she could face criminal charges.

She remembered Joshua's followers dancing and chanting, in thrall to his exhortations to 'bliss', and the young woman, Callie, deliberately taking that whirling step off the rock and into the churning water.

Tess closed her eyes. Had Callie known? Had she realised, as water filled her mouth and lungs, that this was no bliss? But she'd only been a short distance from the falls, and it would have been seconds, if that, before the power of the flood carrying her down the forty-metre drop must have extinguished thought and fear and life.

'Ballard?'

The voice snapped her out of her thoughts and she rose to attention hastily to face Chief Inspector Arundel. *Speak calmly and tell the truth.*

In the interview room, Arundel introduced the other two members of the critical incident inquiry team, and then spent some time outlining the inquiry process and explaining her rights. The procedural issues and their background questions seemed to take longer than their questions about the incident itself. However, they were fair and listened to her responses without interruption, and although they made a few comments she had the sense that they remained open-minded and wouldn't rush to make judgements.

'We'd like you and DS Fraser to accompany us out to the scene,' Arundel informed her at the end of the interview. 'We'll take a short break for lunch and meet here again in an hour.'

An hour. She could stay in the police station – it did have a halfway decent coffee machine – but there might be colleagues expecting to talk and ask questions and she'd overdosed on people just for now.

Outside in the sunshine, she resisted the urge to go for an invigorating walk. Away from the police station, away from people. But Zac was still out there somewhere and she dared not risk coming face to face with him without the weapons on her police vest.

Despite standing on the steps of the police station – surely Zac wouldn't be stupid enough to lurk nearby – she checked the surroundings carefully before she crossed the road to the cafe that served the best salads in Strathnairn.

She scanned the simply decorated room before she entered. No sign of Zac at any of the dozen tables. But at one of the back tables near a bookshelf, Erin flipped through a magazine. Of the National Parks staff, she knew Erin best. Technically Simon worked out of the Goodabri office, but with his call-up for army reserve service two months ago, Erin had filled in. Not only a park ranger, she also volunteered with the SES. They'd worked together with Steve just days ago, locating and retrieving Sybilla's body from the base of the waterfall. Before the flood. Before Joshua had exhorted his followers to find 'bliss' in the raging water.

Other than Steve and Simon, Erin was the only person who would be able to comprehend the tensions of the past week because she'd been there, too.

'Hi Erin. Would you like company, or would you prefer time alone?'

Erin smiled and gestured to the other chair. 'Your company is welcome. How are you faring today?'

'I'm okay. Rough night. Not as rough as for the Frasers, though.'

'A hell of a tragedy. How are they going?'

'Shellshocked, I think. Especially AC Fraser. The sarge is . . .' Being strong. Looking after everybody. Organising the things that needed to be done and holding them all together. Including her. 'He's been a rock. He's planning to take Lily and Tristan. To live with him.' As she said the words aloud, she recognised that her initial impressions of the man were rapidly having a makeover.

Erin may have heard the hint of incredulity in her voice. 'That's a big commitment for him. I did suspect there was more to him than met the eye but that's a huge life change all of a sudden.'

'He's not the only one,' Tess said. 'How's Simon doing?'

'He's coping fine.' She gave an impish smile. 'But he does have me. Now. Hopefully that will make it easier for him to adjust.'

Whereas Steve had two children in his care now, vastly different in age, and only his father as support. And an uneasy relationship with him at that. 'I'm glad for both of you. How's Jasmine?'

Erin took one of the small sugar packets from the dish on the table and rotated it in her fingers. 'She's okay. I think. Stunned by it all, especially Madeleine's death. Simon told her this morning and he's still over at the hospital with her now. They'll discharge her into his care today. Thankfully she was close to Maddie and trusted her, and Maddie had told her to trust us. That's making things easier.'

The young waiter came across with a cheery 'hello' and they both ordered. Tess changed her mind about the salad and ordered vegetable soup and bread instead. Comfort food? Maybe. Something a little heartier than leaf greens, anyway. She did have a demanding afternoon ahead. She also had to offer Erin what insight she could about Jasmine's situation – and get through the conversation.

She cupped her hands on the table, taking a moment to decide how to start. 'Jasmine may feel quite lost for a while. Everything she believed in has been turned topsy-turvy. She's probably been taught that the world outside the cult is full of evil, and she won't know enough about it to be able to judge what's right and what's wrong. Plus she may feel as though she has lost the chance of salvation – I guess in Joshua's terms, bliss.'

Erin could be light-hearted but she was far more perceptive than the blonde looks she sometimes played on. 'You sound as though you speak from experience. You said the other day you knew about cults, and I have wondered.'

With almost anyone else, Tess might have sidestepped the question. But not Erin. Not after working on this case with her. 'Yes. In a way. I grew up in a very strict religious sect. In some aspects it was similar to Joshua's group – reclusive, self-sufficient, revering one man's teachings. But in other aspects, very different. The True Brethren are focused on sin and fear. From what I've read of Joshua's teachings, he wasn't hung up on the concept of sin. Or the inherent evil of women.'

'No. Not with multiple women bearing his children. What happened? You must have left the sect.'

'Yes. I left when I was seventeen and—' She swallowed back the surge of remembered emotion. 'It was very hard, for a few years. I was totally unequipped to deal with the world. But Jasmine is younger and she has you and Simon to help her.'

'You were alone? No family?'

Part of her wanted to simply shake her head, leave it at that. But another part of her yearned to open up a little more, to let a friendship grow. She liked Erin, respected her commitment and the way she threw herself into her work and her life. And Tess could trust her integrity. But it still took courage to speak, and she realised she'd folded her arms on the table in front of her as a kind of reassurance. 'My parents and siblings are still in the sect. They disowned me and the sect preaches no contact with those outside it. My letters are returned, unopened.'

'Oh, hell. That must be hard on you.'

'It is,' she admitted. 'But not as hard as living in the sect.' Despite the logic and truth of it, the emotions that had been bubbling under the surface over the past two days welled up. The similarities between Lily and her youngest sister; Tristan's cautious manner and the lost look in his eyes; both constant reminders of herself at seventeen, terrified of the strange world and grieving for her family and her innocence.

Erin passed her one of the paper serviettes and Tess wiped her eyes, blew her nose. 'Sorry,' she said. 'I'm not usually weepy.'

'You're human, and there's plenty to weep about. I had a howl in the shower this morning myself.'

A group of businessmen, laughing at some joke, took over a nearby table and Tess kept her face down. *Don't cry. Hold it in. You can do it.*

The waiter brought a bottle of water and glasses to the table and Erin poured a glass each, pushing one towards Tess as she changed the subject. 'I've been in to see the new detective in charge. DCI Goddard. He wants me to go out to Serenity Hill with him and Aaron after lunch.'

A somewhat easier topic to address, and the cool water eased her rough throat. 'The CI investigators have asked us to go out there, too. To do a walk-through, I guess.'

'They've asked to see Simon and me later this afternoon. But I guess the CI team are investigating you guys, not Simon, and we're just witnesses. Goddard is presumably the one who'll decide whether to charge Simon with anything. Do you know him? Goddard?'

'Only by reputation. A lot of people think highly of him.' Their meals arrived and she paused until the waiter had gone again. 'To be honest, I'd be very surprised if Simon is charged with anything.' She spoke quietly, aware of people nearby. 'Three of us acted, so they'll have to believe he saw good reason to.

If the hierarchy goes after anyone I'm fairly sure it will be the police officers.'

'Let's hope they don't go after any of you. Goddard said they haven't found either body yet.'

'No. Which is unusual.'

'They may not have been able to get up into the gorge until today. And there was a fair amount of forest debris washed down from the hills. Tree trunks and all. So they may be submerged.'

Tess stirred her soup slowly. It was stupid to feel uneasy about the young woman being pinned under the water when she was dead and long past noticing. And yet she did. Another senseless death. Her appetite had disappeared but she hated wasting food so she ate her soup, anyway. With time slipping away, they didn't linger over their meal.

As they paid at the counter, Tess stretched her toes in the flat shoes she'd slipped on this morning. 'I need to go back to my car, get my boots. I didn't dress for bushwalking today. I won't be long. I'll see you at the station.'

Erin held the door open for her. 'I need to dash to the bank. But I'll walk with you first.'

'There's no need. It's just in the lane on the other side of the station.'

'I heard you had an incident with one of the Serenity Hill guys, rumoured to be the driver of the car last night. And that they haven't arrested him yet. Are you sure you'll be okay?'

'Yes. Go. Get to the bank.'

On-duty police officers used the parking area behind the police station, but with extra officers called in and the day shift already on the job, she and Fraser had parked in the overflow area in the lane beside the station. Tess unlocked the car, pulled out boots and socks from the back seat. As she locked the car again, a piece of paper tucked under the windscreen wiper caught her eye. It was a piece of newsprint. Not an advertising flyer, just ordinary newsprint. The banner of the *Strathnairn Standard*. Today's *Strathnairn Standard*, with the headline 'Police shooting investigation'. And there was her headshot, the one they'd published months ago when she'd arrived in the district.

She stared at it but her hand shook so much she could hardly focus. Someone had used a thick pen over the text to make a crude drawing of a naked female body under the portrait shot. Beside it was an equally crude drawing of a naked man with horns and a tail. And underneath it was written: *Satan's whore.*

CHAPTER 8

'He was here. The bastard had the gall to do this within fifty metres of the police station.' The evidence bag with the newspaper cutting lay in the centre of the meeting room table and Steve turned it over and slammed it face down. Tess, sitting pale and shaken at the table, didn't need that filth in front of her.

'Any security cameras out the back?' Alec Goddard asked. 'Any that might have picked him up?'

'Nothing that covers the lane,' Nick said. 'Only the car park and rear entrance. But if he passed the front of the station to get to the lane we might get something on the front entry footage.'

Steve dragged out a chair and sat. *Think*. Think with his brain and not his anger. 'There's a period of less than three hours when he could have been there. He must know Tess's car. He would have seen it at her place yesterday. Maybe he found out where she stayed last night, followed us this morning.' Crims often came back to the scene of a crime. There'd been plenty of people milling around at the hospital last night. He could have been there, followed her the block or so to the motel. Followed them this morning. Even if he'd been on foot, the short distances would have made following them easy.

Alec, still standing, picked up a marker from the whiteboard, rotated it in his fingers. 'What makes you so sure it's Isaac Matthias?'

'The language. The imagery. The fact that it's directed at me.' Tess lifted her chin, looked at each of them. Nick. Alec. Aaron. Him. All of them men. All of them but him standing, dwarfing her. Her throat moved as she swallowed. 'He believes I am his wife. In the religious sect we grew up in, Satan and demons are real. When I was just seventeen, before our so-called marriage, Zac participated in an exorcism to cast out the demon possessing me.'

Anger burst out of Steve. 'Oh, fuck that for a joke. You surely don't believe that, do you?'

Her face taut, her voice flat, she said, 'I don't believe it. Zac does. Or at least he did. He believed – the elders all believed – that Satan and a demon had caused me to tempt his father, our pastor, to carnal sin. In their minds, there was either a demon to exorcise, or I was willingly consorting with Satan.'

Carnal sin. Her hands on the table clenched into white-knuckled fists added the details the few words glossed over.

Violence filled him and he spun out of his chair and paced to the wall so she wouldn't see it in his face. They'd blamed *her*, a teenager, for a man's weakness and lack of control. Bastard misogynist hypocrites. And he'd be a damned hypocrite, too, if he didn't regain control of his temper and himself, fast.

Nick spoke first. 'Aaron, find Dee and ask her to join us, please. Or Erin, if she's back.'

'There's no need,' Tess said, with a weary resignation. 'You asked why I knew it was him. I told you. I'm probably the only one who knows his face well so I'll work with a police artist if you have one.'

Steve tamped down his anger, focused on Tess, half-aware he needed to hear there'd been some resolution even though it was her story, her life. 'Was he charged? The pastor?'

She gave just one glance up at him and away again, down to the smooth surface of the table. 'No. I didn't know, until a few years later, that I could make a complaint. Officers went out to question him. He hanged himself in the barn that night.'

A coward's way out that didn't count as justice. The bastard should have faced court, been found guilty, spent years in jail.

Tess rose abruptly to her feet. 'If there's nothing more you need me for now, will you excuse me, please?'

Nick opened the door for her and she walked out, head up, eyes straight ahead, not meeting anyone's gaze. Nick nodded to Aaron and inclined his head to the corridor outside to reiterate his last instruction.

Courage. Steve wished he had half as much as she did. Revealing a deep hurt, a woman alone surrounded by four strong, powerful men, not for pity or weakness but because it related to the case and they needed to know.

I'm not protecting him, Sarge. I'm protecting me. Protecting herself from reliving nightmares. From having to recall traumatic memories to strangers. He'd wanted to protect her and he'd failed. Oh, she might be okay physically but emotionally Matthias was hurting her again and again, and Steve had been unable to stop him. And powerless to stop the bastard murdering Maddie.

'What do we know about Isaac Matthias?' Alec asked.

'Bugger all,' Steve replied. 'I ran searches yesterday. Nothing on the COPS system. Nothing on any databases I could access. I found nothing online at all.'

'Leah and I searched last night,' Aaron said. 'Similar results. He has no record, no outstanding warrants, no driver's licence or firearms licence, no social media or other web presence. Either he's using an assumed name or he's kept clean all his adult life.'

Steve marshalled some mental discipline to concentrate on practical reasoning. 'Both Tess and Maddie knew him as Isaac Matthias, so he's probably not using another name. Maddie said he'd been with Joshua's group a few years. They lived pretty much off the grid. We'll have to find out when he left the Brethren sect, and what he did between then and Joshua's group.'

Alec started a list on the whiteboard. 'Do we know the name of the sect? Or anything else about it?'

Steve racked his memory. Tess had told him yesterday. He just had to remember. 'True Brethren. Not the Exclusives, they left them, formed their own group. True Brethren of the Covenant, I think she said. The pastor's name was Abraham. Abraham Matthias. They were in Victoria. Somewhere rural. But that would have been more than fifteen years ago.'

Alec added to the notes. 'We'll look into it. I want to know more about what makes this guy tick. And I want to know more about his relationship with the Simple Bliss folk. Because it seems to me there's a disconnect between a highly devout Brethren group and Joshua's brand of pseudo-religion.'

It didn't add up for Steve, either. 'Maddie said he didn't fit in well. Kept talking about God and sin. But Joshua called himself Joshua Kristos. Maybe Matthias thought he was the second coming.'

'Joshua – Hollywell – was a trained psychologist,' Nick observed, pulling out a chair to sit and stretch his bad leg. 'With almost two decades of experience in manipulating people. If he had a use for Matthias, he will have found a way to make meaning for him in the group's beliefs, and bind him to his will.'

Steve acknowledged the truth of that. 'You're right.' Of course Nick was right. In his time deep undercover he'd portrayed criminal masterminds for months, years without faltering. He could bind a man to *his* will if he chose. Fortunately for the country, he chose not to.

'But Joshua's dead,' Steve continued. 'Did seeing the newspaper report, learning that police officers – Tess and I – shot Joshua, flip him over from wanting to claim his wife to calling her a whore?'

Nick gave a slow nod. 'Perhaps. Or seeing you with her did it.'

'But we're not—'

'I know you're not. But you were at her house. You both stayed in the same motel last night, arrived at the police station at the same time.'

'But that doesn't explain him targeting Maddie. He's got a history with Tess, but when I asked Maddie about him, she didn't give any indication he was anything to her other than just one of the group.'

Alec scrawled 'Motivations' on the board, and added a question mark. 'The more we can find out about him, the more chance we have of anticipating his next move. We'll need to work out, too, if Matthias is connected to the other crimes.' He added more to his brainstorm on the board – the names of the dead women, and 'unknown' for the woman in the woolshed. 'We've focused on Joshua, but perhaps we need to consider others.'

'Tristan saw Joshua with Sybilla at the top of the falls, just before she stepped over.'

'In the dark. From a distance,' Alec commented.

They'd worked together enough and had become friends enough, through Alec's fiancée Bella, for Steve to rib him a little, despite the difference in rank. 'You've been down the coast too long, Alec. You've forgotten how bright moonlight can be out here in the sticks. And it was a full moon that night. Plus the kid is younger than us and hasn't ruined his eyesight on screens.'

'I remember how dark it can be when there's no moon,' Alec retorted good humouredly. 'He's sure it was Joshua?'

'Yes. He's sure.'

'Well, at least Joshua won't be manipulating anyone else now. But we have no evidence yet about who murdered Hayley, and no ID or cause of death at this stage on the dead woman in the woolshed. There's been no sighting of the group members today and until we can speak with some of them we may have no further information to help us.'

Steve stared at Alec's mind-map on the whiteboard. Too many deaths. Too many crimes. And they still had nothing to help them untangle the web of connections to find and arrest Matthias and any other murderer still alive.

•

The sun shone warm on the empty buildings of Serenity Hill, deserted and silent but for the small group of crime scene officers examining the remains of the woolshed.

Once out of the car, Tess took a moment to orient herself to the landscape she'd seen only in moonlight and firelight. On Sunday they'd approached it from the opposite direction, but today they'd come by road, and into the property via the front gates, past the homestead and along the farm track to the outbuildings.

'That's the track we came down on Sunday night,' she pointed out to Chief Inspector Arundel. 'It's the stockyards track that comes off Millers Road about a kilometre west of the main entry.'

Two other cars followed them down from the homestead and pulled up nearby. Aaron with Alec Goddard and Erin in the first one, and Steve, with one of the other investigators from the CI team in the second.

None of them seemed to think it amiss that she'd walked out of a briefing in a moment of weakness. Other than a tactful enquiry from Steve if she was okay, the incident might not have happened. Except it had. And now she had to prove, to them and to herself, that she was competent and completely capable of doing her job properly.

Although the two investigations focused on different aspects, they all walked through the events of the night together. Erin described what had gone on in the woolshed, the drumming, chanting, dancing, the wild exultation whipped up by Joshua's encouragement.

Tess imagined it too easily. Not so much the dancing – that had been banned in her upbringing – but the intense energy and fervour manipulated and directed by one man. One man and his adherents who willingly put aside rational and critical thought to lose their individuality in the promise of bliss. Or heaven. It made little difference what it was called. The promise bound them to the group because to leave, even to doubt, cast one out into the world, never to achieve the promised reward. Pastor Abraham's brand of belief coerced with fear. Joshua's might have been clothed in love and peace, but surely fear underlay it equally as much.

They all waited while Goddard spoke briefly to the forensic investigators, looking at an image on their camera before he returned with the camera in hand.

'Erin, other than Tristan, you're the only adult who met some of the people in the cult. Forensics have a photo of the face of the woman found under the woolshed. It wasn't burned – she wasn't killed by the flames. Would you be willing to look at it and see if you know who she is?'

Erin nodded, with a wry lift of her mouth at his concern. 'Yes. I'm a park ranger, detective. And in the SES. I've dealt with bodies.'

She studied the image he showed her on the camera's view screen. 'That is Tamara. She was one of the sisters. I don't know her surname, sorry. No one used surnames. But it's not Mary.'

She passed the camera to Tess. The woman's face almost filled the small screen. Eyes closed, long hair dishevelled around her face. Small lines around her eyes and her chin put her past her twenties, well into her thirties at a guess. Tamara, Maddie, Hayley and Sybilla – all a similar age. All dead.

Steve stepped closer and she showed him the image.

'Maddie told me Tamara was with Joshua when she came,' he said. 'Her son, David, is older than Tristan. David was Joshua's favourite, by the sounds of things.'

'Obnoxious and full of himself,' Erin commented. 'He'd be about twenty, twenty-one, thereabouts.'

The leader's favoured son over-confident? Not unusual, in Tess's experience. Zac had basked in his father's favour more often than not. Unlike his brother, Elijah, the smarter one, who was governed by his head, not his passions.

'Can you recall the last time you saw Tamara, Erin?' Goddard asked.

'I'm sorry, I don't know. She was there before Maddie and I went outside. We were gone maybe ten, fifteen minutes at most. I don't recall seeing her when we went back inside, but I wasn't looking for her at the time. I don't know if she was still there when Joshua left for the waterfall.'

'Was Joshua inside all the time?' Tess asked.

'I can't be sure, because of that gap, but I think so. He was kind of like the ringmaster in the circus – everything revolved around him.'

Everything revolved around him . . . Tess couldn't imagine him leaving control of the frenzied group for a moment, let alone long enough to murder a woman.

Steve's thoughts followed the same track hers did. 'So if he didn't kill Tamara, we're left with the question of who did? I don't suppose you saw Zac lurking around?'

'I don't know what he looks like,' Erin said. 'He wasn't one of the few men I met. But Tom, the guy who helped us, said Mary was still there, and Simon saw her heading back up towards the homestead.'

'What do we know about Mary?' Goddard asked.

Steve answered him. 'She called herself Mary Saint. She joined the group about three years ago. She appears to have controlled the finances since then, and Maddie thought Mary knew what Joshua was planning. I got an email back earlier from the Federal Police. They've been watching a woman who could be her on suspicion of laundering drug money. I'll send you the email.'

Arundel looked pointedly at her watch. 'We need to keep moving. Fraser, Ballard, can you describe for us the events once you arrived, please?'

Steve took the lead in describing what had happened as they retraced their steps from the woolshed across paddocks and through the trees to the waterfall. Tess could have been pissed off with him except that he included her as he went, and she recognised his strategies: both taking pressure and attention off her, and also establishing his role as senior officer and therefore the one ultimately responsible. She'd had her say to the inquiry team, emphasised that shooting had been her decision, that she'd not interpreted Steve's comments as an order. Whether they believed her or not, she'd told the truth.

The river level had dropped to almost as low as the pre-storm level, but evidence of the flood and the force of the water remained in the debris high in the branches of the casuarina trees and in the two old eucalypts, downed from two metres up the riverbank. Instead of the roar of a torrent Tess could hear the sound of birds above the babbling of the water, and the splashing as it fell onto the rocks below.

Downstream, a crew of police divers worked from the national park side of the river, where the rocks were flatter at the base of the gorge and gave them a platform to work off, now that the river was lower.

After she'd told the investigators her version of events, she strolled away to allow Steve to talk to them without her present. Here at the top of the falls, the multiple channels of the river were once again crossable by rock-hopping, although some debris from the flood was caught here and there in gaps between the rocks or floating in rock pools.

She made her way carefully two-thirds of the way across, to where a large flat rock jutted out over the edge. A small stream of water, only a pace wide, dissected it, falling into the shallow pool below where they'd found Sybilla's body floating, days ago.

Tess stood near the edge, looking down. The breeze, gusting up the gorge, was chilly here, and without a jacket, she wrapped her arms around her torso. Sybilla had stood here, with Joshua. She'd been with him for more than ten years, never contacting her family, listed as a missing person. But she'd stood here, and spoken with him, and he'd kissed her, and she'd then turned away from him and stepped off the edge.

Hypnotism, mind control, drugs or just a blind faith in his lies? Perhaps the means didn't matter. She'd believed enough to allow him to control her. Had exercising that ultimate power over Sybilla inspired him to do the same thing with the larger group?

Or maybe Sybilla had wanted death, yearned for oblivion and freedom from care.

Standing here on the top of the falls, with all the beauty of the wild country around – the rugged hills behind her, the gorge opening in front of her – and the fresh breeze in her face with the soporific burbling of the water, it could be so easy, so easy, to simply step into it, to take that one step and fly into the mesmerising beauty. Just one little step . . .

'Are you okay, Tess?'

Steve's voice, even and gentle. He stood there on the rocks, only a couple of metres away, his face so drawn she realised how she must look. She stepped backwards, away from the edge.

'I'm fine. Don't worry, I wasn't going to jump.' *Just one little step . . .*

His features relaxed into a soft smile. 'I'm glad to hear it.'

She set her back to the gorge and walked towards him and away from the possibility of listening to the seductive voice in her head. How terrifyingly easy it could have been – if she believed in heaven, or bliss. In something better than the challenges life brought.

'Have they finished?' she asked.

'Yeah, just about. Erin's showing them how high and fast the water was. Bit hard to imagine it, now.'

They began making their way back across the rocks. When they needed to clamber down off a high shelf, Steve went first, holding up a hand to steady her descent. A warm hand, firm and steady. Just like he'd turned out to be. Not shallow and flippant like her first impression, days ago.

They were crossing back on a slightly different route to the way she'd come, and as they paused to consider the easiest way to navigate the rocks and rivulets, she found her bearings by sighting the position of the rock Joshua had stood on.

Except from this side, from this angle, she saw what had been obscured from their view on Sunday.

She touched Steve's arm. 'Look at Joshua's rock. See how there's another one behind it, jutting upwards? It's not much lower and that cavity between them looks protected. And there's no debris.'

'Shit. The water probably wouldn't have reached that high. Did you actually see him go into the water?'

Tess cast her mind back, tried to distinguish in her memory between what she'd seen and what she'd assumed. 'No. Not from the angle I was at.'

Steve swore again. 'Me neither. Are you thinking what I'm thinking? That a man who fell or stepped down onto that second rock might not have been washed away? That may be why there's no body?'

'Yes. But he couldn't have planned it. Surely?'

'I don't know. Once the storm hit in the afternoon anyone who knows this area could have anticipated the river rising rapidly. Perhaps he made his plans on the fly. Took advantage of the opportunity. Or perhaps he'd just planned to have them join hands and walk off the edge together or something like that.'

The investigators and Erin began to make their way back through the trees, but she and Steve slowed their pace.

She considered the suggestions, trying to work out possibilities. 'We're fairly certain he planned something. From what we know of him, I sincerely doubt he planned on dying himself. This whole cult was a scam to him, not a matter of his personal belief. So whatever he intended, he planned a way of surviving it. But we shot him.'

'Yes. So the question is, was he able to put his plan into action, or is he dead?'

They paused on the riverbank, studying the rock, the second one behind it not visible from here. The afternoon sun, angling lower in the sky, reflected off the breeze-rippled water.

Steve touched her briefly on the shoulder and said, 'Look, if it's okay with you, let's not tell the others just yet. This might be a total goose chase. I want to talk to Simon – find out if he saw Joshua fall in the water. But if he didn't, and if the body doesn't show up by tomorrow, I might come out here again and have a better look at that rock.'

Tess hesitated. Procedure said they should report their suspicions. But what did they really have? No hard evidence, only suppositions and guesses. The chance of Joshua still being alive hovered close to zero. And whether he'd survived didn't impact on the critical incident team's core task – to determine if she and Steve had been justified in firing their weapons.

'Okay,' she said. 'But if you come back here tomorrow, I'll come with you.'

'Good. But I hope we won't need to.'

Fatigue began to drag at her as they trudged the now well-worn path through the trees. Strange how it seemed further in daylight.

In the open area near the farm buildings, Arundel waited impatiently by her car.

Steve slowed his pace as they drew near. 'Tess, you know you're welcome to stay at the motel with us again tonight. I've still got that second room booked. But I know we're a bit of a crowd so if you don't want to I won't be offended at all.'

This morning she'd intended to go somewhere else for a few days, away from Strathnairn. But events seemed to have overtaken that plan. 'Thanks. I appreciate it. I'll pay you for the room. I'm happy to have Lily again, if that makes it easier.'

He flashed her a tired smile. 'It does. Otherwise I'd be sharing a bed with my father. Or sleeping on the floor.'

'I still have to see the police artist when we get back. I might be a while.'

'And I have to meet with community services to sort out some paperwork. But Dad should be back at the motel so just go there when you're ready.'

By the time they returned to Strathnairn, and she'd spent another hour with the police artist, darkness had settled over the town.

Aaron offered to walk her to her car, still in the lane, and she accepted the offer. He brought a powerful flashlight with him and diligently checked around the lane and in her car, shining the light into the back seat to make sure it was empty. He waited until she'd driven out of the lane.

Her fuel gauge hovered near empty. So did her energy levels, but living out in rural areas meant keeping the tank reasonably full because it was a long way between towns, and petrol stations had limited hours.

She drove a block past the motel to the well-lit petrol station on the next corner. It did double duty as a cafe and take-away, and a few people were around, filling cars or heading inside for food. While the pump chugged into her tank, one of her colleagues came out after paying for fuel and raised a hand in greeting as he returned to his car. A trio of teenagers passed, pooling their coins for hot chips. A burly guy in singlet, shorts and work boots gave her a cheerful wink before he clambered back up into his truck.

An ordinary evening in Strathnairn, like a hundred other country towns across the state. Her tank full, she replaced the nozzle in the pump and retrieved her wallet from the front seat. On any other day, she'd have left the car unlocked. But the ordinariness of the evening didn't stretch to her situation, and she flicked the remote locking before she went inside to pay.

Beside the cashier's counter, the newspaper stand ran low on stock but a few copies of the *Strathnairn Standard* remained, her image staring up at her from the front page. She bought a copy, turning it face down on the counter as she paid for her fuel and a couple of bars of chocolate. If the cashier recognised her, he didn't say anything.

Walking back to her car, she crossed paths with a young man returning a windscreen squeegee to its bucket. He took a pace back to wave her in front of him. But as she glanced at him to say 'thank you,' his gaze caught and held hers, and a smile spread across his face.

'Senior Constable Ballard, isn't it?' he asked, blue eyes as clear and inviting as the sky and with the kind of confident manner that probably made young hearts flutter.

Tess's heart rarely fluttered. 'I'm Tess Ballard.'

His gaze darted for just a nano-second around the area. Tess's caution radar blipped. He could have deliberately intercepted her path. His station wagon, on the other side of the pump from hers, blocked their direct view of the cashier. His hand rested on his hip, half under his untucked shirt. If she was wearing a uniform, her hand would be hovering near her weapon, too.

'My name's David. David ben Joshua.' A car turned in to the driveway, and he moved a few steps away as it pulled in slowly behind hers. 'It's been a pleasure to meet you, Constable Ballard. I look forward to seeing you again soon.'

He didn't seem to be hurrying but his long-legged stride took him quickly to his vehicle and he started the ignition and drew out before she was in her car.

Her instincts said to chase him, but she had no logical reason to. No reason other than suspicion and the sense that he'd had his hand on a weapon, under that shirt.

David ben Joshua. She'd done more than enough bible study in her life to know what he meant.

David, son of Joshua.

She'd shot his father, and he knew it.

•

Steve surveyed the piles of shopping bags covering the queen bed in the motel room and wondered how the hell he'd ever sort it out, let alone fit the contents into his car. How had a couple of changes of clothes for each kid morphed into this? Jeans, t-shirts, jackets, underwear, socks, shoes, pyjamas, toothbrushes, bed linen, blankets and towels, books . . . Okay, so he knew how it happened. He'd given the task to his father, who would have thoroughly and systematically planned it like a major police operation and covered every eventuality. He'd bought entire wardrobes for Tris and Lily.

It made sense to get things here in Strathnairn, which had three times the population and shops that Birraga had. Dungirri, with only three hundred residents, barely managed to support a pub and an agricultural supplies store. No clothes stores there.

And now his dad had disappeared to the motel laundry to wash a load of the new clothes before the kids wore them, and left him with the two of them and the rest of the stuff to sort.

Steve's brain ached. Not surprising, given the full-on, emotionally gruelling day. Reliving the past few days in the interviews and witness statements. Supporting Tristan to give his witness statement. Going out to Serenity Hill again, and that odd, heart-stopping moment when Tess stood on the edge of the waterfall. Then the meeting with the community services case worker. At least he had agreement from them to take the children under his guardianship. He also had a list a mile long of things he needed to do for them, including arranging vaccinations and birth certificates and changing his will.

But now he was bone tired and emotionally exhausted and although all he wanted to do was lock himself away and howl for Maddie, the two kids looked to him for decisions. Decisions and explanations. Their unfamiliarity with so much of what he took for granted meant constant explaining, describing, trying to make sense of things for them. They also looked to him for food. There was no complaining, but none of them had eaten since some hurried bread rolls and a milkshake each from the bakery at lunchtime.

He doubted that was enough for growing bones. He didn't know enough about nutritional needs to be their guardian. He didn't know enough about bringing up kids to be their guardian. He didn't know enough about psychology to help traumatised, psychologically abused kids to cope with grief and disillusionment and fear.

He didn't know enough. He wasn't enough. He'd screwed up left, right and centre in his life and still kept on doing it.

He caught the negative train of his thoughts and slammed on the brakes. This was his life now, he wasn't helpless, and he'd just have to do the best he could.

Damn Proper Parenting 101 and all the 'shoulds' and 'should nots' pounding in his head. This evening surely qualified as a case for Desperate Parenting 101. 'Do you like pizza?' he asked them.

Tristan watched him with that closed, level gaze. 'I don't know,' he said.

'Let's find out then.' He flicked through the flyers in the motel room information book and found the pizza delivery one with colourful images of the topping options. 'How about you two pick a couple of these and I'll order them.'

As he phoned in the order – one large ham and pineapple pizza, one large meatlovers pizza, one lasagne, one garlic bread – a knock sounded on the door. The phone still to his ear, he opened it. Tess. Tess, pale and agitated, glancing back over her shoulder. Her backpack and another bag sat at her feet.

'And a large garden salad,' he added to the order as he held the door open, picked up one of her bags and waved her inside. 'What's up?' he asked her as soon as he finished the call.

She saw Tris and Lily and, with a slight shake of her head, said, 'Nothing urgent.'

He picked up the key for the other room from the table casually as if nothing was wrong. 'I've just ordered pizza and salad for dinner. You'll join us, won't you? I'll carry your bag for you so you can settle in before it arrives.'

She took his cue and when he unlocked the door of the next room and followed her inside, she dumped her backpack on the queen bed and said in a low voice, 'I've just met David ben Joshua.'

It took Steve a moment to process the significance of the name. 'Where? Did he threaten you? Are you okay?'

'It was at the servo. He was thoroughly polite and charming. He said it was a "pleasure" meeting me and that he looked forward to "seeing me again soon". He drove off before I did. I didn't get his car rego.'

She sat down on the edge of the bed and indicated the chair for him, but he remained standing in the open doorway.

'Did he follow you there?'

'I don't know. I only drove the two blocks. If he was watching the police station, he might have. It doesn't count as a threat, of course, but I went straight back to the station and told Aaron.' Her shoulders slumped. 'David knows my car, and so does Zac. I've left it at the police station, in the locked area. Aaron gave me a ride here. It seems wiser not to advertise my presence here.' She met his gaze. 'I'll go somewhere else if you prefer. You've got your family to consider.'

His family. He'd gone from being a bachelor with no one to worry about to being a family man within forty-eight hours. And already Lily and Tristan's safety came first in his mind. But he gave Tess a lopsided grin. 'I think three police officers plus the crew on duty outside should deter any threats. You'll be fine here tonight.'

'Where's your father?'

'In the laundry. Systematically washing and tumble-drying the cargo load of clothes he bought for his grandchildren today. He's even ironing the t-shirts.'

'I used to press creases into my jeans. It's the way I was taught to iron trousers, so I thought at first that they all had to be done like that.'

The memory made her smile a little, and the softer expression made her even more beautiful. She should smile far more often than she did. He should stop thinking about her in that way.

'I think my father still does press creases into his jeans. On the rare occasions he wears them. Because if a thing should be done, it should be done properly. Speaking of which, I should go clear some space on the table for pizza. You will come and eat with us, won't you?'

She agreed, and fifteen minutes later when the pizza delivery guy arrived she came in, a light cardigan over her shirt, and her hair brushed and loose around her shoulders.

Out of consideration for his father's proper ways, Steve cadged plates, cutlery and paper napkins from the motel restaurant but it was so crowded around the small table with five of them that he ate standing up, passing pizza slices from the boxes laid out on the luggage rack.

Somehow, despite the disparate crew and the clouds of sorrow and worry, he managed to keep the mood light-hearted as he encouraged Lily and Tristan to explore new tastes and experiences. His father and Tess ate most of the salad, but they both had pizza slices, too, and joined in a friendly debate over best pizza toppings.

Eventually Lily's head drooped so he encouraged her to change into her new pyjamas – washed, dried and ironed – and clean her teeth with her new toothbrush. The excitement of the new things woke her up enough to achieve those tasks without fuss.

While Bruce returned to his self-appointed laundry duties, and Tess tidied away the remaining pizza slices, he found the small collection of children's books his father had bought. Classics, mostly, ones he remembered from his childhood. Some of them so classic his father probably remembered them from his own childhood.

His throat thickened as he tucked Lily into the single bed in Tess's room, Pooky beside her. Last time he'd tucked a kid in, it had been Maddie, and he'd still been a kid himself. He opened the book he'd selected – A.A. Milne's *Now We Are Six*. One of his favourites. One he'd read to Maddie, when their mother was too sick to read to her. As a tot, he'd loved the rhythms of the words, the sounds marching with the pictures in his head, and the whimsical world where everything was happy.

Tristan listened from the doorway and Tess took her laptop from her backpack and set it up while he read, making him self-conscious. What if she thought him weird, doing different voices? What if he mispronounced a word? Fortunately Lily drifted off to sleep within minutes and he closed the book.

Tess looked up from her screen, tucking a wayward strand of hair behind her ear. 'You're good with kids.'

She rarely made any personal comments so her unexpected compliment caught him by surprise. 'I don't know how. Maddie was my only practice. And a couple of runts of cousins occasionally. Maybe I'm just an overgrown kid myself.'

Tristan left the doorway and Steve heard the bathroom door close. With Lily asleep, it provided his only chance to discuss the afternoon's development with Tess. The strain around her eyes concerned him, but he'd avoided raising any mention of Isaac or David in front of Tristan, whose subdued mood concerned him, too.

Not that he had much experience or skill in being sensitive. But he'd worked with Tess on the case for days, and surely that gave him some responsibility – whether as colleague or friend – to try to ensure her well-being. He kept his voice low, so as not to wake Lily. 'Will you be all right tonight? You've had a hell of a day.'

'Yours hasn't been any easier. I'll be fine. I'm just unsettled, I guess, knowing Zac's still out there. And David. Knowing that they're all out there somewhere. But with you and your father – and Tristan – next door and a car on duty outside again tonight, I should be fine.'

Should. The tightness in her face belied her confidence in the statement. 'They'll all be on the lookout for Zac. Nick's brought in extra officers from around the north-west. There'll be a fair few police around.'

'I know. What puzzles me about Zac is that yesterday he was determined to pursue our "marriage", and now he believes I'm in league with Satan, which makes me his enemy. That's a huge shift in thinking, and I'm honestly not sure he'd come up with it himself. Something happened in the past twenty-four hours to trigger that change.'

He proved himself capable of murder. A too-blunt truth, and Steve didn't say it aloud. Had the man got a thrill from running down Maddie and the others? A taste for the power of killing? Would he have run down Tess if he'd had the opportunity, or did he have a particular motivation for wanting Maddie dead?

Steve had no energy left to maintain anger. Lily slept innocently a couple of feet away, and Tess needed – they all needed – some sleep. Sleep and hope.

'Chances are they'll arrest him soon, Tess. He didn't leave town after yesterday. He must know the police are looking for him, so leaving that newspaper cutting on your car was stupid, risky behaviour. We both know the stupid ones are easier to find.'

She stood abruptly, arms wrapped across her chest, and paced towards the window before pivoting around. 'I'll be honest. I'm scared. I hate being scared. I hate hiding away but I'm not stupid. Zac got away from us in Goodabri, again last night outside the hospital, and no one saw him this morning. He could be anywhere. And then David shows up and makes veiled threats.'

If he could have folded his arms around her, he would have. But in the circumstances, physical contact with a male, even a friendly one, would be as likely to reduce her unease as a rampaging bull bursting in. So he stayed on the opposite side of the small room and dug his hands into his pockets.

'If things haven't settled down tomorrow, you're welcome to come to Dungirri with us, Tess. It's not on the road to anywhere, so any stranger sticks out like a sore thumb and people look out for each other. I've got friends there, and the pub accommodation is decent. Or you could stay with us if you don't mind the madness of setting up a new place.' He slowed down as his enthusiasm for the idea was starting to run away from him. 'But I won't be offended if you want to go off somewhere else by yourself. I'm sure Nick would be supportive if you wanted to take some stress leave. You've got plenty of reason to, in the circumstances.'

'No, I don't want to do that.' She lifted her head high. 'I won't give Zac that much power over me.'

Courageous, proud and strong. Maybe one day he'd be able to tell her how much he admired her strength. Not tonight, when she battled demons and fear, and while a man who'd attempted to rape her wandered free. His interest was probably not reciprocated, so confessing to anything other than collegial friendship would be an additional worry for her.

'I'll leave my side of the connecting door open tonight,' he said. 'If it helps you feel safer, then leave your side open, too. You have my word that I won't take advantage of that.'

She gave him a hint of one of her rare smiles. 'I know, Steve. I do trust you.'

Steve. A small part of him wanted to high-five the air. His name, not the distancing, impersonal 'Sarge' that she'd used until now. She might not have noticed, but he did. One small step forward, and it heartened him as much as her trust did.

With one last glance at Lily, sleeping soundly with Pooky tucked under her chin, he left Tess to her privacy and the personal space she needed.

•

Tess managed to drift off to sleep eventually by imagining Zac sitting in a cell, and officers processing the paperwork to charge him with murder and assault. Mentally running through a detailed checklist of the forms, evidence and statements required by the magistrate always worked much better than counting sheep.

Exhaustion must have claimed her because she slept solidly until just before sunrise, when a squeak of the bed springs in the next room woke her. The connecting door stood slightly ajar and she heard soft footsteps cross the room and the muffled click of the door latch on the outer door. Through the small gap she'd left open in the curtains, she saw Tristan pass her window.

She'd slept in t-shirt and yoga pants so she just pulled a cardigan over the top and thrust her feet into shoes before she opened her door.

He'd gone east, away from the motel entry and the on-duty police car. But he hadn't gone far. In the grassed area near the small swimming pool he faced the sunrise, and as the first beams of sunlight pierced the gaps between Strathnairn's buildings and trees, she caught notes here and there as he sang a low melody, a graceful, slow song while he moved clockwise in a wide circle.

Tess stayed silent, watching, leaning against the doorframe. When he finished, he stood still, head bowed, and his shoulders shook. She gave him a few moments, and then walked down to the picnic table at the edge of the grass.

'Everything all right, Tris?' she asked quietly.

He nodded mutely, but after long seconds he lifted his head. She patted the seat beside her, and he came and sat with her, the sunlight apricot-gold on his face. She let the silence settle around them, not pushing him to talk.

'Is it wrong to greet the sun?' he asked eventually, uncertainty darkening his eyes.

She held that thread of offered trust gently, the fact that he scarcely knew her an indication of the depth of his disorientation in this new world. He had to find his own way, his own answers, but she could give him some tools to help him find them, some lifelines to keep him from drowning now that all the certainties of his old life had been stripped away.

'It's not wrong in itself, Tristan. Not if you want to. Not if it feels right to you, in your heart.'

'I don't know. I just . . . we always did it. Every day. I don't know what's right, anymore.'

'It does no harm to anyone else, so if it has meaning for you, and if it brings you peace or clarity of mind or energy for the day, then there's nothing wrong with continuing, Tris.'

'But is it weird? I mean, other people don't.'

'A lot of people have morning rituals. I started to do Tai Chi, and I probably should go back to it because it felt good and cleared my head.' *You need to relax more, Tess. Your blood pressure is high. You should take up yoga or Tai Chi or something like that.* In two months of classes at her previous posting in western Sydney she'd gradually learned to relax, but she'd let it slide with the move to Goodabri and settling into the new district and the new position.

'Tai Chi? That's the slow dancing thing, isn't it?'

She smiled at the description. 'It looks like that. Technically it's a martial art. For me, it's mostly about focusing my mind and awareness of my body. It's very peaceful, and it opens up circulation and breathing, and I found that was a good way to start the day.'

'It sounds . . . calm. I wish . . . I wish I could feel calm again.'

The lad's appeal struck her heart, and resonated with her own need for calm. If she hadn't left Lily alone, she could have shown him some simple forms, some focused breathing . . . She glanced back at the motel room, and Steve was there, sitting at the table outside the door. He raised a hand in greeting but stayed where he was. He'd be there if Lily woke.

'Would you like to spend a few minutes and do some of the basic movements with me?' she asked Tristan, and he nodded.

In the early morning light, in the quiet with only small birds flittering and twittering in the nearby bushes, she stood beside the young man and talked him through the first basic forms. Then together they performed the gentle, repetitive movements, the steady, deep breathing, and slowly the incessant buzz in her head faded and she was there, present in herself now, the fresh air caressing her face, oxygen flowing, her limbs and spine relaxing their pent-up tension. Present and whole and strong.

Yes, she would definitely take this up again. And too bad if the people of Goodabri thought she was nuts doing Tai Chi in her garden. Too bad if Steve thought she was nuts.

Their impromptu session lasted only ten minutes, but as she returned to the motel room she welcomed the sense of feeling more grounded, more clear-headed, and vowed to herself to dedicate more time to her well-being and emotional balance. Just as soon as Zac was arrested and charged, the inquiry delivered its findings, and Goddard and Haddad found the answers to the murders and the drugs and arrested those involved.

Yes, she'd take up Tai Chi again just as soon as she got her life back. Assuming she did get her life back. Already the concerns crowded back in again, swamping the fragile calm. She had to pack up her things and deal with the day, including finding somewhere else to go because Steve planned to head to Dungirri later.

She considered Steve's invitation to go with them. Considered it and decided not to accept. The Frasers – Steve, Lily, now Tris, and heck, even Bruce – were eroding the armour she'd held around herself for a long time. She was beginning to care. She didn't know how to care. She'd purged guilt long ago, but the circumstances of her upbringing and her emotionally stunted family and community hung like a millstone around her neck, and she knew she wasn't whole enough to give to others the emotion and affection they deserved.

CHAPTER 9

Steve checked his phone for messages. Nothing. Aaron had promised to send him news if they found Joshua's body or arrested Zac. It seemed they hadn't. When Dee arrived to take over from the night shift guarding them she confirmed the lack of news. A quiet night in Strathnairn. No sightings, no developments, no arrests.

Frustration ate at him, gnawing away the benefit of a reasonable night's sleep. Maybe if he'd gone down to join Tess and Tristan in their meditative exercises he'd be feeling more zen now. Although when Tess came out for breakfast she seemed to have lost the soft light in her eyes he'd briefly seen.

As the result of an email exchange last night, Simon and Erin brought Jasmine over for breakfast with them on the veranda of the near-empty motel restaurant. Not only to give the shy, thirteen-year-old girl some time with Tristan and Lily, as close to family as she had remaining from her life in Joshua's group, but also to give the adults an opportunity to discuss developments in private.

While the three young people sat together at a table, Tristan and Jasmine talking earnestly with Lily piping in occasionally, the adults took their own food to a table a few metres away.

'I'm fairly sure I saw him in the water,' Simon said, when Steve asked him about Joshua's fall from the rock. 'At least, I think I did. I didn't see him hit the water, but I saw something white I assumed was him, going over the edge.'

Tentacles of tension wound more tightly around Steve's neck. 'It was moonlight. The water was churning and full of debris. It might have been anything.'

'Yeah,' Simon agreed. 'It may not have been him. Erin, did you see anything clearly?'

'No. I heard the shots. I saw him stagger, just out of the corner of my eye. But I was struggling to hold Willow back from the river so I wasn't watching him closely.'

Steve remembered seeing Erin near the water's edge, only seconds from being dragged into the torrent. There could so easily have been more than two deaths. If he and the others had not fired at Joshua, Erin likely wouldn't have been sitting here. Lucky Simon. Lucky both of them.

Steve took a sip of coffee and set down his mug carefully. 'They haven't found either body yet. So I was thinking about going out to take another look at the rock.'

His father broke his silence. 'It's an active investigation, Steven. You can't interfere.'

Steve took a slow breath before he responded. Time enough to acknowledge to himself that his father's objection wasn't personal, wasn't unfair. In fact, on one level he was perfectly correct. 'I'm not proposing interfering, Dad,' he said. 'There simply aren't resources out here to look into every possibility. This is a wild theory, but if I see the tiniest shred of evidence you can bet I'll be calling Goddard straight away.'

'We can go in on the park side, up the path to the lookout and then the track to the falls,' Simon said. 'It's close on four kilometres from where we can leave the vehicles. I could get you closer in on a fire trail, upstream from the falls, but since they haven't found the bodies yet, maybe it makes more sense to follow the river up to the falls, as much as we can. It's pretty rough in there, though.'

'That makes sense,' Tess said. 'I don't mind the walk.'

'Neither do I,' Steve commented. 'But I've got the kids to consider. It will take us hours, by the time we get out there and back. Dad, could you . . . ?'

One look at his father's face, trying to brave out his trepidation, told Steve he'd have to find some other way. Although he and the kids had coped okay yesterday, it apparently hadn't been relaxed and easy, and his father had spent most of the evening in the laundry. Bruce needed time to come to terms with his grief, his loss, and the children from his daughter's secret life.

'I had planned to return to Sydney,' his father said, 'to see . . . her. Start arranging the funeral.'

The funeral. Maddie's funeral. He understood his father's need to focus on the next, proper steps, was grateful he'd stayed on yesterday to help. But his own priorities had to focus on the children, on getting them out of the motel to some kind of new normality – a house, a place they could make a home. Maddie's funeral, whenever – wherever – it took place, would be a chance for them to say goodbye, an important part of their grieving process, but he wanted to give them some foundation, a place to come home to, afterwards.

'I can look after them,' Erin offered quickly. 'My car's in for a service so Jasmine and I are planning to spend a quiet morning at home together. I'm sure she'd appreciate more time with Tris and Lily before they leave for Dungirri.'

With arrangements sorted, they finished their meal without lingering. Although reluctant to hasten the time with the people who'd fast become firm friends, Steve was conscious of the need to pack up and be ready to leave the motel before their trip back to the waterfall. He hoped to take the kids to Dungirri later in the day. They'd have to stay in the pub at least tonight, but maybe tomorrow or the day after they could move into their new home.

'I want to come to the waterfall with you,' Tristan said when he heard the plan for the morning. 'Please? I was there. I want to see it again.' Lily was outside in the motel's small playground with Erin and Jasmine, but Tris still dropped his voice to a low tone. 'I hate him for what he did. But he was my father. I need to know that he's dead. That he won't hurt them.'

The lad's earnest, troubled eyes pleaded with him and Steve, almost out of his depth, couldn't refuse. The kid was seventeen, nearly a man, despite the odd mix of innocence and self-possession. A traumatised teenager who still stepped up to protect those he'd taken on responsibility for.

'Okay, if you're sure you want to, Tris.'

He'd have to get the lad some counselling. If they could find a psychologist they could trust. One without megalomaniac homicidal tendencies. Or alternatively he could surround Tristan with sane, supportive adults he could rely on. Dungirri had a few of them. People he trusted, people Tristan could trust. And he'd make sure to keep in touch with Simon and Erin and Jasmine, get together with them every few months.

He'd also have to make sure, a small voice in his head reminded him, that he looked after himself. Yeah, when he had the kids settled. When he had time. He could almost hear millions of single parents laughing at the notion.

In the national park they followed Simon's LandCruiser to a camping ground beside the river, west of the waterfalls, and parked at the beginning of the track. Steve had Tristan with him, but Tess drove her own car. The police search for the bodies had moved further downstream, so they were no longer using this area as a staging ground, and there were no campers or day trippers around. They had the place to themselves, with only the birdsong, the mob of kangaroos lazing in the sunshine, and a goanna pacing down to the water's edge.

Steve had reason to be grateful for his father's overzealous provisioning because Tristan now had decent shoes, a long-sleeved cotton shirt, a hat and a water bottle. Tris kept close to him as they walked up the track, Simon and Tess slightly ahead, and despite the steady uphill climb they made good time up to the waterfall.

Steve assiduously kept his gaze anywhere but on Tess's jean-clad butt.

They stopped on the park side of the waterfall. There was nothing autumnal in the heat of the sun, and Steve paused to glug some mouthfuls of water. So did Tess. She'd kept pace with Simon the whole way, her stride even, but perspiration plastered a strand of loose hair to her cheek and she brushed it back behind her ear, tightening her ponytail.

They'd hardly spoken on the track, mostly because Simon hiked at a solid pace, possibly forgetting he had long legs and a commando's physical fitness, and the rest of them, although fit, didn't.

He wanted to make sure Tess was okay, but his first responsibility lay with his nephew. Tristan breathed a little heavily but didn't complain, although he wiped sweat from his forehead and took a second swig from the water bottle.

'How are those new shoes going?' Steve asked him. 'No blisters?'

'No. They're good.'

'Are you okay about being here? I know you don't have good memories of this place.'

He gave a typical teenage shrug. 'I want to help,' he said simply.

Steve liked the lad more and more, respected him for his maturity and his guts and his commitment to doing the right thing. It didn't blind him to the possibility of difficulties down the line, but he wasn't some spoilt kid incapable of thinking beyond himself. Maddie had brought him up well.

They set out after Simon and Tess across the rocks. The river had dropped still further from yesterday, the last of Sunday's storms drained out of the low hills that formed the small catchment. The small channels of water weaving through the boulders and flat rocks were easy to hop over, although some flowed deeper than others. Simon steered them away from a black snake basking in the sunshine, and from some small piles of debris that might harbour others.

The quartz particles in the large granite boulder slanting up from the opposite riverbank where Joshua had stood, sparkled in the sunlight.

They stopped beside it, on the other side of the deep, narrow crack in the rock ledge where the water trickled a good metre or more down. Traces of mud on the boulder showed the height of the floodwater. The boulder balanced against the other slanted boulder behind it, thrown by earthquake or volcano or ginormous flood movements, millennia ago.

'The water didn't reach up there,' Simon commented. 'Not into that space where the upper rock overhangs the lower one. It would have been slippery from spray, but not underwater. The question is, which way did he fall?'

Steve rock-hopped a few metres away, trying to line up with the angle he'd shot at from the trees. He replayed those moments in his mind; Joshua standing there, arms outstretched to his followers, the loud retort of his own Glock and the other two shots almost instantaneously, the man clutching his chest and falling backwards . . .

'He could have fallen onto the rock,' Steve mused out loud. 'But he fell backwards. He didn't have control over how he fell.'

Tess had come to stand beside him. 'It would have been a hard fall. He could have made it into that space, but he might also have hit the edge of the second rock, rolled off into the water.'

Steve ran through the possibilities. A man injured by bullets and perhaps by a fall? Trapped in that space for hours until the water level dropped? He might have survived. Perhaps. But if he had, he might well have left some evidence.

'I'm going to take a look. Although Forensics have probably been over it already.'

Studying the rock, Tess nodded. 'The river was higher yesterday. They might not have thought to check it. They probably assumed, as we did, that he fell into the water.'

She began to follow as he scrambled up the slope of the boulder but he waved her back. 'This is on my head, Tess. If shit flies, it should fly at me. You've got too much to lose.'

She kept her gaze evenly on him. 'And you don't?'

'It doesn't matter as much to me,' he said, and knew it for the truth. His career as a police officer was pretty much over. It would have been good to go out on a high note, but at least he'd be going out alive, and mostly whole.

He stood where Joshua had stood. Up here, five or six metres higher than the water level, the view expanded and he turned slowly, looking out over the riverbank, the river itself, and the waterfall plunging into the gorge.

The breeze coming up the gorge whipped around him more strongly than he expected. Had it been breezy that night? He couldn't remember that detail. The trees where he and Tess had been, fifty or more metres away, scarcely stirred but on the ridge above, where Simon had been, the leaves and branches waved around.

'Did you take the wind into account when you aimed, Kennedy?' he called down to Simon.

The guy snorted. 'Yeah.'

Stupid question. Of course he had. Commando. Trained sniper. With a far better rifle for the purpose than two standard-issue Glock pistols.

Steve knelt on the edge of the boulder, and looked down at the one below. By his reckoning of the angle, Joshua's backwards fall might have taken him off-centre, closer to the edge of the rock. The water spray had left a fine coat of now-dry mud over the lower rock. He couldn't discern much from here.

He jumped down over the edge and landed in an awkward crouch more than a metre below, on the uneven surface of the sloping rock, needing both hands to steady himself. If Joshua had *planned* to step or jump off the rock and fake his own death, he would still have been taking a huge risk. Maybe he hadn't planned it that way at all. Maybe he'd simply been going to wait until they were all in the water, and then just stroll away.

But given that he'd fallen backwards . . . Steve rose to his feet on the slope to examine the edge of the rock. And there, in a darker patch of the thin layer of caked mud, he found a dark splotch of dried blood.

'Bingo!' he muttered to himself. If that was where Joshua's head hit the rock, it would have hit with force, and if alive, he'd have likely been in a bad way. But which way had he gone from there? Rolled down? Rolled off?

Steve rotated on the spot so as not to disturb anything, and hunkered down to examine the area under the overhang. There were some piles of leafy debris wedged in but he couldn't see any obvious signs of disturbance. He used his phone camera to photograph the bloodstain evidence, but didn't collect any of it. Forensics would have to come back, go over the site thoroughly. And they could deal with any snakes or spiders concealed in the debris.

He could see the others, over on the riverbank, Simon and Tess talking and Tristan a few paces away, sitting on the ground, his head down. Steve jumped off the rock and leapt across the few channels to join them.

'Did you find anything?' Tess asked.

'Yes. He fell onto the rock. There's blood. But other than that, I didn't see anything.'

Tristan lifted his head. 'Is he really dead?'

Damn, this had to be harder on the kid than on the rest of them. 'We can't be certain until they find his body, mate. But I think his chances of having survived are very slim.'

'What if they took him away?' Tristan asked.

Steve's instincts went on alert. 'What if *who* took him away?'

'David, maybe. He and Joshua's bodyguards and a couple of the security team went into the bush over there. David gave some orders before he went off that way.' Tris pointed in the general direction of the homestead. 'The security guys went that way,' he pointed downstream. 'I couldn't follow them because I had to look after Jasmine, and find Lily.'

'Who are the security guys? Do you know what orders he gave them?'

Tristan rose to his feet. 'I wasn't close enough to hear. Tom was supposed to be head of security here, but David was taking over. They didn't agree on a lot of things. And Joshua's bodyguards didn't report to Tom.'

Steve swore silently. Tristan knew these people, knew David. He'd discouraged Alec from interviewing him in depth because he'd been through more than enough already. But maybe they did need to find out more from Tristan. His insights and knowledge might well be useful.

'Tom was the guy who helped Erin and Maddie,' Simon said. 'He warned us that Joshua was planning something, that we needed to stop him. But I didn't see him again.'

'He spoke with Madeleine here, afterwards,' Tess said. 'He said people were going into the bush, and that he'd try to find them. I didn't see him come back.'

'I wonder if he's still with the group?' Steve said. 'Wherever they've gone to.'

'He won't be.' Tristan spoke with certainty. 'Not if David knows he helped you. But he might know where the haven is.'

'The haven?' Steve asked.

'Joshua always said he'd made a haven where we could go if the others – if people outside – set against us. A safe place where no one could touch us.'

'Do you know where it is? Or anything about it?'

'No. But David said he did. David said he knew everything.'

Steve's thoughts raced. A safe place where no one could touch them. Had Joshua been speaking literally or figuratively? Because death would be a safe place, too, and establishing the idea of a haven in the group's collective consciousness might have made it easier to talk them into suicide. Except he'd grasped the opportunity and used the flood and the water instead.

If the haven was a physical place, they needed to find it. Alec needed to find it. Alec needed to find it, and to find Zac, and David.

'We should go back,' he told Simon and Tess. 'Once we're in phone range we can contact Alec Goddard, get him to send Forensics out here again. And Tris, when we get back to Strathnairn, will you talk with Alec? You won't have to do it alone, you'll have an adult with you. Maybe me, if I'm allowed.'

If he was allowed. But he was officially off the case, off duty, and he'd already pushed the envelope enough with this unauthorised return to the crime scene. He needed to know how the group worked, where they'd gone, who was a threat and how. Without that knowledge, he had no way to protect Tristan and Lily. Or Tess.

•

Halfway back to the cars, Simon led them down through low scrub to the river, and they walked along a rough track beside the water, clambering over rocks and skirting flood debris where they had to.

The sun, high in the sky, blazed hot and Tess drank more water as she walked. Tired and already on edge, she didn't enjoy the walk. She preferred clear, wide tracks where you could see the snakes metres ahead and didn't have to scramble through places where biting and stinging things might lurk.

But she was a cop and supposed to be tough and this was part of her duty so she just had to suck it up and do it. She figured that Simon, ahead of her, would scare away any snakes so she kept a close eye on the water instead. The police divers had already been here, yet in the rugged water channels and yesterday's deeper water they might have missed something.

Behind her, Steve encouraged Tristan every now and then with upbeat comments. They both had to be weary, too. Tired and heartsick and in desperate need of both answers and of quiet days to come to terms with Maddie's death and the changes in their lives. Only another hour or two before they returned to Strathnairn and briefed Goddard and then, she hoped, they could all get on with their lives. Steve with Lily and Tristan. Simon with Erin and Jasmine. Her with . . . her career. Once she'd had a few days off. Once Zac was arrested.

Simon paused on a higher point a couple of metres above the water and drew out binoculars from a pocket on his backpack.

'Can you see that?' he asked, pointing downstream a little further as he raised the binoculars to his eyes.

She followed the line he pointed. 'That' seemed to be something pale, on the edge of the water on their side where the river widened as it curved a little to the north.

He swore, and handed her the glasses.

She adjusted the focus. A body. It had to be a body. It must have been caught in something when the divers were here. Some pocket in the rocks they'd missed.

Steve and Tristan caught up with her. The grim expression on Steve's face told her he'd guessed why they'd stopped.

'Take Tristan back to the car,' she said. 'Simon and I can deal with this.' They'd have to pass close by it, but Tristan shouldn't witness the sight close-up. Not a body that had been under the water for a couple of days. Not a person he knew.

But Tristan wouldn't be deterred. 'I need to see him. Please. If it's him, I need to know for sure.'

'Let's just wait and see,' Steve said.

Simon set off at a jog, following the track to a point where it was about four metres above the water level. Tess went after him, and he held branches back for her as they navigated down the steep drop through the ragged casuarina bushes to the narrow ledge near the body.

She – it was a she – floated in the water just below them, face up, her long hair tangled around her face, her white dress torn and bloodied. Young. Maybe eighteen, with fine, doll-like features, bruised and battered.

Neither of them reached down to touch her.

'She hasn't been in the water for forty-eight hours,' Simon observed.

Tess's voice rasped in her dry throat. 'She hasn't been dead for forty-eight hours.'

Fatigue made her brain slow. Callie couldn't have survived the fall. Surely. She couldn't have survived for two days, down here in the gorge, alone. It didn't make sense.

Tristan and Steve jumped down the last part of the slope and the four of them crowded together on the limited space of the ledge.

Tristan knelt down to take a closer look. 'That's not Callie,' he said, his voice rough, his fists clenching on the rock. 'It's not Callie. She's the one who jumped into the river the other night.' He turned bewildered eyes up at his uncle. 'That's Rebecca, and she didn't jump.'

Tess turned her face away for a moment to hide the rush of emotion. Another death. Possibly another violent murder. Shooting Joshua hadn't stopped the deaths.

Steve gave Tristan a steadying hand as he rose to his feet. 'Did you see Rebecca afterwards, Tris? Do you remember seeing her at Derringvale?'

Tristan turned his back to the river, gulping in breaths, fending off tears. 'Yes. She was there. And she was back at the homestead the next day, when Madeleine and I went. She talked with my mother but . . . she didn't want to believe. She didn't want to believe about Joshua.'

They stood so close Tess didn't need to reach to put a gentle hand on his arm. 'Tristan, was she one of the sisters?'

He dragged the heel of his hand across his eyes. 'She was one of the new ones. Her and Callie. They'd been trainees for a long time. It was supposed to be her first night . . . with him. We were friends . . . she was so excited . . . but I couldn't tell her . . .'

He hung his head, sobs breaking. Her own heart wrenching for him – not much more than a boy, to have lost another person he cared about – Tess looked over his shoulder at Steve. 'Take Tris back to Strathnairn. I'll wait here with Simon until back-up arrives.'

Simon slid his backpack off his shoulder and began opening a pocket. 'You go with them, Tess. I've got a sat phone, I'll call it in. I can wait until your mob get here. Wouldn't be the first time.'

'Yes, come with us, Tess,' Steve said. The brown of his eyes darkened almost to black. 'Please. We need to know you're safe.'

And she wouldn't be safe with a highly experienced commando? But she understood Steve's concern. He – and Tristan – had too much on their minds without the added worry of her being out here, deep in the bush.

'Just give me a minute to take some photos,' she told Steve. 'I'll follow you.'

While Simon reported the death on the sat phone, she focused her phone camera on the young woman – the girl – in the water. Rebecca, who had been alive late Monday afternoon. Late teens, probably, maybe very early twenties. She had bruises on her face, damp smears of blood on her torn dress. Bruises that took time to form. Whether she'd drowned or whether she was dead before being dumped in the water, she'd been beaten before death. And it had to have happened somewhere nearby. It wouldn't make sense to cart a body far in this country.

Simon was giving GPS coordinates on the phone so she waved a hand in farewell and hastened up the slope after Tristan and Steve, who held back to assist her up the steepest, most slippery parts, his grip firm and steady. They made a quick pace back to the campground, and the uneasiness prickling in her neck reduced a little in intensity once in sight of the vehicles. But not completely.

Hayley, Sybilla, Tamara, Callie, Maddie . . . and now Rebecca. Six of the sisters, dead. Joshua couldn't have murdered them all. Zac, and maybe another killer, were still out there, somewhere.

'Straight back to Strathnairn?' Steve queried when they reached the cars.

Tristan had taken the latest death hard, and he climbed into Steve's car, hiding his face from Tess. The sooner he was away from here, from death and police and fear, the better.

'Yes. I'll meet you at the police station.'

She unlocked her car, dumped her pack on the back seat and drank more water while Steve spoke with Tristan through the passenger door. As she started her car, he went around to the driver's seat so she reversed out of her parking place and drove out ahead of them on the dirt road, staying at a relatively slow pace until he caught up.

There were twenty kilometres or so of park roads before they'd meet the back road between Goodabri and Strathnairn. Winding gravel roads, damaged in places from the runoff from

Sunday's storm, so she didn't speed, and Steve kept around fifty metres behind her.

A couple of k's from the junction she had to hit the brakes and ram down gears to stop the car when a man lumbered out of the bush ahead of her and stood in the centre of the road. Unshaven, his clothes spattered with mud, arms folded in front of him, feet slightly apart. A solid stance. A muscular guy, in his forties at least, possibly older. Not a weak man. He could do damage if he chose to.

She glanced in the rear view mirror. Steve had stopped just behind her.

She looked again at the guy, and recognised the face of the man Madeleine had introduced on Sunday night. Tom, who'd gone to look for the others in the bush.

Madeleine had trusted him.

Relying on that knowledge, Tess got out of the car and walked forward. She heard the footsteps of Steve and Tristan behind her.

As the Fraser men flanked her, Tom nodded at her, cast an assessing glance at Steve, and then spoke to Tristan.

'Are you okay with these people, Tristan?'

Despite his reddened eyes, the lad stood straight and tall. 'Yes. I am.'

'You know they're cops, don't you?'

'Yes.'

'Good. Do you know where Madeleine is? I need to talk with her.'

Tristan shook his head, and stumbled backwards, his

composure starting to crumble again. Steve put an arm around his shoulder.

Tess positioned herself between them and Tom. 'Madeleine's dead, Tom. Zac Matthias deliberately ran her down in Strathnairn on Monday.'

Tom stared back at her, shock draining his face of colour. 'No. No.' When she didn't say anything more, he swore, long and vehemently.

She gave him a few moments. 'Tom, we need your help. The police need your help. Will you come with us?'

Although he didn't move, wariness tensed his muscles. 'Are you arresting me?'

'No. We're not on duty. We're not even on the case anymore.' He'd been with the group for years so she appealed to his sense of community. 'But we need some answers, so we can protect Tristan and Lily. And so the police can find the others and protect them.'

'You really mean that? About protecting the others?'

'Yes. Joshua screwed with everyone's heads, Tom. We're concerned for the safety of the group members. Until we know what's going on, where they are and who's leading them, we can't make sure they're okay.'

He didn't say anything for a long moment, watching her, watching Steve, deciding whether to trust them. 'Someone needs your help. She's hurt. He hurt her. David. He's taken over. He's madder than Joshua. Can you help her?'

A woman hurt. By David. Her gut instinct reaction to David

yesterday validated, she said to Tom, 'Yes, of course we will. Where is she?'

'I'll get her. Wait here.'

He went straight back into the bush. Here it was thick, a mix of eucalypts and native cypress with an understorey of lower growing acacias and other shrubs. He was out of sight in seconds.

Concerned for the injured woman, Tess moved to follow him but Steve caught her arm. 'Stay here. Just in case. He's strong enough to carry a woman if she needs it.'

Reluctantly, she nodded. No sense walking into what could be an ambush.

Tom returned within a couple of minutes, coming into sight with his arm around a dishevelled young woman, who limped heavily and clutched a blue cloth jacket around her shoulders over her white dress. A dress like the other sisters, but dirty, torn. Although Tess did move towards the bush to meet him, Tristan passed her.

'Willow!' He touched the young woman's hand very gently, almost reverently. 'Willow, you're safe. You can trust these people.'

She lifted her head. 'Tris? Oh, Tris.' She burst into tears, sobbing, 'She was right. Madeleine was right.'

Tess approached her. 'Willow, my name is Tess Ballard. I'm an off-duty police officer. Will you come over to my car, so I can see where you're hurt?'

Tom supported her over and Tess opened up the back of her station wagon, pulling out the first-aid kit and inviting Willow to sit on the tailgate. Steve drew Tom and Tristan a short distance away, giving her some privacy with Willow.

The young woman shook as though cold, despite the warmth of the sun. She wore leather sandals, and her feet and her legs were badly scratched, as were her arms. Her face, like Rebecca's, had numerous bruises and much of her long hair had worked free of her plait, tangled and wild.

But at least Willow breathed and was conscious.

'What happened, Willow?' Tess asked gently, offering her a small pack of tissues. 'Did someone assault you?'

Willow sniffed and nodded, taking one of the tissues and blowing her nose. 'It was David. He said . . . he said he's Joshua's heir. Joshua's oldest son. That he's carrying on Joshua's work and that we . . . we have to serve him now. But . . . but he's not . . . Joshua loved us. He really did. It was bliss with him. But David . . . he forced us.' Her voice quavered and she brought her tissue to her mouth, gulping and struggling not to cry.

Rape. That smooth-talking supercilious young man had raped her. Tess's anger rose but her priority lay in giving Willow understanding and reassurance. 'Take your time, Willow. It's okay to cry. It wasn't your fault.'

Not your fault. *Not your fault.* If someone had said those words to her at seventeen, would she have believed them then? Tess shoved the memories back. Willow. Concentrate on Willow.

'He forced Rebecca and me. And Rebecca . . . he hurt her. Hurt her and she cried and I tried to stop him but he said I was disobedient. A traitor. He kept hitting me. I hit him back and yelled at him and pushed him hard and he tripped and fell down and . . . I just ran. Ran out and ran away and kept running when they chased me. I hid in the bush and when it was light again I crossed the river and I thought maybe I could find Erin in the national park. But it's so big. I walked and walked and then it was dark again and I was scared and couldn't sleep. I walked more this morning and found this road, and then Tom found me.'

Two nights in the bush. It must have been Monday night when she'd run from David, and now, Wednesday afternoon, she had to be weak, dehydrated and exhausted. She was extremely lucky she'd found Tom. They were still twenty kilometres from Goodabri, sixty from Strathnairn, with few properties in between.

'Have you had anything to eat or drink, Willow?'

'Tom gave me some water. And he'd found some apples so we had one each.'

An apple. Sometimes apple or other fruit trees popped up in the bush, legacy of an old hut, or a bushwalker throwing out a core. Not often, given the dry climate. Only one apple for thirty-six hours? She'd have to get Willow to hospital for medical assessment as soon as possible.

Tess took out her spare water bottle from the back of the car and a couple of rehydration tablets from the first-aid kit. But before she gave them to Willow, she remembered both about the drugs in the water on Sunday, and the necessity of giving Willow agency and the opportunity to make her own decisions. 'This is just tap water.' She held up the bottle. 'But I recommend that you put these tablets in. They're dissolvable tablets that contain salts and electrolytes that will help your body rehydrate. See? Here's the packet.'

Willow looked at the packet with the kind of dazed expression that suggested to Tess she wasn't really taking in what she read. But after a moment, she put the tablets in the water, anyway.

'Give it a moment for the tablets to dissolve, then drink it slowly,' Tess said gently. 'One mouthful at a time. But drink it all over the next half hour or so.' She waited while Willow drank a little, all the while trying to assess her condition. No obvious major injuries. Alert and responsive. Thirty-six hours after the assault, significant internal injuries could probably be ruled out. But she still needed to be checked over, rehydrated, and have a sexual assault examination and evidence collection, if she could be persuaded. 'Willow, I could clean up your scratches and injuries here, but I think it's best if I take you to the hospital in Strathnairn. Is that okay by you?'

'The hospital?' Willow got to her feet, almost dropping the water bottle, her gaze darting around like a trapped animal, desperate to flee.

What the hell had Joshua told them about hospitals? 'How about I ask Tristan to tell you about the hospital? He's been there.'

While Tristan sat and talked quietly with Willow, Tess left them alone, rejoining Steve and Tom to learn what they'd been deep in grim discussion about.

'Tom will come back to Strath with us,' Steve told her. 'He knows a bit about Joshua's operations. And he knows David and Mary Saint. Plus he's been lurking around and observing since Sunday.'

'They took Joshua away,' added Tom. 'After everyone had left, two of Joshua's – David's – bodyguards took him from behind the rock and carried him away.'

Tess could barely form words around the dryness in her throat. 'Was he alive?'

'I don't know. They carried him. There was blood on his clothes. And . . .' Tom glanced between the two of them. 'I think that the knife I threw was still in his chest.'

CHAPTER 10

Steve interrogated Tom on the drive to Strathnairn. As much as he could interrogate someone while he was driving a car, closely behind Tess.

She had Willow and Tristan with her. No way Steve would have let Tom go in the car with her – a man he didn't yet entirely trust – but Tom hadn't objected at all when he'd been directed to Steve's car.

They passed the forensic team in their van on the way out to the park. Steve didn't stop. Simon had given them the coordinates, and they were familiar enough with the general area. Steve's priority was to get to Strathnairn with Tess and the others. But he needed Tom's information, Tom's perspective.

Although he could have pushed hard for information, he mostly just let him talk to begin with. Give a man space to talk and he'd often fill it, without guarding his words too closely.

'Maybe you'll think I'm stupid, but I believed in Joshua. For years. He gave me hope and gave my life meaning,' Tom ventured in the silence. 'I was committed to keeping the communities safe. We believed that the world outside couldn't be trusted, that they'd try to get to us. But it was Joshua who started to destroy us. Joshua and Mary.'

'When did that start happening?' Steve prompted. 'What did you notice?'

Tom took his time answering, but with the stillness of thought, not the fidgeting of evasion. 'There were small things that started to feel not right. Secrets. Spying on people. But at first I believed it was outside people threatening him, infiltrating us. Then Hayley and Sybilla disappeared, and Madeleine was behaving suspiciously. I thought they were undermining him, contacting outsiders. Erin arrived on Sunday and I thought she was a spy, probably a cop.' He paused for a moment, as if making up his mind. 'On Sunday night, he gave me the drugs to put in the water butts. For freedom and bliss, he said. But when I worked out what he planned . . . I realised how wrong I'd been.'

'Do you know what he intended to do afterwards?' Steve asked. 'After he convinced them all to commit suicide?'

Tom shifted in his seat and for just an instant Steve tensed in case he did something stupid, but the man only made himself more comfortable as he answered, 'I'm not sure. There's a bodyguard called Christopher. He has a pilot's licence. Flies Joshua and Mary around in a four-seat Cessna. He flew Joshua to a landing strip somewhere a bit east of the property on Sunday afternoon. And I know he went back to the plane to prep things to fly them out on Sunday night.'

A plane. Having access to a plane meant they could be almost anywhere.

'I saw David leave with Mary,' Steve said. 'I saw him race back to the homestead and drive off with her. Do you know if he went with her on the plane? And where they went to?'

'I don't think he went with her. He was back here with the car on Monday evening.'

Gradually, from what Tom told him, Steve pieced together the events at Serenity Hill after Sunday night. When the police had finished their examination of the scene and allowed the group members back on Monday, they'd been confused, suspicious, uncertain both about what had happened to Joshua and what they should do next. Rumours flew – about Maddie, about Joshua being shot, and about Tom himself when he'd supported Maddie's statements. So he'd gone into the bush when Maddie left, and watched from a distance.

'David spoke with them all in front of the homestead. I wasn't close enough to hear. Then they packed up everything. Tools, furniture, belongings. There were trucks. The one from here, and four others arrived. David must have organised them. Plus a cattle truck. They left the sheep but the cattle were already mustered. Everything got loaded onto four of the trucks, and the people went in ours. That's how they do it, move around without anyone seeing a large group. In a truck.'

Steve clenched his hands on the steering wheel. Damn, no

way would the police be able to stop and inspect every truck in the district.

'Do you know where they've gone to? Where the haven is? Or whether it even exists?' he asked Tom.

'I'm certain it exists. But I don't know where. Only a few people knew and I wasn't important enough for that kind of knowledge. But I think it's somewhere west of here. And I think David's gathering all the communities together there.'

'What makes you think it's west?'

Tom gave a casual shrug. 'Red dust country. The car comes back full of it. And the truck too, a couple of times.'

Red dust. Plenty of that west of Strathnairn. West of Birraga. He'd worked long enough out of Moree, Dubbo and Birraga to know that the western half of the state wallowed in red dust. An area probably the size of several European countries. Not much help in finding the haven.

'How many communities are there?' Steve asked. 'How many people?'

'Four major communities that I know of. Two or three hundred people. But there are smaller groups of followers all around the place.'

The dappled sunlight on the straight road ahead seemed to dance in front of Steve's eyes as the breeze moved through the trees. So damned hard to see ahead on this case. Everything was constantly shifting. And now there could be hundreds of people involved. *Hundreds.* Shit.

'What is David planning? Do you have any idea?' *Please, not a Jonestown. Not here. Not anywhere.*

'I don't know. I didn't know what Joshua was planning either, right until the end. I believed in him until he ordered me to make sure Madeleine went to the waterfall and didn't come back.'

'He gave you that order? Directly?' Other than Tristan seeing Joshua at Sybilla's death, they had no evidence, yet, to place him at Hayley's murder. But if he'd ordered Madeleine's death that would be evidence he was targeting the sisters, or at least the older ones who had been with him since the beginning.

'Mary did. She often passed on Joshua's orders. Sometimes David did, too.'

Steve's head spun with questions. Joshua's orders? Or their own? How much control were they exerting over the group? Who else might be making decisions? 'Tell me about Zac Matthias. Was he close to Mary or to David?'

'Zac? He wasn't important. Just one of the group. Mary wasn't here all that often and she rarely came down to the cottages. Zac's not the kind of man she'd ever have looked at twice. David – I don't know.' He laughed, guttural and bitter. 'A few days ago I wouldn't have said anything bad about him. Joshua's son. Joshua's eldest, chosen son. But now . . . He beat those girls, and raped them. Willow and Rebecca. Sisters. We honoured the sisters, their service to Joshua. But I was outside the homestead in the night and I heard him, heard them begging him to stop. When Willow ran, I followed, to protect her. But then I lost her again, until this morning.'

'Do you know what happened to Rebecca?'

He turned his face to the window, and Steve heard him swallow. 'I saw them. Around sunrise yesterday. I'm not sure who – I was too far away. Two men. They tossed her over the side of the gorge. I waited until they were gone, then went to see, just in case . . . There was nothing I could do for her. I haven't told Willow.'

Steve slowed behind Tess's car as she indicated for the turn to the south on to the Derringvale–Strathnairn road. Not much time left before they reached the police station and he handed Tom over to Alec. And although Alec might – *might* – share some information, technically he shouldn't share much with an off-the-case detective, and Alec was a follow-the-rules kind of police officer.

'What can you tell me about David? What's your impression of his character?'

'David is greedy. For power. For attention. For women. He's young, and he's smart. Joshua has been taking him places for the last four or five years.' Tom angled in his seat towards him, and Steve felt the man's watchful gaze. 'Madeleine said it was all a con. That Joshua tricked us all. Brainwashed us. Is that true?'

'Yes. His real name is Peter Hollywell. He's a psychologist. He wrote papers and gave speeches about how Joshua used cult techniques of hypnosis and mind-control and manipulated his followers. It was all one big game to him.'

Tom breathed out a heavy sigh. 'Then David knows that. I think he's known it for years. He can be charming and friendly but he uses people. He finds out secrets, what they're afraid of, what they want, and he uses that information.'

'Is that what he did to you?'

Half a kilometre went by before Tom answered. 'He knows I murdered a man.'

'He knows you threw your knife at Joshua?'

'He'll recognise my knife. But that's not what I meant.'

They weren't far from Strathnairn, and he had a murderer in the car. 'Who did you kill? And when?'

'I killed a man and dumped his body in the Mallee scrub down near Mildura. More than ten years ago.'

'Why?'

'He was a vicious bastard involved in one of the bikie gangs, and he raped a woman at the farm I worked at. My mate and I pulled him off her but he had a gun, and he escaped on his bike. I chased him in the ute and he came off his bike on a dirt road, broke his leg, dropped his gun. He was writhing on the ground and I picked up the gun and shot him twice in the head. Dragged him into the scrub. Buried the gun. I don't know if they ever found him. I never went back to the farm. I've been living off the grid ever since, no surnames, no banking, no phone, in case they find me.'

'The police?'

He snorted. 'The bikies. The police will just put me in prison. But I'm a dead man if the bikies ever find out.'

'You were involved with them?'

'They involved themselves with me. Not my choice. Attacking that woman was the last straw.' He blew out another breath, and out of the corner of his eye Steve saw the man's large hands spread out on his knees. Open, unarmed. 'I guess you're going to arrest me for that. I'll face up to it. I did it and I'm done running.'

'I'm off duty. I've got other, more urgent worries on my mind. The crime occurred in Victoria so it's not my jurisdiction. If you give everything you know about Joshua's mob to the police, I just might forget to chase up with the Victorian police.'

Steve believed in justice, but bikies didn't forget or forgive. Sending the guy to prison for a bikie murder would only result in his violent death. Tom might yet redeem himself. Maybe he already had. He'd saved Maddie on Sunday night, found Willow today. And he'd thrown a knife to stop Joshua luring his people to their deaths. That made four of them who'd acted in that moment. Steve's gut instinct said he could trust the man. Probably. He never entirely trusted his instinct anymore. He'd been terribly wrong, more than once.

Tess phoned as they approached the outskirts of Strathnairn. 'We're going to pick up Erin and the girls. Erin and Jasmine will go with Willow to the hospital. She'll feel more comfortable with them there. Can you take Lily with you?'

'Sure.' In his car. With a guy who'd confessed to a violent murder. But his car had the booster seat, and it would only be for a few minutes. He followed Tess's car as she turned into a lane in a semi-rural area. Erin waited with Lily and Jasmine at the gate of a farm cottage. They loaded up quickly, and Tristan slipped in beside Lily in the back seat.

As he pulled in behind Tess's car in the hospital drop-off zone, his phone rang again. Nick Matheson.

'Where are you?' Nick asked.

'At the hospital. Tess and Erin are about to take Willow in. I've got—'

'Get Tess and the others. Come straight to the police station. We've got a situation.'

'What the f—?' He pulled the phone from its console, his car door open already.

'There's a mob gathering outside. David ben Joshua is all over social media claiming police brutality and the murder of his father. Says that we terrified his followers by herding them to a "concentration camp" at gunpoint. The mood is getting angry out there. I want you and Tess in the safety of the station right away.'

•

The security gate into the police car park behind the station locked shut after them as several protesters came running down the side street. They shouted through the bars as Tess drove around the corner of the building and parked right near the secure rear door into the cell area.

'Okay, you can sit up now,' she told her passengers, hunkered down as she'd instructed. 'We're out of sight here. I'll get you inside in just a tick.'

Parked beside her, Steve had Lily out of the car and he handed her to Tristan while he loaded up with a couple of bags and passed another to Tom.

Tess grabbed her backpack from the car before she swiped her ID card at the door and ushered them all inside. She led them to the custody area, trying to think, plan, what best to do with the disparate group now they were here in the station. Willow, reeling on her feet, and leaning on Erin, needed first aid and someone she trusted to give it. Jasmine, Tristan and Lily needed somewhere quiet and safe. Tom needed to talk with Alec. She and Steve needed to find out what the hell was going on.

'Willow, there's a first-aid room here. Would you be happy if Erin cleans up your cuts and bruises? You'll feel better after they're seen to, I'm sure. Is that okay, Erin?'

'Of course.' With reassuring words, Erin steered the young woman into the small room. Not the hospital care that Willow should have been receiving, but Erin's advanced first-aid training would have to suffice for now.

Tess turned to the teenagers. 'Jasmine and Tristan, can you look after Lily? I'll take you upstairs to the staff break room and we'll find something for you to do while we talk with the detectives.'

Steve lifted one of the bags he carried. 'I've got some books and things. I'll settle them and then find you. Can you take Tom through to Alec?'

At the landing at the top of the stairs, Aaron stood by a window overlooking the front entrance to the police station and the street. He waved Tess over and made room for her by the window.

Tess introduced Tom quickly – first name only, because that's all he'd given her. But she used Aaron's full name and rank. Despite the differences in their ages, Tom nodded respectfully.

She looked out the window to survey the scene below. Maybe sixty people, adults and teenagers, crowded on the footpath at the base of the stairs leading up to the station. Most wore the distinctive simple clothing of the Serenity Hill people, but she recognised few of the faces. Not that she'd seen many of them in good light the other night.

'Do you know any of them, Tom?' she asked.

Tom remained near the side of the window, just enough to see out. 'Some of them. Some aren't from Serenity Hill. That guy at the front isn't.'

A young man with dreadlocks had his back to them, speaking to the crowd. Through the double-glazing she couldn't hear the words, but the group became increasingly agitated, shouting towards the building, waving fists. None of them carried placards, and that didn't surprise her. There'd been no use for stationery at Serenity Hill, and people with no money couldn't wander into a shop for cardboard and markers. It didn't make them any less vocal though.

But the shouts died down and people stilled as she caught a glimpse of movement directly below. A news crew, hovering on the edge of the crowd, rushed forward.

'That'll be Nick and the top brass. They've gone down to speak with them,' Aaron said.

Sure enough, Matheson stepped out to address the crowd, along with the two visiting Chief Inspectors, Alec Goddard and Heather Arundel. Even from behind they all appeared commanding – straight backs, formal uniforms. She could only imagine Matheson's face, but he carried a portable speaker and his words carried as he addressed the crowd.

Tess noticed a second news crew arrive, as Matheson assured the protesters that their concerns were heard and that the formal investigation would establish the facts. He introduced Arundel, who advised that they would be calling for witnesses to Joshua's death to provide statements.

'Most of them wouldn't have a clue what happened,' Tess muttered. 'But they'll tell her what they've imagined.'

Aaron shot her a sympathetic glance. 'Arundel's not stupid. She'll be able to sort the facts from the talk. But it's all over social media, so she's got a big job ahead of her.'

'Peace-loving community leader gunned down by police,' Steve said drily behind them. 'Oh yeah, that's a rallying cry.'

Tess moved aside slightly to make room for him. 'But they don't use computers or phones,' she pointed out. 'They're not on social media.'

'Not the ones who live in the communities, no,' Aaron said. 'But it seems there are plenty of sympathisers out there. People who have bought the books, been to the website, but haven't made the big commitment. This last couple of hours, they've been chattering like mad online.'

The crowd began jeering again, the leader argumentative, leaping up the steps to shout in Matheson's face. Nick didn't move. She couldn't hear what was said, but after one startled moment the man backed off a step, whirling around to start whipping up the protesters again.

Someone started beating a drum, and another joined in.

A projectile flew through the air – maybe a small rock – hitting Arundel in the face so that she staggered backwards.

Alec Goddard escorted Arundel back inside, but other officers came out to stand with Matheson, forming a line at the top of the steps.

'I've got to go down there,' Aaron said. His boots, pounding down the stairs, echoed the drumbeats.

'We can't go,' Steve said to Tess. 'One sight of either of us will throw oil on the fire.'

A cold unease sat like a stone in her gut and she nodded. Even as they watched, other protesters came running down the street, some of them with placards. More followed, doubling the numbers within minutes.

The double-glazing of the window didn't shut out the yells, the chanting and the incessant drumbeats.

The thin line of police officers stood firm at the top of the steps. They had no riot squad here, no riot equipment, and her colleagues – her friends – were unprotected except for their standard equipment vests.

CHAPTER 11

'Tom, you go and stay with the kids,' Steve ordered. 'Guard them and keep them right away from any windows.'

Aware she also couldn't risk being seen by those outside, Tess bolted down the stairs after Steve. They met up with Goddard as Jacob, the technical officer, buzzed him and Arundel through the secure door from the reception area. Grim-faced, Goddard had an arm around the Chief Inspector, blood running down her cheek from her temple. 'Steve, we'll need back-up. Call in an emergency and get every officer available from around the district. Tess, first aid for the inspector, please.'

'I'll be fine,' Arundel insisted. 'I just need to sit down for a minute.'

She wavered on her feet, not at all fine, and Tess took her arm. 'This way, ma'am. We'll just get that blood cleaned up.'

Arundel didn't protest, and Tess left her in Erin's capable care and rejoined Steve and Goddard, now in the small comms room that contained the main telephone switchboard, two CCTV screens and the radio desk below several large maps on the wall. Jacob had the feed from the front CCTV camera up on the larger screen.

The crowd had swelled even further, blocking the street. Around a hundred and fifty people or more were gathered now.

Goddard swore. 'Steve, you'll need to direct things from here. If Arundel's okay she'll get HQ to coordinate reinforcements. Tess, you know the town. As reinforcements come, you and Steve will need to decide the best routes and deployment. We'll keep in touch by radio.'

'You're going back out there?'

Goddard paused briefly in the doorway. 'Yes. There's only a dozen or so of us. Until back-up arrives, our primary goal will be keeping the station secure. Keep yourselves and the others out of sight. We'll try to keep them calm. If they don't know you're all here, it will be safer.'

Safer . . . Tess gritted her teeth. At the bottom of the screen, the security camera showed the thin line of police standing shoulder to shoulder. Nick in the centre. Aaron. Dee. Matt, who was keen on Dee. Samantha, just new from the Academy, two guys from the critical incident team and the five other day-shift officers. That was all.

Steve sat at the radio. 'Strathnairn station, urgent. Signal one, all available staff. Potentially violent protest outside station.'

The maps on the wall of the region emphasised their isolation. Even if Steve could call back-up in from Tenterfield, Inverell, Moree and Birraga, they'd be at least an hour away, most of them longer.

Tess pulled out her phone. 'I'll start contacting the night shift and off duty,' she told Steve. 'But there's not many of them. Jacob, can you access the contact list?'

Jacob – middle-aged, unflappable – nodded towards a red folder on a shelf while he set up a laptop. 'Front page in there. I don't rely on electronic versions.'

His gaze glued to the security vision, Steve asked between radio calls, 'Jacob, there are at least two news crews out there. Can you check the news stations, see if they're broadcasting?'

'I can do that,' Erin said from the door. Arundel's voice sounded out in the corridor, on the phone already.

Jacob glanced around the small, already crowded room. 'You want me to set up in the incident room? There's more space, and I should be able to feed things through to there.'

For fifteen minutes Tess stood out in the corridor and made phone call after phone call, working her way down the list of station officers, while all the while the radio buzzed in the background as Steve called in and coordinated back-up. Occasionally she heard Matheson and Goddard giving orders or asking questions over the radio, both steady and professional, totally focused on keeping the powder keg from exploding.

But the crowd had swelled still further, blocking access to the station – and the police cars and equipment – for the local officers recalled to duty.

'Meet the others at the corner of Burke and Church streets,' Tess passed on the orders to the last officers on her list. 'Block traffic and turn back protesters if you can. We think they're coming into town that way.'

Steve's phone buzzed and with a quick glance he snatched it up. 'Simon. Where are you? Good. Yes, they're all here in the station, safe. For now. Listen, I need someone on the ground out there. Numbers, movements, strategy, groupings, whatever's useful. Yeah, back-up's coming within the hour. Great. Thanks.'

Erin and Inspector Arundel had already moved across the corridor to the incident room but Tess stood by Steve's chair, both of them watching the screen.

'There's a new front man,' she said, calmer than she felt. 'And more placards.'

'Yeah. There's a new front mob.'

She studied the figures she could see, grainy and blurred in the camera's narrow field of focus. 'They're not from Serenity Hill.'

'Joshua's mob have fallen back. See, there are some over there. They were amateurs. But this new mob, they're different.'

Dressed differently, behaving differently. 'They're organised,' she said. 'Experienced.'

'Yes.' He rose, slipping his phone into his pocket, reaching for the portable radio. His face drawn and lined with worry, he asked, 'You don't have your service weapon, do you?'

'No. I handed it in to Haddad on Sunday night. Arundel probably has it locked up as evidence.'

'Mine, too. I'll go check on the kids, and bring Tom down. We need to know more about these new people. Maybe he knows them.'

She followed him out the door and crossed to the incident room. Arundel, with a dressing on her head, reported on her phone while Erin worked at a laptop. Jacob had the CCTV footage projected up onto a large screen, and television with live coverage from one of the news crews.

Tess stopped in front of the TV. A breaking news report showed footage of the protesters outside the police station. Well over a hundred in the camera shot. These images, clearer than the CCTV, showed her own face on numerous signs, with damning captions. 'Public Enemy'. 'Killer Cop'. 'Murderer'. Even 'Senior Constable Killer'.

She couldn't see Zac anywhere, but it didn't matter. These people, with their fury and their barely restrained violence threatened her just as much as he did.

•

Lily was fractious, hungry and scared, and the older ones weren't much better.

'I found some biscuits in the cupboard,' Tom told him. 'But they weren't much.'

Four o'clock in the afternoon, and some of them hadn't eaten since breakfast. Steve kicked himself. He'd not noticed his own hunger, but he had kids to worry about now.

'Let's go downstairs. I've got some food there,' he said. What he'd raided from the motel mini-bar this morning. 'And I'll find some more.' The vending machine behind the reception area. One problem solved. For now.

With muesli bars, chocolate and soft drink, he left Jasmine and Lily under Willow's care in an interview room beside the incident room. Closer to him. Closer to his protection. No need to concern them, yet, about the seriousness of the situation, although Willow with her huge dark eyes had a fair idea.

He took Tom and Tristan back with him to the others and glanced at the CCTV images. For thirty minutes, Nick and the others had held that line. But the early protesters had given way to the newcomers, and they moved closer, more aggressive, yelling and jeering. Even Nick with his steely command of others wouldn't be able to hold them much longer. No hope for reinforcements coming through the station from the back; the smaller tiled images from the rear CCTV camera showed a crowd at the car park entrance, too.

Erin had a laptop open on the table, Tess and Heather Arundel standing behind her.

'Okay, this is what seems to have sparked it off,' Erin said, clicking on a video.

Steve nudged Tristan forward and with Tom they gathered around to watch the video.

David ben Joshua's face filled the screen, and Erin turned up the sound.

'I am devastated to have to deliver the shocking news to our friends that our beloved leader, my father, Joshua Kristos, was brutally murdered by police on Sunday night. Armed officers burst into a peaceful gathering of friends and fired multiple rounds.

They drove two terrified young women, our sisters in bliss, into a flooded river where they have tragically perished. They then set fire to our living quarters, and as you can see –' the image changed to the destroyed woolshed, carefully framed to exclude the intact cottages, *'the damage is total. We have lost everything. Our tools, our work, our simple belongings.'*

'But that's not what happened,' Tristan protested. 'It wasn't like that at all.'

'We know that, Tris,' Steve assured him. 'But there were only a few of us who weren't drugged. It will be our word against his.' He struggled to keep the bitterness out of his voice. 'And a lot of people believe him.'

'I am David ben Joshua, and I vow to you, to all my friends, that Joshua's work will continue. We are Joshua's children, and we will rise like the phoenix and fly ever higher, beyond our oppressors, and pursue our sacred dreams to live in simplicity and bliss.'

The cynic in Steve waited for the appeal for donations. He didn't have to wait long.

'If you can help us replace our equipment . . .' David pleaded, and the details of sites where people could donate came up on the screen.

'I'll get the internet fraud team to look into that,' Arundel said. 'Send me the link please, Erin. And keep searching for anything else of relevance.'

Arundel held herself straight but gripped the back of a chair for support, clearly not yet recovered from her injury. Like Steve, her gaze drifted back to the CCTV screen. So did everyone else's.

'Tom, Tristan – do you know any of these people?' Steve asked while his thoughts raced. David had posted his video online through a social media account. He'd caught a glimpse of the number of 'shares' at the bottom of the link – thousands. More than ten thousand in just a day, maybe two. The guy had reach far beyond the dozens in Serenity Hill, and in other communities.

Neither Tom nor Tristan recognised anyone on the screen. Steve hadn't seen David or Zac at all in the CCTV video. But there were all these people, protesting Joshua's death. If David was orchestrating it, he was doing it from a distance. And how the hell, and when, had he become so adept at social media, when Joshua had barely scratched the surface?

Tess abruptly turned and left the room. Erin began to rise but Steve shook his head and followed Tess out himself.

She stood in the corridor, her back against the wall, sucking in slow, deep breaths. 'Did you see it, Steve? They're focusing on me. Not you. Not Simon. I don't know why. But all their posters are of me.'

He'd noticed. Part of his brain had been looking for placards denouncing him. 'You're right,' he admitted. 'No posters of me. But why you? Why so much focus on you?'

'There was that photo in the damned newspaper,' she said. 'I assume the online version, too. That personalises it more than just a name. I'm a woman and I shot Joshua. In some people's minds, a woman in a position of authority is an aberration in itself. With that mindset, a woman shooting a man, a powerful man, is layer upon layer of evil. It's much easier to whip up a furore against a non-traditional woman than against a man.'

'It's not fair, Tess. It's so, so wrong.'

'I know it's wrong. But it's the way it is.' She gave an attempt at a grin. 'Next thing they'll be criticising my appearance. You know, my uniform makes my butt look big.'

Her semi-joke, a momentary denial of reality, begged for understanding. He forced a half smile. 'Oh, anyone who comments on the size of a woman's rear has to be an idiot.' But he couldn't hold the smile, and he reached a hand to cup her shoulder, to reassure her with his touch. 'You're not going to face this alone, Tess. You know I'll stand by you.'

She made no move to step away from the physical connection. 'I know you want to. But you have Tristan and Lily to think of. They're young and vulnerable and they need your protection more than I do. They come first. Their safety and yours has to come first for you.'

She only spoke the truth, and they both knew it. She straightened her shoulders, stepped away from the wall. 'We need to go back in.'

On the CCTV image, the guy at the front of the group – shaved head, maybe in his thirties – suddenly charged forward, up the steps, a placard on a wooden post held high in his hand.

Nick's voice came clear and blunt over the radio: 'Stand by for casualties.'

Steve didn't wait for Arundel to give orders as the images on the screen showed a number of the protesters rushing forward behind their leader. 'Tess, Erin, get the kids into the safest part of the station and stay there. Tom, Jacob, you're with me. Now.' He bolted out of the room, the two men at his heels. 'Jacob, I need the front door set so it can only be opened from inside. Can you do that from the reception desk?'

'Yes.' Jacob dragged his pass on its lanyard over his head. 'Or you can use this at the keypad beside the door.'

'Thanks.' Steve pushed through the door at reception while Jacob went behind the desk. 'Tom, I'll need you to help me at the door. We may need to get people inside in a hurry. Jacob, stay at the desk and be ready to open that door.'

He flicked the foyer lights off, counting on the bright afternoon sunlight reflecting off the cement outside to blind the protesters to his presence in the dullness inside. A risk, but there'd been no photos published of him. Unlike Tess, with her face on fifty or more placards.

Outside, the police line still held, but barely. At least ten protesters attacked the line, the police limited to using batons in the close quarters. Too dangerous to draw a gun even to fire in the air – a raised gun would quickly become an easily snatched target.

Without breaking line, Nick defended himself against two protesters with his bare hands, sending them stumbling back down the steps. Alec pulled a man off young Sam, the new recruit. Dee struggled with a guy twice her size. No hope of arresting anyone in this scrum. Not enough officers.

Steve clenched his fists and fought the urge to rush outside to help. He mightn't be recognised here, but out there . . . he couldn't risk inciting them further. Although most of the protesters held back from charging the police, the mood was becoming ugly. Projectiles started to fly. Aaron ducked and a stone missed his head by inches and slammed into the reinforced glass door.

Wave after wave charged at the police and beneath the seeming chaos Steve saw the pattern. They were aiming to weaken them. Break them down. Put pressure on the line without provoking them to firing. And every wild charge, yelling and shrieking, fed the manic energy of the rest of the group, the bruised retreaters carried off as warrior heroes on the shoulders of the others.

Steve swore under his breath. Theatre. The people leading this were orchestrating a show but the police were the circus animals, trapped in a cage. Sooner or later, when they had the crowd whipped up high enough, they'd rush in to overwhelm them.

'They're not our lot,' Tom muttered beside him. 'I don't know them. A few right in the back, yes, but not these ones.'

Time stretched on held breaths, minutes dragging as Steve watched, helpless. Nick and Alec must have realised the tactics, but they didn't signal a retreat. Probably because the glass doors and windows, strong though they were, wouldn't stand up to a full-scale assault. The protesters couldn't be allowed to enter the station.

More stones, bricks, garbage and even plants ripped from the gardens in front of the station pelted the officers and the walls of the building. Down on the street, flames from a burning garbage dumpster danced high into the sky.

He leapt forward when Dee staggered and fell to the ground, motionless, a rock coming to a stop on the cement beyond her.

His face a mask of anger, Aaron dragged her back several metres towards the building, shooting a pleading look inside before he returned to the line.

Steve yanked open the door and Tom held it open while he dashed outside and scooped Dee up to carry her to safety. No time for a neck brace or a stretcher; the rock had hit the side of her face and her bleeding head rested against his shoulder, blood oozing from her ear as well as the gash on her cheek. He carried her through the reception area. Jacob buzzed open the door and Tess met him on the other side, grey eyes clouded with concern.

'Erin's getting the neck brace. Bring her through to the incident room.'

They'd need an ambulance, paramedics, maybe even the rescue helicopter to fly Dee to Tamworth or Newcastle or Sydney. They could have none of them, yet. If her head injury was severe Dee could die before they could get help to her.

'I've got medical evac on standby,' Tess said as they hurried down the corridor. 'Inspector Arundel's not doing so well. She passed out briefly. She and the kids are in the custody area. It's more secure there.'

Tess supported Dee's head as he laid her on the large table in the incident room. Erin hurried in, carrying a large first-aid box and a head brace and immediately started to assess Dee.

'There are two Moree cars on their way, ETA fifteen minutes,' Tess reported. 'Three Inverell cars, ETA seventeen. A Birraga car, half an hour away yet.'

Too far away. They might not have fifteen minutes.

From the comms room Nick's voice on the radio ordered the use of capsicum spray and tasers. On the CCTV screen, the protesters surged forward en masse.

Steve took Dee's taser, OC spray and cuffs from her equipment vest. As he reached for her Glock he said to Tess, 'Go down to the custody area and look after the kids. If need be, lock yourselves in a cell.'

Her hands still gently on the sides of Dee's head as Erin readied the head brace, Tess said quietly, 'I've got a job to do here, Steve.'

He had no holster so he tucked the Glock into the waistband of his jeans. He had no coherent words, either. Only the gut certainty that if the protesters made it inside and found her, they'd probably kill her. The children might be okay, but Tess . . .

No words, but as he passed her on his way out, he pressed a quick, hard kiss to the side of her face.

He didn't wait to see her response. Out the door, back through reception, out the front door of the building. The police battled with thirty or more protesters, some rushing for the open door. He mightn't be able to stop them, but he'd die trying if he had to.

CHAPTER 12

Tess's phone buzzed in her pocket as Erin slid the head immobiliser into position. Four buzzes before she could remove her hands from Dee's head and answer the call.

Leah Haddad spoke immediately. 'We're two blocks away. The lane seems clear. Give us five minutes and then open that back door.'

Tess breathed out. The plan might work. 'I'll be there.'

On the CCTV screen, the image in the corner of the rear camera view showed a smaller crowd at the gate than a few minutes earlier – but the main image showed a larger crowd at the front. She couldn't bear to watch the fighting.

Her phone buzzed again. Simon. 'I've picked up McCallum and we're near the service station at the end of the street. Where do you want us?'

With a nod to Erin, she left the room, talking as she ran to the custody area. 'Leah's almost in place with the SES truck on the lane to the east. ETA five. There's an ambulance waiting in Church Street. Inverell cops should be coming past that way in ten or so. Ask them to clear people away from the car park gate to give the ambos access.'

'I'll see what I can do,' Simon said, and hung up.

Arundel, pale and battling concussion, had the young ones in the custody sergeant's office. Lily was curled on her lap, crying. Jasmine sat on another chair, Tristan kneeling beside her. Willow huddled against a wall.

'What news, Ballard?' Arundel demanded.

'Reinforcements are nearby, and will gain access through the rear door. They'll be through here in four –' she checked her watch, 'three minutes. They'll rush through.' Four pairs of young, frightened eyes watched her. 'You'll all need to keep out of their way, okay? There'll be about ten police. They won't hurt you.' She met Arundel's direct gaze again. 'Can you stand by to buzz the car-park gate open, ma'am?' The custody sergeant's office had a view of the car park and she indicated the control panel for the gate above the desk. 'Kennedy and McCallum may be able to clear the way for the ambulance. And we have a critical case who needs it.'

The senior officer nodded. 'Yes. Good work, Ballard.'

Tess reached in front of her to press the intercom to the front reception. 'Jacob, reinforcements coming through from the rear shortly. Be ready to let them through.'

'Thank God,' she heard him say as she left the area.

At the rear door, Tess touched her security pass to open it. The afternoon sunshine streamed in, hot after the air conditioning. From here, she couldn't see the gate around the corner of the building, but she could see the fence between the car park and the lane. Almost two metres high, with a row of razor wire on top. Ask a commando how to access a building . . . While Simon sped back into Strathnairn she'd relayed his suggestions to Haddad, just arrived back in town from Sydney, and they'd made the plan, deliberately keeping off radio to ensure security.

The noise, the drumming and the shouting from out the front drifted loud here, but under it the rumble of the approaching truck sounded, and through the gap between the fence and the wire she saw the top of the vehicle pull in to a stop. Doors slammed, and within seconds a ladder towered half a metre over the wire. A male cop – she couldn't see who – scrambled up it, balancing for a moment at the top before dropping the couple of metres down to the ground, landing with a skilful roll. Already a second ladder was against the fence, quickly manoeuvred up and over and held steady in place by the first guy while officers rapidly scaled the first ladder, then crossed to the other to descend safely.

Only when Haddad reached her did she radio for those out front to hear, 'Back-up arriving from rear. One minute. Repeat: back-up arriving from rear.'

Tess led them at a run through the station, standing aside when Jacob held the door into reception wide open. Tom stood ready at the front, and Haddad didn't need to slow her steps as she ran through, straight into the melee, followed by the others.

Tess couldn't see Steve. Nor could she see Aaron or Nick or Matt in the seething mass of people and fighting. Alec Goddard dragged an immobilised protester – he must have been tasered – over to the side of the building, at least partially out of the way. Tess thought she saw the blue of a police uniform on the ground and then recognised Sam, the new probationary constable, staggering to her feet, clutching her arm. Haddad grabbed her by the shoulders and pushed her towards the station. Jacob and Tom, on post at the door, assisted her to stumble inside.

Her eyes red and streaming, pain making her sob, she stopped, disoriented in the relative stillness. With no one outside paying attention, Tess stepped out into the open to the young woman's side.

'You're safe, Sam. You're going to be fine. Paramedics and more back-up are on their way. It will all be over soon. You've done well, really well.'

Despite her assurances, when she guided Sam to Erin's care in the incident room, a breathless journalist on the television news reported, *'We're broadcasting live here from Strathnairn where a peaceful protest against the alleged police shooting of religious leader Joshua Kristos has exploded into violence. Protesters say police are using tasers and tear gas against them and we've heard reports of gunfire.'*

'Bullshit,' Dee muttered from her prone position on the table. 'If we actually had bloody tear gas it'd be a different story.'

Tess moved to beside the table, into her friend's limited field of vision. 'Conscious, aware and opinionated. You're looking better than you were, Dee.'

'Erin better keep an eye on my blood pressure. That shit on the news isn't good for it.'

Tess watched the report on the screen. 'The journo is at least two blocks away, down by the park. They can't see what's happening here.' But the images showed plenty of protesters milling on the street, and they'd dragged park benches onto the road.

The journalist brought one of the protesters in front of the camera. *'You say you're expecting further police action?'* Dressed in black, her long hair half-stuffed under a military-style cap, the wide-eyed woman answered, *'Yes. They've called in special ops against us. We're expecting a water cannon and more tear gas, so we're building a barricade here against their oppression.'*

Erin looked up from the sling she was tying for Sam. 'That woman's definitely not from Serenity Hill. I doubt she's one of Joshua's.'

Tess agreed. Somehow, everything had spiralled out of control, way beyond Joshua and Serenity Hill and the deaths of the women. But she couldn't make the pieces fit, couldn't work out where and how the escalation had happened.

The CCTV showed the police had made only a little headway, as the protesters were still on the steps.

'It's true isn't it?' Sam asked, a tremor in her words. 'Special ops are coming, aren't they?'

'Yes, they're on their way,' Tess assured her. She didn't add that they were coming from Sydney, and still at least six hours away.

•

Something shifted the mood. Steve couldn't discern what. Maybe the use of tasers and spray, although they'd hardly deployed them in the close-quarters confrontations. More likely the arrival of the additional officers. Leah and the recalled locals on the station steps; Inverell cops on the east side of the street; Moree cops on the west. Not a lot of them, but enough to push the remaining hard-core group of protesters on to the street in front of the station and to let an RFS tanker through. Flames shot through the roof of the cafe across the road, its windows smashed, tables and chairs overturned, fridges emptied.

From where he stood on top of the steps he could see the growing barricade at the park. A small group pushed a wheeled freezer from the cafe towards the makeshift wall of park furniture, garbage dumpsters and shopping trolleys.

Leah came to stand beside him, her breathing still heavy from the confrontation. In her dry tone, she commented, 'I wonder if they'll work out that special ops will be coming from the east, behind them, not from here?'

Steve's throat burned from thirst, from whiffs of capsicum spray, from shouting and fighting. 'Let's keep that our secret, for now.'

He must have sounded bad because she cast him one of her shrewd looks. 'Go inside, Steve. Check on your family.'

He nodded. They could do without him here, for now. He'd reached the door when she added over her shoulder, 'By the way, Tess was brilliant. You can tell her I said so.'

Tess was brilliant. Of course she was. A damn fine police officer. Better than he'd ever been.

'The kids are upstairs,' Tom told him as he passed through the foyer. 'Jacob took them a few minutes ago. Out of the way of the ambulance.'

Ambulance. Good. Dee needed it. The new kid with the broken arm probably needed it. Maybe even Arundel.

Post-adrenaline exhaustion: yeah, he had it. He could barely think straight. Fatigue weighed on him and he pushed his energy-depleted body up the stairs with effort. But when Lily saw him at the door of the staff room and rushed into his arms, and Tristan gave one of his rare smiles, he knew he'd do the same thing over and over again if he had to.

Tris's eyes narrowed when he saw his ripped, bloodied shirt. 'You're hurt.'

'No. It's someone else's blood.' Dee's. He hoped she was in the ambulance, and okay. 'But I never liked this shirt. Good reason to toss it, now.'

Good ol' Steve Fraser, keeping it light, joking around and avoiding the hard stuff. Or trying not to worry his nephew? He didn't know anymore. The lad would understand when he saw the bruises that would undoubtedly start showing soon. But at least Lily wouldn't.

He looked beyond his children into the room. Willow was there at the table, and Jasmine. No Tess or Erin.

Behind him Jacob said, 'You should go in and sit down, Sarge, before you fall down.' He'd found a bottle of lemonade somewhere, and a plastic container filled with dried fruit and nuts and several chocolates. Perhaps it was his own snack stash.

While Steve dragged out a chair at the table, Jacob brought cups from the cupboard and put them out with the food on the table. 'Help yourselves,' he said as he left.

Lily leaned close against Steve's side, and he pulled her up onto his lap.

'Have the bad people gone?' she asked.

'The police are chasing them away, honey. You're safe here.'

The large TV in the corner was switched off. Good. These young ones didn't need to see what had happened. What could still happen. They had enough nightmare fodder already, without seeing how close danger had come to them today.

Willow regarded him with uncertainty. 'Are we really? Safe?'

He didn't lie or gild the truth. 'There are a lot of people here now to protect you. The protesters have retreated. The worst should be over.'

Lily lifted her head against his shoulder. 'Are we going to that place you said? Drunggy? To our house?'

The plans he'd made this morning seemed an aeon ago. 'We won't be able to go to Dungirri tonight, unfortunately. We'll have to stay here for another hour or two.' Until the mob had dispersed, its leaders arrested. Until they knew what and who they were dealing with, and where further threats could come from.

Lily had more prosaic questions on her mind. 'Where will we sleep?'

'I'll have to work for a while longer, but when you get tired,' he pointed to the few lounge chairs and sofa at the end of the room, 'you can have a sleep there.' His phone vibrated with a message. Amazing he still had it in his pocket, given the rough action outside. Alec. *Briefing in 15 mins.*

They watched him, Tris and Willow and Jasmine, as if they'd learned that phones rarely communicated good news. He gave them what he hoped was a reassuring smile. 'Another meeting. You guys should get some sleep while you can. It might be a late night.'

Before he shifted Lily off his knee, Simon and Erin arrived. Simon, with a massive parcel of fish and chips, the salty scent wafting from the butcher's paper and making his gut rumble.

'I don't know about anyone else,' Simon announced, deliberately cheerful, 'but I'm starving. And these fish and chips are the best in Strathnairn.'

Trust a soldier to find food in the middle of a battleground. Steve tucked in with everyone else, glad of the hot, filling food. But his gaze kept going to the doorway.

'Tess is downstairs,' Erin said to him quietly. 'The ambulance is about to take Dee to the hospital. She was good for a while, but lost consciousness again. They may have to medevac her out. Tess is phoning Dee's sister to let her know.'

Dee. Bright, always upbeat, competent Dee.

Steve washed the salt and grease off his fingers at the sink and went downstairs to find Tess.

•

The ambulance drove through the gate and one of the police cars from Inverell pulled out in front to escort it, lights flashing.

Tess closed the back door of the station, listening to ensure the lock clicked properly into place. She didn't dare take any chances with security. Not yet.

Emotion welled and she closed her eyes and rested her forehead against the doorframe. Just for a moment. Just to draw some breaths and courage and energy to get through the next few hours. The protesters still roamed the streets. It wasn't over yet.

The soft squeak of rubber soles approaching on the linoleum floor alerted her to someone's presence.

Steve. Steve with a ripped, bloodied shirt sleeve hanging down from a shoulder with a ragged, red scratch mark across it. Steve, who'd kissed her in that last moment before he'd gone out to face the mob.

'How are you doing, Tess?'

'I'm okay. Better than you, by the looks of it.'

'Just a scratch.' The corner of his mouth quirked for just an instant. 'Maybe a bruise. Or two. I've played worse rugby games.'

He might have been telling the truth. She doubted it. But at least most of the blood on his shirt wasn't his. 'A squad car's already taken Sam and the inspector to the hospital. The ambulance has just taken Dee. The rescue helicopter's on its way from Tamworth. They'll fly her to Newcastle.' The lump in her throat clogged her voice.

'She'll be in good hands, Tess.'

'I know.' She dug for her handkerchief and blew her nose. *Pull yourself together, Ballard.*

'I'd offer a hug but you probably wouldn't want it.' He jerked a thumb back at the ripped cloth on his shoulder. 'I should find a clean shirt before the briefing. I've got one in the car. I think.'

She could have done with the hug. She should have offered to check the scratch on his shoulder. Confusion and uncertainty collided with the emotions she'd barely steadied. She turned and pressed her access card against the scanner. Practical action. She could do that. 'You'll be okay to go to the car. There's a team guarding the gate now. I'll see you in the briefing. Make sure the door's locked properly when you come back in.'

Stop babbling. Go. She barely raised her eyes to his as she passed him.

'Tess.'

She stopped mid-step, her black boot stark against the grey lino.

'I apologise for stepping over the line when I kissed you.' The rasp of his voice barely sounded like the Steve she knew. 'I'm the senior officer. I didn't mean to offend you. I'm no threat to you, Tess. I promise you that.'

She remained still, out of her depth, reaching for clear thoughts in the abyss of emotion. No threat? Not physically, no. He'd never hurt her. He'd barely ever touched her, respecting her personal space. It was the wall of reserve around her heart, around herself, that his presence and his considerate attention to her had been dismantling, stone by stone, until now little remained. And she didn't know whether to pick up those stones and rebuild the wall, or let them lie scattered in the grass, undisturbed.

Yet she did know that he hadn't offended her. Surprised her, yes. Confused her, yes. Zac's reappearance in her life and his assaults had sure done a number on her confidence and sense of self.

Steve hadn't moved. She needed to move, to respond. *Get your act together, Tess. You're better than this. Stronger than this. Tougher than this.*

Sucking up courage with oxygen, she lifted her head and faced him. 'You didn't offend me.' Fact one, clearly stated. She *could* do this. 'There's too much going on right now to know for sure what I think, what I feel.' Another fact. He waited, motionless, a bruised warrior. A gentle man. The contrast held no inconsistency. 'But I do know that we're friends, Steve. I value that. I value you. I'm not going to complain about a kiss between friends.'

The lines of his face relaxed, no longer as taut and serious as if he faced a jury. Or a mob. 'Thank you, Tess. I value our friendship, too.' He paused, as if on uncertain ground, searching for words. But his phone buzzed, and hers, and voices sounded in the distance. He gave a wry smile. 'Duty calls. I'll see you in the meeting room shortly.'

Duty. Always duty. Tess walked back through the custody area and along the corridor to the incident room to do the job that defined her sense of self and self-worth. Serve the police force and through it the community. But underneath the beat of her pulse and the habitual mental ordering of tasks and strategies, a small voice chanted, *'What if there's more? What if you can be more than this?'*

No time for that now.

The live news report on the TV as her colleagues gathered showed protesters – *rioters* – running through the main street, some brandishing flaming torches, others throwing rocks through windows, and at least one more business and a vehicle on fire.

•

Tristan waited in the corridor outside the incident room, relief easing his frown when Steve approached.

'Do you want me –' he began, 'in there? In the meeting?'

Through the semi-open door, Steve could see some of them taking their seats – including Erin, Simon, and Simon's mate, McCallum.

'Yes, Tris. Come on in.'

He waved the lad in and they took the vacant chairs beside Tess as Alec opened the briefing. He and Leah and Aaron all showed signs of the confrontation earlier in blossoming bruises and, in Aaron's case, a blood-spattered shirt. Tom was there, too.

'I'll aim to keep this pretty short,' Alec began. 'As you're all aware, it's still fairly wild out there. Nick's continuing to coordinate the police response so he won't be joining us. However, I've invited Erin and Simon to join us, along with Gabe McCallum. Simon and Gabe were instrumental in freeing up access for the ambulance earlier and can contribute some valuable intelligence.'

Steve had heard snatches of comments about a borrowed van. The full story could be interesting.

'Our purpose now is to bring together as much information as we can from the last few hours,' Alec continued, 'to try to establish who is out there, which group or groups they belong to, who the key leaders are, and how they're communicating. This protest began around two this afternoon with a group of people from Serenity Hill. It may have been led or incited by David ben Joshua. But am I correct in saying there have been no confirmed sightings of him?'

He scanned around the table, allowing time for anyone to speak up. No one did.

'Right,' he said, standing by the large whiteboard someone had brought in. Typical Alec, thinking best on his feet with a marker in his hand. Under the heading '*David*' he scrawled, '*Social media – location*'. 'We may be able to pin David's location using his social media postings. We'll prioritise and allocate tasks shortly. Next – the group movements. Tom, Tristan, Erin – you recognised some people from Serenity Hill out the front early on?'

Erin answered, 'Yes. They may have moved around to the side. I saw a couple of people I recognised on the CCTV in both places.'

'Simon, you and Gabe had contact with that group. What can you tell us?'

Simon leaned on the table. 'Most of them were Joshua's crowd. After I picked Gabe up from the motel on the edge of town, we came in past the showground and saw a van parking there beside two others. A light commercial delivery-type truck, about three tonnes, similar to the one at Serenity Hill. People got out from the back, dressed like the Serenity Hill folk. We waited a little further up, and they walked past, up towards the park and here. When Tess said the access gate needed clearing, we went back and –' he shot a crooked grin at Alec, 'borrowed one of the vans. Drove right up to them and told them the riot police were coming with tear gas and David wanted them to get to safety. There were around thirty-five of them, already jittery. Most didn't need any persuading.'

Steve could almost have cheered the audacity, but Alec raised an eyebrow. 'I presume,' he said drily, 'that they're not still locked in the back of a van?'

'No. We drove them up to the highway, handed over the keys to a guy who could drive the truck, and told them to get to a safe place while we "rescued" more people. They turned west on to the highway.'

'They didn't recognise either of you?'

'No. We kept a low profile and mostly stayed in the shadows at Serenity Hill on Sunday and hardly anyone saw us there.'

'Good. Tess, what were your observations about the protesters?'

'The majority of them weren't Joshua's people,' Tess said. 'Early on, yes, maybe up to a hundred of them. But the later ones – the violent ones – they were all in off-the-rack clothes. And the photos of me, the placards – someone's been printing those. Enlarging the photo and printing it on an A3 printer. Some of the captions were printed, not painted.'

'Tess is right,' Steve said. 'We know David's been using social media. But he couldn't have manipulated the situation into that so quickly, could he? Two hundred people showing up in Strathnairn on a Wednesday evening?'

'In Sydney you might get that kind of spontaneous crowd,' Leah said. 'Maybe even Newcastle or Wollongong, but Strathnairn's seven, eight hours drive away from Sydney.'

Alec's phone chimed and he took a moment to check it. 'Okay, I've just confirmed one lead. I thought I recognised a face from Sydney. A guy at the front of the crowd. He was a small-time anarchist a few years ago. I asked a colleague to run a search on him and apparently he's been ranting about Joshua Kristos's death for days. There was mention of a possible protest against the "murderous police state" yesterday. It seems Joshua had some following in anarchist circles, too.'

Tess's brow furrowed in thought. 'Rejection of established authority and freedom of the individual. You could interpret some of Joshua's teachings that way, I guess.'

Tristan leaned forward, half raised a hand.

Alec saw it. 'Yes, Tristan?'

Steve gave him an encouraging nod.

'The police state will attempt to crush us one day,' Tris said nervously. 'I remember Joshua saying that sometimes. I never understood what he meant, though.'

Alec added '*Anarchism connection?*' to the whiteboard. 'Thanks, Tristan. That's helpful.'

Tess gave Tristan a gentle smile, and partly in answer to him, as much as to the rest of them, she added, 'Instilling fear of authorities or fear of outsiders is a tactic that leaders like Joshua use to bind a group together. If people are afraid of the world outside, they won't want to leave the group. But it's also a way of keeping a group's activities – even its existence – hidden.'

'There's plenty wrong with the government,' Steve added, 'but it sure isn't a police state.'

Alec laid his phone back on the table. 'Insufficient police resources, to start with. You can't run a jackboot police state when you're struggling to fill basic staffing. Organised crime is better resourced than we are.'

'The protesters are pretty well resourced, too,' Leah said. 'Not just printed placards. Plenty of phone cameras among them. They've been uploading pictures and videos online. Select shots of cops with batons, people affected by pepper spray, a guy who'd been tasered. We're such a brutal mob,' she added with caustic sarcasm.

Alec ran them through a few more questions, allocated some tasks. That done, he continued. 'Steve, Tess, Erin, Simon – I'm concerned about your safety. And yours, Tristan, and the others. It may be a few hours until you can leave the station, but we need to find a secure location for you all.'

Steve agreed, but couldn't think where. Not the motel, with the mob still out on the streets. He was too tired to drive to Dungirri. Tess would be, too.

'Riverbank,' Erin said. 'It's a National Parks property, about twenty kilometres west of Goodabri. An old homestead we're doing up as a lodge. It's not ready for the public yet, but there are beds there, and room for all of us.'

'I've been there, sir,' Aaron said to Alec. 'There's only one access road. If we can spare a car for the turn-off and maybe one for the driveway, well, it won't be perfect, but probably as secure as anywhere else in the district for now.'

'Tess? Simon? You both know the place? Do you agree?'

Simon nodded slowly. 'Yeah. As Aaron said, not perfect. But not many people know it's there. If we can get out of here without being followed, it'd be long odds for anyone to find us there. Gabe, you want to come, too? The more, the better.'

Steve was pleased that the taciturn man nodded. That would make two police officers, two ex-commandos and a park ranger. A pretty good team under the circumstances, to protect the girls and Tristan. And each other.

'I don't know the place well,' Tess said, 'but it is out of the way. I agree it's probably the answer, at least for tonight.'

'Should I go there, too?' Tom asked.

Alec considered the question for several seconds, exchanging a glance with Leah. 'We'd prefer you to stay here, if you're willing, Tom. Your experience of the functioning and structure of Joshua's group could be critical in helping us to resolve this situation.'

Tom nodded, without argument, and slumped back in his chair.

They'd almost wrapped up when another news report began on the muted TV screen, the dramatic images capturing everyone's attention. A panning shot showed more burning cars down the street from the station. Alec found the remote and enabled the sound.

The reporter talked breathlessly about protesters still running amok around town, and terrified residents staying indoors. The camera zoomed in on a small group in a park, a guy waving a burning flag at the end of a pole.

Steve's breath stopped. Not a flag. An effigy.

He heard Tess's gasp beside him.

The flames licked around a stuffed paper bag made to look like a head, with a face pasted on it. Tess's face. Tess's face with a black witch's hat flopping above it.

But the shot lasted only a moment before the camera focused on the grinning guy maniacally waving the effigy.

Zac Matthias.

Fury roared in his head and clouded his vision. 'That's him on the TV. Zac Matthias. He's in the park. Now.' He had just enough presence of mind to touch Tess's white fist on the table before he bolted out the door after Leah, Aaron and Alec.

CHAPTER 13

In the break room Jasmine and Lily slept curled together in the largest armchair, and Willow on the sofa. Tristan dozed fitfully in another armchair.

Erin had gone with Simon and Gabe to collect some supplies and bedding from her place, if they could get there safely.

Tess had her laptop open on the table and tried to work while she watched over the young ones and waited for news.

So much didn't make sense yet. The relationship between the anarchists and Joshua's followers. Whether there was any connection between Zac and the anarchists. And what connections, if any, there were between David ben Joshua's social media blitz this morning, and the riot late this afternoon. She'd watched the media reports and he'd not shown up on any of them. But the protests had focused on the 'murder' of his father, and the coincidence of the timing, the similar language and claims, strongly suggested a connection.

The similarities made her increasingly uneasy. If David ben Joshua had the semi-organised and better resourced anarchists under his influence as well as Joshua's Simple Bliss communities, it gave him far more power than his father had ever held.

The fluorescent light overhead glared on the screen and Tess blinked her tired eyes to focus more clearly while she typed in Joshua's website address. The page loaded more quickly than she expected. She'd navigated through the site days ago, searching for information about Joshua. A clunky, old-fashioned design using frames and slow-loading images. But there'd been no images of Joshua, and no videos, only his audio lectures and links for his books. Whoever had designed the earlier pages was fifteen years out of date in web design.

But the page that loaded now was sleek, streamlined and professional. An image of David and his father on the front page, Joshua's face in a softened profile looking at his son, so that the viewer's eye fell on David's face in full profile. Movie-star attractive, with dark wavy hair falling below his shoulders, ocean blue eyes, a contemplative smile. And thirty or more years younger than Joshua. The new order taking over from the old. And something in that flawless, masculine face made her think that if Joshua hadn't been dead when they took him from the rock, he would be by now.

She pushed her chair back from the table and stood to stretch her tired muscles, tense from too much activity, too much stress and too little sleep.

The red light from the fire in the cafe still glowed through the window across the room; the cafe where she'd had lunch with Erin, just a day ago.

She dared not go closer to the window to see down to ground level better. The flicker of flames haunted her enough already. The woolshed on Sunday. The cafe and burning cars today. Zac's paper-bag effigy, with flames burning the image of her face.

She rubbed her arms, the air conditioning cold on the goosebumps on her skin.

Firm, fast footsteps approached. One person.

Steve stopped in the doorway, his eyes bearing the news before he found words to tell her.

'You didn't arrest him,' she said flatly.

'No. I'm sorry, Tess.' He took a few steps in. 'We chased him across the park, but there was a car waiting for him. White. Possibly David's Subaru. We were on foot and too far from the vehicle to pursue. Alec's put a call out but . . .'

She understood the rest of the unfinished sentence. Not much chance, with the chaos on the streets. She hadn't realised how much she'd hoped for Zac's arrest until it didn't happen. Her body started to shake, and she couldn't stop it. Stupid that she couldn't stop it. It was just a reaction. A physiological reaction to holding herself together for so long, alone.

'You know that hug you offered earlier?' The shaking affected her words, and she tried to smile at him like a friend and probably didn't succeed. 'I could do with it now. If that's okay with you.'

In an instant he drew her to him, and she wrapped her arms around his waist and rested her cheek against his shoulder, his body solid and warm against hers. His heartbeat sounded under her cheek, his first uneven breaths slowing into evenness along with hers as they stood there, together.

Despite the unfamiliarity, the vulnerability of being so close to a strong man, her muscles relaxed a little and the paralysing fear loosened its grip around her body.

'I'll be all right in a minute,' she murmured, but she didn't want to leave the strength, the security he gave her.

'It's okay, Tess,' he said. 'Take all the time you want. It's been a damned rough week.'

His arms tightened a little more around her, and he rested his face lightly against her hair. A rough week, yes. But for him even more than for her. She shouldn't draw any more strength from him . . . *Compassion generates its own energy.* She'd read that once, although she'd never understood it or believed it, until now.

Could she give comfort, strength, to him? She didn't know how, other than holding him the way he held her. And the awareness of her own pleasure in their closeness, of the stirring of desire within her, left her unsure of what she *should* do, of what she wanted to do right now.

But Simon's voice carried along the corridor and Willow whimpered in her sleep and Tess drew away from Steve reluctantly.

'Tess . . .' He reached out a hand, touched the side of her face in a gentle caress. 'Thank you for—' Words didn't come easily for him, either. 'For giving me your trust,' he finished, as Erin and Simon arrived, and the brief moment alone together ended.

They had to pack up, get everyone to Riverbank, get things organised and the kids settled for the remainder of the night out there.

There'd be no time to sort out the state of her emotions or her heart for a while yet.

•

They drove in convoy the sixty kilometres through the darkness to the Riverbank homestead. The lights of the three cars ahead of him illuminated the bends in the back roads and helped Steve concentrate, despite his fatigue. The police escort car, Simon's LandCruiser, then Tess's station wagon, with Gabe's utility bringing up the rear behind him.

Lily slept soundly in the back seat, Pooky tucked in under the seatbelt with her. Tristan, sitting beside Steve in the front passenger seat, seemed determined to stay awake, and between them they finished off the last packet of potato chips from the police station vending machine. Tomorrow, if it was safe enough to go into Goodabri, he'd buy vegetables. Heaps of them. Healthy vegetables and fruit and low-fat protein to counteract the junk food of the past few days.

Carefree bachelor to responsible guardian in less than a week.

Overworked detective to time-rich man on extended leave in less than a week.

Single man with no attachments to a man more than halfway in love with a policewoman with haunting, silver-grey eyes and no need for a relationship-failure like himself. In less than a week.

Throw in finding and losing his sister, having to arrange a new home, and worrying how to keep the kids, Tess and himself safe from potentially hundreds of deluded cult followers . . . oh, yeah, no wonder his brain spun madly and wouldn't shut up.

'Could I make a video?' Tristan asked out of the blue. He'd been silent, deep in thought, for ages.

A teenage boy interested in technology. No surprise there. He'd probably be chewing through data playing online games by the end of the week.

'Making a video is relatively easy,' Steve explained. 'A phone like mine can do a basic one. I've got software on my laptop you can use to edit it. What kind of video do you want to make?'

'One like David's. Except telling the truth. I thought maybe they'd listen. Because I'm Joshua's son, too.'

Shit. Not so simple. 'Tris, technically you could. But that kind of thing – it gets really complicated. I think it's best if we keep you right off social media for now. There are millions of really weird people out there and I don't want you to become a target of them.'

'But people who knew Joshua need to know what really happened.'

'They will. It will take some time, though. It's an open police investigation and DCI Goddard and his team are gathering evidence so that anyone who's committed a crime will be charged and tried in court before a jury. Evidence helps us prove that crimes occurred beyond reasonable doubt.'

'Will David go to jail?'

'Quite probably. As long as we can find evidence to convince a jury that he has committed crimes.' Steve spoke with more confidence than he held. No one had seen David at the riot. They might charge him with assault and rape – but that would be Willow's word against David's. Murder? The police would need to find physical evidence on Rebecca's body, and witness statements pinning David to her killing. Interfering with a dead body? Except David had sent others to move Joshua. The manufacturing of crystal meth? No, nothing definitive found in the machinery shed to prove ice was even made there, let alone David's involvement in it.

The guy might walk scot-free, laughing at the police.

Thank the universe and Maddie that Tristan was totally unlike his half-brother.

Another kilometre went by under the wheels, and a question that had been niggling him rose to the surface. There were eleven years between Tristan and Lily. Hayley didn't have children other than Jasmine, and she was Simon's daughter. Sybilla apparently didn't have children. Willow didn't have children.

'Tristan, how many children are Joshua's? How many siblings do you have?'

'I don't know. There's David, and Fleur and Rory. Tamara's their mother. Fleur and Rory were at the hospital.'

A girl about Jasmine's age, and a curly-haired toddler. The kids who'd been taken from the hospital the night Madeleine was killed. The night the Bliss people packed up and left Serenity Hill.

David, about twenty, Fleur thirteen-ish, Rory two-ish. Big age gaps for a committed sexual partnership.

'Sybilla had Melody,' Tristan added, 'but she got the coughing sickness and she died. She was only little. Younger than Lily.'

Whooping cough? Immunisations for both Lily and Tristan were on his urgent to-do list. He'd make an appointment with the doctor in Birraga. But Sybilla had been with Joshua for around ten years. Ten years and one child.

'What about in the other communities?' he asked. 'Do you know of any siblings with other mothers?'

'At the old place – before we moved to Serenity Hill – there's a boy, Harrison, and a girl, Rhiannon. They're a bit younger than me. Their mother left when they were little, though. I don't remember her and nobody talked about people who left. I think there are other children, but I don't know them.'

Six sisters in each community, Maddie had said. Four communities, according to Tom. Twenty-four women, give or take a few over the years. Some of the women had been with him for close on two decades. A man could have fathered a whole lot of progeny in that time, but Joshua hadn't. Condoms? Low sex drive? Low sperm count? Whatever the reason, it didn't matter now.

David claimed to be the eldest son. It might be just as well there wasn't a whole tribe of others, looking to him for leadership.

The vehicles ahead slowed and indicated for the turn-off into the national park. Lily woke with the change in speed.

'Are we there yet?' she asked.

Typical kid. He'd better get used to it. 'We're just turning in to the national park now. We'll be there soon.'

Riverbank was only about ten minutes away. But safety, healing and normalcy . . . they all still had a long, long road ahead of them.

•

Tess opened her eyes to bright sunlight and the cheerful bubbling of a child's laughter somewhere nearby. Her quilt over her, the wooden slats of a bunk bed above her . . . it took a moment for her brain to wake up and recognise her surroundings.

Riverbank. A bunk room in the homestead that she'd shared with Willow and the younger girls. Lily's bed was empty, and Jasmine's top bunk. But she could hear Willow's breathing from the bunk above.

She checked her watch, reluctant to disturb Willow if it was still early, and had to look at it twice to see if the second hand was moving or if it had stopped last night. Ten thirty. She retrieved her phone from the floor beside the bed to confirm it. Yes. Ten thirty-one. She hadn't slept this late in years.

She rose as quietly as she could, reaching for her jeans.

'I'm awake,' Willow said. She lay on her side, the sheet clutched under her chin. She'd cried not long ago, a tear still damp on her cheek.

'How are you doing?' Tess asked. 'Did you sleep?'

'I'm okay.' She sniffed, another tear escaping. 'I'm just . . . thinking. It's quiet here, and I have to sort it out. In my head.'

Quiet time to reflect and make sense of the nightmare. She'd need it.

Tess placed her hand over the young woman's. 'Willow, I've been somewhere like you are now. I felt so lost, and everything was unfamiliar. It took me time to find my way. But you're not alone, and we're all here to help and support you while you find your path.'

Willow's fingers gripped hers. 'Does it stop hurting so much?'

She could almost see herself in Willow's troubled eyes. 'Yes, it eases. It's like a cut that heals with a white scar. It never totally goes away, it's part of you, but you're so much more than that.'

Senior constable, quilter, friend . . . and whatever she was to Steve, and he to her. The scar of the terrified seventeen-year-old who'd run from Zac and his father and the sect into a cold mountain winter remained, but yes, she'd become so much more than that, and it no longer defined her.

'Stay here in the quiet if you want to. Would you like me to bring you in a cup of tea? Or some water?'

'No. Thank you. I'll come out in a little while.'

Mulling over her own thoughts, Tess left Willow in peace. She'd told more people in this past week about her early life than she'd ever told in sixteen years. And now her friends, Steve and Erin and Simon, had taken others as lost as she'd been under their care. Willow, Tristan, Jasmine and even little Lily had to learn to understand this new world.

Perhaps she could help. Her experiences and the strengths she'd eventually found through her own struggles had given her an understanding of the challenges, emotional, social and practical. It wasn't exactly within her police duties, but she could be more than a police officer.

In the kitchen with its too-bright 1970s curtains and orange tiles, she made coffee and, following the shouts of laughter, found an impromptu game of backyard cricket underway in the side paddock. Not a particularly skilled one, but Steve helped Lily bat while Simon showed his daughter how to bowl and everyone whooped when bat and ball actually connected. When Tristan had a go with the bat, he even gave Erin and Gabe some exercise in the outfield.

Nobody kept score.

Nobody heard the car approach until a door slammed shut.

Tess beat Simon around to the front of the house by seconds.

Leah Haddad stood beside her car.

The relief after the burst of panic made Tess's head spin.

Leah held up her open hands. 'It's okay. Just me. And the car at the corner demanded my ID before they let me through.'

The adults gathered around the kitchen table while Tristan and the girls retreated to the shade of the back veranda with some books.

Leah accepted some coffee from Simon. 'I've got some good news to start with. We've arrested eight people in relation to the riot. Special ops rounded up forty others and are escorting their bus back to Sydney. There was another busload, apparently from the Central Coast. I wouldn't have thought that a hotbed for radical anarchists but I guess it's rampant suburbia there these days. The vans Simon reported seeing at the showground were all gone by the time we got there. Seems like Joshua's crowd didn't want to hang around for the fireworks.'

'What's the bad news?' Steve asked before Tess did.

Leah didn't sugarcoat it. 'We didn't find Zac Matthias. Or David ben Joshua. And nobody's had any time to find out much more. Nick ordered most of the locals home this morning after eighteen straight hours of active duty. There's a skeleton crew of out-of-towners on today.'

'You could do with Steve and I back on duty,' said Tess. She could go back, but Steve couldn't easily, not with Lily and Tristan.

Leah scotched that idea flat. 'Hell, no. But if you want to do some online research while you're twiddling your thumbs out here in the sticks, let me know what you find.'

'We can do that,' Steve said. 'Courtesy of National Parks internet connection.'

Leah drank some more coffee and checked the time on her phone. 'I'll have to go back soon, but there are a few things I wanted to update you all on, face to face. First up, there's no sign of Joshua's body at Serenity Hill. Forensics are running DNA samples from the blood found on the rock, but results aren't in yet.' Her tone softened. 'Simon, the preliminary autopsy report on Hayley is in. Not much we didn't already know, but they did find tissue under her fingernails. There are also partial prints on the knife that aren't yours or hers. We've got nothing to match them with, yet. But we may eventually get answers on that, and it will be clear evidence as to who killed her.'

Simon clasped Erin's hand on the table. 'Thank you. That's good to know.'

Leah checked some notes on her phone. 'I've got other reports to sift through, and data still to come in. While Forensics were out with Rebecca's body yesterday – it was just yesterday, wasn't it? Anyway, they found Callie, too. Post-mortems on both of them, maybe tomorrow. Along with the woman, Tamara. What else is there . . .'

Steve cleared his throat. 'Maddie?'

Leah met his gaze. 'Only what we expected. Death due to impact injuries. There are tests still to analyse but other than being underweight, she appears to have been healthy.'

Tess brought her laptop into the kitchen after Leah left. The others had gone outside again, but Steve stood by the kitchen window, staring out.

'It seems like we've got some work to do,' she said.

He turned slowly, eyes bleak. 'Let's just leave it for an hour or two, can we? Do some normal things for the kids. There are sausages we can barbecue. Some movies we can watch. We don't have to leave here today, and they need something – we all need something – that's not tied up with death and violence.'

•

The afternoon of peace cleared some of the whirl in his head, let him think clearly again. Nothing was normal; his previous 'normal' had been relegated to history, over and past, and until he had them all safe there couldn't be a new 'normal', but gradually the insistent voices of apprehension in his head and the adrenalin-charged drive to investigate and find answers quietened a little, sometimes for minutes at a time. Quiet enough for him to focus on Tristan and Lily and their need to be safe and reassured and to forget, for even a short while, that danger still threatened them. The other adults, even Gabe, shared the same priority, and with games outside and an early barbecue for the evening meal before a Wallace and Gromit movie, there'd been laughter, and fun, and Tristan, Willow and Jasmine no longer looked quite so guarded and wary. Lily asked question after question, ate heartily, watched the movie wide-eyed until the notion of make-believe clicked and she giggled until the end, and fell asleep before Steve finished reading her a bedtime story.

And all afternoon, he was grateful for Tess's presence nearby, an easiness developing between them that he hadn't realised he'd craved so much. Although never on their own, they connected through concern for the young ones, and shared laughter and tasks as together they prepared a light supper for everyone.

He'd fallen for her, totally and completely. None of the other women he'd been involved with – fewer than most people believed – had ever touched his emotions the way Tess did. And at some level, at least, she liked him. Damned if he knew why. But he had Tristan and Lily now and a new life to build and no solid foundation to offer her anything. And he couldn't rest easy, relax, until they were all safe.

For an hour after everyone else had gone to bed, he and Tess worked at the kitchen table. Or rather, Tess worked, and he tried to keep his eyes and his concentration on his own research but he was constantly aware of her there, across the table, brow furrowed as she typed search terms intermittently, and jotted occasional notes on the writing pad beside her.

'Bingo,' Tess murmured after a period of silent research. She looked up from the laptop screen and had to blink to refocus her eyes. But her smile beamed with triumph. 'You'll want to look at this. David's been a busy young man. And he has some rather interesting friends.'

He came around to look over her shoulder, bracing a hand against the back of her chair as he bent to see the screen.

'Okay, here's David ben Joshua's profile.' She pointed to a date with the cursor. 'Only new, started on Monday.'

Her nearness scrambled his thoughts but he straightened out a thread to make sense of her point. 'The day after his father presumably died.'

'Yes. But look here, at the people he's linked to. Christopher Sinclair is one of them. I'll get to him in a minute. But here's an interesting profile – Anarky Dave. Anarky's been around for a year or so, on a few sites. Anarky is the first one to post about Joshua's death, the first one to use inflammatory language, and the first one to call for protest action. Yesterday morning he started reposting David's posts with added anarchist commentary. He's only a kindergarten anarchist, though. Not a lot of depth or familiarity with anarchist political theory or history, and he's not connected to the major groups.'

Startled, Steve dragged his gaze away from the screen to see if she was joking. 'You're familiar with anarchist political theory?'

She continued to focus on the computer, her face serious. 'I studied some in political science at uni. Interesting theories.

Unfortunately they don't work so well in practice.' As if she noticed his surprise, she gave him a quick grin, her eyes sparkling with amusement. 'Relax, I wouldn't be a cop if I believed in anarchism. Now, here, we have an older, less active profile. Dave Kay-Haitch.'

He snapped his thoughts away from Tess, intelligent, knowledge-hungry Tess studying political science, and back to the topic at hand. 'Kristos Hollywell?'

'It fits. Dave Kay-Haitch is also friends with Christopher Sinclair. And Christopher Sinclair is connected to this lady, Marianna Sinclair. None of them have actual profile photos, but look, young Dave posted a happy holiday snap about three years ago and linked to them.' She clicked on the image link. 'A lovely family photo on someone's rather nice yacht.'

The image loaded slowly. Steve whistled as the first faces became clear. 'That's Joshua. And Mary. And there's our David, too. But that last guy I don't know.' Younger than Mary, in his twenties maybe. Young enough to be Mary's son. Or her husband, if she went for younger men. Except she lounged in a deck chair beside Joshua in a way that suggested intimacy.

Tess rose to her feet and stretched her arms up high. 'Mary Saint, Marianna Sinclair,' she said as she loosened stiff muscles. 'A contraction of Saint Clair. I haven't found out much about Christopher, yet, but he has a plane and a pilot's licence.'

Another link of Joshua's network clicked into place. Steve could have whooped. 'Tom mentioned one of the bodyguards, Christopher, flies a Cessna. He flies Joshua and Mary around.'

'Handy, having a pilot in the family,' Tess commented. 'I wonder what the relationship between Christopher and Mary/Marianna is? Didn't you say the Feds were looking into a woman who could be her? Now we've got another name to give to them. Another two names, since Christopher seems to be involved with her.'

'And more leads to follow to find David and Zac.' The dread weighing him down lightened somewhat. They might crack this case yet. Thanks in a large part to Tess's contribution. 'You are planning to become a detective, I hope.'

She pulled the clip off of her ponytail and her hair settled around her shoulders as she shook her head. 'Not at this point. Front line works for me. Prevention rather than investigation.'

'You're pretty darned amazing, Tess Ballard. Remind me to tell you that sometime.'

'Just doing my job,' she said, but she held his gaze, as if asking for understanding.

And he did understand. Being a police officer was central to her sense of self, more than it was for him. He'd joined because three generations of Fraser men had served in the police force before him, and he'd stayed to prove himself to his father. Maybe, in part, to prove himself to himself, especially the past few years, and yes, he was proud of what he did, of the police officer he'd eventually become. But Tess had joined out of choice, and served with dedication, and she made a damn fine officer.

He risked touching a finger, feather light, to the soft blush of pink that rose on her cheek. He thought she might be startled, pull away from his touch. Instead, her fingers brushed the back of his wrist, as light a caress as he gave her.

He cleared his throat. 'The women I've liked have all had the good sense to fall for better men than me.' Like Bella, who'd left him years before she met Alec Goddard. And Jenn, who'd never looked twice at him. But what he'd felt for them came nowhere near the power or complexity of his feelings for Tess.

Her beautiful grey eyes, silver like moonlight on water, held him captive. 'When I first met you, I thought you might be one of the self-important, cocky jerks that sometimes gravitate to detective. They bring out the worst in me. But although you sometimes pretend you are, in truth you're not like that at all. And you deserve honesty.'

Uh-oh. He braced himself for *Nice guy, but* . . .

It didn't come. Her hand closed over his wrist, his hand, and she held his palm against her cheek. He took the risk of another gentle caress with his thumb, and she smiled gently and leaned into his hand.

'I'm not sure what I'm doing,' she said softly 'Why me, why you, why now. I didn't want to like you at first. My relationships with men haven't been exactly sterling. But you're not them.' She gave a small, self-conscious laugh. 'And I'm probably talking too much but I need to work it through. You're not them. You're dedicated, and honest, and courageous, and I want to be courageous and take the risk to find out more about you. About the possibility of us.'

The possibility of him and Tess . . . With so much uncertain, he wanted to believe, even if just for a short time, that the possibility existed. It awed and humbled him that she trusted him enough to lower her habitual guard, emotional and physical.

She trusted him. He wasn't sure he deserved it but he wanted to believe he'd become the man she believed him to be. He closed the small space between them and she moved into his embrace, her head against his shoulder, her arms around him. And once more, as in the police station last night, the unfamiliar sense of rightness flowed through him.

They held each other for a long moment before he found words to express a fraction of the thoughts in his head.

'Do you remember last Friday night at the charity ball in Goodabri?' he said quietly. 'You wore a dress the colour of moonlight. I always seem to think of you as moonlight. I didn't ask you to dance, and that wasn't because we were trying to find out more about Hayley's murder. I didn't ask you to dance because it was the first time I'd seen you out of uniform, with your hair soft, and that dress made you look like a goddess. You took my breath away.' She still took his breath away, and for want of other words he fell back on good ol' Steve Fraser's humour. 'We already had enough to worry about without me gaping like an idiot and succumbing to asphyxia on the dance floor.'

He felt the vibration of her laughter against his chest.

She lifted her head and murmured, 'And there I was thinking you looked as cool and calm as James Bond in your dinner suit.'

'I had to hire it. Not my usual attire. Took me half an hour to get the cufflinks in.'

Her eyes shone with her smile, with pleasure and trust and the warmth of desire, and he almost wished he had Bond's smoothness with women before he instantly dismissed that as too facile, not sincere enough nor respectful enough for a woman like Tess. Not sincere enough for what she meant to him.

'If you tell me to stop, I'll stop. I always will, Tess. No means no. Any decent man knows that.'

'I know you know that,' she said, and she touched his mouth with hers and kissed him. She tasted of coffee and the chocolate from the station vending machine they'd finished off tonight, and hope and peace.

Peace. Now that was an unexpected word.

He held back, afraid his need might be too much, that he might be clumsy, and this was Tess who deserved every gentleness and care and no reminders of Zac or the pastor or anyone.

But she drew his face down to hers and explored his mouth with hers and their kiss deepened and deepened until he had to draw back, breathless. He rested his forehead against hers, and she cradled his face between her hands.

'Steve,' she said. 'Don't be afraid. You won't hurt me and I want this. We need this, both of us.'

'I'm not good enough for you.' The harsh whisper felt as though it came from roots buried years, decades inside himself.

She brushed his mouth with hers again. 'You are more than good enough,' she whispered.

Her trust flowed like a salve over his doubts.

'One day,' he promised her, 'I will make love with you and show you how beautiful you are, to me.'

A shadow flittered across her face and for a heart-stopping moment he feared he'd misread her thoughts, gone too far.

The warmth of her palm on his heart, and the honesty of her candid gaze allayed that fear. 'There's an empty double room. Stay with me tonight, Steve. There's no knowing what tomorrow will bring, but we have now, and I want to be with you now.'

His heart thudding, he kissed her, long and sweet and slow, giving her time to change her mind. To be sure. But eventually she stepped back, her breath uneven and her shy smile full of promise while she closed her laptop, and led him out of the kitchen. At the door of the women's bunk room she stopped, nodding down towards the open door at the end of the corridor.

'I'll meet you there,' she whispered.

In the bunk room where Tristan and Gabe slept, where he'd slept last night, he rummaged quietly in the dark for the small box he kept in his washbag, more out of hope than actual need. Until now. He closed the door silently behind him.

Her bare feet silent on the wooden floorboards, Tess carried a bundle in her arms, and he held the door of the empty room open for her. She dropped a sheet, and the quilt he'd glimpsed on her bed, days ago, on to the double bed. Without words – how could he have found words for this moment? – he helped her spread them over the mattress protector.

Moonlight angled through the wooden venetian blinds on the window and it seemed a sign. Tess and moonlight. It touched her skin with silver, danced over the rich colours and patterns of her quilt.

Its soft light illuminated them both as they undressed, slowly, discovering, caressing, touching and tasting. She tasted the light between shadows on his chest, on his stomach. When they lay side by side, her hair dark against the sheet, her eyes reflected the moonlight, and he kissed her face and traced the lines of light and shadow on her body with his hands, his mouth, his tongue. The desire to love her, to cherish her and give her pleasure, overrode his own physical hunger.

He kept his control on his desire and watched her face, determined not to frighten her, but he only saw her eyes darken in passion, her lips part in breathlessness, and when her hands gripped his hips and drew him towards her, insistent, he finally stopped thinking and joined with her, holding her tightly and as need and passion bound them together, kissing her on the mouth to quieten their cries as release crashed over them in wave after wave of ecstasy.

Afterwards, when he surfaced and became aware of the cool air on his skin, he pulled up her quilt, and he held her in his arms underneath its warmth while she slept. Eventually he slept, too, deep and peaceful.

Lily called out in the small hours, scared by a nightmare, and Steve rose without disturbing Tess and dragged clothes on and grabbed his phone before he found his niece in the corridor, sobbing quietly. He took her into the lounge room and she snuggled under his arm and returned to sleep.

Wide awake now, his thoughts raced with the desperate need to ensure the safety of his family, and of Tess. He wanted there to be a chance, a possible future, for Tess and him. If anything happened to any of them, he'd be shattered forever. While Lily dreamed of happier things he pulled out his phone and continued his search for answers.

•

Tess woke before sunrise. Steve hadn't returned. She'd heard him, earlier, speaking in soothing tones to Lily. She pulled on her clothes and went in search of him, and found him asleep on the sofa, Lily protected under his wing. The gentleness with which he held his niece showed the heart of him. A different gentleness to the tenderness with which he'd made love with Tess in the night, but no less a demonstration of his capacity to give of himself and to love. It took a special kind of courage to do what he'd done – accept the sudden responsibility of Tristan and Lily – and he'd done it wholeheartedly, with grace and no complaint. He might doubt himself sometimes, but she'd never respected a man more. Never liked a man more than him. Never desired a man, wanted to make love with a man, more than with Steve.

Wide awake now, she went out onto the veranda. The pearl-grey light of dawn drifted over the still paddocks, soft and dreamlike. Very little stirred. A kangaroo and joey grazed beyond the fence. A flock of small birds twittered in a kurrajong tree.

Peaceful, quiet, the beginning of a fresh new day. Anticipation hummed within her. A good morning. A good day to make progress on the case, to further explore her relationship with Steve, to unfurl the woman within her, the woman she could be.

A white station wagon came down the road, slowing as it passed the turn to the house. Stopping. A Subaru, or something similar. Like the car David had driven. But there were thousands, tens of thousands of those on the roads. And there should be a patrol car at the turn-off, checking any vehicles to come this way.

The veranda gave her a good view down the dirt road, which continued past the homestead to a fishing spot by the river. Probably just a fisherman or a tourist with an early start, heading back east, driving slowly to see the scenery.

The boards of the veranda cool on her bare feet, she headed to the bathroom on the corner. When she returned a few minutes later, the light had an apricot tinge and she paused again, leaning on the veranda railing. To the east, the glow of the rising sun tipped the tops of the trees with gold . . . and reflected off the rear window of the white car, parked again at the corner.

She ran to wake Steve, but the car had already gone, disappearing down the east road in a cloud of dust.

•

Steve phoned Strathnairn immediately but with no radio, they had to wait ten minutes for answers to be relayed back.

The police car at the turn-off had pursued a van answering the description of the Serenity Hill one, acting suspiciously. They'd lost it, and hadn't seen the Subaru.

Tess studied the map on the kitchen table. 'There's no one on duty at Goodabri with me not there. And fat chance of a patrol car being out this far from anywhere at this hour of the morning.'

Steve put the coffee he'd made in front of her but remained standing, too worked up to sit. 'Let's just hope they're stupid enough to go back to Strathnairn for breakfast.'

If Alec, or highway patrol, could arrest Zac . . . The thought skidded into a dead end. They didn't know if it was Zac, or David, or even anyone connected with Joshua's group. In dull light from two hundred metres away, Tess had only seen a car similar to David's.

So why did his gut keep screaming that it was Zac *and* David?

Because Zac had a phone, and so did David. Not a lot to go on. But Zac wanted something badly – Tess – and that made him a good candidate to be used and manipulated by a smarter man. And David could well have learned a lot about manipulation from his father, and given it a more contemporary twist.

The video David had posted late last night – the video Steve had watched in the small hours of the morning on the sofa with Lily – showed the young man expressing dismay at the violence of the riot, and distancing himself and Joshua's followers from involvement. They followed the path of peace and bliss, he insisted, not violence. It came across innocently and sincerely enough on the surface. Because most people didn't know that David ben Joshua was also Anarky Dave, ardently recruiting people for the protests across multiple social media channels and advocating violent opposition to the police. He presented two very different personas to the world. Two identities, each manipulating truth and fiction and the people who believed in him, for his own ends.

The sounds of running water, of voices, drifted from the bedrooms. The others were waking and dressing. Within minutes they'd be gathering here and he still didn't have answers.

His phone beeped with a message. Alec, replying to the text he'd dashed off a few minutes ago. And the words on the screen provided a possible answer to the gnawing question of how their location had been discovered: *Tom left sometime yesterday afternoon. No one saw him go.*

The trust he'd given Tom might have proved to be a huge mistake.

Tess shot to her feet when he showed her the message. 'I'll go and get my things. I'll have to leave here.'

He paused her flight with a hand on her arm. 'Let's wait a little while and see if Alec finds them. If he doesn't, we might all have to leave. But we don't have to rush off just yet.'

She held firm, unconvinced. 'But it's me Zac's after. It's me the others want.'

'Yes. But it's you, and me, and Tristan and Lily that David wants.'

'Tristan and Lily?'

Weariness washed over him. If he could just go back, back to last night and that short time when they'd held each other, and when the resolution of the case had seemed closer. Before he'd sat wide awake in the darkness with Lily, and turned his restless thoughts into further research to protect them all.

'There was another video on David's website overnight,' he told her. 'He says he's gathering the children of Joshua. Joshua's children will "shine the light of hope for the world and lead them to bliss". There was a photo of him with a few others. A happy family portrait.'

'He wants Tristan and Lily? But Tristan doesn't believe. Tristan knows the truth.'

'Yes.'

'You think he wants to silence Tristan?'

He didn't want to think it. He couldn't think anything but it. 'There are too many bodies, Tess. Joshua had his reasons for silencing Hayley and Sybilla, and maybe even Tamara, before the planned mass suicide. But David's running his own show, taking advantage of his father's death, continuing the group instead of abandoning it. Rebecca is dead, and Willow could easily have been. He's capable of murder. Lily's young enough that he might be planning to play benevolent big brother to her, but we all know, David included, that Tristan knows too much and won't be persuaded to play along. So yes, I think Tristan is in danger.'

He had to protect him. His quiet, reserved, courageous nephew who needed to have a future ahead of him and a chance to learn and discover the world, to find his own passions and interests and become whatever he wanted to be. And Lily, so young and exuberant and vulnerable. And Tess.

He had to protect them all. He loved them all.

•

The Strathnairn police didn't find the car. Highway patrol had a description but no one was out on that long stretch of the highway between major towns, let alone the minor roads to Goodabri. Tess repacked her bags, ready to leave. The sharp sense that they'd come looking for her wouldn't be silenced. Both Zac and David had reason to hunt for her and they, or whoever had been in the car sent to find her, could be anywhere. On their way back to Strathnairn, or somewhere east or south, or they could have looped around on any one of myriad back roads and be going anywhere, in any direction.

Forget needles and haystacks. Trying to find a single car in the thousands of square kilometres of north-west New South Wales ranked near impossible. They'd need at least some narrowing down of location and even then a large dose of luck. And if they found the car, it didn't guarantee finding Zac or David with it.

But she'd made up her mind, and she planned on using those impossible odds to their own advantage. She left her hair loose, and slid sunglasses on to the top of her head. With the sunglasses over her eyes and the straw hat she kept in the car on her head, there'd be little resemblance to the photo of her in uniform with her hair twisted back tightly in a knot.

In the room next door, Steve's phone burst into the Darth Vader theme from *Star Wars*, and through the thin walls she heard him answer, 'Hi Dad.'

She had to smile. Maybe once things quietened down, he'd get around to changing that ringtone, now that he was on better terms with his father.

She carried her bags out of the bunk room and closed the door behind her. The door of the guys' bunk room stood open, Tristan carefully packing Pooky into Lily's little backpack while Steve spoke on the phone.

'Okay. Stay there in Dubbo, Dad. We'll meet you there. We'll be a couple of hours. I'll call when we're closer. See you soon.' He saw her in the doorway as he finished the call. 'Dad left Sydney last night, planning to go to Dungirri to help us there, and set off about midnight. His night vision's not what it used to be, but he made it as far as Dubbo. Seems as good a place to head towards as anywhere.'

She nodded non-committally and left to take her bags out to her car. She'd have to tell him her plan soon. But not yet. Not while he had time to argue against it.

In the kitchen, Simon had coffee brewed and had pans of bacon, eggs and hash browns sizzling on the stove, almost ready to serve. Gabe, leaning against the bench, munched on a slice of toast.

Simon waved her to the table. 'Sit down and eat a decent breakfast before you go. Erin and the girls will be out in a minute.'

She'd have preferred a simpler breakfast but she had hours of travel ahead and food made sense. 'Have you decided where you're going?' she asked Simon.

'Yeah. Down to my stepfather's home in the Hunter Valley.' He buttered a slice of toast, slid two eggs on to it. 'Willow's coming with us. Ray's a good bloke, very gentle, very perceptive. Meeting him will be good for both Jasmine and Willow.'

Tess helped herself to coffee from the pot on the table. Perhaps having a gentle, perceptive stepfather helped explain why Simon, despite the demands of his army career, remained grounded, emotionally stable. Not something she could ask him about, though, especially as the others could be heard coming down the passageway to the kitchen.

Gabe rinsed out his coffee mug, 'I'll be off.' With a bare nod to Tess and a brief 'I'll be in touch,' to Simon, he left, the screen door on to the veranda closing silently behind him.

'Gabe's gone already?' Erin asked as she ushered Lily and Jasmine into the kitchen.

Simon served up more plates of bacon and eggs with military efficiency. 'Yep. Back to Strath to collect his gear from the motel. He said he might scout around a bit.'

They all ate the hurried breakfast with limited conversation, although the adults tried to keep things light for the younger ones.

Tess excused herself as soon as she'd finished and washed her dishes. Outside at her car, she busied herself checking the oil and water.

She found her chance to explain her plan when Steve brought his bags out to his car, the kids still inside the house.

'Listen, Steve, this is my plan. We travel together to the highway and some way down the road towards Dubbo. But when I know we're not being followed by anybody, I'll turn off and head east. They know my car, and they probably know yours, too. Hundreds, maybe thousands of people have my picture. So being together more than doubles the risk of you and the kids being found. I'll hire a car in Gunnedah or Tamworth and leave mine there.'

He heard her out before disagreeing. 'No, Tess. There's no need. Alec's going to send an escort car with us down the highway for a hundred k's or so. We can be sure then that no one is following us. Then it will be less than two hours to Dubbo. We can meet up with Dad, go on in his car or hire one. Or even fly out of Dubbo to Sydney or Melbourne.' He gave a crooked grin. 'Or Paris. You know, anywhere we want. Nobody's going to expect us back at work for at least a few days.'

The fact of the escort car made a difference. And she hadn't thought of flying somewhere. Not Paris, not without passports, but Perth, Darwin, Adelaide, Hobart, Cairns; plenty of places to go to where people wouldn't think of looking for her. She still wouldn't go with them, but she could fly to a city, find a room in an airport hotel, and hide away for a few days until the dust settled and the investigation made progress. She had her patchwork piecing, and she could download books to read, watch movies and order room service. It almost sounded like the ideal break. For two or three days, anyway.

'Okay,' she agreed. 'That's a good plan.'

A good plan that meant she didn't have to say goodbye, just yet. Saying goodbye was going to tear her heart into shreds. But her head knew it had to be done, for Steve's sake, and for Lily's and Tristan's.

Once out on the road, following the cloud of dust ahead that was Steve's car, she cranked up the music and tried to enjoy the sunshine and the landscape. Aaron in the escort car drove about a hundred metres behind her. Not far now, to safety. In a few hours she'd be on a flight out of Dubbo. She'd have to fly via Sydney, most likely, but maybe she'd go to Hobart. A long way away from northern New South Wales, and where the weather mightn't be tempting enough to emerge from her hotel and risk recognition.

They saw no other vehicles on the back road from Goodabri to the main road, and few once they turned on to the highway. There was an occasional car, travelling north, but no white Subaru. She didn't see anyone travelling behind the police vehicle.

After well over an hour down the highway, Aaron flashed his lights and they pulled over into a truck parking bay as they'd planned. An opportunity to wait ten minutes and ensure that no one followed behind them. With the coast clear, Aaron waved a hand in farewell and left.

Back on the road, she counted down the kilometres. Only an hour to go. Fifty minutes. Forty minutes. Still very little traffic.

A blue sign indicated a rest stop ahead, and Steve flicked on his indicator, slowing for the turning.

'Toilet stop,' he said apologetically when she pulled up beside him in the picnic area. He opened the back door for Lily and helped her out of the seatbelt. 'Looks like it's just a one-stand shed,' he said, nodding towards the toilet, about fifty metres away down a footworn path in the dirt. 'If you could take Lily to the throne room, Tris and I will go and water the trees.'

Tess slung her backpack over her shoulder. Among other useful things, it contained toilet paper, wipes and her water bottle. A habit after travelling in regional Australia for a while, rural toilets being often inadequately equipped. 'Okay, Lily, let's go!'

Lily dashed and she raced after her, letting her win. Tess checked the facility first. Clean, equipped with the necessaries.

She waited outside for Lily. The guys had walked into the bush, out of sight. Watering trees. Yep, it was easier being a male.

When Lily finished, she told her to wait for her. Might as well take the opportunity while she could. She heard a vehicle approach as she washed her hands and quickly went outside. A truck, a delivery van or moving van, without any company name, parked beside her car. Lily was halfway along the path.

Plenty of people stopped in rest areas.

Few people stopped close to another vehicle when there was plenty of other space to park.

'Lily!' she called. 'Slow down. Wait for me.'

The van blocked the line of sight between her and the direction Steve had taken. She couldn't see who drove it.

She caught up with Lily, grabbed her hand, and veered off the path, intending to loop around and give the van a wide berth. But the driver's door opened as another man came around from the passenger side, cutting off her planned route. David. He strode towards them, smiling, while the driver, a man she recognised as Christopher, opened up the back of the van.

She didn't dare call for Steve. Like her, he carried no weapons, and he was at as great a risk from these two as she was. Tristan even more so.

'Hello, Lily,' David said, crouching down in front of her. 'This is a lovely surprise, finding you. How about you come for a ride with your big brother, hey?'

Lily turned to Tess, uncertain. They'd shielded her from almost everything these past few days, and she didn't understand the danger David represented.

'Leave her alone,' Tess said. 'She's just a little girl, no use to you. It's me you want.'

He rose to his feet, calm, cool, drawing Lily back against his legs, with his hands possessively on her shoulders. 'She's my sister. Of course I want her with me. And your husband wants you. I promised him I'd bring you back.'

Two other men jumped down from the back of the van and others watched from inside. Joshua's followers, in simple, loose clothing. Six that she could see, all men. Too many for her to deal with. Too many for Steve and Tristan to deal with. And if David hadn't expected Lily, just her, then maybe he didn't recognise Steve's car. She slid her pack off her shoulder, keeping hold of the strap. If they let her take it she might get a chance to use the Swiss army knife, tucked into a pocket, or even the small scissors in her patchwork tin . . . Christopher grabbed her from behind, and cold steel pressed against her throat. 'Drop the bag. Now.'

She had no choice. Nothing she could do, but stay alive for now. While David took Lily to the front of the van, Christopher shoved her towards the waiting men, who dragged her up into the van and thrust her face down onto a stack of hessian bags in the back. The doors slammed shut. She coughed in the dust that rose but as the engine revved and the van accelerated, the men in the back held her down while they tied cords tightly around her wrists and ankles.

CHAPTER 14

Steve cursed himself for the few extra minutes they'd spent watching a wallaby joey the moment that he saw, through the edge of the trees, the three-tonne truck parked close to Tess's car. A truck. They used trucks to move people and belongings, Tom had said.

A man shot the bolts closed on the back of the truck. Steve couldn't see Tess or Lily at all, but the guy picked up Tess's blue backpack and tossed it into the bush before he headed back to the cab of the truck.

Steve pushed Tristan back into the scrub and down low to the ground, and swiftly pulled up Alec's contact details before handing him his phone. 'Hide,' he said. 'Whatever you do, don't let them see you. If they see you and chase you, run like the wind. When it's safe, press this button. That will call Alec Goddard. He'll know what to do. Okay?'

Tristan nodded, 'But—'

'Go. Hide in the trees. Now.'

The moment Tristan obeyed him, Steve bolted for the rest area. The truck was already reversing.

David sat in the passenger seat.

Steve raced, leapt up on to the footstep as the truck began to accelerate forward, grabbed the metal bracket for the side mirror with one hand and yanked on the door handle. Locked.

David, his face just inches away through the window, laughed. Beyond David, Lily's wide eyes stared into his.

He had to stop them. He had to get into the cab.

He clung on to the mirror bracket as the driver took the turn on to the highway too fast, the rear wheels fishtailing on the dirt until they found their grip on the highway surface.

He raised his elbow to smash in the window but David pushed the door open, hard, slamming it against Steve's legs so that he lost his footing on the step. The truck swerved and he hung from the mirror bracket, his arm straining as he scrabbled to find something solid for a toehold. David yanked the door back and threw it open again, and Steve caught one last sight of Lily, screaming, as he lost his tenuous grip and fell from the truck, rolling over and over in a ball of pain as he hit the dusty verge beside the highway at speed.

•

Face down, her hands tied behind her back, the wild swinging of the truck threw Tess sideways, wedging her between the pile of sacks and the side of the truck. The others muttered protests at the movement but within a few seconds the engine roared in acceleration and the truck sped ahead.

Tess lay motionless. Her vision blocked by the sacks, she closed her eyes against the dust and concentrated on listening to the sounds around her. Her companions in the back moved around a little, settling. Someone opened a bottle and glugged down liquid. Someone else asked, 'How long, do you reckon?'

'I dunno. Probably a few hours.'

'Might as well get some sleep then. Toss us that cushion, will you?'

'She okay?' It sounded like an older man.

A voice near her, deep and hard, answered, 'Who cares? She can rot there.'

Not much sympathy then. She'd have to sit up in a while, get to know them by sight, try to determine who might help her and who wouldn't. For all his faults, Joshua had preached love and bliss, not violence. She had no chance in hell of besting at least seven men with her limbs bound, but identifying potential helpers, or at least people who disliked violence, gave her a better chance of taking advantage of any opportunity that might arise.

But for now she lay still. In the rough handling shoving her into the truck, her jacket had twisted back, and she could feel the edge of her phone in the pocket. The police could locate her by tracking her phone signal if she was in range.

Attempting to make no sound, she gradually worked the phone up and out of the pocket, the bonds on her wrists tight and painful. With her movements awkward and limited, she felt for the buttons on the side, and switched it to silent. Damn touch screen phones. It was impossible to dial a number or send a text without vision or speech, especially with her hands tied behind her.

Should she put it back in her pocket or leave it in the truck? No one had searched her, yet. She imagined that wouldn't last. When they got to their destination in a few hours, wherever it was, she'd be hauled out. This lot mightn't think of phones, but David and Christopher would.

She rolled back slightly, her hand meeting the rough texture of hessian where the floor of the truck met the wall. One of the sacks must have slipped from the pile. With only a small amount of wriggling, she lifted the edge of the hessian and manoeuvred the phone underneath it. There. Steve and the other police would be able to locate the general area of her phone, if it was in range of mobile reception. Which meant, out here in the west, only if it was on a main road near a town. And towns were few and far between.

They'd turned north, onto the highway. Back towards the north-west of the state. A vast area, sparsely populated. But if the signal on her phone could be traced as they went through towns or communities with mobile phone towers, then the police could narrow the search a little.

Steve wouldn't give up. David had Lily with him, and Steve would give his life to rescue his niece.

But the sharp swerve the truck had taken as it left the rest area haunted her. Steve couldn't have been far away. If he'd tried to stop the truck . . . A waking nightmare kept returning, of his body, bloodied and broken on the road, as Maddie's had been.

•

Agony ripped through his ribs and his shoulder but he pushed himself to his feet and staggered from the side of the road into the scrub. He gripped his left arm with his right and held it against his chest. Dislocated shoulder. A familiar pain. One of the reasons he no longer played rugby. And it hurt like the hounds of hell tore at it.

They would come back for him, and he could scarcely walk, let alone run. If not for the leather jacket he'd pulled on this morning against the chill, his arm would be more shredded than the side of his denim jeans. The deep grazes on his leg bled, his hands dripped blood down his shirt, and he could feel warmth oozing down his face where he hadn't managed to protect it with his hands.

He limped twenty metres deeper into the trees, but the truck didn't return. Maybe it wasn't going to. Why? Why weren't they coming back for him? Why hadn't they waited for him and Tristan when they must have seen the car?

Because all they have is your name.

Detective Sergeant Steve Fraser. That's all there'd been in the newspaper. No photo. And if they'd done a web search on his name, after wading through a million other Steve Frasers they'd have only found a few police reports, and damn few photos. He'd once aimed for undercover work and, as a matter of principle and caution, he'd kept way out of the media spotlight, and he had no social media profile at all.

On Sunday night at Serenity Hill, and at Derringvale, he'd

stayed in the shadows. As far as most of Joshua's people were concerned, he'd have been just another cop in a search and rescue uniform.

Maybe no one had seen him with Tess, and put two and two together.

But they'd found her, twice. More correctly, they'd found her car. Through the fog in his brain the distinction became significant. Zac had left a message on her car. David had been near it at the service station. Both had had the opportunity to fit a tracking device. Simple. A device in a magnetic case took only seconds to attach to the underside of a car.

As a result, now they had her and Lily. And it was only a matter of time before Lily mentioned Uncle Steve, and they'd do their arithmetic.

He had to get Tristan to safety before they returned.

He made his way back towards the car. Not far, but he had to grit his teeth for each body-jarring step. As he came out of the trees at the edge of the rest area, Tristan ran towards him, the phone to his ear.

'He's back! But he's hurt. Hurt bad, I think.'

'Alec?' Steve checked, taking the phone. 'David has Lily and Tess in a white three-tonne truck heading north. Mitsubishi, I think. New South Wales rego with seven-three at the end.'

'We're getting cars out from Strathnairn and highway patrols are alerted,' Alec said. 'How badly are you hurt?'

'Dislocated shoulder, a few gashes. I'll live.' Yeah, even if he had to lean against the car to stay upright. 'Listen, I have to get Tristan to safety. They didn't know me but they'll work it out quickly and come back for him.'

'Stay put,' Alec said. 'There'll be help there within minutes.' Steve heard him speak to someone else. 'Get an ambulance there, too. One person injured.'

The sun was warm, his jacket was hot, flies buzzed around the blood on his face and he thought he might puke from the pain. 'Dad's in Dubbo,' he said to Alec. 'You'd better get him here, too.'

He handed the phone back to Tristan and let himself slide down to the ground. Better. Easier when he wasn't trying to stand. 'I'll be fine in a minute,' he reassured Tristan, who was reporting his unexpected sit-down to Alec.

In a minute, in a few minutes, not long, there'd be cops to protect Tristan and paramedics and painkillers and if they didn't put his shoulder back into place he'd damned well do it himself. And his father would be there and there'd be hell to pay for losing Lily. But he'd find her. He'd find her, and he'd find Tess. He had to.

•

The constant discomfort of lying un-cushioned on the floor of the truck eventually drove Tess to struggle to sit up, pushing the stack of sacks with her legs and shifting around so she could lean against them.

Most of the men dozed, but three of them watched her, with no move to help.

The temperature climbed, stuffy and hot, and sweat trickled down her face.

'Get the vents open, Duncan,' the hard-voiced guy to her left said, and an older man she'd thought had been sleeping rose and slid open vents in the sides and on the roof. The noise increased with the rush of air but the temperature began to drop.

Interesting that they'd adapted the truck body to carry breathing passengers. Not in a great deal of comfort, but there were large cushions, and a few rugs, and some low canvas seats hooked into the side of the truck.

Duncan, the older guy, returned to the cushion he'd been lying on and tipped his water bottle high to take a drink from it. He lowered it, and with his eyes on her, swirled the remains in the bottom. Not much. But he got up again, came over to her, and held it for her to drink from.

Warm water, and only a few mouthfuls, but wet and soothing in her dry throat, and she thanked him.

'You should have let her go thirsty,' the hard guy said.

Duncan shrugged and returned to his place. 'David wants her to stand to account for what she did. She can't do that if she's fainted from dehydration.'

He kept watch on her, eyes narrowed thoughtfully, and she remembered him from the night at Serenity Hill. Perhaps in his late fifties, Gabe had brought him back from the waterfall, unsteady on his feet, and crying. She'd wondered briefly, then, if he'd understood more of what had happened than the others.

She must have been wrong, because he wanted her to stand to account for her actions in shooting Joshua.

•

Painkillers and a relocated shoulder gave Steve a much clearer brain. A nurse cleaned the worst of the abrasions and cuts, but he didn't wait in the emergency department for x-rays or stitches. When the nurse protested about the gash on his hand, he took some tape, dressings and a couple of latex gloves.

While his father, grim-faced and uncommunicative, brought Steve's car around from the police station, he enlisted Tristan's help to tape the cut closed and cover it with a dressing. He tore the fingers off a glove with his teeth and drew the remainder on over his hand to hold the dressing secure and protect the wound.

His father refused to hand over the car keys. 'I'm driving. We've got a trace on Tess's phone. They've taken the western highway up towards Birraga. Goddard is on his way there.'

In the passenger seat, Steve took his arm out of the sling and made calls while they were still in mobile range. Alec. Leah. His colleagues in Birraga, Kris and Adam.

The phone signal dropped out. No emails, no phone calls, no texts probably for an hour yet. He didn't have a satellite phone. Neither did his father. He didn't have a radio in this car either, but his father had borrowed a portable from Dubbo. Assistant Commissioners could do that. But they were too far from Birraga yet to get any relevant comms on the police channel.

An Assistant Commissioner could also have driven as fast as he wanted to in an emergency. Bruce exceeded the speed limit but didn't push it as Steve would have done. Or maybe it was his own anxiety that made the speed seem slow.

Tristan sat silent in the back seat, his arm resting on Tess's backpack. He'd had the foresight to retrieve her other belongings from her unlocked car. He'd refused to be left behind in the care of the Dubbo police, and neither Steve nor his father had pressed it. Pooky had started the trip in Lily's booster seat. Now he was on Tristan's lap.

Frustrated by his inability to do much, Steve turned to the nearest source of possible information. 'Tris, I need you to think. Can you remember anybody talking about places to the west? Anything that might give us a clue to where the haven is?'

The lad thought for a minute. 'There were some people that came for a visit not long after we moved to Serenity Hill. An old couple, a lady and a man. Joshua asked me to clean their car. It was a big four-wheel drive, very dusty. With that kind of red dust.'

Red dust. Tom had spoken about red dust. 'Do you remember their names?'

'No. He didn't introduce me. They were on the veranda and I didn't even see them properly. But I did hear them telling him their place was a wildlife refuge. A refuge is kind of a haven, isn't it?'

'It is. Very similar.' Steve tried to keep hope from sprinting too fast. An 'old' couple with no names, in a four-wheel drive. Not a lot to go on. 'What else can you tell me about them?'

'Well, they gushed to Joshua. They believed in him. But the lady, she was sick. In a wheelchair, with tubes in her nose like they have in hospital, and a big metal bottle on the back. But I think they gave him money, 'cos Joshua kept thanking them.'

Money? Or land that was a wildlife refuge? The north coast didn't have a monopoly on ageing hippies and environmental warriors. The west of the state had a few, too.

'The thing is,' Tristan continued, 'there's this guy who came to live with us about a month ago. I don't know if he's the same man or not, but he went with Joshua and Christopher one day, and they were gone for days. He's very sad, and he doesn't talk much. But there was a wallaby caught in a fence once, and he knew what to do.'

Sounded like a wildlife warrior. Plenty of them about, too. Working it through aloud, he said, 'She died and he donated the refuge? If they donated the land, though, it won't show up in a sale. Not through an agent, anyway.'

'It might not,' his father said, speaking for the first time since they'd begun driving. 'But look for death notices for a wife. Funeral directors might know. There can't be too many of them out this way, or too many deaths in the past few months. It's too soon for bequests to have come through, but maybe there have been transfers of title deeds.'

'Good thinking, Dad.' Steve started to type a text. 'Do you know this man's name, Tris?'

Tristan shrugged. 'People just call him Duncan.'

Duncan. Better than nothing. He typed the text, copied to everyone, Leah, Alec, Aaron, Nick. *Wildlife refuge owned by Duncan and deceased wife possibly donated in last 3 months.* He pressed send on that one, although his phone showed no reception, and followed it with a second text listing places to check, and a third to his friend Jenn at the *Birraga Gazette*. He held his phone up on the dashboard. Low data texts needed only a smidgen of signal to transmit.

The good old-fashioned paper map open on his lap didn't need a signal to show him the towns and roads, which was why he kept several in the car. He studied possible routes David could have taken, considered the areas most likely.

Out here, the western plains stretched into the horizon, with cleared land for wheat, cotton, cattle and sheep interspersed with vast tracts of mulga scrub on dry, infertile sandy soil. The midday sun beat down, hot even in autumn, and the wildlife rested in the heat, so they'd seen little activity for the last hour. Only some emus, racing along beside a fence.

As they approached the small community of Bandar Creek, where the police tracking had received signal from Tess's phone over an hour earlier, a flurry of text messages and voicemail notifications beeped.

'Stop here, Dad,' Steve said, 'while we've got contact.' There were no other communities between here and Birraga, and unless there'd been a ping from Tess's phone closer to Birraga, then David could have taken any of at least four back roads from here, fanning out to the north and west of the state.

They parked in the shade of a kurrajong tree near the tiny community school, and his father and Tris stretched their legs for a few minutes while Steve stayed near the car, checking his messages.

Alec and Leah would be mostly out of range themselves while they travelled to Birraga. Nick messaged that the phone trace had received no pings at any towers since the one at Bandar Creek.

Steve swore and pulled out the map. David had turned off the road somewhere between here and Birraga. But which road? To where? They couldn't go wandering all over hundreds of kilometres of back roads in the vain hope of working out where.

He texted the others that he'd meet them in Birraga. They needed more information, some way to pin down the location of the haven, some way to discover what David planned when he arrived there with Tess and Lily.

He sent emails to the local estate agents, asking for details of land sales or title transfers over the past few months. But he'd worked out of Moree, Birraga and Dubbo for enough years to be familiar with the country to the west. The vast distances and harsh unpopulated outback held a million places to hide, and if they didn't get a break soon, Tess and Lily could easily disappear into that wilderness, forever.

•

The constant jarring of the uneven dirt road never seemed to end, and Tess couldn't find a comfortable position. Her arms ached, her neck ached and the muscles in her legs kept cramping painfully. Unable to stretch them out or massage them, she could only flex her feet and try every relaxation technique she'd ever heard of. None of them worked.

She had no way to monitor the passing time, but they must have been on the road for hours. They'd headed north from the rest area, taken a left after a while on to another good, sealed road, and then the left on to this rough, bumpy, torture-device of a road. Or roads, because there'd been a few turns since then.

The sun shone through the vent in the roof, lighting a small patch of floor and catching dust particles in its beam. But eventually the light angled, and the direct beam disappeared, and the journey continued without stopping, into the afternoon.

Her companions mostly slept, and there was little conversation.

But when the truck turned again, onto an even rougher track, and stopped with the engine idling for a few minutes before edging forward slowly and another stop and start, the men started moving and stretching.

Duncan undid the cord around her feet and she stretched her legs, attempting to return some function to her muscles.

'Why'd you do that?' the hard voice asked.

'So she can walk,' Duncan retorted. 'Unless you want to carry her?'

The guy just snorted.

There was another stop, the engine still idling. But she heard a car door slam, and within moments the sound of the bolts on the back sliding open. Hard voice and one of the other men pushed them open.

'Out,' Christopher said. 'Her, too. Quickly. He's in a hurry.'

The men jumped down and Duncan hauled her to her feet. Her legs wooden, she shuffled to the door. Duncan, already on the ground, lifted her down from the truck.

Dizzy, unsteady, with the sunshine bright in her eyes, she looked around to get her bearings. The scrub was thick, the mulga scrub of the north-west, and the only building nearby was a rough tin shed in a small cleared patch of red sand surrounded by mullock heaps. Hardly a haven.

As Duncan led her towards the shed, the truck engine revved, and it turned around a rough turning circle. Tess caught a glimpse of David, and a red-eyed Lily on his lap, before the truck drove off through the trees and out of sight.

Her phone remained in the truck, also out of sight. She doubted there'd be enough signal anywhere for miles, but at least if there was it would lead Steve and the police to Lily.

The fact that David had her on his lap gave her a little hope for Lily's well-being.

Her own well-being was a different matter. She was alone with Joshua's followers and with no way for Steve or the police to know where to find her.

CHAPTER 15

The disorientation of walking into his office in the Birraga police station brought Steve to an abrupt halt. Yes, same mess. Same whiteboard covered in his scrawls. Same Tardis coffee mug beside the keyboard. Definitely his office. The one an overworked but mostly upbeat detective with few cares beyond the job had walked out of nine days ago to drive to Tenterfield to attend a regional crime summit.

Turn a man's world upside down and his perspective changed. *He* changed. This corner of a regional police station no longer contained the majority of his focus, his definition of himself. But for now he needed the resources and comms in this office and he'd contemplate his personal metamorphosis when he had Lily and Tess back and all of them safe, together. His arm ached, his leg ached, his entire body hurt. He'd be a mass of red abrasions and black and blue bruises if he took the time to look. He didn't have time to look.

He downloaded emails to his desktop computer, sent lists from the estate agents of recent property sales to the printer. He had five minutes until a briefing with Alec and a hastily assembled team of local officers on duty. Not many, since six had been in Strathnairn overnight assisting to clean up the riot. Fortunately Adam Donahue, the constable usually working out of Dungirri was filling in for absent colleagues in Birraga today, and Steve had already co-opted him for assistance.

He needed all the help he could get. Desperation burned within him.

His phone buzzed and he snatched it up from the desk. Jenn Barrett from the *Birraga Gazette*.

Jenn didn't waste any words on pleasantries. 'Bettina Henderson, wife of Duncan, passed away on December twelfth. Private funeral. But the death notice was paid for in cash and I don't have an address. I'll ask around, see who knows them. I'll call back the minute I have anything.'

A name. Henderson. At last, something to go on. And a death notice in the *Birraga Gazette* implied they lived somewhere locally – although out here, 'local' could be two hundred kilometres away.

'Adam!' he yelled out the door as he grabbed the lists of property sales from the printer and started scanning the columns. Adam appeared in seconds. 'Duncan Henderson. I need licence details, car rego, anything with an address on it. Get someone on it now.'

His leg painful, but without enough time to sit, he propped on the edge of his desk while he flicked through the few pages of sales. Houses in various towns and communities; blocks of land, both town and rural; larger properties, mostly working farms for cotton, wheat, cattle, sheep.

He noted as relevant but not urgent, a comment from the Moree agent beside the record of the Serenity Hill sale, six months ago. *Relisted for sale Friday.* Relisted for sale two days before Joshua's grand farewell statement – a mass suicide he'd probably planned to walk away from.

Interesting, but not helpful for pinning down the location of the haven.

He scanned down the column of vendor names. No sign of Henderson. He shifted to the column of buyers' names. On page three, the name Pax Clementia Holdings leapt out. The Latin master at the private boys' school he'd endured for a year would be astonished by what remained wedged in his brain.

Pax Clementia. Peace, mercy, clemency. A shift from serenity, simplicity and bliss, but not far.

Pax Clementia Holdings had purchased two hundred acres of land north-west of Birraga two months ago. From a vendor whose surname wasn't Henderson.

At his computer, Steve pulled up a map and searched for the address. Out in the middle of nowhere, well off main roads. The map had bugger-all in the way of detail. The satellite photos showed a number of buildings, a dam, the brown of a dry or ploughed paddock, and the rest the dull green of native vegetation. Scrub, probably.

He set the printer whirring again with both the satellite images and the map, as his phone buzzed with a text from Adam. Duncan Henderson's address. Near the address he was looking at, but not the same property.

Shit. He grabbed his phone. Kent Marshall, the only solicitor in town now, did everything – court cases, property, wills.

'Kent,' he said the moment the man answered, 'a police officer has been abducted, her life is at risk and I need some information from you to find her. Bettina and Duncan Henderson – are they clients and, if so, is there any connection between them and Pax Clementia Holdings?'

'I can't give out confidential client information. Do you have a court order?'

Damn the man and his professional standards. 'I could get one, but she'll probably be dead by then. I need a simple yes or no. Have they donated or planned to donate or bequeath money, property, anything to anyone connected with Pax Clementia?'

The printer finished whirring. Kent stayed silent for long seconds. 'Yes,' he said eventually.

'Thank you. If you're still processing anything, do Duncan Henderson a favour and delay it as long as you can. If they're who I think they are, they're a mob of scum.'

Steve stacked the printed papers on top of his laptop and carried them under his good arm to the briefing room. His father and Tristan arrived as he did, bringing packaged sandwiches and bottles of water. Food. Breakfast seemed like days ago. Painkillers worked better with food. He ripped open a sandwich packet and took a few hurried mouthfuls as everyone gathered.

The Birraga station commander sat with Alec Goddard at the front of the room. Aaron from Strathnairn introduced himself to Adam and the other locals. His father, insisting his presence was observational only, sat with Tristan at the back.

Just as Alec rose to speak, Simon arrived with Willow. 'We'd only got as far as Inverell when we heard the news. An ex-army mate there with a mustering helicopter brought us,' he murmured as he took a seat beside Steve. 'Goddard hopes Willow might be able to help. Gabe's driving across.'

Alec opened by plotting pins on a map up on a wall showing the trace from Tess's phone, and adding another pin for the single, faint ping from Tess's phone at a tower north of Bandar Creek.

Steve added the information he'd found, the location of the two properties, the possible connection between Duncan Henderson and Pax Clementia. Henderson's address lay a few kilometres west of the Pax property. But the tower that had received the ping was a good thirty kilometres further east.

'Have you got any solid evidence to show a connection?' Alec asked.

Hearsay from Tristan, the inadmissible intimation from Kent Marshall, a faint ping from a phone tower and his own unreliable gut instinct. 'No,' Steve admitted. 'Willow, do you know Duncan Henderson? Or have you heard of Pax Clementia Holdings?'

She stood up, her hands clenching by her side betraying her nerves. In jeans and a blue shirt probably borrowed from Erin, with her hair in one long plait down her back, she could have been any young woman not long out of her teens. 'There was a man called Duncan. Joshua asked us to be particularly attentive to him, to help him find peace. He worked with the farming men. I didn't see him often. The other – the holding thing – I don't understand what you mean. I don't know those words.'

Steve didn't attempt to explain companies and company types to her. 'Pax means peace. Clementia is related to mercy, to clemency and forgiveness. Did Joshua talk much about those things?'

'Sometimes. When a member of the community strayed from our principles, he always said there was a path to forgiveness. That we should be merciful if they earned forgiveness. He wrote a pamphlet about the bliss of forgiveness not long ago. But I guess that was all lies, too.'

He'd track down that new pamphlet on earning forgiveness. The medieval church had built its wealth on selling forgiveness in the form of indulgences. Joshua wouldn't be the first charlatan to copy the idea.

But while Willow's information deepened his own certainty, it still didn't provide them with any firm evidence that Pax Clementia or Duncan Henderson were connected to Joshua or David.

With nothing to justify a search warrant, Alec wouldn't order them to go there until he had better evidence. He allocated tasks, stressed the urgency and told everyone to reconvene in thirty minutes.

Steve shoved himself to his feet. Thirty minutes. Thirty minutes plus an hour to get out to the first property. David would have reached there with Tess and Lily well over an hour ago.

Those with allocated tasks left the room swiftly. His father spoke with Alec while Willow and Tristan hugged each other and talked quietly.

Steve signalled Simon to come with him. Back in his office, he unlocked the secure cupboard holding his rifle. A personal weapon, not police issue, but he kept it here for security.

'It's going to take too long,' he told Simon bluntly. 'I need to get out there, start scoping the two places. But I could do with a driver.'

Simon propped a shoulder against the doorframe, arms folded over his chest, his backpack at his feet. 'Is this where I'm supposed to tell you to let the police officers with four functioning limbs handle it?'

Rifle, check. Ammunition, check. 'Like you left it for the police to find Erin and Jasmine?'

'I did keep in touch with you guys.'

'You did. And I'll report in once I'm there.' He had a spare daypack in the cupboard. Paper maps. GPS. First-aid kit. Camera. Painkillers.

'What if they're somewhere else?'

'Then I'll have fucked up, big time. But I might find that out in time to send the others elsewhere.' The equipment vest was already in the car.

Simon slung his pack on his shoulder. 'Where's your car?'

'Out the back. You don't have to do this, mate. It may be nine parts stupid and one part not exactly legal. Or something. So you should stay in the car.'

'When I'm better at skulking around in the bush? Sure. Hand over your keys and that pack. Let's go find them.'

They left via the back entrance, unnoticed.

•

The floorless shed concealed a mineshaft. The others disappeared down a ladder below ground, but Duncan ordered Tess to sit by the wall of the shed, and looped a chain through the cords around her wrists then padlocked it to a large steel ring attached to a wall joist.

'We won't be long,' he said, but he didn't move away immediately, studying her with narrowed eyes.

She risked a question. 'What's going to happen to me?'

'David will decide.' He left her without another word, climbing down the ladder into the earth and out of sight.

A mine, concealed by the shed. A haven. A hiding place. When she'd first heard the haven mentioned, she'd imagined somewhere like the Serenity Hill homestead. But who would suspect an old shed in the bush? There would be hundreds of them, scattered around the vastness of the west. The police might never find her.

Sunlight shone through the gaps in the walls of the shed, and she watched the slow progression of the stripes of sunbeams and shadows across the red sandy dirt.

David would decide her fate. Did that mean he would return here? Or would they take her to him? If she could see Lily, she might discover David's intentions for the child. If she could see Lily, and Alec and Steve could track her phone signal, she might stand a chance of being found.

The 'ifs' chased each other around and around. Maybe an hour passed. Maybe longer. Occasionally the sound of voices drifted up from below, but she couldn't make out actual words.

Helpless, thirsty and chained, she refused to give in to hopelessness. She stretched muscles to keep from seizing up. Feet, legs, back, neck, shoulders, hands.

North-west. If she'd judged the twists and turns of the truck correctly, they had to be somewhere beyond Birraga. The mine, the mullock heaps and the landscape didn't narrow the options much. Thousands of square kilometres from Queensland down through Lightning Ridge and across to White Cliffs and beyond were dotted with small opal mines.

And in those thousands of square kilometres there'd be a handful of phone towers and relatively little area with phone reception. Steve wouldn't stop until he found her and Lily, but he'd have to have more to go on than whatever signal her phone might have sent when within range of a tower.

She'd have to trust him, Alec, Leah and the rest of the team, and be ready to take whatever opportunity arose to escape. She had no doubt that David intended her harm, most likely her death. The only positive so far was the absence of Zac. He certainly intended her harm.

The narrow beams of sunlight edged up towards the wall. The sun must be low in the sky, heading towards sunset.

The ladder creaked and a woman came up from below, followed by Duncan and another man. They'd all changed, all dressed in loose white tunics and leather sandals. Duncan unlocked the padlock and released her wrists from the bonds before the two men gripped her arms and took her out, around to the side of the shed.

Tess recognised neither the second man nor the woman from the night at Serenity Hill, but in the dark and confusion then she hadn't seen everyone. The woman filled a bucket with a few inches of water from the tank beside the shed and handed her a ragged square of cloth.

'Take your clothes off,' she said, 'and wash. Now. We don't have much time. Shoes and socks first.'

'Obey her,' Duncan growled, but both he and the other guard turned their backs, standing solidly less than two metres from her. Duncan held the cord from her wrists in his hands. A sign her freedom was only temporary.

Reluctantly, Tess knelt to unlace her boots, scanning for escape possibilities. If she could charge between the men, take them by surprise, she might make the scrub beyond . . .

The woman whacked her across the head. 'Hurry!'

Tess yanked off her boots and socks, her bare feet sinking into the warm sand. No choices. Not yet. Shirt off. Jeans.

'Everything,' the woman told her. She pulled the white cloth Tess had assumed was a scarf off her shoulder, and shook it out. A tunic, like the others wore. 'Wash and then cover yourself with this.'

Standing naked outdoors with three hostile people made for a speedy wash, even if two of them weren't watching. The small square of cloth, dampened in the almost-hot water from the corrugated iron tank, took on a reddish hue as she washed off accumulated dust.

When the woman handed her the tunic, she pulled it on over her head gratefully. It hung in folds around her, down to her knees.

They refused to allow her to put her boots on again.

Duncan bound her hands again, but this time in front. More comfortable, and potentially leaving her hands more useful. She'd be able to push, pull, strike and grip if she had the chance. But if she had to run without shoes, the rough ground in the scrub would tear her feet to shreds.

People began to file out of the shed, all in white, all silent. One by one, ten, twenty, thirty, forty at least of them, walking in a long line across the sand to a path leading through a gap in the trees. The woman joined the line at the end, and Duncan and the other man gripped her arms and made her follow. The loose sand underfoot gave way to packed dirt, worn bare but scattered here and there with leaves and twigs that stung her bare feet.

A few hundred metres on, the path led to an open, sandy area. A dry creek. A flat-bed truck was parked on a stony crossing through the sand, a couple of wooden benches on the back, and the side of it decorated with woven tree branches, like a dais. In the middle of the creek bed, some distance from the truck, a huge pile of neatly stacked timber and tree branches stood two metres high and three metres long.

The group formed a circle between the truck and the woodpile and began to sing a slow, haunting melody as Duncan took her to the back of the truck where a chain hung, ready for him to padlock her wrists.

Then he joined the others, and the song split into harmonies that wove through each other and floated in the air as the sun sank lower to the horizon, spearing golden apricot light into the treetops as they all waited.

•

A kilometre from the entrance to the Pax property, they struck lucky. Or, at least, Steve hoped it was luck. The white station wagon, barely visible in a cloud of dust, turned out of the homestead track and on to the dirt road ahead of them, driving west in to the glaring light of the sun, close to setting.

'Do we follow it?' Simon asked.

Steve went with his gut. 'Yes. Keep back though. The dust should hide us.'

Just a few minutes down the road, the cloud of dust ahead turned into another property. Duncan Henderson's place, according to the GPS.

Simon drove past the turn-off without slowing, not pulling up until they were half a kilometre further on, where the scrub grew thicker and the cessation of their dust cloud wouldn't be noticed. Ahead, the road dipped down to a cement causeway over a dry creek bed.

Simon undid his seatbelt. 'We're going to take a stroll in the bush, I presume?'

'I am. You should stay here. It's perfectly legal to park on the side of the road.' And not legal to trespass. Simon already had enough to face with the inquiry into Joshua's death.

'Someone has to watch your back. Besides, I seem to recall you hurtling across the countryside to back me up and protect Erin on Sunday.'

Steve didn't press the point. A park ranger and a soldier, Simon understood perfectly the legalities and the risks, and he respected the man's willingness to assist in spite of them.

He swallowed a couple of painkillers with a glug of water. He'd held off as long as possible, but an hour of travel over dirt roads exacerbated every ache and bruise. Before they left the car, he messaged Alec using Simon's sat phone, advising him of the white car leaving one property and travelling to the next. It didn't confirm that David was here, but it added one more piece of circumstantial evidence, which was maybe enough for Alec to officially target the place in a raid. A career DCI in charge of an operation in an isolated area had fewer choices than an off-duty detective sergeant at the end of his police career.

Simon compared the landscape to the grainy satellite photo. 'The creek runs up through the property. I'd suggest following it in, but at this time of day there could be thousands of corellas settling to roost, and they'll make a hell of a racket if we disturb them.'

'How about we go in through here,' Steve marked a line on the photo with his finger. 'Cut across through the trees to this cleared area. I can't see a building but if there is one, it might be around there.'

'Okay. Watch out for old mineshafts. This area is full of them. If there's a dirt heap, there'll be a mine nearby.' Simon glanced across at the sinking sun. 'Let's move. There's less than fifteen minutes of sunlight left.'

And maybe half an hour of twilight. A week past a full moon, there'd be no moonlight for hours yet.

Steve swung his backpack on to his good shoulder along with his rifle and they set off into the scrub. He let Simon take the lead for now. There was no sense wasting the skills of a highly experienced commando when it took half of his own concentration to move one leg in front of the other at a fast pace. When the adrenaline and painkiller kicked back in, he'd move more easily. He repeated the promise to himself again and again.

They paused at the edge of the scrub where the track into the property ended at an old tin shed and at least ten large mullock heaps. *Where there's a dirt heap, there's a mine,* Simon had said. He indicated the shed, mimed a downward movement with his hands.

Steve got the message. The mine entrance was inside the shed. But he was more interested in the three vehicles parked nearby – the white Subaru wagon, the 3-tonne truck that had taken Tess and Lily and a new LandCruiser.

This was hard evidence that they were somewhere nearby. He crouched awkwardly in the cover of the trees and sent a message to Alec on the sat phone. The presence of the van used in an abduction would be enough for him to bring a team in. But it would be an hour at least before they arrived, and darkness would have fallen by then.

Nothing moved in the small clearing. No sounds other than birds either, until Simon, creeping silently forward to the shed, gave a low, soft whistle.

Steve edged out of the scrub to see what he pointed at. A metal bucket. A pair of boots and a neat pile of clothes.

Tess's clothes. Shirt, jeans, practical black underwear.

Rage obliterated pain. They'd made her strip, here in the open. Tess, with all her reserve and the trauma of past rape and assault.

Simon tapped him on the shoulder, pointed to the sandy ground. Even Steve could see the line of tracks, the flat shapes of some kind of footwear, and the single set of bare footprints in between them.

•

Four men carrying a bier with a figure swathed in white walked solemnly down the path. Zac was one of them, his head bowed as he carried his share of the load.

Tess redoubled her efforts to twist her hands free of the wrapped cord.

David walked behind the bier, the very picture of a benevolent brother clasping hands with Lily on one side and holding a toddler with dark curls on his other hip. Others followed him in the short procession: A couple of boys and a girl in their mid-teens; a younger girl, early teens, and two even younger, maybe nine or ten. All of them dressed in white like the others, except the fabric of their clothes fell more softly around their bodies, long to their ankles, tied at the waist with decorated cloth belts. There were no coarse sack tunics for Joshua's children.

Mary Saint – Marianna Sinclair – brought up the rear of the procession with Christopher, her white tunic dress as elegant as a fashion plate.

They'd gathered the whole family. Criminal, probably murderous adults with innocent children in their power. Tess broke another fingernail working at the knots in the cord.

The men with the bier lifted it onto the truck, in front of the benches, and the gathered faithful made small sounds of grief and distress. Someone had put a set of steps beside the truck and David helped the children and Mary up to take seats on the benches.

David leapt up, demonstrating fitness, youth and masculinity, and stood in front of the gathered assembly, his arms out wide to capture their attention. 'The soul of our beloved father Joshua has ascended to bliss, and now we, his children, gather to send his sacred shell into the beyond.' He projected his voice strongly, like a professional stage actor, making it deep and resonating with sincerity. 'We are indebted to the purity of his vision, his exemplary dedication to guiding us to bliss, the decades of service he gave with no thought for his own well-being, and above all, the selfless love he shared with us all, his children of the body and children of the spirit.'

Tess swallowed the urge to shout the truth, to contradict his every word. But while everyone's rapt attention was on David, she worked at the knots with her teeth. She didn't think Lily had seen her. The child sat quietly, hands in her lap, head bowed, and Tess could not gauge her state at all.

She didn't think Zac had seen her either. But his presence gave her a desperate desire to loosen her bonds and escape. How she'd rescue Lily, she had no idea.

David continued singing Joshua's praises for several minutes, but finally signalled to the pallbearers to lift the bier again.

'It is fitting that at the end of this beautiful day,' he proclaimed, 'as the sun takes its warmth and light from us, that we farewell the warmth and light that have guided us for so long.'

As Mary began to sing, the pallbearers carried Joshua at a funereal pace through the group so that each person could touch and caress the shrouded figure. Everyone joined the wordless song, the poignant melody floating in the last apricot-gold rays of sunlight.

A funeral pyre. They planned to cremate Joshua's body on the stacked pile of wood and branches. Tess tugged uselessly at the tight knots, fighting back sobs. She wouldn't be able to stop them. They'd burn Joshua's remains, hot and fast, and even if the police found this place there'd be little left for a coroner to examine. No answers to his cause of death.

The song ended as the pallbearers took the bier behind the funeral pyre. Battery-powered lights flicked on at the edge of the truck, illuminating David as he raised his arms again to draw the group's attention back to him.

'We have cleansed our bodies and our hearts will be made pure again. Tomorrow we will celebrate life and new beginnings. I am rewarding faithful servants with great gifts. To my cousin, Christopher, I will give my beautiful sister, Rose, so that they may share bliss and continue Joshua's line. And to Zac, who has dedicated himself to us, I will give my lovely sister, Fleur. We will celebrate their pairings at sunrise, the dawn of a new day.'

Bile rose in Tess's throat. Like some kind of medieval king, he was playing lord over his sisters' lives and forcing them into marriage. Barely a teenager, Fleur looked terrified. If he used such a young girl's virginity as a reward for Zac, what fate awaited Lily if she remained with him?

'But first we must complete the purge of those who have betrayed Joshua, who have betrayed us. The non-believers stand in the way of the path to bliss, and are not fit to be among us.'

Duncan and his fellow guard appeared again at Tess's side, unlocking the padlock and dragging her to stand in front of David.

Lily gasped and started to stand, but Mary pushed her back to the bench, her hand tight on the girl's shoulder, her face hard as she whispered something into her ear.

David looked down at Tess from the truck, the lights reflecting the triumph in his eyes. 'Tess Ballard, you fired your weapon and killed my beloved father, our cherished leader, while he was peacefully worshipping the natural world. We have brought you here to answer for that crime.'

Alone, with more than fifty people against her, she had nothing left to lose. Her only hope lay in stirring the conscience of any doubters in the group. 'Joshua was a fraud and a murderer,' she shouted, loud enough for them all to hear. 'And so are you. You murdered Rebecca—'

The blow to her head knocked her to the ground. Not Duncan, the other guard. But Duncan bent over to haul her to her feet. And in one instant, his face close to hers, he muttered, 'Is it true?'

'Yes,' she hissed. 'And worse.'

He hit her this time, a hand across her face.

She doubted, then, that she'd heard him correctly.

As he dragged her to her feet, other hands gripped her, yanking her back against a hard body, and Zac yelled close to her ear, 'She's my wife. I am the one who should punish her.'

David waved a regal hand, his eyes alight with laughter. 'Take her, Zac. Take her away and make sure she understands her sins. Punish her for the loss she has caused all of us.'

And Zac said in her ear, 'You'll burn with Joshua, witch. When I'm done with you I'll throw you on the pyre with him and you can burn your way to hell.'

•

Simon grabbed his arm and stopped him when he would have bolted out of the trees. 'Wait,' he hissed. 'Wait until they've separated. Then we go.'

Tess struggled with Zac, fighting him as he dragged her backwards into the midst of the group. Steve hated that Simon was right. If they charged in now, they'd have to deal with fifty of them. And he couldn't fire a rifle, not into the crowd.

David leapt down from the makeshift stage, guiding the children down, and there was Lily, obedient but frightened, so small and alone in events she didn't understand.

The sun was setting, sending long fingers of red through the wisps of cloud in the western sky, but a fire flared in an old oil drum, and while Tess still struggled with Zac, David led the procession, taking rush torches from beside the drum and lighting them, circling the pyre, chanting a meaningless chant that swelled, growing louder and faster.

Steve and Simon followed at the edge of the trees. 'You watch for a chance to go for Lily,' Simon muttered. 'You can carry her. I'll go for Tess.'

But even as Steve reluctantly agreed, his gaze darting between David and Zac, Simon suddenly pitched forward and a blur of a figure in white raised a thick branch, ready to strike again. Steve swung his rifle, hitting the man hard in the guts but the impact jarred his bad shoulder so painfully he could not keep hold of the weapon. The guy gave a shout of alert before he toppled.

Simon gripped the man's ankles and hissed at Steve to run.

Steve's pulse drummed in his ears as he bolted forward. Lily and Tess were fifty metres apart. He couldn't get to both of them. He couldn't save both of them and stop David cremating Joshua.

One man against fifty, all of them alerted now to his presence. David set his torch to the pyre. Zac had his arm around Tess's neck, dragging her to the fire.

Lily or Tess.

Lily or Tess.

The thudding of his boots drummed the chant of the impossible choice in his head.

Lily screamed.

CHAPTER 16

Her head spinning, Tess gasped for breath and clawed at Zac's arm. Wiry and strong, driven by mania, he didn't even flinch as her ragged fingernails dug into his flesh. She could hear the crackle of flames, see the smoke beginning to drift.

She wasn't ready to die. She scrabbled to find footing, anything to give her leverage against Zac.

There were yells, and she heard running, and a child screamed, loud and long. And then Steve's voice yelled, 'Run, Lily!'

Adrenaline and determination shot through her and with one foot finding flat ground, she used all her strength to slam her other foot into Zac's leg. He swore and staggered and she used the instant when his grip slackened to twist and ram her elbow into his ribs. As he grunted and doubled over, she hit him under the jaw with her bound hands.

He pushed her down and fell on top of her, hands gripping her shoulders to pin her down. His face contorted in rage, he half straddled her, his knee digging into her stomach. He hit her again, a blow across the face, and she swore at him and angled her hands to punch him in the balls. She hit the goal, hard, and he jolted back, gripping himself with one hand.

'Die, bitch,' he roared, raising his other hand to strike her, and she jerked her head away to the side, not far enough, groping for sand to throw in his face.

But the blow never fell.

His weight dragged back over her legs.

'Run,' Duncan said. 'Run as fast as you can.'

She pushed herself to her feet, dizzy and nauseous, and staggered a short distance away while Duncan grappled with a semi-conscious Zac.

Lily. She had to find Lily.

The fire was taking hold of the pyre, casting eerie light over the creek bed as the flames danced and grew.

Far too close to the flames, Steve fought with David, the others circling around them. And Lily, brave little Lily, ran for her life along the creek bed away from them, Christopher in pursuit behind her.

Tess sprinted to intercept, the sand dragging at her bare feet. The thud of bootsteps overtook her. Simon. 'Get Lily,' he shouted as he passed.

He tackled Christopher hard, as Tess reached Lily. She dropped to her knees, slipping her still-bound hands over the girl's head to hold her tightly against her. 'You're safe, Lily. It's me, Tess.'

And Lily cried and clung to her, and Tess lifted her and carried her into the bush, her own sobs mingling with the child's. Because Steve still fought for his life and she could do nothing to help him but protect his niece, too young and small to protect herself.

•

His head rang with pain, his shoulder hung at an angle again and David circled, preparing to move in for the kill. The heat from the fire prickled his back. Holding David's gaze, Steve feinted a charge, dropping back a few steps to his right. One more feint, and the heat radiated on his cheek, not his back.

He had David's arrogant pride to thank for the fact that the others hadn't joined in. The man insisted on dealing with him alone. And on playing with him before the kill. Good. It evened the odds. One broken down thirty-something cop against a man in the over-confident strength of his youth.

But he still had a trick or two up his sleeve. 'David ben Joshua, I'm arresting you on suspicion of the attempted murder of Joshua Kristos.'

David just laughed, but as the others shifted uneasily Steve tossed over his shoulder, 'You lot might want to tear down that pyre and rescue Joshua. In case he's still alive.'

'He's lying,' David said loudly. 'You're lying, you bastard. You shot him. You shot my father.'

Steve feinted again, fell back a few more paces around. 'I shot at your father to stop him persuading all these people to commit suicide. But I don't think I hit him.'

Not a lie, that. More than fifty metres at night with a handgun. He doubted he was that good.

But now he had David lined up near the fire. If he charged, David might assume another feint. He could push him into the flames. And he'd likely go in himself.

He wasn't ready to die.

He kept talking. 'Joshua fell on to the rock behind, just as he planned, but he had a knife in his chest. And you took him away. Was he alive then, David? Is he alive and drugged in that shroud?'

At the edge of his vision, people started dragging burning timbers from the pyre. Someone yelled for water. Goaded into fury, David charged.

Steve stepped to one side a microsecond before impact, using his good arm to follow through with a hard elbow to the back as momentum hurtled David down to the ground.

As Steve staggered, barely able to stand, David groaned and began to push himself up. But a figure in blue bolted out from the trees, a thick branch in his hands and as David rose, the man swung the branch hard into his head.

David crumpled in a heap on the ground. Tom stood over him, branch held ready to strike again.

Steve fought for even breathing. 'Where . . . ? How did you get here?'

'A fair few defected after the riot. I talked with them and one of the guys had been out here before. I hitched a ride with your mate McCallum. Go,' he added. 'Your kid's that way. With your girlfriend. They're okay.'

They're okay. Steve clutched his arm to his chest and dragged his feet through the sand. The crowd around the pyre were throwing sand and water at it, and had the edge of Joshua's bier in grasp to pull it down.

There'd be a body for the coroner. Despite the suggestion he'd made to the others, Steve doubted Joshua was alive. David had no use for a living father.

One foot in front of the other. There was still enough light around to see that Simon had Christopher down on the ground, binding his hands.

Another man had Zac immobilised.

Gabe McCallum had the little kid, Rory, by the hand, coaxing him and Fleur out of the bushes they'd run to.

Your kid's that way. With your girlfriend.

Steve found the path through the scrub, kept shifting one foot after the other, leaving shuffle marks in the sand.

The trees cleared and he lifted his head. The three vehicles were still there. Somewhere nearby, sirens sounded.

His father held Mary handcuffed against the LandCruiser, reciting a caution.

Tristan held his little sister and Pooky tightly in his arms. Close beside them, Willow stroked Lily's hair.

And Tess . . . Tess met him halfway across the sand, walking straight into the circle of his good arm, and he pulled her close.

The small clearing filled with police vehicles, people, voices. Officers ran past them.

He held Tess. Or maybe she held him. 'Forgive me,' he said.

'I had to choose. You or her. It tore me apart. I couldn't have borne it if either of you . . .'

She lifted her head from his shoulder and cupped his face with her hand. 'There's nothing to forgive. I had to choose, too, and we both made the right choice. We're police, and the vulnerable come first. They always come first.'

The vulnerable come first. They stepped aside for more officers and paramedics to pass down the narrow path.

Tess kept her arm around him and he couldn't bear to let her go, to lose the closeness. He glanced across at his family, his father lifting Lily gently in his arms, drawing Tristan into his embrace.

'They're safe,' Tess said. 'And now they're safe, this is my next choice.' She raised her face to his, and kissed him.

He caught her mouth with his, gentle, tender with her bruises, and his. He lifted his head when someone coughed and asked to pass.

'Go and be with your family,' Tess said.

His family. Tristan and Lily, his first responsibilities. He loved them already. But he loved Tess, too.

'Will you come with us?' he asked. 'For a little while at least?'

She linked her fingers through his. 'I'll come with you. But they need you now.'

He limped across the ground towards his father, his niece and nephew. His children. They did come first, for now. But Tess's hand remained in his, warm and secure, and when he embraced his family she stayed with him, by his side.

•

'How badly is he hurt?' Leah Haddad nodded towards the ambulance where a paramedic stabilised Steve's arm, while Bruce Fraser hovered close by with his granddaughter on his hip.

Propped against the bonnet of a police car, Tess eased her socks on over the abrasions on her feet, relieved to be back in her own clothes again.

'He's pretty battered and bruised. I think he'll be okay. So will I,' she added, before Leah became the twentieth person to ask. Paramedics, police and now Leah seemed to need convincing that she wasn't about to collapse in a heap.

The small cleared area near the shed teemed with people and vehicles. Police cars and vans, two ambulances and a Rural Fire Service tanker occupied most of the limited space. An SES crew must have left their truck on the road, walking in with first-aid kits, tool boxes and water bottles, trekking along the well-worn path to the creek.

'Everything under control at the creek?' Tess asked. Mary sat, straight and scornful, under guard in a nearby police car, but there'd been no sign yet of David or Zac being brought up from the scene.

'Yes. We've restrained and cautioned David, Zac and Christopher. There'll be plenty to charge them with. Murder, abduction, assault, drug dealing. It's going to be a busy night.'

'Will there be enough for the prosecutors?' It worried Tess, the lack of evidence on some of the charges.

Leah smiled like a cat with a mouse. 'There'll be enough to convict David. Abduction of you and Lily will be straightforward. Assault – Steve, Willow, and we'll probably get him on Rebecca, too, and hopefully her murder. As for the others, everything's unravelling now. Part of that is thanks to you, finding the connection between Mary Saint and Marianna Sinclair. The Feds connected a heap of dots with that information. They've wanted the Sinclairs for a while on drugs and money-laundering charges. Seems like they've been living it up for years on other people's misery.'

Tess finished lacing her boots and stood up cautiously, bracing for pain that didn't come as sharply as she'd feared it might. 'David referred to Christopher as his cousin. Are the Sinclairs and Joshua – Peter Hollywell – related?'

'That's where it gets interesting. Newspaper archives only recently put online a report that a man named Peter Hollywell died in a hiking accident in Colorado, a week after graduating as a psychologist, twenty-five years ago.'

Tess grappled to make sense of that. There couldn't be many psychologists named Peter Hollywell. 'He died? So Joshua isn't Hollywell, either? But who—?'

Leah's wide smile said she'd not only caught the mouse, she was eating it with lashings of cream. 'The only witness to his death was a fellow student, an Australian exchange student by the name of Joshua Sinclair.'

'Jesus,' Tess breathed out. 'He really was Joshua.'

'Yeah, but not Kristos. Nothing divine about him at all. You'll be interested to know,' Leah added, 'that I took a quick look at his body. The post-mortem will have to confirm it, of course, but I'd be willing to lay a bet that the cause of death will be a slit throat.'

'He survived the fall?'

'Yes. He also survived being shot at. The only wound I saw other than his throat was a clean incision on his upper chest, presumably from Tom's knife. No bullet wounds at all.'

No bullet wounds. Tess reached for the bottle of water someone had given her, suddenly a little light-headed. '*None* of us hit him?'

'Nope. Not by the looks of it. Two cops and a soldier, and none of you can hit a stationary target.'

Over a distance at night. Tess took a long drink of water and didn't protest Leah's dry teasing. 'I'd do the same thing again if I had to.'

'Of course you would. You're a good cop. So would I, in the circumstances.'

Aaron and another officer came along the pathway with Zac between them, handcuffed and head hanging low. Aaron steered him away from Tess and towards a police van. He didn't look up, didn't see her, and Aaron closed the door behind him, shutting him out of sight.

She left Leah and went to Steve, who pushed himself off the gurney despite the paramedic's protests, and caught her hand with his uninjured one. 'He'll go away, Tess. With luck he'll never be free again.'

'He never was free,' she said. 'He never learned to think or to question. He's been trapped in blind belief and used by others all his life.'

Would she have become like him if she hadn't run? Would she have endured the marriage, borne children, become so fearful of exclusion, like her mother, that she'd never step out of line? No. She'd made her choice that day, and run from all she knew, alone and frightened. And she'd found her way, made her way, and become her own person. A woman with enough strength to give and to accept.

Some of Joshua's followers appeared along the path. Those in the lead stopped, hesitating when they saw all the lights, the vehicles, the people.

But Willow and Tristan went towards them, hands held out in greeting, drawing them forward, reassuring them that the police would help them, guiding them to a place to sit.

There was a grace to both of them, a kindness that went deep, and the capacity to think, to question, and to love.

'They're going to be okay, those two,' Tess said quietly to Steve.

'They will,' he agreed. With his good arm, he drew her close. 'We will. All of us. We'll get through all this, and we'll be more than okay.'

CHAPTER 17

Gum trees bordered the long straight road from Birraga to Dungirri, their shadows flickering and dancing on the bitumen. The scrub kept the morning sun mostly out of her eyes but every now and then a break in the trees allowed the beams to shine through, making Tess squint and highlighting every dead bug and smear on the windscreen. Ahead of her, Steve's car, driven by his father, kept exactly to the speed limit.

In the two days since the events out west, there'd been hospital treatment and police interviews and several rounds of x-rays and scans for Steve and little time for them alone, together. But he'd healed enough to travel, and he wanted to get Lily and Tristan out of the Birraga Hotel and settled into somewhere they could call home.

She could have gone back to Goodabri yesterday. But she'd stayed, ostensibly to help Steve and his father with Lily and

Tristan, all of them still unsettled although David, Zac and the others were in custody and had been refused bail.

Maybe she would go home, later today. The road to Dungirri led on eventually to the highway and the route to Goodabri, so for now she followed Steve.

Eventually, a crooked sign announced 'Dungirri, Population 350' and another sign beyond it required her to slow to the residential area speed limit. A few scattered houses marked the beginning of the town.

Having dropped her speed and shifted down into third gear, Tess looked around as they drove down the main street. A showground with a tilting grandstand but neatly mown grass on one corner; diagonally opposite it, a century-old two-storey pub with wide verandas. Rows of shops flanked either side of the main block, one with an ice-cream sign outside, most of the rest boarded-up and empty, like many a country town. But the garden beds in the middle of the wide road were neat and well tended, with hardy native plants and a splash of floral colour here and there.

A few more houses, and then Bruce Fraser turned on to a road off to the left. She took the turn after him. Just two houses down, at a traditional rural Australian place with a 'For Sale' sign on the gate, Bruce stopped the car and Steve, Tris and Lily piled out. Tess parked out the front as Bruce did a U-turn and headed down to the pub to check in for the night.

As she got out of the car, she noticed the police station just beyond a vacant block across the road. One side the station itself, the other half the residence. Older than the Goodabri station, going by the architecture. Early Federation era. Maybe nineteen twenties. Probably fine for a single cop but cramped for an officer with a family. At least Dungirri, like Goodabri, still had a local police presence.

The Frasers were on the veranda of their house by the time she walked down the short drive.

'Wait there, kids,' Steve said. 'The agent's left the key around the back. I won't be long.'

Lily bounced with excitement and clutched Tess's hand. 'It's a whole house! Just for us!' she informed Tess. 'We're going to live here. Isn't it pretty?'

'It is,' Tess agreed. A weatherboard house, probably a century old, but freshly painted in a cornflower blue with white trims. Nothing fancy, but the type of modest house that millions of Australians made into homes. A few native shrubs and an expanse of dry grass made up the front yard.

Footsteps sounded within and Steve pulled open the front door. 'Welcome to our new home, guys. Have an explore. No furniture yet, but we'll get mine out of storage tomorrow.'

Lily darted straight down the central hallway, Tristan not far behind her – in distance or enthusiasm. They pushed open a door to the right, and disappeared inside.

'Bert Dingley owns this place,' Steve explained as he waved Tess in, 'but he's getting on in years. He's moved in with his brother in Birraga. The house has been on the market for a while, but it's hard to sell anything in a place like Dungirri. So I've got a six-month lease. I've only seen photos and a plan, so I hope it's liveable.'

Memories of searching for decent rentals in Sydney haunted Tess. 'You're lucky you were able to organise this so quickly.' And a nice house, too, if the light and airy living room was indicative of the rest.

He turned around slowly in the centre of the room, scoping the space, and his face relaxed for the first time since she'd met him into an almost-boyish exuberance. 'I reckon I could put the TV there, sofa across here, bookshelves on that wall there. It should all fit in fine. Come on, let's explore the rest.'

They went from room to room, crossing paths with Lily and Tristan, opening cupboards and wardrobes, looking out windows, planning furniture.

It wasn't her house. She had a job and a place to live back in Goodabri.

But after all the death, violence and tension of the past week, she let the family's excitement carry her concerns away, just for a while.

Living room, dining room, large country kitchen, three good-sized bedrooms plus a built-in veranda at the back that made another living space. A carport and a large shed and a not-too-overgrown veggie patch with some late season crops still surviving. Carrots, parsnip, potatoes and fennel, along with plenty of herbs.

Steve stood gazing at the shed, eyes wide, broad smile, arms folded. Just standing, staring at it. She had to grin. There was a man who'd just fallen in love with a shed. And a fine-looking shed it was, even she could see that. A fine-looking man, too, even with bruises on his face and his arm in a sling.

'So, what are you going to do in it?' she asked him.

He hadn't heard her approach and he glanced around, startled. 'In what?'

'The shed. You've clearly got a case of shed lust.'

He laughed out loud, a rich, infectious laugh that crinkled his eyes and made her grin again. 'Oh, yeah. I've never had a decent shed before. I'm fantasising about carpentry. I did some at school, and always wanted to do more.'

Carpentry. An interesting insight into the man. A down-to-earth, functional creativity. The light and life in his expression when he spoke of it hinted at an unfilled passion within him.

Lily came racing out of the house, the screen door slamming behind her and they both spun around, on alert.

'Uncle Steve!' She tugged at his hand, excited, not scared. 'Uncle Steve, there's girls outside. And they've got a *puppy*!'

He gave his niece the gentlest smile. 'A puppy? Well, let's go and say hello, then.' He didn't hold out his hand to Tess, but his smile invited her, too. 'Would you like to come and meet the neighbours?'

A guy in a wheelchair waited at the gate with the three primary-school-aged girls. And the puppy, a black and tan ball of fluff on a red leash. It was a kelpie, probably, maybe a bit of border collie. A couple of months old and right in the irresistible stage.

The girls sat on the dry grass between the fence and the road, in a little circle around the puppy. Tristan stood guard at the gate, uncertain about the strangers, although he nodded at something the man said.

Steve greeted the guy warmly and introduced Tristan, Lily and her to Ryan Wilson. A friend, he introduced her as. They'd made no decisions, no promises.

'We heard on the grapevine what happened, and that you're renting here for a while,' Ryan said. 'We're just heading to the pub for lunch and saw your car, so thought we'd say hello. And I'm sorry, mate, about your sister. Means a bit of a change for you now, I gather.'

'Thanks. Yep, Tristan and Lily will be living with me. Life turned upside down, you might say,' Steve's mouth curved into a crooked grin, 'but I find I like the view from this angle.'

It still impressed her that he'd accepted his sudden, unexpected family responsibilities with such calm and grace. Ten days ago, when she'd first met him, she wouldn't have believed it possible. But now she knew that the irreverent, sometimes cynical persona had been a mask protecting deeper feelings and emotions, and an integrity that could be relied on.

One of Ryan's girls – around Lily's age – made room for her to sit with them, and Tess watched the little girl reach out tentatively to the puppy, giving a little squeal when the fluff ball barked at and then licked her fingers.

'Beth said to tell you if there's anything you need for Lily, just ask,' Ryan told Steve. 'With three girls we have things to spare. She's at church this morning but she'll meet us at the pub for lunch.'

'Thanks, mate.' Steve gave a self-deprecating laugh. 'You'll both probably get sick of me bugging you for advice.'

'Anytime.' Ryan included her in the conversation with a friendly curiosity. 'How long will you be staying, Tess?'

'Just passing through. I'll have to get back to Goodabri soon. I'm a senior constable there.'

With a job and a life there and . . . and the puppy barked again and scrambled onto Lily's lap and even Tristan laughed as his sister tried to hug the squirming ball of fur.

Ryan grinned. 'Well, if you're looking for a change of scene, the police sergeant here has just gone on leave for six months.'

She didn't miss the light of hope in Steve's eyes. 'Kris is on extended leave?' he queried.

'Yeah. Gil officially owns the pub now, and she's moved in with him. And she doesn't believe that policing and pub ownership mix.'

While Steve and Ryan caught up on local news, Tess leaned on the fence, watching the girls and the puppy, studying the street and the town. Not a rich town, Dungirri, but then every small town out here in the bush struggled with shrinking employment, an ageing population and the shifting economic policies that favoured large centres over small communities. Yet the Memorial Hall beside the police station gleamed with fresh paint, the paddock across the road was freshly mown and a poster on the power pole nearby advertised a Dungirri Progress Association meeting.

No decisions, no promises. Not yet. Too early yet. They both needed time. But there were possibilities, and there might be opportunities.

A week ago she'd set off on a wild ride with Steve through the night across paddocks towards risk and uncertainty. It could be a metaphor for life, really. But she'd trusted him then, and she trusted him now. More importantly, she trusted herself. Trusted herself to be able to give to others, beyond her work. No longer on the outside, looking in.

Lily laughed out loud, the puppy wriggling in her arms and Tristan and Steve crouched beside her, patting the puppy, sharing her joy. They'd be a strong family, those three.

Lily looked up at her. 'Tess, the puppy's name is Rufus. 'Cos he goes "*ruf, ruf*". You can come and pat him, too.'

'Yes, join us,' Steve invited, his eyes sparkling as warm as the sunshine. 'You'll come to the pub for lunch, won't you? You'll stay a while?'

She knelt beside him, with his family and his friends, the puppy's fur so warm and soft under her hand that she couldn't help smiling – at the puppy, at the kids, at Steve. 'Yes, I can stay for a while,' she told him.

As they all walked the block to the pub with Ryan and his daughters, she debated with herself about staying longer than lunch. She didn't have to be back at work for a week . . .

Her phone buzzed in her pocket just as they reached the entry to the pub's leafy courtyard. Not a number she recognised, and she stayed outside to answer it as people greeted Steve and he went in with his friends.

A woman's voice asked anxiously, 'Theresa? That's really you?'

'Yes.' Wary, concerned some of Joshua's people might have found out her phone number, she asked brusquely, 'Who is this, please?'

'I'm Verity.' The woman's voice wavered. 'Please, I . . . we . . . we need your help.'

Verity. Her little sister. There was a low brick fence around a tree at the edge of the pavement and Tess sat on it, her legs too shaky to stand. Laughter drifted from the pub, but she was out here, alone but for a couple of birds twittering in the leaves overhead and the sister she'd not spoken to in sixteen years on the phone.

Her mouth dry, she managed to ask, 'Where are you, Verity? What's happened?'

'At the hospital in Albury.' The words rushed out, Verity's voice teary and distressed. 'My baby got sick. Pastor Elijah said the Lord would cure the worthy but she got sicker and Mother said she needed the doctors in the hospital and she argued with Pastor Elijah and we . . . we left. Mother and me and my children. We left and we can't go back and I don't know what to do.'

They'd left the sect. Tess closed her eyes, struggling for clear thinking in the jumble of emotion as her life shifted around her. First things first. 'How is your baby?'

'She's getting better. The doctor says she can go home tomorrow. But we . . . we don't have anywhere to go.'

Tess pushed herself to her feet, checking for her car keys in the pocket of her jeans and quickly calculating time and distance to Albury, down on the border with Victoria. She had no choices, only one possible course of action. 'Stay there at the hospital, Verity. I'll drive down to meet you. I'll get there later tonight.'

CHAPTER 18

Ten days later, Rookwood Cemetery, Sydney

The light breeze played in the trees bordering the cemetery lane, and as Steve helped Lily out of the car a few autumn leaves fell in a shower of gold around them.

Holding her hand, they followed behind as his father and Tristan, and two of his cousins, carried the simple coffin decorated with flowers and rainbows across the grass to the small graveside gathering of mourners, of family and friends. His Aunt Liz and more cousins. Leah and Heather Arundel and a couple of colleagues of his father's. Simon and Erin, with Jasmine and Willow. And Tess.

He smiled on seeing her, the tight band around his heart easing. She hadn't been sure, when last he'd spoken to her, if she'd make it back in time. But she'd promised she would try.

They laid Maddie to rest beside her mother in a simple service and when Steve faltered for a moment in the reading he'd chosen, Tess was there, across the grave from him, her eyes shining with tears and compassion, encouragement and love.

He'd lost Maddie, twice, but this time, after a life of peace and simplicity, she'd left behind a precious legacy: Tristan and Lily. She'd entrusted their care to him and already he could no longer imagine ever returning to the emptiness of his life before they'd come into it. And in the events around his sister's death he'd found Tess, and he thought Maddie would be happy about that, too.

The sun shone, the leaves danced in the breeze, and somewhere in the trees a magpie carolled, long and sweetly.

Towards the end of the service, he stepped forward again for his final tribute to his sister.

'Everything Maddie did, she did out of love. Her gentleness, her compassion, her love and concern for others and for the natural world are the gifts she has given us, gifts to hold and to cherish and live by.'

Instead of a solemn hymn that didn't fit the circumstance he and his father had agreed they wanted something for the committal that the kids knew, something uplifting with meaning for them.

'This was one of Maddie's favourite songs when she was a child,' he told the small gathering. 'When we were planning this service, we discovered that she sang it with Tristan and Lily, too. It's 'The Rainbow Connection', from *The Muppet Movie.*'

The first plucked notes of the banjo sounded from the speaker and although the embarrassment of doing this in front of some of the state's most senior police heated his face, he opened his mouth and began to sing, his voice as croaky as Kermit's, about rainbows and lovers and dreamers, and the magic on the other side. Their hands in his, Tristan and Lily joined in, and his Aunt Liz, and Willow and Jasmine and Erin, and his father wiped his eyes with his handkerchief and Tess stepped up and joined hands with Willow on one side and Liz on the other, and they all formed a circle and sang as the coffin was lowered into the ground and Maddie returned to the earth she loved.

After the service, after he'd embraced Lily and Tristan and his dad, shaken hands with the senior police, accepted hugs and condolences from Liz and his cousins and Erin and even Simon, he found Tess waiting for him. Without words, she stepped forward into his arms, wrapping hers around him and they held each other close, body to body, until her strength helped him find his own again.

•

Most of them went to his cousin Kate's house nearby for refreshments and sandwiches after the funeral. Kate's kids carried off Lily to explore the playhouse in the garden. His Aunt Liz – a retired teacher – answered questions from Tristan, Willow and Jasmine in a conversation about study options. And Kate – a passionate environmentalist – cornered Simon and Erin in the kitchen. His father, finalising things with the funeral home, had yet to arrive.

Steve poured two mugs of coffee and found Tess out on the back deck, watching the young children. He handed her a mug and sat beside her on the garden bench.

They'd had so little time together he almost wanted to simply sit and enjoy her quiet company, but they had things to say and maybe not much longer to say them in.

'How's your baby niece?' he asked, because they'd both been so caught up with other demands there'd only been time for a few text messages and brief phone calls. 'And the rest of your family?'

'Baby Constance will be fine. The infection has cleared up with no signs of lasting damage. Verity and her children – she has three under the age of five – are staying with my mother in supported accommodation that the Albury women's refuge runs.'

'They won't go back?'

'No.' Her mug in her hands, Tess blew softly across the hot surface of her coffee to cool it. 'I went there,' she said, her tone matter-of-fact. 'I went back to the community to collect some of their things and I didn't let Elijah or anyone stop me from seeing my brother and my other sister. They didn't throw me out but they're not ready to leave yet. I told them to contact me when they did.'

He could imagine her facing them. In Victoria she had no police authority, but she'd have carried her own authority, her sense of justice and fairness. 'You expect that they will leave?'

She nodded. 'The group is disintegrating and Elijah is losing control. Some of the elders have died, including my father. There is dissent, and that brings questions. My mother wasn't the first to challenge Elijah's authority.'

If he'd imagined her mother at all it was as a downtrodden, subservient woman, but he'd learned there were complexities in cults and sects that he still strived to comprehend. 'That was brave of her.'

'Yes. I don't know if her fear for her grandchild's life overcame her fear of eternal damnation, or whether she stopped believing. She'd lived outside the sect, outside the Brethren, in her youth, so she knows a little of the world, of how things can be.'

She took a sip of her coffee, and then looked across at him, with a confidence and self-assurance in her eyes that hadn't always been there. 'You know something? It was empowering to go back to the sect. To see the smallness of it, to learn that it has no hold on me anymore. I'm glad I went.'

Her courage and her quiet pride in facing her past awed him but he wasn't sure he had words to express it.

Out in the garden, the playhouse had become a castle that the kids were defending against dragons, cunningly disguised as Kate's two tabby cats, lazing in the sunshine. Lily joined in the game with enthusiasm, lapping up new experiences, observing and learning all the time.

I hope she grows up as strong as you, he wanted to say, but he wasn't sure where he stood with her, and she'd go, soon, back to Goodabri and he'd take his family home to Dungirri and maybe it was all just too impossible.

In the silence between them, Tess watched the kids play, too. 'Lily seems to be doing well,' she observed. 'How are you all going?'

How could he sum up the progress? 'Lily loves school and is writing her name on everything. We're working our way through the alphabet book. Tris did a couple of days' mustering work out on my friend Mark's property, but he's also enrolled in an online general education certificate. We bought him a laptop yesterday when we came down to Sydney. Dad's going to retire from the police force.'

'And what about you? You didn't mention yourself.'

Yeah, he'd reported facts, like a briefing. 'I'm okay. I'm managing. The house is almost organised, Lily and Tris are settling well, and HQ approved my extended leave without a blink.'

She shifted to sit sideways on the bench, one arm leaning on the back rest, facing him instead of out over the garden. 'Will you go back to policing?'

'To full-time active duty? No. But there is some plotting going on to establish a police youth club in the district.' Led by the unlikely team of his father, and the ex-con owner of the Dungirri pub who had mafia money to turn to a good cause. But that was a long story he'd share with Tess another day . . . if they ever had another day. 'Anyway, there might be an opportunity for me in that. But Tris and Lily have to be my priority. They'll need stability, and someone there for them. They've experienced so much trauma.'

Tess set down her mug on the deck, out of the way, and folded her hand over his. 'What you said about Maddie, that everything she did, she did out of love, is true. The fact that Joshua manipulated her and used her doesn't change who she was, it doesn't diminish that love. She loved her children and they'll remember that more than they'll remember the rest of it.'

He linked his fingers with hers because he needed, at least for now, the connection. 'I know. I'm just hoping I can live up to that.' The knowledge that he'd failed Maddie, that his love hadn't been enough when they were teenagers, still hurt, but he wasn't a teenager now, facing impossible odds.

'You will,' Tess said. 'You are.'

The simple directness of her assurance made it possible to believe again that he could succeed, that he could be what they needed. 'Will you come and visit us sometimes?' He tried to camouflage his hope with lightness. 'Buck up my courage in the face of kindergarten homework? Organise the shed when it gets too untidy?' *Share with me and laugh with me and make love with me and let me show you how amazing you are?*

A soft smile, a little shy, curved her mouth. 'You haven't heard? Nick's still concerned about Joshua's followers in the area so I've been transferred. Dee's going to take over the Goodabri station and I'll move in to the Dungirri station at the weekend and start as acting sergeant on Monday for six months.'

There was pride in her eyes, a hitch of excitement in her voice. He knew how much her career meant to her. Of course she'd have leapt at the chance to be acting sergeant. 'Congratulations. You're going to be a damn fine police sergeant, Tess. Dungirri will be lucky to have you.'

He still had hold of her hand and he wasn't sure if he should let it go, let her go. He must have allowed his uncertainty to show, because she touched her other hand to his cheek and when he searched her face she held his gaze, honest and open.

'Steve, I had a choice of acting sergeant positions. Dungirri or Maitland. Maitland's larger, more opportunities, but I chose Dungirri.'

She'd chosen Dungirri over Maitland. He breathed again, but he waited for *why*.

She continued, serious, laying things out because that was the way she did things. 'Steve, I'm not making any promises. Neither of us can do that yet. You've got Tris and Lily to care for and . . . well, I've now got my family to support, too. I'm not sure what's going to happen there. But I chose Dungirri because it would give us a chance, if we decide to take it, to explore the possibilities. Of us.' Her courage faltered. 'If that's what you want.'

A hundred doubts fell away and for the first time a sense of peace, of rightness, quieted the chatter of uncertainties and eased the loneliness he'd carried in his heart.

'Yes,' he said simply. Yes to Tess. Yes to his family. Yes to the future, and whatever it might hold.

Her smile blossomed and he cradled her face in his hands, planning to kiss her so gently that she'd never doubt his love, but Tris laughed with one of the girls just inside, then the screen door slammed and his cousin called them to lunch and Lily came racing across the lawn, calling his name.

'Welcome to my new life,' he whispered to Tess, and although her cheeks flushed she still smiled as they hastily rose to their feet.

Lily pounded up the steps to the deck and tugged at his arm. 'Uncle Steve! Did you know dragons have wings? And you can *ride* them?'

'Can you?' With his good arm he swung her up onto his back. 'Like this?' He spun around the deck, holding on to the light burden of the child securely, making her laugh as he dipped and wove between chairs.

He put her down when they returned to Tess. 'Time for us to go in and get some lunch, Lily. We've got a long drive back home this afternoon.'

Eight hours, give or take, to Dungirri. To home. It had been right to bury Maddie with their mother, but the city had ceased to be home to him long ago, and even after just a day here he craved the open spaces, the fresh, dry air of the west.

'Can we ride a dragon home?' Lily asked.

Someday he'd find a way to explain about dragons and myths. Not today, when she needed rainbows and hope and love. 'We have to take the car, sweetie. But you can have a nap in the back and dream that you're riding a dragon, okay?'

He held the screen door open for her and ushered her inside and kept the door open for Tess. As she passed him he touched her shoulder and said in a low voice, 'You know that empty paddock between my place and the police station? If you want to go on a wild ride in the moonlight with me anytime, just let me know.'

'I already did.' In the shadows just inside she brushed his cheek with a kiss. 'And I'd do it again. With you.' He wasn't sure if she meant their desperate ride to Serenity Hill, or the night they'd spent together at Riverwood. It didn't matter. It was enough. He was enough. Tess was more than enough; emotionally strong, capable, courageous, she'd drawn wisdom, not bitterness, from hard experiences. He hoped he'd learned to do the same.

Her fingers closed around his, and they rejoined the others, together.

ACKNOWLEDGEMENTS

First and foremost, I am so very grateful for the many readers who have bought my books, borrowed my books, read them, talked about them, reviewed them, and contacted me to tell me they've enjoyed them. You, dear readers, are what makes writing a book a joy.

My agent, Clare Forster, is forever encouraging and helpful. The team at Hachette are wonderful: Rebecca Saunders, whose faith in this book has made it a reality; editors Karen Ward, Chris Kunz and Clara Finlay, whose suggestions have made the story stronger; and the sales and marketing team who ensure my books get to readers.

Sergeant Gemma Gallagher has once again patiently and enthusiastically answered my many questions about police procedure and equipment, even responding to messaged questions on a quiet night shift. Any errors or artistic licence are entirely the responsibility of my own imagination.

Writing a book can be a challenging, difficult and lonely business, but I am fortunate in having strong circles of author friends who reassure me in the difficult times and celebrate my successes with me. The batty friends, the sane friends, the ones in the cave and the ones in the cellar – you know who you are. But I will make special mention of Anna T, who over long lunches and numerous cups of caffeine has been a wonderfully supportive friend in a challenging year.

Gordon has now survived the writing of my sixth book and is still with me – an indication of his courage, patience and dedication. He serenely cooks meals and puts them in front of me during deadline weeks, understands my near-constant distractions, answers seemingly random technical questions, and his mad suggestions when I'm stuck on a plot point always make me laugh. Thank you, Gordon, for everything.

Finally, I want to express my gratitude for my beloved mother. Mum was always my champion, and she loved the characters and places I created as if they were real. Sadly, she did not live long enough to read the final version of Steve and Tess's story, but she encouraged me through the challenges of writing it. I've dedicated this book to her memory. She was truly an inspiration, and I would not have been the writer I am without her influence in my life.

Also by bestselling romantic suspense author Bronwyn Parry
– the Goodabri novels

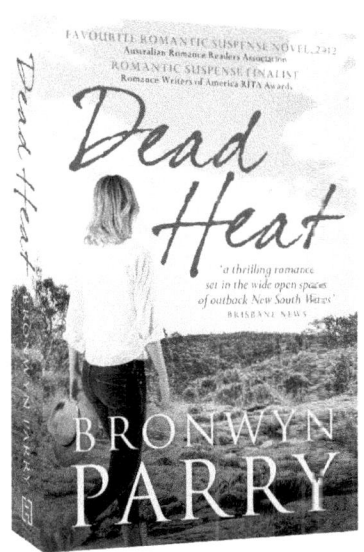 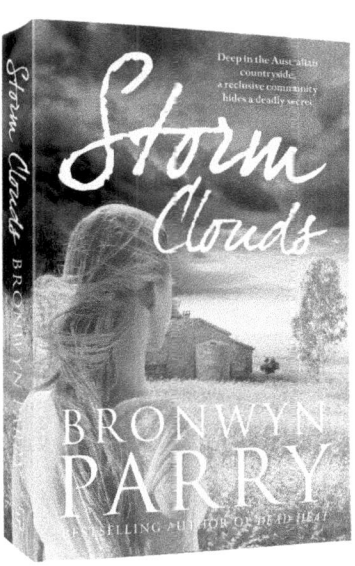

Read on for a taste of

Storm Clouds ...

CHAPTER 1

The late afternoon sun shone straight at the dusty windscreen, semi-blinding Erin so that she didn't see the small landslide of rocks and dirt across the rough fire trail in time to avoid it. The four-wheel-drive Hilux utility tilted as one wheel mounted the edge of a rock, and then dropped suddenly as the rock spun off to the side. Metal scraped on stone, the steering wheel dragged to one side and the right front wheel went *thunk, thunk, thunk* before the vehicle stopped.

She swore as she switched off the ignition. A flat tyre. The last thing she needed at the end of a twelve-hour workday. She swung out of the ute, knowing exactly what she'd see. Sure enough, the Hilux had thrown a tyre off the rim.

Changing a tyre? No worries. As a National Parks ranger working in rugged country, she'd changed a fair few, and she methodically chocked the other wheels securely and gathered what she'd need – the jack, the wrench and the spare tyre from beneath the truck.

But changing a tyre on an isolated bush track miles from anywhere when the wheel nuts were so frigging tight she had to battle for minutes to loosen them? Despite her strength and fitness, Erin ran through her entire vocabulary of swear words twice before she'd removed the first one. She brushed hair that had escaped her ponytail out of her eyes.

'Where the bloody hell are you when I need you, Kennedy?' she muttered into the silence.

Simon Kennedy. Fellow National Parks ranger. Friend. And army reserve soldier who'd been gone on deployment for close on two months. Maybe in Afghanistan. Or Iraq or some other war-torn hellhole. He had to be overseas somewhere, because in the two months since he'd been abruptly called up for army reserve service there'd been no word from him. Two months without an email, a text. Nothing.

She used her pent-up frustration as well as her boot on the wrench and the third wheel nut finally loosened. Hallelujah. She might get this tyre off sometime before nightfall.

She wouldn't make it home before dark, though. Twenty kilometres back to the Goodabri National Parks office to leave keys and swap the work truck for her own ute. Seventy kilometres back to Strathnairn. She *should* go into the National Parks district office there and return some borrowed equipment, but no one would need it before morning. And she just wanted to go home to the cottage she rented on the edge of Strathnairn, pig out on some comfort food – she'd done more than enough physical work this week to justify a dozen cheese-laden pizzas – watch some mindless TV, and have an early night.

Assuming she could get this tyre changed.

A stick cracked in the undergrowth and she stilled, gripping the handle of the wrench. She spent most of her days out in the bush alone and had never scared easily – until three months ago, when her colleague Jo had stumbled across a body, and a drug lord's minions had terrorised the park. They'd all since been arrested, but Erin still responded warily to any sudden sound. Now she scanned the bushland around her for the source of the noise.

Ten metres away among the trees, a six-foot, well-muscled male watched her. Fortunately not a human one. A full-grown red kangaroo, powerful and dangerous if threatened. But this one only studied her, his upright posture showcasing his height and strong shoulders, until he decided she was no threat and resumed grazing the native grasses in the scrub.

'Good decision, big boy,' she murmured. 'You stay over there, and I'll stay over here.' Unlike the time a few months ago when she'd inadvertently disturbed one and Simon had stepped between her and the kangaroo to protect her. No Simon to step in this time, but she could always jump into her utility in the unlikely event that the roo changed its mind about her. Very unlikely. She had far more chance of being bitten by a venomous snake than being attacked by a kangaroo.

The fifth wheel nut defied all her strength and curses for a good five minutes. Giving in wasn't an option – she was going nowhere until she changed the tyre. They were so short-staffed she had no colleagues closer than an hour away, and they'd both be finished for the day anyway, so she'd just damn well have to manage by herself.

By the time she'd removed the last nut her shoulders and back ached from the exertion. She replaced the wheel, fastened the damaged tyre in place of the spare, put away the jack and the wrench and removed the rocks she'd used to chock the other wheels. Climbing into the driver's seat, she stretched her neck and rubbed her shoulders before turning the key in the ignition. There'd been way too many long, lonely days with too much work.

No point whingeing and moaning. She put the truck into gear and eased her way over the loose rough ground. Home, a hot shower, and pizza. Definitely a good plan.

In the small town of Goodabri – population barely three hundred – she parked in the yard behind the National Parks office, closed and silent after hours. It took her only a few minutes to leave the work ute keys, collect the paperwork she'd need for a meeting tomorrow, and lock up again. In her own ute, she reversed out into the back lane, on her way home at last.

Only one other vehicle moved on Goodabri's main street – a white LandCruiser, a block ahead as she turned into the street. She caught her breath. A white LandCruiser with two spare tyres on the back, and indicating a left turn.

Simon. Simon Kennedy driving back into Goodabri as unexpectedly as he'd left two months ago.

The rush of pleasure at his return dragged with it the undercurrent of uncertainty that had plagued her during those two months of silence. She'd regarded him as a friend – a good friend.

But what good friend didn't happen to mention in almost a year of working together that he still served in the army reserve? Dammit, she'd liked him. More than liked him, although – for reasons that had nothing to do with him – she'd quashed any errant fantasies of anything happening between them. And she still couldn't quite believe that she'd never known, that he'd never told her, and worse, that she'd never suspected he hid something so important. So much for being able to read people.

And there she was again, on that round-and-round-and-roundabout of emotions and second-guessing and trying to work out how to make sense of her feelings.

She shook her head, as if she could shake the confusion out of it. Her hang-ups, not his. Plain and simple, they were friends, and he'd been away, serving the country. So she'd do the friendly thing and go welcome him home.

Goodabri had only a few streets, and she followed Simon's route left off the main street then right into the next, and pulled up five houses down in front of the weatherboard house he rented.

He stood at the back of his LandCruiser in the driveway, a kit bag resting on the tray. Old Snowy McDermott, his neighbour, leaned on the fence post between them, settling in for a good long yarn. Snowy could talk the hind leg off a horse and usually missed most social cues, but Simon saw Erin and excused himself to Snowy as she got out of the ute.

As they walked the fifteen paces towards each other, the light cheeky comments she might normally have made turned to dust on her tongue. For months they'd worked side by side in the relaxed way of equals, trusting and relying on each other in their physically demanding duties for both their National Parks jobs and volunteer SES service.

He wasn't in uniform now. Not the army uniform she'd never seen him wear. Not the National Parks uniform, nor the SES uniform they both wore often enough outside work. Just faded jeans and a white t-shirt that stretched over his fine physique and highlighted the deep hazel of his eyes. Eyes that reflected the warmth of his easy grin and gave little hint that he'd been anywhere but a relaxed holiday away.

The early autumn sun had started to set, casting a golden outline around him, almost as if nature wanted to make a gilded statue of the soldier hero. Whereas she . . . she was no hero.

They stopped half a metre from each other, within touching distance, but neither of them made a move to touch. He was out of her reach in too many other ways. Maybe the caution that had stopped her making a fool of herself in the months before he'd left had been good sense, rather than cowardice.

She resisted wiping suddenly sweaty hands on her uniform trousers and summoned up a grin, aware of Snowy watering his garden close by. Keep it simple, keep it light. Just the warm, familiar teasing she'd missed in his absence.

'If I'd known you were coming back today, I would have volunteered you for the regional planning meeting in Moree tomorrow.'

His eyes sparkled. 'Phew. I've had a lucky escape then. Who drew the short straw?'

'Well, since Jo's on light duties and not allowed to drive, I got the long straw, the middle straw *and* the short straw.'

'Jo's back at work?'

'Yes, working half-days. But it's not quite three months since her craniotomy so she's not allowed to drive yet.'

'So you've been doing all three of our jobs, all this time.'

'Yeah. You owe me. Although I suppose if you've been off saving the world, that might cancel the debt, soldier.'

His cheerful, relaxed expression slipped and the light in his eyes dimmed for a moment before he gestured with a jerk of his thumb towards the house. 'Come on in and tell me the news while I dump my gear, and then I'll shout you dinner at the pub.'

Back at his LandCruiser, he grabbed his kit bag with one hand and then slid a metal case out. His rifle. Invaluable in feral animal campaigns. She'd usually managed to put out of her mind that in the army, his targets didn't have four legs. His past army service had been abstract in her head, something she rarely considered in detail, because on the few occasions he'd spoken of his experiences he'd sounded carefree, as if his deployments, even in Iraq and Afghanistan, were barely more adventurous than an outback camping trip. But then he'd gone again, between one shift and the next, with scarcely a word of explanation to her. Nods and murmurs from senior National Parks staff who'd known him longer suggested there was more to his role than he'd ever let on, leaving her with the distinct impression that he'd been – was still – a commando with significant experience in covert operations.

No wonder he was such a valuable member of the volunteer SES squad and a capable National Parks ranger, especially in dealing with the law-enforcement aspect of their roles. Maybe the signs had always been there, and she just hadn't recognised them.

But the fact that he was still in the army – that changed things, changed how she felt, although she'd spent the past few weeks trying fruitlessly to put a finger on how and why. Not that there was any point in trying to understand it, since she mattered so little to him that he'd not contacted her once since his abrupt departure. They were friendly colleagues in a small community, nothing more. So she'd keep things at that level.

She grinned with a good imitation of her usual cheekiness. 'Well, since you apparently couldn't remember my email address all this time, I'll let you shout me dinner.'

She'd not often seen him discomfited, but now he grimaced. 'Sorry. Not much internet access where I've been.'

Obviously not a local army base, then. But he headed towards the house without any further explanation. He set down his bag and the rifle case to unlock the front door and from behind she saw the sudden wariness tensing his spine as he pushed it open.

The odour hit her. Pungent, nauseating, *dead*. 'Sheesh, Simon, did you leave dead fish in your —'

'No.' His hand moved towards his hip, reaching instinctively for a sidearm that wasn't there. 'Keep back, Erin.'

She stayed on the doorstep while he entered, as alert and cautious as if walking into a terrorist's hideout instead of a typical Australian colonial cottage. There were four doors off the short central passageway, two on each side. In the dimmer light inside she watched as he approached the second on the right, the only door not closed. Although he had no gun to hold ready, he used the partially open door as cover to glance into and check the room.

Whatever he saw startled him with a visible jolt. He swore and dropped his guard, striding into the room.

In a few steps Erin covered the length of the passage and followed him through the door. His study had been ransacked, computer equipment smashed, books and DVD cases torn apart and thrown on the floor. But she stopped hard when she saw what Simon had discovered, and nausea rolled in her stomach so violently that she barely resisted the urge to turn and run.

He knelt by a woman sprawled on the floor, his hand on her wrist to check her pulse. But there could be no pulse. There had been no pulse for hours, maybe days. Numerous wounds on her torso had stained her white dress dark red, and blood from her slit throat had dried in splatters all around her on the polished wood floor. Her eyes stared blankly at the ceiling.

'How . . . ? What . . . ?' Erin's throat wouldn't make a full sentence.

Simon turned his head slowly to look up at her, eyes shadowed, his mouth a hard line. 'I don't know how she got here, Erin, or why. I haven't seen her for years.' But he didn't move away from the woman, and there was an intimacy of sorts in the way his fingers rested loosely on her wrist.

The closeness of the room, the stench, the buzz of flies filled Erin's head, almost suffocating rational thought. 'Who . . . ?'

'She's . . .' His voice came out as ragged as a storm-ripped tree. 'She's my wife.'

www.ingramcontent.com/pod-product-compliance
Ingram Content Group UK Ltd.
Pitfield, Milton Keynes, MK11 3LW, UK
UKHW021329180426
11947UKWH00017B/1517